Tales OF THE *Mistress*

Tales

OF THE

Mistress

Dorette E. Snover

For all the Mistresses who have guided my life,
including my brother, Jeremy. My husband, Rich.
My two sons, Erick and Jaryd, and their loves, Abbie and Ana.
And of course, my darling granddaughter, Izzy.

For even more gratitude, please read the
complete acknowledgements on my website:

DORETTESNOVER.COM

Epi's Journey

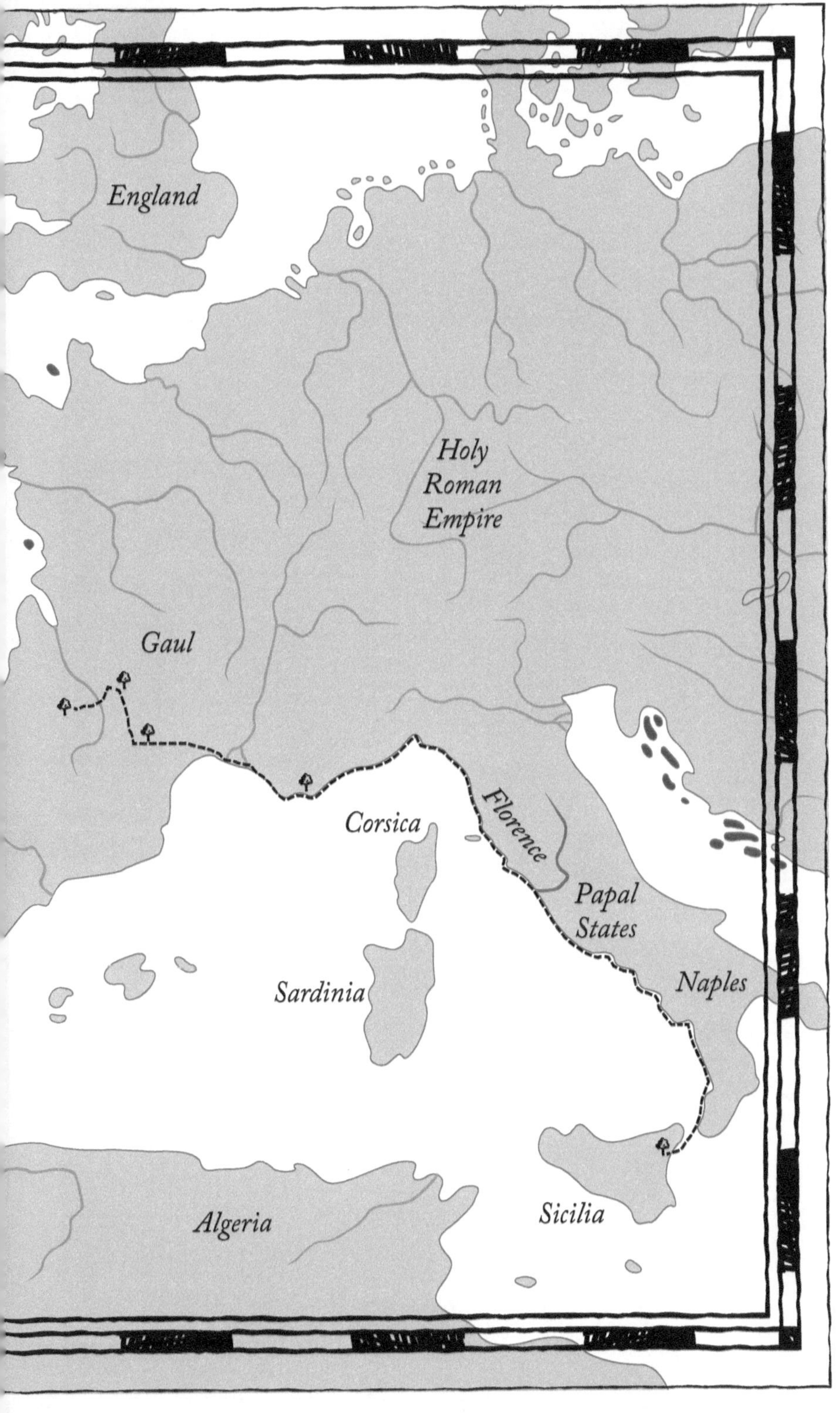

England
Holy
Roman
Empire
Gaul
Corsica
Florence
Papal
States
Naples
Sardinia
Algeria
Sicilia

OPENING PSOMI'S BOX OF SEEDS
The Ceremony

September 1, 1556–Ceres, France

I study Maman's eyes. Flames of blue, saffron, and apricot flicker in her green orbs from the torches perched beside the new wood-fired oven. We're safe at last inside the freshly swept stone-lined bread terrace. Outside, the winds bend the trees and circle the bread terrace, enraging the flames in Maman's eyes to go higher. Most people would see her calmly smoothing her hair, waiting, and never guess the truth. But I know Maman's eyes. She's angry. I cringe and wonder what I did? Or what's missing? She said something I didn't hear. It's always that.

The shallow bowl on the wood kneading table holds our offering. Flour; white and soft. Guild flour. The others who are coming for the ceremony are to bring Psomi flour. The ceremony has not even begun, but I only want one thing, for tonight to be over so Maman and I can leave together as she promised.

The others are late. We must begin. In Maman's eyes I see a distant path, winding through fields, and beyond those fields, more fields. A path that disappears into the mountains. Her eyes blaze with these reflections. Before the ceremony begins tonight, she whispered.

Listen.

Oc.

Prend le Boite.
On part ce soir.
Listen.
Yes.
Take the box.
We are leaving tonight.
The wind rushes Maman's words across the bread terrace. I grab her arm, but she turns, stepping away from me. The others arrive through the archway of rose canes. Did they hear her? I look up as Auvillar, the head of the Guild, arrives with Claude, the miller who grinds flour for both Psomi and the Guild.

My stomach clenches. Claude set a bucket of water on the table beside the bowl of flour. Auvillar's hands are empty. I've never seen anyone with skin so dark. He must grow wheat, and spend a lot of time out in the sun.

I try not to, but my eyes dart to the log sitting on the shelf to the left of the wood-fired oven's mouth. Maman rested three scallop shells on top of the log. The shells hide the brass handle. The log is really Maman's cleverly hidden box, a box that looks like a tree log, carved from her apricot tree. The box hides the wheat and grain seeds Maman grew and collected for Psomi.

"We don't need you. Go on, get out of here," Maman motions my brother, Antoine. He's so quiet, I had forgotten he was here. He drops the basket of bundled twigs, then falls on his knees to pick them up, a stupid look on his face. The twigs were collected from the maze of trees. I fall on my knees and hand him some bundles. I don't even know him, my mouth opens to say good-bye, and I am sorry to leave you when we just met yesterday. I'm sure it's my fault you were brought back here from Nerac. I want to help you understand. But I don't have time to explain the North Field and the maze of trees. Show him how to make Psomi's bread of dreams. Why does Psomi have this problem with the Guild? Maman turns and narrows her eyes at me, as if listening to my thoughts. I open, but then close my mouth. Antoine puts the basket of twigs on the table by the bowl of flour and the bucket of water and backs up through the archway. I watch him run down the path in the shadows of the evening.

I wedge between Claude and Maman in front of the oven. The man who came back with us from the market, Auvillar, hoists himself and sits on the kneading table. He hums while Maman arranges the bundles of twigs in the oven. Auvillar swings his legs, his fine boots made of thin leather. He sighs. "Baking all of Nerac's crowns for the King is an honor. Close to the fields, the wheat. And the mill. The Gelise River. Is good, this much Guild work, yes? Isn't it, Claude?" Auvillar brought nothing and knows nothing. If he did, he would never sit on Maman's table. You don't sit where bread is born.

Claude, his tall sharp legs like the river herons, is quiet, looking in the mouth of the oven as if he's looking in the river for a fish. The same river that grinds the wheat. I feel sick that he hasn't brought any Psomi flour.

Auvillar is squatty and smelly and noisy like the river ducks, *le canard*. He reminds me of a *leurre*, a duck whose job it is to make noise and bring in the other ducks, but then once the other ducks are netted and captured by the king's hunters, he leaves.

And then there's Maman, like a *crevecouer hen*, her movements broken between the noisy duck and the quiet heron. Her hair tufts like apricot feathers as she turns and tilts her head to listen. And speak. Her foot scratches at the meal that fell on the stone terrace, like one of our hens.

I barely hear Maman's words to them. But I recognize her tone.

Prendre la vie du feu, Oc, take the life of the fire.

The first fire in the new oven is a special ceremony to join Psomi and the Guild. Maman said but because it's my tenth birthday, it's MY ceremony into Psomi. But that part is a secret. Our secret. Auvillar thinks it's his ceremony, for joining the Guild and Psomi together. Maman doesn't want the Guild here. And now Auvillar hasn't done his part, by bringing Psomi flour. I stare at him and play along with Maman.

I wish I could use the first fire in the new oven, to make a new bread. One that combined Psomi's bread of dreams, with the Guild bread crowns for the King. The King could never be satisfied with a flat flimsy Psomi bread. He only wants big round crowns so dense they take weeks to chew.

Maman says to never make the bread of dreams in the Guild oven. So many things are a mystery with Maman. She didn't explain why. She didn't tell me everything about our journey, it's a secret she said. We made a fire last night in the North Field where the maze of trees had stood. But that fire is our secret too, it's lighting the path to where we're going. Fires that bake the bread of dreams are supposed to burn away everything old and make way for everything new to grow. That's what she said. I'm pretty sure I remember her words.

My oldest sister, Margot, comes inside the bread terrace. I lift up my hands as if to welcome her bowl. I always hope for the best. I hope she will be my true sister and help me. Maybe she has brought Psomi's flour. I chew my lip and move from one foot to the other. I stand next to Maman. I pull on her arm, and she nods and pats my hand and smiles as if nothing is wrong.

But Margot frowns at me, her disapproval as strong as ever, and her arms are empty and I am scared that since she arrived, there are more Guild people inside the bread terrace than Psomi people. Maman doesn't know that I heard something terrible from Auvillar and Margot at market. So terrible, I can't even think it. Maybe I misheard? That must be it. Surely, they didn't really say what I thought they did. Before market I could be happy about my secrets with Maman, but now with Auvillar and Margot's secret, they want to destroy the very thing that Maman wants to protect, Psomi. Everything she does is to save Psomi. It scares me that she wants to join with the Guild. I have to get her out of here. She's doesn't know it, but she's in danger.

I look at the box sitting on the shelf. Are the *Trakhanas* still inside? Last night we sat in the North Field sitting beside the stumps left from the maze of trees. Maman placed the small pot over the fire. She cooked onions with thyme, black cumin, and a little coriander. Maman touched the side of the pot, testing its heat. She nodded that it was cool enough. I added some of our *levain*. Maman tested the side of the pot again, and nodded. I added the wheat seeds we had collected during our small harvest and stirred. It looked like a big curdled mess, like someone threw up. *I know,* she said. *But it's Trakhanas,* she said. *It's the Mistress's way of feeding baby doves. And preserving our seeds,* she said. *We'll form little cakes out of this mixture and hide them in the box. They will look like food. No one from the Guild would be caught dead eating bird food.*

Maman says when you're scared, just breathe. I blow out a breath. My burnt fingers touch the stone shelf at the oven. Did I turn ten in the field when yesterday disappeared into the fire's flames? Or do I become ten when the fire is lit in the oven inside the bread terrace tonight? Maman knows. She knows everything. I push out another breath. Auvillar and Margot stare at me. Their stares make me feel so much older than ten. I overheard their plan in Nerac about Maman, and just overhearing it made me so tired. Auvillar smells up our bread terrace. Margot talks and walks like a crow, her black hair like crooked feathers. Margot reaches out and touches the bread trough. If Margot knew we make the *levain* by adding water to a bit of the dough left from the bread of dreams and that *levain* then also goes into the bread crowns for the Guild, she might just die.

I watch Maman. I watch Margot. How they look at each other. My hands on the wood table. The feeling of my fingertips burning takes me back to last night. After we made the *Trakhanas, we put the seed cakes in the box,* didn't we? Then we walked back to the North Field. It's possible Margot watched us. I walked with Maman swinging the basket with our bread of dreams dough, hidden under the straw. I fed the fire with Maman, and when the stones were hot enough, we flattened the rounds of dough and laid our bread of dreams, pebbled with apricots and thyme, onto the hot stones.

I asked her, what are the bread of dreams, Maman?

Bread of dreams are flat and don't take long to puff and brown. We make them in the same field where the grains grew, Eleone. They come from the Mistresses who had to always be ready to leave.

I turned our breads over the fire like she taught me, and that's when I burned my fingers. She laughed at the maze of trees. When they grew and lived, there was one tree, protected by one Mistress, she said. But the trees were already gone. We had chopped them down days before. Why did the Mistress not protect their tree?

We are leaving, she said. She never said what would happen to Margot, her oldest daughter, who wasn't coming with us. Maman laughed again, this time at the wheat shooks in the field. To Maman everything feels like a game, like a secret. But to me, her world feels dangerous, like death. Psomi's bread comes out of the fire alive, hot. She dropped one on my lap, smeared it with duck fat, and sprinkled it with salt. I folded it in half. I stuff the bite in my cheek. I worried that Margot was watching, jealous, left out, ignored, and would be even more angry. Margot is Maman's oldest daughter and shouldn't she be first in line for what Maman says I am to do? I don't know what happened to Margot and Maman, but I hate Margot, and Margot hates me. I don't know why, but that feeling scares me.

Far away above the rose canes the stars are safe. When I was little and hungry, I felt safe gobbling down the bread of dreams while watching them twinkle.

But last night when Maman said slow down, really hear the dream, I held the bite of bread in my cheek. Maman said that the bread of dreams comes from many fields and many hands. Bread of dreams fill your hungry places better than the Guild crowns that come from one field, one hand. I don't know what this dream is, but it feels very dangerous, hidden, and Maman's promise, to keep the dream alive, to keep the Tales of the Mistresses alive.

My burned fingers throb, Maman please hurry. We have to leave Claude and Auvillar and Margot so you can be safe. The moment of silence lasts a long time as we all stand inside the bread terrace.

Maman gathers the twig bundles from the basket Antoine left for us.

This fire will let all the Psomi Mistresses who could not be here with us tonight, know that Psomi is joining the Guild.

Auvillar's face falls, he did not know this.

Margot's face reddens. She did not know this.

Maman lays the bundles of twigs in the mouth of the oven.

Maman lifts one of the torches, and I stepped back away from her. But Maman wraps my hand with hers and we touch the flaming torch to the bundled twigs in the mouth of the Guild's new oven.

"With this light we pledge Eleone to Psomi, to gather and teach people everywhere how to save seeds and make fire from Psomi's trees, giving life to the bread of dreams. Breads made over fires from the Mistress trees, Psomi wheat, flowers and fruits from the trees."

As soon as Maman says this ceremony is for me, my heart falls. I knew it.

Maman knew it. She didn't have to say it. She didn't have to give Margot any more reasons to hate me. Auvillar is going to hate me for taking away his light.

"No. This ceremony isn't about her." Auvillar blubbers at me. "It's about…the Guild."

"You forgot I am the one to do this." Margot pushes Maman.

"You? Save seeds? You gave up that right. You were thrown out of Psomi today. You're lucky that the Guild wants you." Maman says calmly.

"Margot, we're joining the Guild with Psomi who thrives on camaraderie, and lives together," Claude looks down and scuffs some fallen kindling along the stone floor and into the dirt covering the newly planted rose canes.

"Margot, enough. This fire and oven are pledged to the Guild. For the next steps in the plan we need the box. What have you done with it?" Auvillar asks.

"You're right. I am the one who saves seeds." Maman says, looking at Margot.

"I watched Madame hand it to you after the meeting in Nerac. She said the box kept the seven grains. That will save us from years and lost fleurins by traipsing around the countryside collecting Psomi's seeds. I don't, and the Guild certainly doesn't, have time for such craziness!"

"Madame gave it to you? The box is mine!"

"Yours? You can't even bring me Psomi flour." Maman says and looks up. Her shoulders stiffen, her back straightens.

Margot spits at Maman. But Maman says nothing.

I can't imagine what would happen if I spit at Maman. I can't imagine wanting to spit at Maman. But I can imagine spitting at Margot. If Maman is planning to take Auvillar to Psomi's secret and sacred fields, Margot won't be far behind. Maman told me she doesn't know where the fields are. She has to find them. On the way. That is our plan.

Auvillar really is stupid. I glance at the box on the shelf. Everything is moving so fast, I feel like I am hidden, like the box. But the scallop shells are still in place and keep us from seeing that the log is Psomi's box. It rests, the brass handle hides under the scallop shells. I am afraid if they looked at me, I would pop open and spill out the secret of the log to save Maman.

Maman eyes the log, too. "Seven grains? Auvillar, no, no.

You misunderstood. It's nine. And not yet, but the box *will* hold the nine grains." I watch her do something I can't believe. Maman takes the shells off of the log and hands the log to me. "There are a few seeds here, and Eleone will keep these seeds from the North Field safe. To find the nine grains we have to find Psomi's sacred fields, and we still need the Guild's help. Like you promised."

"How clever, so, this is Psomi's box." Auvillar slides off the table and stands by me.

Margot steps closer.

I back up. My heart falls. Auvillar turns to me. His eyes are cold and black. His hands are on the box. I pull the box back, the bark rough on my fingers. I can't let him have it. Margot steps close to me too. She wants the box. Maman's eyes are calm. Maman why would you say that you are leaving, and I will stay and keep the box? "Psomi's not far. It lives in the North Field, right?" I ask Maman, wanting to show her that I know where the seeds are, she can trust me. I hand the box back to Maman.

Maman swallows, leans in and brushes my hair, and ignores my words. "The fields will call you. And the Mistresses. Epi, they live too far away to be here tonight, but they hear you, and so you must listen for them when you're walking."

"Who's Epi? You mean when we're walking. Because I'm going with you." I'm getting scared. What is Maman talking about? She looks at me strangely. Why are things changing?

"Look in the fire, daughter, what do you see?" Claude takes my hand, eager to take the heat off Maman and return the focus to the ceremony being for the Guild. But what does that mean? He's not my father. So much depends on me going along with what I don't know. I'll not say another word, or else I'll say something even more stupid.

"Pah! Flames, what else is there to see?" Auvillar's chin juts out. "Hmm. She's so beautiful, what a fine daughter. She'll be safe. Of course. We'll go forward as planned, Antaia. The

Guild will unite with Psomi, so we'll all be the same. All the same. Psomi and the Guild will work together to save the seeds. There. Easy. I wouldn't lie. It will be easier for Eleone because she won't have to go against the Guild. I can tell, Antaia. Now let's get on with it. Eleone, show me the seeds in the box. Now."

I shake when Auvillar's voice booms out Maman's name as if Maman could be many people. Many places. An-ta-eeya, and when he got to the last part, Eeeya, I watch Maman change, and grow older; and her skin takes on shadows like the bark of Psomi's box.

"Perfect, we'll take the life of the fire with us. That will begin the change."

I slip two fingers through the handle and turn the box upside down. I notice the carving on the bottom. My thumb traces a great broad tree, its roots spread below ground as wide as the branches above that reach into the sky. "What kind of log is this?" I ask. Is it her tree? The apricot tree?

Auvillar grins, his yellow teeth showing. He touches my hands, gently pries them away and takes the box. Maman steps in front of me. Auvillar knocks her away, and the box clatters to the stone floor. It opens. He picks it up and shows that it's empty. Where are the *Trakhanas* seed cakes that we put in the box? I try to remember. I don't remember. Maman sucks in a breath. Did she know this? A calmness overcomes her, but it's like I am standing at the edge of the pond by the millhouse with the Gelise River furiously streaming inside. Where are the seedcakes that we put in the box? I look at Maman, but she stares at Auvillar.

We all watch the box lying on its side, gaping open as if it should tell us what happened to the seeds. As if the box is somehow the one at fault, not me, certainly not Maman. Or any of the Mistresses who Maman told me each had a tale about the seeds. She tells me this while we're making our breads. The box changes, and ages like Maman. All of this feels like it takes a long time, but the box was only on the floor for a second or two.

I lock eyes with Auvillar and reach for the box. My fingers can stand a lot of heat, as they turned our bread over the hot stones. The box feels hot like one of our bread of dreams. I drop the box. I see the tree Maman told me about. A large tree, so large it can protect horses and make bread, make fire, and protect one of Psomi's sacred fields. I don't know how a tree protects a field.

Auvillar picks up the box and offers it to me. My hands shake and fall by my side. I won't touch him, not after I heard him and Margot talking at Nerac's market about killing Maman. He shoves the box at Maman. He has no idea who she really is. Or me, her daughter, either. I should have picked up the box and run away with Maman while I had the chance.

I think back to the day before. While the dough of the bread of dreams slept in the trough at the bread terrace, we walked to the North Field. We cut Psomi's wheat and piled the straw in tall shooks around the field. The doves flew out of the dovecote and around us, gobbling down some seeds. Then we boldly walked across the bridge carrying the seed heads to the bread terrace. Maman and I climbed up on the roof of the woodshed that stands behind the bread terrace. We tucked and hid Psomi's rich wheat heads in the straw thatching of the woodshed. The colors of the wheat that had waved at us in the field, shone in the moonlight; the black, purple, red, and golden hues I thought lived only in the sky with the sun. Maman scanned the river and the path carefully, and we climbed down. She brushed her hands and said *remember these are the seeds of life, of Psomi. It hurts all the Mistresses that the Guild has disturbed this time of planting, but we will keep these here, for if we return. We will plant the Trakhanas with the Mistresses on our journey.* In the bread terrace, she shook her head as if she to get rid of a headache. She lifted our dough from the bread trough and heaved it onto the table. In short fast bursts, she cut the dough with the walnut handled lame, and threw rounds of our bread of dreams at me to flatten.

I remember this and watch Maman kiss the box and lay it in the mouth of the oven, on top of the lighted twigs. I stand back, expecting Auvillar or Margot to lunge at her, and hit her, or me. But he stands still.

"Psomi's fire will burn long after the Guild fire goes out. Watch the box in the fire, Epi." Maman says. I thought I was supposed to take care of the box.

My mouth opens. Fire grows in the wood oven. What is she doing? Fire flickers around the box. Am I becoming part of Psomi while the box burns? A rush of anger sparks up and down my neck. I don't know what's happening. My breath stops. I see the tree Maman told me about again. A large tree, its roots below ground fan out and look as large as its branches above ground. The tree protects horses. Its nuts can make bread, its wood can feed fires, and its Mistress protects Psomi's sacred fields. I close my eyes. My heart feels like a shook of wheat that catches a spark and explodes into flames.

If Auvillar touches Maman, I will grab her hand and run to the Gelise River. Get on the barge. Hide under the bridge. Then head back to Nerac. I can find it. The river took us there. I have to keep her safe. Whether I am Epi or Eleone. I don't even care as long as we leave together.

"We'll keep the crowns going. The box is safe. Right, Epi? Now that the Guild and Psomi are united, you can leave, go find the fields." Claude puts his hands together, like he's praying and acts as though it's all been done and decided. And I am staying here. Claude motions Auvillar and Maman to leave. But the box is far from safe, it's on fire and my name has changed, and Margot will kill me, and even I know Claude's trying to act like everything's going as planned, but it's not. Maman is supposed to be his enemy, but its strange that her leaving will break Claude's heart. Claude must know Maman is in danger with Auvillar, and she's just pretending to go with him. Claude loves her but does nothing. Claude is afraid of Auvillar, like me. Claude is afraid of Margot too. He's pretending Maman and Auvillar are leaving. How did burning the box unite the Guild and Psomi? The *Trakhanas* were not in the box. I am glad Auvillar won't get the seeds. Because no seed is worth Maman dying. My palms stretch down the side of my legs. Ready to run. It's not too late. I wait for Maman's signal that we are going. I rub my eyes free of the smoke.

"Don't worry, Epi." Maman pokes the box, the flames grow. "The box of Psomi is yours."

I turn, waiting for Maman to explain why I want a burned box of seeds, and why she's calling me Epi.

"Never." Auvillar roars. "The box is the Guild's. As you promised."

"I am keeping my promise too. We agreed to join Psomi and the Guild. And Epi is perfect, he is the boy who bakes the best Guild crowns in the world. Don't you see? I'll take you to the fields. But take one look in Epi's eyes, and see that he will join them, the Guild and Psomi. Believe in Psomi to survive."

"How does this join the Guild and Psomi? Who is Epi? You're mad. And now you're threatening me?" Auvillar storms at her. His jaw is set. He'll never let her out of his sight. He wants what she has. The seeds of Psomi. But where are they?

"It's not a threat. Believe that Psomi will survive." Maman says.

Claude interrupts. "Antaia? You must leave."

"She's staying right here." Margot huffs.

"Look again. Epi will bake all the crowns for the Guild. Lots of crowns for the King. Epi is the best bread apprentice. I've seen him. Taught him." Maman looks wild. She has just thought of this plan and is telling me at the same time. I can't breathe. She wants me to pretend. But I have never made a single crown. I stop talking. Listening. I am too scared. Scared that Maman will be hurt. Caught. I let out a breath. My ears flatten and close like a dog when he is scared. They all sound like when I'm under water in the river. Maman what is our plan to leave? What about us?

Psomi? A wave of heat comes from the oven, from the burning box, and I move back, away. We are leaving. It doesn't make sense that I have to be in the Guild. That I must pretend to be a boy? Bake Guild crowns? I rub my hands together. I shake my head. Maman what are you doing?

"Leave Eleone out of this." Claude picks straw off Maman's shoulders with tenderness. "Come sit with me." Claude says my name Eleone like he's forgotten and confused too. He says Eleone, like Auvillar says Antaia. But his saying Eleone makes me feel anything but safe. I can pull on a hat, and become Epi, a boy. Whatever it takes to get away with Maman. It won't be easy for Claude to be left behind. He can't bake the Guild crowns either. He's a miller. He knows Guild wheat, and Maman taught him about Psomi grains. I can't let Maman leave with Auvillar. I feel so sick. Maman stands straight and tall and leans her elbow on the shelf of the oven. My finger tips burn hot.

"Your daughter pretending to be a boy? She won't fool any-one." Auvillar says.

"Your daughter?" Margot spits out at Maman.

"After I leave, the Guild will breathe down on you. It's bet-ter. If you believe it, they will." Maman is playing a game and I uncurl my ears to listen. Maman's spirit swirls around me. My ears fill with mud by the Gelise, and keep me from hearing her.

Then, something. Outside the bread terrace, my new little sister, Térèse, sniffles and whimpers. This is her first night with us. Is she crying? Térèse withers at the sight of a cloud overhead. She repeats one word. Maman. Over and over. Antoine shushes her. Trying to calm her.

"Daughter, sit." Maman nods at me to sit on Claude's lap.

My legs shake and I sit down. But then I jump up as if I have just woken. I can't rest. "Maman's right, I'm Epi. I've always been Epi. I'm ready to make the crowns. I can do that." The mud sucks me into the water. I have to protect Maman by stealing their attention away. Claude pats his lap. Looks at my hair. My hands.

"See?" Maman held out her hand. "Epi. Ears. Epi means ears. Listening is more important than speaking."

"Eleone, sit." Claude says. He seems as resistant to my name change as I am.

Claude takes my hands, then holds a length of my hair. "Soft as green pear wheat in the field."

"Epi." Maman says this name again. "Call him by his right name."

"She will always be Eleone. Antaia."

The fire turns, changes. Maman reaches for the carved handle of walnut that pokes up from the crack in the table. The handle of our small but sharp bread knife, the *lamè*, to Claude. We need to leave the bread terrace now and get as far away from all of them as possible. I can't get up. I close my eyes. All I can see is the fire in the oven. I open my eyes. I have to speak to Maman without saying anything.

"Am I ten yet? I feel so small. Maman?"

"Tuck Psomi away, your time as Eleone is over for now. Bring out Epi to join the Guild. You'll have everything you need. You'll bake the best bread crowns they've ever seen." Maman holds out her hand, her eyes calm. Claude and Auvillar fall under her spell too, I take her hand. Squeeze it. She squeezes mine back.

A feeling like the sunflowers turning to the sun radiates through my chest; I understand Maman is playing a game and we will walk out under the archway with this new plan of me being a boy. I don't even care. Just leaving is all I want. She wants to shock them into standing still. It's working. I hold her hand tightly, squeezing it to let her know I hear her.

"I am ready. My legs and my feet. My heart is now Epi's heart. I hear you. I am ready." I didn't add, I am ready to jump up and run with her. I am already Epi, since Maman wants me to be. But I don't know why. She'll tell me when we're alone and it will make sense then. It has something to do with the Guild.

"Epi you have to listen, *follow the doves* fluttering to the tall rye, the wheat growing near peas and bees, beneath figs and cherries, in rows the pattern of shells, and climbing the sunflowers. Wheat that grows tall and fat-close to the ground, talking in wisps and beards, with hues of lavender and rose from the sky and peach and bronze from the fire. For the day when you join all of Psomi together." Maman beckons me, and I give her my hand. I want to be like her, and yet be quiet. There's no need to speak our secrets. Maman's eyes widen, and I fall into their pools. Into the wide green water of her eyes where the clouds drift overhead, and fields of wheat stretch up into the mountains.

Margot stands behind Maman.

"I'm listening…but where is Psomi?" How am I going to join all of Psomi together when I'm not sure where it is?

"Epi. Ssshhh. Now. Your name means ears. Ears don't talk. Ears of wheat listen to and remember the doves."

"The doves?"

"The doves." Then she leans closer, "Take the box," she whispers. "Take the life of the fire."

The box smolders inside the oven. I move towards it, then a wave of heat hits me. I step back. Margot rushes in. I remember her words to Auvillar in Nerac. They didn't know I was hiding in the courtyard behind the apple tree, listening.

"Auvillar, do you know that Margot's tree is the walnut tree. Thick-barked and bitter." Maman says.

"You know nothing about the Guild. The walnut tree is the strongest."

"Maman, they plan to kill you. After they get the seeds. But now there are no seeds. How can a daughter say she's going to kill her mother?"

"And how can a mother leave a daughter." Margot laughs to Auvillar. She pushes the box out of the fire. "She's taking Epi, not you."

Oh, no, Margot hates Maman so much.

"I trusted you." Auvillar grabs me and shouts at Maman. "And now you're trying to trick me?"

"Leave Epi alone. He has nothing to do with it." Maman tucks me under her arm. Auvillar pulls me away. His hands feel like they're on fire.

Claude pushes Auvillar away. "Antaia, go. She's not safe with you." Claude wraps me in his arms and pushes Maman away.

Margot grabs me, I kick her. Maman reaches my hand and pulls me away from Margot.

The fire burns in the oven. My nose tingles from the smoke. Does she hear me? I feel like I am shouting. "Oc, Maman. Oc. Psomi." I answer yes, in the tongue of Psomi. Her people. Our people.

I push my back into Maman. She wraps her arms around me. She holds me. I feel her shaking. Margot turns her anger on us. Auvillar pushes us down.

Empapaouter! Maman shouts at Auvillar, then she kicks me away and she rolls towards the rose canes, I crawl towards her.

Prend la vie de feu. She whispers.

Margot lunges at Maman, wraps her hands around Maman's neck, and squeezes. Maman goes limp. My chest heaves. A cry escapes me. I fall on top of Maman in the rose canes, listening and shaking her to wake up. My eyes close. The stone floor feels cold. I stroke her cheek, crying. Maman, I shouldn't have told you. It's my fault.

"At last, the box belongs to me!" Margot hisses. It feels sad that Margot wants an empty box. A burned box. She picks up the smoking box, screams and drops it in the rose canes. Little orange flames lick at the dry canes.

"Claude! The water!" I point to the bowl on the table.

Claude brings the bowl, and pours it into Maman's mouth, and she sputters. Coughs and gags. Margot throws the bowl of flour on the flames. The flames explode in bursts of red and yellow. I shake Maman and drag her. She crawls and I pull her through the archway and outside the bread terrace. She wraps me under her arm and whispers. *Prend la vie de feu.*

"I'll take the life of the fire," Margot grabs the torch from the holder beside the oven. Auvillar wrenches Maman away from me, her arm behind her back. Leaves rush away from the trees in russet and yellow over the bread terrace. Maman will never find me in all the leaves.

I pound after Maman, across the bridge. A duck swims in the pond, safe from the fire, but there is no barge to get me to Nerac and Madame's shop. Margot waves the torch around. She walks on the towpath by the river. I hope she stumbles into the pond and the waterfalls drag her under the millhouse to be ground like flour.

Maman's dove flies ahead. I run up the hill of the North Field. Smoke overhead. Everything is burning. I cover my ears. I stop and listen. Even listening fills my ears with smoke. I stop. She told me my new name, Epi, means ears, but I cover them to listen, searching for Maman's voice. My eyes squint. I slowly open them. The wheat shooks stand as they did last night in the North Field where we made the bread of dreams. Maman hovers at the top of the hill. She waves a torch in her hand. Is she waving goodbye or beckoning me to hurry. I can't hear her.

I crest the top of the hill. Smoke swirls around me. I rub the hair out of my eyes. Maman's dove flies out of the dovecote and lands on a shook of wheat. I rub my eyes with the back of my hands. The shook catches fire, crackles and burns, and I run past it. Her dove flies overhead. Twisting and sparking.

"Epi. You have to listen. *Follow the doves.*"

THE FIRST TALE

Trakhanas—Psomi's wheat seeds and the
Apricot Tree. Greece, Ikaria. Maman.

"Prend La Vie De Feu"
Take the Life of the Fire

SEPTEMBER 1, 1563–CERES, FRANCE

CHAPTER ONE
Life on the Bread Terrace

WHEN I WAS ten, she left me. The Guild tells me I killed her and that's why I am alone. My heart longs for her, and to know what happened. I can't stop thinking about her, my Maman, my mother. To them she was the great Antaia, Mistress of the Psomi. The enemy of the Guild. They wanted Psomi to join the Guild. But they lie. They only wanted to know what she knew. Have what she had. Then kill her.

But to me she was none of those big things. She was my mother. Keeper of the apricot tree. Warm, with me, her hand over my heart. She never said don't cry. If I even felt sad, she knew, and held me. But then, in our life, I had no reason to feel sad or alone. No reason I can remember until the last day.

Before that, the days with her were filled with walking and planting. And we might be quiet. When we kneaded the bread, when she was there, with me, and like a fire in me. She was around me. Her warmth helped me grow. Helped me see.

Helped, no, that's not the right feeling. She loved me into growing. Watered me. Fed me. Dug our sleeping places at the bread terrace and filled the sleeping hollows with stones warmed in the fire, and duck feathers.

We are the Mistresses of the Psomi world, she said, we lived in the world of Psomi. We were not afraid of living outside. We were safer in the world of trees and wheat and fire.

The feeling of losing her and the part of me that went with her, wakes me. I sit up, staring into the tangle of rose canes overhead as if the sound I might be hearing, might be her. Maman is coming back to my little world, right now, this very second. I am ready. My heart ticks so fast, and sends signals out to my legs, to leave, to go to the North Field, and find her. To try again.

Inside my legs I am still her little girl, she is so deep in me that I know I must be deep in her too. Maman must feel my movements, as I sense hers, wherever she is. And that it's the Guild who accuses me of her murder, that keeps me hidden and baking the crowns of bread for the King in Nerac on the bread terrace of Ceres.

Anyone ever accused of murder by the Guild is trotted out for a show, and then shot or stomped to death like the rats found in their grain bins. But not Maman. Because she escaped. And this really embarrassed them. And angered them. This must be the reason they have said nothing.

They had no show, and they were without their great Antaia. But they got me, and even though I am a girl, and girls are not allowed to bake, they don't know or are too embarrassed to reveal that fact that the King has a girl baker. The biggest problem for them. I feel so stupid. So stuck. I could never stop baking the 27 crowns of bread for the King each week on the bread terrace where I live. How could I? They count. They even charge me rent to live here. As if they have any idea. They own the bread terrace. But the Guild can't own me or the mouth of the oven. I feed the mouth of the oven better than they feed me, her son, Epi.

This place is still my land, my sacred place. So, I can never leave. Or let them know. And except for when they come to collect their crowns, I can be alone. I like that best. I can be alone and think about Maman. When I do, it's like she's here. And nothing has changed. I talk to Maman and tell her what I'm doing. I make the King's bread—I have to—but it's a terrible feeling that I have to make Guild bread, and the best Guild bread so I can forget them, the Guild.

The bread terrace is set apart, alone too. But only a few steps away the bank goes down to the Gelise River, which once flowed through the millhouse and under the bridge. The road skirts the North Field and the dovecote, and if you don't get lost or murdered in the field, the road will take you into Nerac and the Guild home.

Our bread terrace, for it was built by Maman and me, may as well be on an island, far away across the sea. It sits on a pedestal of laid stones, encased by an iron trellis. Up and through the iron trellis grows Maman's roses. I am pretty sure that the iron trellis came first, but Maman may say that the roses grew over it to strengthen the iron. In the end it doesn't matter. The roses grow and twist with the iron, from feeling the warmth of sunlight. The roses and iron give enough shelter from the sun to spark the fire inside the wood-fired oven. I love the fire because it reminds me of Maman. But I hate the fire too because it gives her strength back to the Guild's bread crowns baking hidden inside her bread terrace.

They say I am hidden, too, but I can't believe that. Anyone could wander from Nerac on the road. Pass the field, down and over the bridge and led by their nose, follow the scent of hot bread, and the oven-dried herbs and roses. They could go further and pass through the rose cane arch to the bread terrace and stumble dumb-founded onto me. Why don't they? People are hungry. Everyone is waiting for the harvest. Do they believe stories about Ceres? They could step around the hot mouth, the fire burning in the wood oven. Steal my *levain*. The bread starter. They don't. But would I stop them if they did? Maybe they would bring a gift of wood, so my brother could rest and I wouldn't have to pay the Guild. They could sit on the table with me, watch the flames lick at the ceiling and bake the Guild's bread crowns that I must make and count them. The crowns keep me stuck on the bread terrace.

But what could I do? Could I pass through the rose canes that arch over the iron trellis? How far could I get? My shoulders tingle with fear. With wanting to reach out and touch the trellis. I feel shivers of joy even to think I could leave. I can't imagine what would happen to me if I left. I step back. I couldn't do it.

It's possible that the Guild has forgotten, and I am staying here for no reason. So, I hide even from myself. I have to. Nothing the Guild could do would be worse than how I feel. Sad. Punished. As dark as the bread terrace.

Something I did killed my mother, the great Antaia? You'd think I would remember what. The Guild never said. How. What. I've had seven years to sweat before the fire. Maybe this fire is part of the very fire that the Guild says killed her. One of the last things I remember was following her. But I returned from the field, from chasing her because I didn't want to lose her. They told me I had killed her.

No one in Ceres remembers who I was before, Eleone. But Maman took Eleone with her. That night, and that part of me is gone forever.

How horrible it is that I am still here, feeding the wood oven, still feeding this oven with Guild wood. I poke the fire inside the oven. The wood breaks and crunches, making the same sound as when Maman ground our wheat in the little flour mill, between two stones.

I have to think she's coming back. I can't believe for a minute that she is dead. My thoughts Térèse around. Never ending. I pick up Maman's shells from the shelf over the mouth of the wood oven. I listen to them. But they are quiet, as always. The curves take me back to being with her, standing here with her. I hold them close.

I sit down on the wood kneading table, looking into the oven fire. The flames destroy the wood, and I wonder if I entered some foul state of mind, and like the fire here, I did kill her. And she really is dead. A thought so horrible I push it away.

I hold the shell to my ear and listen again. Is it the wind or is Maman calling me? And why would I have been mixed up? Well, I'll tell you. Because we were having a fire ceremony so I could join Psomi to be with her. But what changed, I don't know. At the end of the ceremony, I was Epi. Maman was gone. And I was in the Guild. I learned their tricks, and their plans.

As Epi, I am stuck here. But as Eleone, I am lost back then with her. Maman was stronger than all of the Guild. All of us. She must be nearby, weighing out—and waiting in another apricot treehouse, that's just like the one the Guild made us— Maman and me—chop down. I have to stay here but they don't, my brother and sister, they leave, but they always come back.

I've asked my sister, Térèse, to search for Maman's tree. But she tells me, in an exasperated tone, standing in front of my oven. "Despite how much you want to believe it, there is no apricot tree or roots, or anything like that in the field, Epi. Are you sure it was even here? I know how you imagine things. Apricot trees can't live here. They live far away in the warm land of oranges and olives, near the sea."

I don't know how to convince her. She could ask my brother, Antoine. He's a woodmonger and would remember Maman's oddest trees. He would find evidence of her apricot tree. Maybe there's a sapling growing in the middle of the woods where a bird dropped the stone. I love them, my brother and sister, but our situation is troubling. They think I'm crazy. They were not here when Maman and the maze of trees was here.

I circle around the kneading table. And stare into the oven. At the Guild's bread crowns lifting their scents towards me. The cold crowns that went in, should be baking up into a cross hatched crust of grain flavored with the *levain*, the hours of work, and my sweat that drips into them.

But this morning something's wrong. The fire isn't hot enough. And I don't have any more of Térèse's wood. I won't buy wood from the Guild. I slip the bread peel under a crown and pull it into the mouth of the oven, turning it with my fingers. It's barely warm, and I close the oven door to keep in any last hope of heat that these crowns will finish in time for Antoine to take with him.

The problems here are many.

Right after Maman disappeared, Claude—the Guild leader and my stand-in father—changed. He said he was glad that I killed Maman, his enemy. But his mind is questionable. If he catches my dove, *Aubada*, in the bread terrace, he always asks if there was a message from her. Maman threatened the survival of the Guild. Claude believes though I was small, he always knew that I would protect the Guild and not the Mistresses of Psomi. But he feels like my enemy, too. Boys can't be Mistresses. And girls can't be in the Guild. If he really believed I killed Maman, he would be sad. And afraid of me. How could I learn anything about her? He is very strange, or maybe it's me, and I don't re-member any of what happened, as I am sure he loved Maman. I am sure my feelings about that night are true, he was protecting her and me. I don't know what happened to him afterwards.

But here's the thing, I know my feet stand on the Guild's bread terrace. But my heart and soul are with Maman. I don't know or care anything about Psomi, either. It's Maman I care about.

I slam the oven door closed. Usually, there's plenty of wood, and I have to be careful not to burn the crowns. Why is the wood causing me trouble today of all days? At least two of the crowns have to be perfect, for Antoine to enter in the apprentice contest. I hate the crowns. And the Guild who makes us pay for our wood. Or steal it.

I look around. My face must change when I remember her, surely. And returns to a softer time, when my face…when she…I set the stones down. When I was with her, when I was Eleone, her daughter. If anyone is watching me, when I think of her and see my face change, I would be discovered and arrested because girls are not allowed to bake. Least of all for the Guild.

Surely it wasn't me as Eleone, who killed Maman. But that only can mean one thing, that it was Epi, who I am now, who did it. And then I am trapped in this Térèse, because I don't believe I killed her at all. But since the Guild does, and has charged me with murder, that's the only thing that matters. It doesn't matter what I think. What I feel. What I do. Except to keep baking their crowns.

I put the shells in my pants pocket, pressing their curves against my leg. I take her saw hanging on the nail and saw through some rose canes and feed them into the mouth of the oven. The flames crackle. Smoke drifts over the crowns. All of Maman's Psomi, her people, and her stories, lost in the same fire that took her. And that haunts me, that I have lost that for her and for all of us who had so much hope that the Guild would be the one to die.

I look around for something else to burn. If Maman never birthed me, then she might still be alive. And I could see her, talk to her. Or if I had paid attention to her, listened to her teachings, I might have kept enough of her alive in me that I can save her, even from this distance of the bread terrace. But I didn't listen.

When I was in her, and with her, my hand warmed in hers as we walked in the rows of her wheat to her apricot tree. I was in her world. It wasn't a listening world. It was a feeling world. A world of aromas of black cumin, and thyme, bay leaves, drifting over fields. She added these and mixed them with our wheat seeds and dried them, calling the little cakes *Trakhanas*. To give to people she knew, to add to their breads on far away fires. People blew through flutes made from trees, sunflowers, or bones, she said, to start the fires. Then these flutes made music. I know I am crazy. The strange music is beautiful, and the feasts that swirl their scent make me want to follow the night wind. Where the owl's call. Where the trees rustle overhead. But when I lean out of the bread terrace to listen, the sound is just the doves flying through the leaves, their rustling, and the tree roots growing towards water. And towards her secrets, that are far from me. Like every other moment since she's been gone.

And so, here, I will forever live on the bread terrace. And only here.

During the day I sink into my straw bed inside the rose canes. Pull up my blankets and pillows made of goose down. They are so soft and the oven warmth is soft too. The aromas of bread wrap me. Soon, I will sleep. Forget the reason, the reason I am alone.

When the darkness comes, I push thoughts out and use my hands to light the oven's fire again. How much I love my beautiful bread terrace. I say, I am happy. Covered over by an iron trellis, and rose canes, in front of the fire I forget sometimes that first it was hers. We built it together. I touch the shells that she lay on the shelf beside the mouth of the oven. They are cold but I keep them, for her shells hold and remember what I cannot. They could bring her back. I know if they cannot bring her back that it's because of me, it's my fault. When I was small, I burned hot as her fire to save Psomi. What she wanted. To join her, please her. We both fed each other's heart. I believe that, and remember that only, and if I can remember what happened, how the fire separated us, maybe I can. No, I could never be with her again.

I open the oven door and scoop some ash into the bucket, will that help you, fire? Dare I admit in the darkness, how very much I wanted to be like her, and thought I could be, because I knew better. I saw a crack in her. Was it nothing more than a hiss of steam? And then maybe I changed? Was it the day that she left, had I seen something in her that changed me into her son, Epi, instead of her daughter, Eleone? Or was it something she saw in me that displeased her and so she changed me, taking away any chance to be like her? When she said, you are now Epi, because Epi means ears and you have to listen. I don't know if by listening she meant I should obey. Or to see. I never wanted to displease her, and if I listened, would I find that what I felt in my heart about our closeness, and about Maman hearing me even when I didn't speak, was never true.

I am happy that I knew her. That I loved her. I tell myself this. That the time that I had with her is all I ever needed.

In the last seven years I've pondered how it is that I am alone. But I cannot remember. And in that small wisp of smoke that comes before the fire ignites, Maman is close. Does she see me? Miss me? She must still be my mother in the life where she lives, on another bread terrace. I prefer to think this than whether the Guild has her working for them or maybe they killed her a long time ago but blamed me. And whatever keeps her there, must also keep her safe. So, I am glad she is away, and I am not there, which would be unsafe for her. And she thinks I am safe here, because she made me into Epi. But I am sad we are not together.

In the time before she left, the bread terrace was different. Antaia's hair was soft, like red wheat. When she sheltered me on her lap on the kneading table, her hair waved and fell over me like a roof, thatched with precious seed heads.

The night of my ceremony, my hair was cut.

Inside her, like then, inside our bread terrace, lived all dreams. The sun and the clouds passed over us as we worked inside the bread terrace and sowed her fields. The warmth of her hands worked its way down onto the waving heads that bent and followed one another, rows of grains that brushed the winds to move, and filled our troughs with golden dough inside the bread terrace.

Her soft blue veined hands mixed the *levain*, the sour and milky mother, our bread starter. We bubbled and laughed and slept with the trough beside us. It fermented safely under our down covers. When my eyes opened in the dark my eyes saw another Maman, another person, maybe a woman, an old bent man or laughing child under the covers where the trough slept. I rubbed my eyes and they disappeared.

From our *levain* came soft breads, full of the fields and flowers. Our breads are flat and bake quickly. Some are chewy and some, crisp; it depends on the time of year. And what we find in the fields.

In the oven I slip the peel under the Guilds child-big crowns, to turn them. Oh no. I can't pull them out. They're stuck together. Each one needed more and more room. They push at each other. Their skins touching. There's no way to save them. When they come out, they have to be pulled apart. When they are, this leaves a scar on their skin and the Guild refuses to accept these crowns.

What two breads could be more different? One kind is treasured because it's different and the other is good enough only if it's exactly the same as every other one. I feel sad wondering if this is true about Maman and me, since she left me behind to be in the Guild.

I drink in the aroma of the *levain* and am filled with some peace. My hands stir the sourness and bubbles, tastes that grew in me. That's why I do it. That's why I make them. Our breads. To keep Maman safe. It's wrong that I make them in the Guild oven. But there's no way I can light a fire in the field at night.

I rake the back of my neck, sweaty and gritty like the bread terrace floor. When I get so mad at the Guild, I don't stop making their bread. I just make more of our breads. Our breads use everything the Guild leaves behind. Térèse used to forage flowers and herbs, wild and pilfered fruits. Things the Guild can't see and won't miss. Can't count, and don't understand. She brings me root vegetables dug from the garden, and grasses that grow heads of wild grains. I grind them and mix with our *levain* and fling the breads (Maman would say sing them) onto the stone floor of the oven, after the crowns have baked. I hope our breads are a remedy, a soothing from Maman for annoying the oven with baking the Guild's crowns who take up the most from the oven.

I hold her shells again. Maman made a special bread with them over a fire in the field. She fed the fire with branches from the maze of trees. When it burned down to hot coals, she laid on her shells, and when they were hot, we draped the soft breads over the stones and the shells. Some breads took on the shell's ridges, their valleys, the path to the sea where the shells were born. Other breads we lifted warm and brown and smooth after baking on the hot stones, as if the breads had comforted the stones like the river that once flowed over them. But I must be a Guild baker because I am too scared to do this.

I make what I can and cry. Térèse hurries them away and leaves them under the bridge. I hope that maybe the aroma of my bread of dreams will call her, and Maman can find her way back to me. That is if she's lost and not dead. Or even if she is dead and lost. I just don't know, but I can't stop making them.

This morning my stomach roils with smoke. It's Wodin's Day. The day of the apprentice test. The logs lay perfectly stacked in the oven, but the fire has quieted. There are only a couple of scrawny limbs of oak under the oven. Not enough to finish the crowns. My brother, Antoine, will be back soon. I tilt my head to listen for his steps.

CHAPTER TWO

Psomi Wheat & Guild Wheat

I KICK THE ASH bucket and it spills on the stone terrace. The Guild owns me. My brother. This bread terrace. I'm not sure if they own my sister, Térèse, but I am sure they think they do. They don't own my past, my memories.

When Maman grew Psomi's wheat with flowers and carrots in the North Field and we made Psomi's bread of dreams. The same wheat that grew under her sweeping hands, died under the Guild's strict order to grow by itself and tall, just like their wheat strains. But worse than that, the Guild claimed Psomi's wheat belonged to them. Their wheat was dying, true. Yet, they knew that Psomi's wheat was stronger, but trickier. To grow Maman's wheat according to the Guild doctrine would assure Guild survival. They needed Maman, but she left. Both the Guild and me.

Maman must have picked my brother and sister the same way she picked the feral Psomi wheat. By listening to her heart. My brother, Antoine, is older. And my sister, Térèse, is younger. Like heads of wild wheat that didn't meet the Guild's standards, but Maman saw strong seeds where the Guild only saw trouble and disobedience. Each seed head was different and therefore not good for the Guild. When they say it's not good for the Guild, they mean not compliant. Not moldable. Not obedient. Antoine and Térèse are the same and yet so different. Sometimes sweet if they are out in the sun all day, but sometimes sharp and bitter if they are hungry and raw from the cold rain. Maman said they were sturdy-strong and would grow and bend like the young *Rouge de Bordeaux* wheat in our North Field. I met Antoine and Térèse the day before Maman left. The Gelise River moved swiftly on the way home from Nerac. I sat in the barge behind Maman and the man whose name I can't remember. Was Claude with us too? Maybe he was waiting here for us to return. Antoine ran in front of Maman's horse, Miele, as she trotted along the towpath, pulling the barge. Térèse rode Miele's foal, Beauté, and cried when Beauté left the path and galloped through the trees, which was all the way back to Ceres. I put my fingers in my ears to shut out her cries, because it made me want to cry and I couldn't help her. This was the day before Maman left. They found even threatening me was not enough for the Guild to own Maman.

CHAPTER THREE

The Falcon and the Dove

I RUN MY HAND over the Guild plaque set in the stone-arch of the oven. It's a falcon, his talons wrap the part of the G that looks like a branch. The bread crowns of the Guild and Psomi's bread of dreams are as different as the falcon and the dove. As spring and winter wheat. Before my ceremony, the Guild knew and loved my mother, Antaia.

That Guild welcomed her to bake their crowns.

That Guild watched us build their oven, and we built it better. We used their oven to dry all the wheat, and bake their crowns, but never to bake our bread of dreams. So they watched us in the field, tending, and growing our wheat. They whispered, yes, ok. It is good. Even better. Let them grow their Psomi wheat, and make our crowns better. Let them share their seeds. They can teach us.

That Guild wanted to learn.

On the stone shelf beside the oven mouth, in full view of the falcon, sits a nest from my favorite dove, Aubada. Beneath the oven sits the Guild basket designed to perfectly hold seven, but only seven of their crowns. To bake their crowns the Guild demands that the fire in their wood ovens must come from logs of oak cut from their forest. The tree harvesting is done by my brother, Antoine. He's not a falcon or a dove, he's a woodmonger and fells the oak trees while I sleep during the day. I hate that he cuts wood for the Guild. But I doubt that he hates that I bake their crowns. I couldn't do his job, and he couldn't do mine. The only comforting part is when I hear a tree falling, I know Antoine is nearby.

Some time ago, my oldest sister, Margot, who is more like a falcon than a dove, insisted on squeezing inside my bread terrace with my brother, Antoine. She measured. She evaluated. How many more crowns could the oven bake? She stared. The King demanded more. It was complicated. How would I pay the tax increase? More taxes? I asked. Your doves are eating all the grain, she said. Margot is clumsy and smells deeply of rot. Like a fat grape she got stuck inside my thorny cage of roses, and all I want to do is push her out. Her rancid breath hurts my eyes. But I thought of Maman and spoke deeply as Epi. She stumbled around, spilled flour and made sucking noises when she breathed. I don't know if it is because I hide so well or because she is so stupid, but Margot didn't see Eleone, didn't remember her little sister, me. Was it just Margot who didn't see? Or has all the Guild forgotten who I am? I am "hidden" as long as I stay here. How could the day that changed my life when Maman left, not have changed hers, too? She lost her mother too. But she blames me. I almost hear her say, be careful. I will never forgive you or see you. You are Epi. You killed our mother. You can never leave the bread terrace.

But just as different as falcons and doves are, my sister, Térèse makes her garden grow, and instead of cutting the plants down, she plants them together. Beans and squash stretch to the sun or to the rain or to the moon, together. Térèse and her garden live beside the bread terrace. I hear the beans and cress and red orach growing while I sleep too. They pretty much hang on her every word. They love her and want to grow to please her. Térèse sleeps in a little straw hut she built, but I am sure she sleeps with one eye open to be sure the *courgettes* have all they need to grow at night. She rakes furrows and tells the curly tendrils to climb up their trellises like good little peas. She builds trellises from pilfered oak or willow. She catches water from the night and sprinkles the bright green and red lettuces. Just as quickly she turns and yanks out stray radishes and thins out her leeks, throwing them outside the garden.

Our doves fly from the dovecote to her garden. Térèse says they prefer seeds to dried up lettuce. I don't know where she finds it, but she brings me heads of millet, ripe with seeds. Unlike plump Margot, Térèse slips like a tall thin leek inside my thorny cage. Inside the bread terrace she sits on a stump, like a little dove with her mouth open. I cook a pile of millet with water in the wood oven and spoon some into her, drizzled with her honey, and she coos like a dove. She takes the rest of the heads of millet with her on the path, winding up to the dovecote. She feeds them the millet and shovels up their droppings and hauls the dark piles of stench to the garden. It's like when the Guild hauled stones from the field to build the oven. These two beings, the stones and the stench, come from so close to the same home, but are as different as the crowns and the bread of dreams, the falcon and the doves, and my brother and sister, as they can be.

I sniff. And slide the metal door away from the mouth of the wood oven and measure the heat on my hand. Seven round crowns of bread sit on the floor of the oven. I push a terracotta plate of cherry tree bark and juniper next to them.

Petals of Maman's roses fall on my shoulders. I scrape the pink, dry petals and buds from the shelf into my hand, then drop them into the grinder and turn the handle. Their scent is smoke and roses. I close my eyes. I turn the handle again. A pile of flour sifts out. Not enough to make even one bread of dreams. It was the apricots that Térèse found and brought that made me remember making them. I cried. Térèse scowled. And refused to talk. That's not like her. She stuffed the bread of dreams in a linen sack and left quickly. I'm getting tired of my promise to keep you safe, she said. I feel so much confusion watching her walk to the bridge. She said she left the bread of dreams on a rock under the bridge. I love her too. Maybe Térèse was left under the bridge in Nerac, as if she was a bread of dreams when Maman found her. And I hope the aroma of apricots in the bread of dreams would call Maman to come back to the bridge of Ceres, that she would find Térèse and me again. If I can keep baking the bread of dreams, I hope one morning I will wake to find Maman standing in the bread terrace with the sack of them, asking me to forgive her. I breathe slowly. Next time, I said I want to see who takes the bread of dreams. But Térèse got mad. And she asked just who would make the Guild crowns if something happened to me? I closed my eyes, as she stormed away. Térèse warned something would happen to me because I was making the bread of dreams. With my eyes closed, I stretched out under the rose canes and waited for her return. In my dream I watched villagers and passers-by, travelers, wanderers, to take my soft bread of dreams from the sack. The people rush by like clouds. Some had teeth and tore into the breads. Others smile sweetly and stuff them under their tunics, to warm them and keep them till later to eat under the stars. I don't see Maman, but maybe I don't remember what she looked like. I shake my finger at the falcon in the Guild plaque set in the stone arch of the oven. Sometimes I think that falcon leaves the plaque and swoops down to kill Maman's doves while I sleep. So, I don't.

CHAPTER FOUR
Aubada, the Dove

S OFT COOING SOUNDS come from outside the bread terrace. Her beak pecks at the stones, and clawed feet scratch. My eyes fly to the falcon in the Guild plaque. More cooing sounds come from the path. Is it a dove or Térèse cooing to one?

Smoke billows out the chimney of the oven. Térèse worries that when I start the fire in the wood oven the smells of the smoke and the bread baking calls people as far away as Nerac. But I only bake at night when they sleep.

She tells me people in Nerac are unhappy with the Guild and don't sleep, especially at night when they are looking to steal or hurt the Guild. Maybe it's true but maybe she tells me this to scare me into staying here. So, if I bake crowns, Nerac's people are still hungry, and if I baked the bread of dreams the Guild would be angry. The sky is like a bruised purple and blue. My arms feel heavy and frozen. No matter how many crowns I make, they only go to the King, but I want to feed the hungry people with my bread of dreams. What would the Guild do if they found my bread of dreams?

Branches rustle. Stones plonk in the river, thrown from the bank. Low voices come across the water. Footsteps rustle along the path. I lean out of the archway. The thick rose canes arch like ribs over the iron trellis and block my view.

The oven door is barely warm. I slide it away from the mouth and take out the plate of bark and leaves, then slide the door back. The brown bark and green leaves turned white in the fire. I'll grind them into flour. And add it to the roses. It's still not enough. I empty my basket on the table. Nothing here to grind. If Térèse isn't still mad at me, I hope she will find more apricots on her way back from Nerac. Then I can make more bread of dreams tonight.

I slide the oven door away. The metal scratches against the stone shelf. No heat wooshes out, the Guild crowns have flattened in the dwindling fire. My heart falls. I slam the door back in place. I stoop. my hands in the spilled ash. Not even a spindly little twig of oak under the oven. Maybe Antoine's selling logs, but I would never buy them. I slide the metal door back in place over the mouth of the oven to keep in as much heat as possible.

Antoine, my brother, might be angry with these crowns, especially if he knew I had used his oak to make a fire to make my bread of dreams. But the crowns are not even a little brown. He'll be back any minute wanting to take them to the Guild shop in Nerac to enter in the apprentice test. I cringe thinking I would disappoint him, but I would get blamed because I am the spare bread apprentice, *talmelier.* I get blamed if the crowns are bad, but I don't get the credit if they are good.

Suddenly, there's a fluttering at my feet. I jump away, worried that I might crush the mouse that's been after the grain. But it's not a mouse. It's my dove Aubada, a far distant nestling of Maman's old messenger dove, who birthed all of the other doves in the dovecote. She coos and pecks at the crowns on the wood table. She hops, then stops. What's on her foot? I sweep some crumbs from the table in my palm and bend to show her. She hops away.

I crawl slowly and bring my other hand over her. Her warm body stills under my touch. Her feathers are so silky. My finger examines the string wrapped around her foot. How did she not get stuck on the way to the bread terrace? Maybe she did. She faces away and bends her head, touching her beak to my outstretched finger as she walks out on it, as if my finger is a branch. She turns sideways and inches onto my other hand. Her beak tickles as if a small bug were walking on me.

She struggles and I let her go. She comes back. Let me help you. I cuddle her close, but she pecks at me. She comes back, twittering and hops through the rose canes.

I crawl in and find her. Let's nestle in the straw. You're safe here. I can't sleep yet, because I have to figure out how to get the fire going with no wood in sight. Aubada pecks my hand, and scurries deeper into the rose canes.

Where are you going? I crawl past my bed. The rose thorns scratch a trail of blood on my arm and blood drips on the leaves. Once out of the rose canes, I brush the leaves off my shoulders and stand. My legs shake under the dawn sky. The stars of Cassiopeia flicker above. I hear Térèse's tale about the star's path in the sky that mirrors one on earth. Aubada? Aubada! I squint. My dove pecks around the winter honeysuckle bush. And just beyond that, is what? Covered with the rose canes? A fallen tree? A broken tree?

I breathe hard, then I hold my breath. I step back inside the bread terrace. My head hurts to think about what that is. What happened, and how it came to be? I have a very big knot in my stomach. Maybe it's another bread terrace growing? And not a tree. I look again. It's so close, living beside the bread terrace, like the garden. I back up against the rose canes. Whatever it is, it scares me.

I crawl on my knees and scoop up Aubada. I hold her in my loosely closed fist tucked against my side. I crawl, my head down, and slide one hand along. My knees follow. Thorns scratch and hold us, but we go further inside the rose canes, and tumble in the straw bed. Aubada, I need sleep. The wood oven is quiet and needs to be fed. And how am I going to get this string off your foot? I run my finger over her soft head. She chirps, and struggles to get away. I can't let you go. What if the Guild hunters find you? And where is Antoine? I glance up at the falcon in the plaque.

CHAPTER FIVE
Paillard Visits

I'M SITTING IN the rose canes with Aubada, and I'm not doing anything wrong, I'm not. But when somebody comes, I feel like I've been caught.

"Epi, you here?" a voice asks. "Did Aubada come down here?"

I recognize the voice. With a mix of wanting to be alone, and wanting to let him know she's ok, I hold my breath. Aubada hops further away into the rose canes. I crawl out and stand up, brushing off my pants. Maman's old dove keeper, Paillard, rushes through the archway, and gets snagged by the thorns. His hair is stringy long. His neck moves back and forth as if he's pecking while he walks. He can barely find his way down the hill, past the bridge. He can't tell if it's day or night. And he forgets that people can see him, even if he can't see them. It's getting way too light outside for him to be sneaking around.

"Epi, you have to trim back the roses."

"Aubada's got a string wrapped around her foot. She can't fly. I don't know why she hopped all the way down here."

"It's the bread. She'll always follow you." He turns and lifts his nose in the air. "Where is she?"

"Aubada's hurt." Since he went blind, he sees the world through the doves' eyes.

Paillard turns. He leans towards the rose canes. Touches the edge of the table and sets the sack on the table that Térèse took to the bridge. "I knew something was wrong. You're usually making quite the racket when you take the crowns out of the oven. Did Antoine take them to Nerac?"

It's too much to explain to him. And to most people. I can go for days being the only one stumbling around the bread terrace. I like being alone. I feel safe. People are the problem. When I see no one, and no one sees me, I don't have to explain anything. Even when blind Paillard comes in, I look around and the bread terrace changes. It becomes small and close, and even though I like thinking about Maman when I'm alone, as if she is still here, I can. But when he comes in, I know she's not here and he knows it too, and he doesn't know whether to tell me the story that she's coming back for me, or that she went away because she is busy with our work, or that lately he's been saying, yes, maybe, probably, she died. Then I gasp, feel foolish and stupid and lost. But he's blind, and I'm not, so then I am even more sad to see less than a blind man. I hope he can't see what a mess I am, but since I feel it, I know he can too. So, what is that about? I crawl out of the rose canes and take his hand. He pulls me out. I want to cry and grab a hold of him, his big shoulders, and scrunch up in a ball, and never let go. At the same time I hope he'll soon be gone so I can go to sleep and forget all this ever happened and how much I just hate myself.

"Epi, the Guild is coming for you." Paillard picks up the sack of dream breads on the wood table. The E on the sack identifies it as mine. I am not even smart enough to use a different sack. He then stoops under the table and whistles to Aubada. "Was there a message?"

"What? How do you know that? And since when, did Aubada have a message before?" I take the sack, open it. Shudders travel out to my fingers. The breads rest with some fleurins in the bottom of my sack. "Why would someone leave fleurins and not take the breads?"

"No one's going to take illegal breads. Like Maman's bread of dreams. Are you crazy? You're the only baker around here."

"The Guild knows nothing. If I catch her, can you hold her?" Aubada hops around the bread terrace, the string tied on her foot catches on the thorns and canes.

"You been up all night? You want to crawl in your bed? Listen to me. Get out of here. They don't like it."

"I only started making them because Térèse bought me some apricots."

He cups his hands around Aubada. "Apricots, here? No. Let me tell you something."

"Pah, the Guild doesn't scare me." I must be brave for him. But stay and face the Guild or leave? Both sound horrible. The Guild was responsible for Maman disappearing. I knew they could make me disappear. What I didn't know was, why they hadn't. Was I a shining example of what happens to someone charged with murder? Being kept prisoner by the Guild? "I bake all the crowns for their King."

He touches my face. "It's like, it keeps going. The shell, the snail that feeds the doves. I am blind. But I see all the things. Beautiful sunflowers? The trees budding in spring? Sure, that's good, and good things are easy to see. But I see the hard look on Claude's face, too, or when Margot storms across the bridge in the middle of the night. The disappointment in Antoine's eyes. I'm blind but I see all these things. I see that staying here isn't safe anymore for you. Look what happened to Aubada."

"Are you saying the Guild tied a string to her leg?" I pat his hand, and pet Aubada, too.

He sighs. "Wake up. Apricots don't grow around here."

I push the sack aside and sit on the table. It's strange to hear him say apricots don't grow around here. Térèse didn't tell me where she found them. It's worrisome that fleurins would be left but no breads taken. I bend my head to work on the knot on Aubada's small foot. My fingers are too big, and the knot's too small. Aubada flaps. "I'm not leaving you. Or you." I rub his shoulder. What would my leaving do to him?

He pries my hand off his shoulder. "Epi, I'm an old blind man who talks to doves. Listen to me. The Guild does care. There used to be so many more doves coming to the dovecote. I don't know what happens to them. Maybe they will return to Morocco. Maybe they're lost. But it's a sign. Aubada got away. And so should you. Go to Nerac. Get lost in the Fool's Feast."

"What about the King's crowns?" I am getting so tired of making them. I blow a breath out of the side of my mouth. Go to Nerac? Is that north or south? And then? What? I look at the knot of string on Aubada's foot. It's so small I could cut it off with the bread knife, the lame. I pick it up, from a crack in the table. I keep it sharp to slash the crowns, and it glints in the slant of the sun. If it slips even a little, I will end up cutting her foot and that would hardly help her. I put the lame back in the crack in the table. But if I leave the string, the tail of it might snag in the thorns and trap her, then a hawk could swoop down and tear her apart. Might she trust me enough to let me hold her so I could loosen the string? She hops away and flies over our heads.

"The Guild only cares about the extra crowns they can sell. Are you kidding, I could never find Nerac." At the mere suggestion of leaving, I am sure my feet have grown roots like a rose cane deeply cracking the stones of the bread terrace. I hug the sack of my breads. The scent of rose petals and apricots floods through me. Maman, the bread of dreams, I can hear you saying it. They help hungry people. A fire burns in me to face the Guild. Maybe I am crazy like Paillard says.

"Are you listening? Maman said you never listen, and that's...."

"What?" I touch his shoulder and open the sack, take out one of the breads. "And that's what? What did she say?"

"That's why she named you Epi, for ears so that part of you that would hear her even when.... she was dead. If she died, I mean."

That's not what I remember. Maman said to listen and follow the doves. As easily as I wished Paillard would stay, now I wish he would go so I can forget he said anything about Maman dying. The bread of dreams feels a bit greasy and heavy, next time I won't use as much duck fat. It's pebbled with apricots and roses, and some fall to the stone floor. Aubada flutters and pecks at the soft roasted fruit, hopping on one foot, tucking her other one up and against her belly. A hawk could fly in here. It's never happened, but it could.

"Say, uh, speaking of Maman, I followed Aubada, and she showed me something I had forgotten."

"What?"

"Just outside." I say quietly. "The canes have grown over it, but I think it's a thatched roof. A *poulailler* for chickens? An *ecurie* for Beauté? An *abri de jardin* where Térèse keeps her seeds?"

"Epi, whatever you're talking about I'm sure it's not safe, and you're better not to know. When you leave, take the breads, but don't take the millhouse bridge. I'll distract Margot. She doesn't know I brought them back to you. She's very angry about your breads." Paillard lifts a bread of dreams and smells it, then tucks it inside his coat. "*Calquecop Le Pa Que Be Quand Las Denses S'en Soun Anandos.*"

I can't remember what that means. I can't have Margot catch Paillard. I can't have him get in trouble. I can't have a hawk take Aubada. I can't even sit down. I can't imagine being more tired.

"Epi, you can remember. Listen. Sometimes the bread arrives after the teeth are gone. And I want to enjoy your bread of dreams while I still have teeth."

I want to touch his face. I want him to touch mine. "You can't trust Margot. Why on earth would you tuck one of my breads in your coat." It's crazy to think he could find and cross the bridge at the millhouse where Margot and Claude live. The bread will surely fall out and he'll never know it until he gets back up the hill to the dovecote. I tell myself I don't care what the Guild thinks, but they would delight in making a spectacle of Paillard.

"I'll take Aubada with me."

"And what if the Guild is waiting at Maman's dovecote?"

Paillard nuzzles Aubada against his cheek.

"Paillard, are you listening?"

He walks out through the archway of rose canes. He talks to Aubada. His steps set stones loose and tumbling; maybe enough stones to fill the dry riverbed. He disappears down the path.

I set the sack with my breads on the table. The Guild coming to check on me is stupid. Isn't it? Not even Margot would waste her time on me. I'm doing everything she wants. That the Guild wants. Making crowns. Making them money.

Aubada flies into the bread terrace and pecks the stones for crumbs. What? Have you come back looking for your dove friends? Maybe they are close by. Maybe they are hiding in the rose canes too.

CHAPTER SIX

The Woodshed, Finding the Box

A UBADA FLIES UP into the rose canes. I reach for her. She flits away. I go out through the archway. She's alone. The sun blinds me even though it filters through the overgrown canes. I shield my eyes from the light. Holding on to the iron trellis to steady myself, I listen for rustling in the leaves. Rose petals fall. I snap my head and see above. Aubada hops on one foot, then flits deeper into the canes. The canes have grown over a thatched roof. But like I asked Paillard, I don't know what this place was.

A *poulailler* for chickens? An *ecurie* for Beauté? An *abri de jardin* where Térèse keeps her seeds? I lift some of the canes. Really? Doors? Aubada chirps above me. So strange. I push on the doors, but the canes have grown into a strong web, keeping the doors closed. I stand on my tiptoes. The thatched roof, dry and crackly, bursts open with a tree growing out of it. That's why I thought it was a tree. Aubada, chirps, chirps loudly, then there's nothing but silence.

I wrap my fingers around the canes, and the old thorns sink deep into my fingers. I pry them out and kick them. But they are thick and strong as if their only job is to protect whatever is inside. I go back and take the saw that Antoine hangs on a nail outside the bread terrace and saw at the thorny canes.

Aubada? Aubada! Chirps come from inside the *abri de jardin*. She's looking for the seeds that Térèse kept in here. They could be rotten and festering, or growing something. Térèse hasn't talked about it in a long time.

The door handle sticks. The wood creaks. I pull again. The door gives a little but sticks at the top. The door pulls away a little more. Then, finally they creak open. Then the door falls away. A thick scent of apricot flowers, rich with honey and bees buzzing, floods my nose. The walls are tall, made of dry bales of straw. Heavy logs line the bottom. Stacked three or four on top of each other. The boughs of the trees bend their arms with flowers. Aubada flutters up and out of the thick branches. The scent is sweet. But rotten and fermented. So strange. If this belongs to Térèse, it's not like her to let it go, and not clean it up.

I lean into the *abri de jardin* further. But this is not dirt and old cabbages. It's a pile of trees. Could it have been Maman's woodshed? But why would she have stored these trees like this, in secret? I pull one of the branches towards me. The light comes through and blinds me. But the branch has fruit. Fruit, as if the tree is still growing.

Suddenly I am transported back to a place with Maman that was safe. The maze of trees. I must have been so little. Maman told the story of when she carried me, before I could walk. When I was a crying babbler, my arms spinning the air as if I could fly like a dove. So, she strapped me to her and we walked. We walked in the North Field. We made a path around the trees. The trees lifted their boughs in spring with flowers, and in the fall with fruit. The doves got fat. The trees got taller. I got older. I didn't pay attention.

Why did Maman cut her trees down? We sat at the trunk of the trees and counted branches or watched bees pollinating the flowers. Maman told me stories. I don't remember them, but only how they made me feel. The scent of the bark, sometimes rough and sometimes smooth, reminds me. Her stories told tales of another world.

The trees were all different. Some were big enough to hold us. Care for us. Keep us safe. Trees that let us make our home in them. Let the doves' nest and live in them.

When the field was dark, we cut the branches. Maybe with this saw! I felt mad. We sawed and tore till the trees were in small enough pieces for us to carry. As we made the trees smaller, and smaller, I felt smaller and smaller too.

Maman loved these trees. Why did she cut them?

My fingers find the round end of a log, run down the thick wide grooves. Apricot bark swirls with white patches like the clouds overhead. Little green shoots feather along the branch. I would never have found you except for Aubada. I forgot you. And you've been dead for years. I step inside, Aubada swoops in and rests on the tree, hopping along the branch.

The apricot branch sticks out, full of green leaves. I pull out the branch. If the Guild asks, I will just say, go ask Antoine, he's the woodmonger. He chooses the wood for the oven. But we are both apprentices of the Guild, and I am the spare one, who takes the blame for everything. And as the spare, it's my duty to keep him safe too. I get up, pulling the log out. Finish the crowns. Get some sleep. Let him go to Nerac. Leave me be. Where IS he?

Aubada flies close. Her wings brush my head. Something glints in the light of the torch. Wedged in between the branches is a metal handle. My hand snakes in. A mouse squeaks out and up my arm. I jerk back.

The handle slips away, falling deeper in the branches. Aubada chirps noisily. Shoo. The branches sink under my weight, but I grab the handle and lift the log out. There are grooves cut in it and a clasp like lock. It must be an ordinary log. But it's not. Ordinary logs don't have handles. As if ants are crawling on me, the hairs stand up on the back of my neck. A layer of dirt cakes the bottom. Aubada coos on the rose arbor, I look up.

"Aubada come down." But then she flies off. I run to the archway to see her fly over the thatched roof.

I tumble the log with handles and the apricot log inside the leather carrier. Light breaks open the sky with streaks of flame and scarlet.

Safe back inside the bread terrace, I set the leather carrier on the table. It flaps open. Chills race up my back. I lift the apricot log to sit on the table beside the sack of my breads. I stare at the door to the oven. I lift the handle of the strange log to sit on the oven shelf. What are you? My excitement dances and I pick it up and hold it in my arms. Oh, you're a box. I quietly put the log back on the shelf.

You're a box.

I let out a big breath and hold a linen cloth over the handle of the iron door. It scrapes as I move it away from the mouth of the oven. Inside the oven, it's cold and deadly quiet. The crowns in the oven are quiet. Is it too late? The fire is dead.

I look at the box, which looks just like a log of the tree. Except that it has a handle. How did this box get inside the woodshed, and buried in the apricot tree? What happened? I remember something about this box. And something about the night Maman disappeared. It's all a blur of the oven and footsteps. Voices and heated words that make my stomach close up tight.

I look back in the oven. Focus on these crowns. Get them finished for Antoine. It's my job. Who I am. I can't let him down. In Nerac, they think he makes them.

I sneak another look—what is this box saying? I remember Paillard's words. The Guild is coming for you. I lean in and listen to the box. Worried. Scared.

I set the sprouting apricot log in the mouth of the wood oven. The new green branches spring back at me. I turn the bread peel around and with the end of the handle, push the log with feathering branches next to the crowns. I hold them in place and cringe, feeling some wildish part of me gleefully dancing, because I found free wood! I touch the delicate branches with the flame from the torch. I breathe in and watch, then blow on the flames. The small leaves fizzle and pop. The new green branches illuminate like threads of lightning in the sky. I run my fingers along the top of the log, which looks like a box, and then lift it by the handle and place it in the entrance of the oven. Could the fire from her trees open the box since they are from the same tree? Or might the box burn up completely? I slide the box further into the mouth of the oven and step back.

The ladle in the water bucket glints in a ray of sunshine. The cool water tastes good and runs down the side of my mouth. I wipe it away with my sleeve. I glance in the mouth. In the oven, the flames lick and whiten the ceiling as if the fire came from Guild wood that burned for a full day and night. The fire from the apricot log curls in flames over the box, warming it with the scent of something delicious, like Maman's bread of dreams with cherries and wild onions, or with pears and thyme. It's been a long time since I've eaten anything filled with so much love.

In the distance footsteps crush leaves on the towpath by the river. I look in the oven, hoping that my eyes can hurry the fire and the crowns to finish baking. Antoine's coming. Hurry! He really should have left by now. There'll be no living with him if he has to wait another year to enter the Guild test. He'll have to pick up the crowns and run to the top of the hill to catch the wagon. Is that how he gets to Nerac? The river must be too dry, but how far down, maybe he leaves the barge at Brax? He only needs one perfect crown from these five to enter the Guild shop. Everyone knows Guild crowns have to all look the same. But who even remembers what a bread of dreams looks like?

I watch the fire from Maman's apricot log work over the crowns and the box.

The Guild is coming here to question me. I say it out loud. Me? The spare talmelier, Epi, the quiet one. I say it again. They don't trust me. It still doesn't make any sense. Between Antoine and me, I am the good Guild apprentice, a good worker. Dependable. Quiet. Certainly stupid. My feet push into my crusty boots. I never make waves, until last night. But no one knows me.

Inside the wood-fired oven, the apricot branch bursts into flames, and showers sparks over the flattened Guild breads. The apricot log glows as if it has a bright red sun inside. Hissing and singing.

My hands clasp together, then still under my arms and then rest on my hips. I wrap a worn linen around the box that sits in the mouth of the oven. I whisper. "Box, what is your story, where have you been." The box feels small and big wrapped in the linen. It's warm against my chest. I shake it, something rattles inside. I sit on the wood table. The wrapped box on my leg. The linen smolders, and the box jumps down on the stone floor. Dirt flakes off the bottom. I pick it up again. My fingers tremble and press and push the lock. But the box's mouth stays clamped shut.

The bread lame scrapes off a little dirt. I blow away the dust. Then I scrape a little more. Am I scratching it or is something etched on the wood? A circle? I scrape more. I look up from my work on the box to hear the oven sizzle, then hiss. I put the box down and open the oven. Smoke pours out along with a terrible burning smell. I wave away the smoke and slide the peel in. One by one I pull out the crowns and slide them on the table. I stand and look at them, steaming like piles of horse *merde*. They went from looking like soft bellies of frogs to blackened stones. All I wanted was for the crowns to bake quickly. I guess the wood from Maman's woodshed could burn up the bread terrace.

Five bells chime from the church on the hill. My heart falls. It's too late. I've been up since midnight, and this is all I have to show for it. My own bread of dreams brought back to me, the crowns burnt, Aubada injured. And a mysterious box that I can't open. The chimes jar me, and I knock against the bread peel, which was leaning against the table. It clatters on the stone floor next to the box. The garden gate opens and closes. Great. Of course, Antoine is coming to collect his crowns. He's bound to be in a foul mood, after digging holes or moving loads of stones for a new wall for Térèse. His footsteps get closer.

"Where the hell have you been?" I ask Antoine before he enters. I slide the darkest crowns in the bottom of the basket on the table. My sack of breads rests beside it. Maybe the crowns won't look so burned when they cool, but there's a chance they'll look worse too. Footsteps crunch closer. My heart leaps. I wish most of all that Antoine would see me. I want more than that from him, but if we could be on the same side, be friends. If I am honest, that wouldn't be enough. He's become such a taskmaster, maybe it's because he thinks he's been chosen to be the next Guild leader. I have no idea how the Guild hierarchy works. Will he share that job with Margot, when Claude retires? And here I am the spare talmelier, but the one who actually does all the work. Or maybe Antoine's afraid, because he really doesn't know anything. He can't be the next Guild leader. He could never tell me that he doesn't know anything. I wish I knew what to do. I can't very well want him to protect me from the Guild, because I am the one protecting him. I quickly throw a linen over the box and put it in the sack with my breads. A shadow appears in the archway. I pick up the peel to protect myself, or to look busy, whichever will keep the Guild away.

"It's about time you came back." I look at who came to the bread terrace. My heart quickens. My chest tightens. It's not Antoine at all.

CHAPTER SEVEN

Térèse Visits, Brings Garlic Flowers

YESTERDAY SHE STOOD across from me, her mouth turned in and turned down, and her face just as red as the tomatoes she tells me she wants to find. My youngest sister, Térèse and I haven't spoken since our fight yesterday. She spent the night in the garden talking over her ideas about love with the peas. Maybe she's settled on how to convince me or maybe she's found someone else to focus on. Or maybe she's snipping off the chives before they can set seeds.

"You're stupid and you don't know *merde*. Your words can't keep me away." She thrashes through the thorny rose canes, but I am pretty sure her words are intended to push me away. She rolls her shoulders forward and backs through the canes, and into the bread terrace. She turns to watch her step. Her long dark hair hangs over her eyes. She steps in further, and the canes catch her sleeve. Her arms wrap and hug something against her belly. She shakes her head from side to side and her hair swings off her face.

"Snails and roses! The cause of all my troubles!"

"What are you wearing? A dress made of fur. Feathers? And flour sacks?" The fur sleeve snags on the thorns of the archway. I was hoping she wouldn't stop in to see me before heading to Nerac. I feel so awkward about yesterday. Since she said she loves me, she's been really angry. It's because I haven't said I love you back to her. But if I did, then what? I don't know what to say because she's Térèse, and I'm Epi.

"Epi. You can't even see out of the bread terrace. Cut these canes back." She pulls the basket free and the green stems fly all over the stone terrace.

I stoop to the stone floor, my shoulder against hers. She grunts in frustration at me. And pushes me over. She gathers the stems into a bouquet. If you look closely at the green heads, you can see they are the tiniest, the most perfect seeds of the garlic. I watch her braid the stems and smell them. Has garlic always smelled like Térèse? Or has Térèse always smelled like garlic?

"Uh, oh." She stands and lifts the linen covering the basket of burnt crowns on the table. "Epi, you never burn the crowns. What happened? I guess Antoine won't be entering the contest this year either." She opens the sack of my bread of dreams, the corners of her mouth turn in. "Why are—who brought your breads back here?"

"They were here when…." but then I quiet and didn't finish saying that it was Paillard who was here and brought them back and told me the Guild knows about my breads, and I have to leave. I don't know what that means for me, yet alone for Antoine, who works in Nerac and knows nothing or what that would mean for Térèse, who brought me the apricots which started me making them. I lift the sack of breads away from her and put it further down on the table.

She hands me the bunch of garlic flowers. "I'm still angry with you, but Happy Birthday, Epi. I should let you fend for yourself. But here." She touches my arm, then rubs it, and my hand, and all my concerns about the breads disappears.

I look in her eyes, and shrug away from her touch. She opens the basket and tilts it towards me. I shrug. "I can't do anything with this garlic." I push away the basket.

"Listen, Madame buys my seeds, all kinds of…seeds and especially wild carrot leaves. She says they work best when they're dry. But they grow best under the wheat, which is so hard to find."

"That's what Madame says? Hmmpph, she doesn't know much. She sounds as stupid as…you."

It hurts me to see her eyes fill with hurt at the sharpness of my words. But I have to get her to leave me alone. It hurts me to hurt her. But she doesn't know who I am. Who I really am? And it would be much worse to hurt her by leading her on when I know who I am. But this is terrible because she brought me the apricots, and that's when I started remembering and making the bread of dreams. She understands the risks—and yet she takes the sack of breads to the river, to the table there, so I don't have to leave. But now she's also taking wild carrots to Madame? It's too risky to stir up trouble. That can't be good. Maybe she won't bring them to me anymore. I want to show her the box, but then she would know I left the bread terrace. She would be really mad about that.

"Madame's not stupid at all. But never mind. What's wrong?" Térèse asks.

I stare at her. "Do I embarrass you? Do I look stupid? When did you stop asking me to go with you to Nerac? Or even to look for wild wheat?" I sigh. Her face looks even more open and searching, tries to convince me, without saying anything. She does think I'm *coille, stupid*. She's often said that about other boys, that the thoughts in their heads don't amount to the *merde* from one chicken. I somehow thought I was different, but maybe not. Maybe I'll never understand what she's thinking. And maybe it's because I want that too much. Because I know how lonely I am. She must be lonely too.

"You're so grumpy today." She folds her hands around mine.

"Me? You're the one who's like a falcon. Térèse. Look. Maybe I've been here too long. I can't even make one good crown for Antoine, for the test. He only needed one crown, and look." I don't want her to feel any kind of sorry for me. "Let's go to the garden, show me your beans."

She stands in front of me. "It's not very far. But no."

I step forward and put my face in hers again. I've watched Antoine do this to me. This is what it means to be a boy, push your way in. "Take me to the garden."

She steps back. "Why? Someone might see you. It's not safe."

I step back. Put my hands on the burnt crowns. My fingers circle the raised and slashed crust, the sharp edges. They feel like the darkness of night, burning in a fire.

"You wake me up talking to the peas or the fig tree. Look at your arms, all your stings, I can help. I know how to draw the wasps away. Take me to the tree." I need to stop shaking.

"Epi, these are bee stings, not stings from fig wasps." She squints and leans into me as if I have a bug on my forehead. "Stay here. I'll be back."

"I can get my own figs if that's what you're doing. It's not much farther than the woodshed." I follow her outside the archway.

She turns around and pushes me back. "Epi, you can't."

"I had to, Aubada flew here and then she fell through the roof—and then she—because of the string, her foot, well, it's broken. Probably."

"What? Men can't take care of doves! And look. Look up. See that full moon?"

"Of course. I'm not blind, I'm not like Paillard."

"Epi...no. Look, you really are stupid. That's the moon of dispute." She pushes me to sit down. "You walked over there?" The way she said there, made it sound like it was as if I had walked to Nerac.

I sigh. "Aubada, she. Needed me. And then. Oh, never mind. But Térèse, Maman's trees, the cut ones, they are growing." Now she'll understand why I left the bread terrace. Why I have to save Aubada.

She touches my forehead. "You don't seem sick. But it's not like you to lie." She crosses her arms over her chest. "And ok, I give up, where's Aubada?"

"With Paillard. I think." If she's this upset about the woodshed, me going there, then there's no way I can tell her about the box.

"I always tell you where I'm going. Did you even call out to me when you got this wild idea?" Térèse grabs my hand.

"Just say it. I'm stupid."

"That's not the point." Her gaze falls on my hands. She reaches out and touches me, then frowns. "Look at you, I mean, really. You're not stupid. I would have gone crazy staying in the bread terrace."

"I'm glad you understand."

"But you have to stay safe. Stay here."

My heart sinks. Stay Safe. What is going to happen to me? My feet feel glued to the bread terrace and at the same time staying here feels like a death trap. Tears sting my eyes. I wouldn't even know my way beyond the bridge. But for the first time ever, I don't think it's safe here anymore. Our eyes meet. Her brown eyes search mine, dark eyebrows raised.

She closes her eyes and opens them, like a cat watching a mouse. "But Epi, I have to ask you, er, tell you something. You and Antoine both have Guild jobs. And I am starting work today, too."

"For the Guild? Not the Guild?" Térèse wants a job. This is a surprise. She's already so busy. Maybe she wants a job to forget her garden. Maybe she wants a job to get out of Ceres. She could never leave her garden, like I could never leave the bread terrace. Maybe the Guild wants her garden? No, she's leaving me. That's got to be why.

"What's the big deal? You bake their bread. Antoine chops wood and delivers bread to the Guild."

Sun comes through the canes, lighting her brown and gray speckled fur sleeves that curve towards her dried elbows. I wish she'd let me rub them with a bit of duck fat to smooth them. She cleverly stitched this dress together from bits and pieces of bread linens, maybe that she stole from the Guild, and from deer-skins. Her round cheeks like cherries in the sunlight streaming through the rose canes. Her hair shines. Is she still washing it with moss? How tall she's grown. "Maybe you could sell your peas and lettuces to the Guild?"

"But no, I don't think we need another family member to sell out to the Guild. Besides, Madame Bouquin gives a much better price."

"You're working for her? The stupid seed lady?"

"Madame Bouquin has a shop. In Nerac. On the street that runs along the Baise, it's called Le Graine. Do you remember?"

Why am I supposed to remember all these things that I had forgotten. Will everyone please just leave me alone? I close my eyes. "It's a shop? Along the Baïse?" Memories stir in me. Strange aromas.

"Le Graine, yes, you could say it's a garden shop."

"How do you get there?"

"I used to walk through the fields. But now I take the wagon."

"Wait…so this isn't your first day." I really had no idea what she was talking about.

"Epi, Madame's, it's complicated. It's the best place to sell your breads. Screw the Guild and what they think. It's perfect. She's on our side."

Our side. Even though I work for the Guild, Térèse still thinks I am on Maman's side. The box, I should tell her, before she finds it. She moves closer, did she see it? I feel around for it with my foot and push it further under the table. I should say something. I search my brain for what Antoine says when he leaves. Nothing, that's when my whole body comes alive, both when he comes into this space and when he leaves. I act busy, waiting to see what he says. But now with Térèse the same feelings wash over me. I sense her hands wanting to weed the hair from my face, but it's everything I can do to not reach for her face too.

I'll miss you. I need you. You're a good sister. But I don't say it. I back up into the wood table. Térèse steps into me and holds the back of my head. Her lips press mine and her mouth presses softly into my mouth. She tastes warm and spicy, like cloves or cinnamon or a tree bark. Her other hand squeezes my shoulder and then snakes to my belly.

"What? No!" I push her away. Even though I wish for such closeness. It's very confusing, how in this moment of leaving the bread terrace, the oven's warmth and the breads on the table, I feel a collision of all of us being here but at different times. The bread terrace holds or offers up some kind of magic from the night Maman left. A magic where we're all the same. Locked in this dance. It must be because I am Epi, supposed to be a boy, but I am a girl. How can I know what I want? Antoine would never step forward to kiss me. But I feel chills imagining that if I stepped into his space and kissed him.

"Térèse!" I wipe my mouth, and then quickly wipe the back of my hand on my leg. Her mouth tastes like chives.

"Look, I love you. Promise me you'll stay here. I won't be back till late tonight."

The feelings wash over me and I stir them into warm ashes. There's a spark in my stomach. "Bring something that will be good in the fire, like mushrooms or like a rabbit ready to roast?" I blurt out, horrified that I asked Térèse to bring me a rabbit. She's a Cathar and doesn't believe in eating meat. Cathar's believe that eating the flesh of an animal is the same as eating the soul of the animal. And even worse, that the soul of the animal can get stuck in you if you eat it. But on the other side is Maman who believed that if you ate meat, it fortified that animal's strength in you. And made you more like that animal. But that is no answer either. I wonder what eating rabbit does, does it make you more timid, or jumpy? There is no animal I know of that

I would rather be more like than a dove; silent and beautiful. Flying out of here. Knowing which way to go. But I could never eat one. So, I'll settle for being like an onion.

"I can't do that, Epi."

"What can you bring me, then? What should I be more like?" Then a wild thought. Maybe in Nerac I would be safe from the Guild, even though I would be in the town owned by the Guild. Maybe they would never see me. Or look for me there, since I am confined to the bread terrace.

"If I can find any, I'll bring you tomatoes. Love apples."

"What are they? Is that a fruit or a vegetable?"

"How do you not know these things? It's both. A fruit—according to its family, but the way people see it, it's a vegetable."

"So you think they might be in Nerac? Are there a lot of food sellers at the Fool's Feast?" I hold the table, getting dizzy just thinking about leaving the bread terrace and standing in the open of the garden.

The fire in the oven crackles. Smokes.

"There it is. That funny look again. Promise me. You've got to stay here. The moon makes everything more visible."

Térèse must know something about the box. About the edges of the day Maman left. How did the box get so much dirt on it? Maybe it was somewhere else before it was in the woodshed. Maybe it means Maman is still alive.

"Take your garlic and carrot leaves." I push her out of the archway.

"They could help you remember. But you're not ready. Maybe tonight, I won't be late."

"Bring something. I have to make more bread of dreams."

"Epi. You have to stop. Get some rest."

"Goodbye." I look in her eyes.

She bows her head and ducks through the rose canes, knocking off a few petals that I missed drying, grinding into flour. They float to the stone floor.

I look around the bread terrace. What would I do if Térèse didn't come back? This pile of stones called an oven looks different. I feed the fire, surrounded by thorny rose canes. Maman, can you imagine how long I've been here? The box hides under the table. Térèse demands I stay and Paillard insists I leave. But what would Maman say? Paillard seems to think she's alive? But if she is, why wouldn't she come back here?

I set the box in the mouth of the oven again. Then after a few minutes of heat, I throw a cloth over the box and remove it from the oven. Take the bone handled bread blade, the lame, from the table. I pick up the box and turn it, gently. Blow the dust away and hold it to the light. Something is etched into the bottom. A shell? I scrape, gouging the wood. My breath leaves me. The box falls on the stone terrace. I kick it away.

Near my feet, the box sits quietly. A tree is carved on the bottom. A large tree with a canopy of branches as big overhead as its roots extend underground. I can't believe it. Either that I found this box or that I'm getting ready to go. Because where is Antoine? He hasn't shown up. He's late. Or he's dead. I have to find out. I stuff the burnt crowns inside the sack with my bread of dreams. I take the box, wrap it with a linen cloth. It's smaller than either the bread of dreams or the burnt crowns. And it fits in perfectly.

THE WEIGHT OF leaving the place where Maman could find me drags me back. But I have to find out what happened to Antoine. And this will be easy. Nerac is just over the hill. If there's a chance that Maman is still alive, maybe, she will even be there, waiting for me. And then, I can give her the box, and we'll come back, as if nothing ever happened. I have to get these crowns to Antoine. What happened to him? I throw the sack of bread over my shoulder. Tuck the box under my arm. I whisper, *Aubada stay*

close. But she flies ahead. I hurry after her. I can't lose my dove. Beauté's neighs and snorts, but she doesn't come to me. Then I stop in my tracks. A terrible horrible thought does come to me. Did Claude sell Beauté to the Guild? I click my tongue against the roof of my mouth to call Beauté.

She answers. But sounds far away.

The mist from the river swirls, cloaking the path. A strong breeze starts in the treetops and clears the mist enough to see my mare, Beauté, pull a wagon and shakes her head. Oh, it is her. To see her makes my heart stop and run at the same time! Does she even know me anymore? How I want to leap on her. She loves working and pulling and plowing, but not like this. Not with the Guild. She was just a colt when Maman left. A black colt. I feel her emptiness too. Deep down in my stomach. A dark panic creeps over me. Hair prickles on the back of my neck. I couldn't live if she looked at me strangely. If Beauté has forgotten me. I would cease to exist if she doesn't know me or would be afraid of me. Of me.

I fear being seen, but I step out to see her better. She's mostly gray. All Camargue horses are born black, Maman said, to protect them, keep them hidden from the Guild. But when did she turn white? She's not safe, either. I don't take any comfort in Térèse's words. "Stay safe, stay here."

The driver cracks the branch across Beauté's back. The wagon looks heavy, full of peasants, farmers and talmelier. Beauté bumps into the air. Chains hang off the sides of Beauté's harness and attach with iron hooks to the wagon. Her legs lift. She shifts back. My oldest sister, Margot, steps in front of the wagon.

A rooster crows. Térèse is in the wagon and stands up. She shouts at Margot. "I will not. Not today or any day."

What are they arguing about? I want to run to Térèse, but I can't let Margot see me leaving Ceres. Maybe she is the one who found my bread of dreams. Maybe there are more Guild members waiting. Waiting to question me like Paillard said.

We have to get past Margot, and up the hill. Tell Paillard at the dovecote. The dizziness hits me. Dizziness at what I am doing. I feel invisible. Shaking so much from fear that maybe I have disappeared. A bird lights in a tree on the other side of the Gelise but I can't tell if it's Aubada or not. The mist thickens and shudders run down my spine. I untie the boat and drag it out. Staying under the bridge, and away from Margot. Would she send me back to the bread terrace? No, worse. She would beat me. I can't trust her. Where are the oars? I feel around and pull out the handle. It's the old bread peel and I use it to push off the bank. I am thankful for Beauté making noise. For the wagon clinking. For the passengers coughing. Above us Margot's rough voice asks, "Térèse. You will, because you owe me. Bring him to me. Or double the toll." Margot wants to take me to the Guild and question me about the breads.

Once across the pond, I leave the boat, it drifts out. But I stand still. To stop making noise. It takes everything I have to slowly climb the bank and not run. I follow the towpath by the Gelise River. I brush through the bushes, then veer off the path, turning left into the North Field. The ground is hard, dry as a bone. My throat tightens, I can't swallow. Aubada flies over the field towards the top of the hill. The dovecote waits like a prize, I have to tell Paillard I am leaving. The dovecote, a fat little house perched on skinny legs, like a heron stalking fish by the river.

I lean forward and climb the hill. I trip and fall. I run and search the sky for Aubada. The sack slung over my shoulder feels heavy, like I'm carrying rocks. I set it down. My breads and Antoine's crowns together in the same sack must be the reason. Plus, fleurins and the box. It's been years since I've been this far from the bread terrace. I gulp air, but none goes in me. I stand still. Frozen. My legs don't work, they shake too badly. I turn around and stare at the space where I know the bread terrace must be. Might Margot have gone herself to the bread terrace? Will she find the woodshed and the thatched wheat roof, all of Maman's trees inside? Will I be in trouble again? I look ahead and scan the field for movement, for Aubada. The tip of the dovecote's roof juts up at the top of the hill, still a hike away. A flurry of dove's swoops over the field. Might she have rejoined them?

"Paillard?" I circle the dovecote, panting, but can't hear anything besides the birds and can't make out anything in the field below. It's like from here the rest of Ceres is cut off. I step in the dry and fresh mounds of *merde* underneath the dovecote and look up. I remember scooping it up and spreading the *merde* out over the field to dry. People would come by to buy it, or even steal it. Now it's only used by Térèse and only sometimes.

Halfway up the ladder, I look down.

Maybe I missed Paillard? Maybe Margot stopped him. Maybe he's out by the road waiting for the wagon. Maybe he can't hear me over the wind. But then I hear a groan from inside the dovecote. "Paillard, did you like the bread? You're right." My hands climb, my feet go up the ladder. "I'm listening. I'm leaving."

CHAPTER EIGHT

Epi Finds Claude

I CLIMB FURTHER. INSIDE the dovecote. The smell is dusty and ripe. The doves flutter and coo above. My eyes adjust. Doves flutter around. I duck. Feathers and dust fly around my head.

"Paillard? Hello?" My fingers tremble. Doves walk out of their holes and onto the roosts. Some lift off, and some land and walk in. What's he talking about? They're here.

Each nest holds a pair. It feels like the bread terrace, or the woodshed, but smaller. I know this feeling. The nests are all around the four sides and reach up to the roof, there are perches for the birds, and they are arranged so that all the droppings drop down here on the ground. Still on the ladder I reach for the small sunflower sitting in one of the nests. Maybe one of the birds is sick, and that's why the sunflower was left. I flake a few grey and white sunflower seeds into my palm.

"Chase them away. If the Guild finds them, they'll kill them." A voice pierces the soft coos of the doves. He coughs. He sounds very strange.

"Paillard? Where are you?"

Then my eyes adjust. Another figure rests on the other ladder, but I look again, and he's kind of stuck on it, he's clutching it, his one arm grabbing his other arm through the rungs. The voice is not Paillard's. It's Claude, my one-time father.

"Claude, what are you doing?" I can't call him father. He's my stepfather, one time father, I guess. There was one time when it felt like he was a kind of father. He took care of Maman but after she left, I really don't know what he did. He certainly didn't help Margot with the millhouse, or at least not much, she wouldn't let him. Whenever I saw him walk by the bread terrace it was like he was staring me down.

"The doves eat the grain that the Guild needs." He says.

"No, doves help plant the grain. The Guild was always better at killing than growing."

"Epi, I forgive you. We both know, we all know. Antaia died because of Bouffe, because of you."

"Bouffe?" My stomach sinks. Bouffe, bouffe, I say under my breath, but nothing comes to me. It feels like a word that was important to me once.

"Her fireflute."

"Her fireflute," I remember I was so upset. My stomach did turns. The doves flutter above me. In a panic they fly off. Their nests are empty.

"Epi, I know you were just practicing how to make a fire with Bouffe. You didn't mean it. Did you?"

"Mean what?" I get a strange feeling in my stomach at Claude's mention of Maman's fireflute, Bouffe. I had forgotten all about it. And what did I do? Or did Bouffe do it? Was there a song? A fire? I am not sure at all. But he remembers.

"So maybe you did. You are quiet. But not stupid. You wanted to take Antaia's place." He struggles to get up. He turns sideways and leans against the wall where the dove nests begin above. One walks out onto the perch and hops on his head and then pushes off, flying to the top of the dovecote.

He steps closer, into a shaft of sunlight. He lifts my chin. I step back. I hang the sack on a perch. He's bleeding from the arrow in his back.

"Oh my god, Claude. What happened? Who did this?" I suddenly get very cold. And want to bend over in the middle, fold completely in half.

"The Guild needs you. We'll take care of you. Epi. You can make it right."

"Claude, who did this?" I shake my head. "Stay with me, Claude. Don't sit down." And when did this happen? Why would someone shoot Claude? Then I get sick thinking maybe it was meant for Paillard? Did this happen when Paillard came to tell me it was too dangerous for me to stay? Did he come back and see that Claude was shot? And then left? Maybe he's back at the bread terrace. Maybe Margot has him.

"Antaia, I forgive her, too. When she left. They made me. It hurt me to say she died."

I had to think, what was he talking about. His words come from a faraway place. "You mean you had to say Maman died? Does that mean she isn't dead?" What in the world? His words sound strange. It hurt him to say she died. Because she did die, or because she didn't? I'm scared to hear more. Is he dying? His words settle on me like a dark cloud.

"Can you ever forgive me? They will show you." He squints at the doves, and waves his hand, then it falls into the feathers and straw.

"Where Maman is?" My chest feels hollow and Claude's words feel stuck in my hair, like a spider web.

"The fields."

My heart pounds in my chest. So, will the doves show me? I slip away, biting my lip. And Bouffe, what does her fireflute have to do with it?

"Eleone."

"Did Margot make you say Maman was dead? Where is Maman?" I shake inside and feel hollow again. I bite the inside of my cheek. I never say any words, and the sun has barely come up, and I'm out of words to even think.

"Get to the Guild shop."

"Is that where she is?" Maman is working for the Guild. My heart falls.

"Tell Antoine. He's a good son." His eyes search mine. Then flicker. Gazing far away. His chest puffs out, his breath disappears. He slumps over then his hand slips off the ladder and he tumbles down into the *merde*. His hand opens, sunflower seeds in his palm.

"Claude!" Blood seeps from his wound, trailing down his chest. He called me Eleone, my Psomi name. Tears stream down my cheek. What happened? I grab the sack with both the crowns and the bread of dreams, gold *fleurins* and the box.

I have so many questions. Did the Guild shoot Claude? Why? But then a chill runs through me. Or maybe they thought he was Paillard. All I can think is that I have to get to Antoine, he isn't safe either. This is all my fault.

Aubada flutters down. Her beak pecks at the sunflower seeds in Claude's open hand. Her one delicate foot tickles. The other one, broken and wrapped with the short string, hangs limply. I look more closely. Could Claude have been right? Maybe there was a message attached. But that means either of two things. That the message was tied on by someone who lives somewhere that Aubada flies. Or that someone here was sending a message, and who would do that, and who were they sending it to? My stomach burns to find out.

CHAPTER NINE

Epi Goes to Nerac

OUTSIDE THE DOVECOTE, the noises close in. I lean and stand still. Its Beauté's hooves pounding on the road and a swell of voices. The wagon that was stopped by Margot at the bridge climbs the hill. A man in the cart belches. A whip cracks. Beauté!

I lift Aubada up. Her foot clasps around my pointer finger. I brush her twig-like foot with my thumb, the small string still attached to her broken foot. Close my eyes. I stroke her head. Aubada, what do you know? If I can follow you, maybe you'll show me the fields and Maman. Maybe Maman wrote a message to me. If I can keep you safe, we'll find her. I bring her to my cheek. She struggles. Stay with me. Wait, so I can see where you go. I set her on the rafter above me. She hops around.

I have to leave here. I wipe the tears away. Is it possible that Maman is still alive? I can hardly breathe, looking at Claude. No, Aubada, we'll let the wagon pass.

Aubada hops around.

We'll go back to the bread terrace. Because no one knows I was even here.

Aubada flutters up and lights on a rung above me. Aubada, wait. out of the dovecote.

But I can't. Too much has happened. I have to find Antoine, if he doesn't know I have to tell him what's happening. My fingers pick up the sack. It feels much heavier than before I got to the dovecote.

Where is she? I push my way through the sunflowers. At the top of the hill, I run out in the fog. No Aubada. I look back and the dovecote sticks up above the fog. Aubada circles the dovecote, rounds the hill, and disappears into the thick fog of the field, where once Maman's maze of trees grew.

The cart driver pulls the reins back and Beauté rears up.

"Out of my way." The cart lurches ahead.

"Please! I have to get to Nerac." I run behind the cart. Where is Térèse? The last I heard her was when Margot was telling her that Térèse owed her. What happened? Did she make Térèse get off the cart? I'd be afraid to learn Margot forced Térèse to go back inside the bread terrace. Opening the doors of the woodshed? Realizing the trees of the maze are inside? That the thatched roof holds wheat that Maman grew, that we grew and harvested?

He looks me up and down. "You're not from here, are you? I know everyone in these parts. Ah, so you're a little thief, running away. Which side are you on?"

I scan the faces of the people on the cart. I don't see Térèse. Did some of these people take my bread of dreams? So many chills run through me, as if I am naked in front of him. I bake all the crowns for the Guild, but nobody knows who I am. Suddenly the sack I'm carrying feels heavy, with Guild crowns and the box, and my bread of dreams. I swing it behind me.

"I have to get to Nerac for the..." What can I say, I don't know what's in Nerac except Antoine and the Guild. And some strange shop where Térèse got a job selling seeds.

"Shake your sack again."

I hide it behind me.

"Fifty *fleurins*. That's about what I hear in your sack."

"Never mind, I'll walk."

"It's 15 kilometers full of hunters and robbers, boy. If you don't get killed, well, you'll wish you had."

Aubada swoops over us. She flutters towards the dovecote. Then disappears over the hill. But what about Aubada? Does she know how to avoid hunters? I don't, I had no idea, they were real. I have to keep her safe.

"Follow that dove." I tell the driver. But where is Térèse? Why isn't she coming to help me? She doesn't want the driver to know she knows me.

"You're a dove hunter. You let one get away. No worries, the King's woods are full of their falcons, especially on Feast Days like today. They'll find her."

I draw back. Aubada has to face the falcons! It's everything I can do to not run after her. He shakes the reins, and Beauté shakes too.

"Out of my way. Move over. Or I'll step on your chicken. Epi, what the hell are you doing?" Térèse walks over and around people on the front of the cart. Then she turns to the driver, "This is my betrothed."

"The fig-keeper is betrothed. Well, bust my heart." The driver bows to Térèse. "But it is the Fool's Feast today, little fig-grower."

Térèse grabs me and pulls me close so the driver won't hear. "Epi, get back to the bread terrace. You have no idea what's going on."

"Neither do you," I say. Térèse's hand squeezes mine. Can she tell mine is shaking? I reach into the sack. Touching the breads, shift the box aside, the burnt crowns. On the bottom, the *fleurins*, a few months' worth, jingle in my hand. "I'll give you ten now and forty once we get to Nerac."

"You're a better hunter than you look, to have so much Guild gold. Unless, maybe I was right, and you're a hired thief?! Sit up front, young man, where I can keep an eye on you."

Beauté snorts out a foggy breath. I touch my face to Beauté's cheek. I let go of Térèse's hand. The driver takes it instead. Térèse walks to the back of the cart.

"Get in, while this horse is still lively." He smacks Beauté with the branch and she rears up, then launches us galloping viciously ahead, pulling the cart as if she's trying to shake free of it, up the hill. Beauté passes the turn where the path of sunflowers leads down to the Gelise. This is as far away from the bread terrace as I've been for seven years. I turn around, looking for familiar sights, anything I might remember if I had to find my way back. I watch the hill disappear and my home, Ceres, sink away.

When the cart jolts over a rut in the road, I turn back and face where we're heading. Has Margot jumped on the cart too? I get shivers just thinking about her sneaking up on me. She can't ride a horse. She doesn't have a horse. I squirm in my seat. A terrible scent drifts up from behind. No, it's much closer. I lean against the driver, and he smiles. He smells like a chicken who's been dead for a month. I almost fall off, and so I lean closer. He puts his hand on my leg. I jerk away and grab the seat so I don't fall off.

Signs appear along the edge of the Kings Forest.

Do not enter.

No hunting.

Stay only on the marked path.

No gathering wood.

By order of the Guild.

Nothing looks familiar. I close my eyes. I can't think of anything else but seeing Claude. The smells and the stench of the driver is like a fog covering me. I still see Claude. I want to cry. I hold my breath. I'll die. This smell. The leaves, the scurrying of hooves, and white tails bounce and then disappear over the fields. This is it, Maman, where I'll die. I tried to find you. I did. I didn't get very far. I look behind me. The millhouse is at the bottom of the hill. I try to find where the bread terrace is hiding. I can't find it. The cart jolts again. Beauté struggles up another hill. I feel sad to think even Maman's trees won't remember me. In her woodshed. They see me leaving and wonder why Maman cut them and I left them too. I'll be back. I'll return by tonight. I am so tired. I touch the hat I wear at the oven. My heart aches to leave. I don't feel like I was ever there. Or ever here either, on this cart. I ache to find Maman too. I won't be long. Once I give Antoine the crowns and ask him—about Maman. He'll have answers about the box. He is the lead talmelier—he must know something. I can come right back on this wagon. Hopefully with Maman. But with a different driver.

I turn around, as we crest the hill, and off in the distance is the dovecote. It disappears as we go down the hill, and follow the sign, an arrow points straight ahead. Nerac 10 km. How long will Claude lay there, dead, inside.

CHAPTER TEN

The Feast of Fools

ON THE CART I breathe as quietly as possible. But I'm not used to breathing around other people, and I can't even hear my own breath, over the coughing and sputtering. I bend my head, my hands over my ears, scoot away from the driver, who is the most obvious breather on board. Maybe he's laughing? Or about to die. I'm not sure. I inch further away. Aubada flies ahead of us, into the forest. I tuck the sack under my knees. I get a hot flash that the box, the *fleurins*, burnt crowns and the bread of dreams that Paillard brought back to me—any of them are certain to get me arrested. For how could I prove that I bake the King's crowns? Conversations drift up from the back of the cart.

"Have you found any?"

"What?"

"Wild wheat for the Guild challenge?"

"None of those fields are near here, near Nerac. You'd be lucky to find a stray millet weed that escaped the crazy gardener of Ceres."

"The Guild is good; the Guild is true. The Guild feeds me. The Guild feeds you."

We arrive at the bridge into Nerac. I scan up and down the waterway. Wild colorful birds fly under the netted trees lining the waterway, screeching. Below the chateau there's only a trickle of water. Aubada, small and white, is protected from the red crested birds with long blue tails because she's on the outside of the net. How far south along the river is the next dovecote? I should try to see King Henri. I can explain everything. Maman. Me. Psomi. Now that Claude is dead—King Henri must be the head of the Guild again. Since I bake his crowns wouldn't it be best if I was the one who let him know?

Térèse lifts her basket of garlic over her head. "Epi." She grabs me. "Just what do you think you're doing? I have to get to work. Are you sick or something?"

"Which way is the Guild shop? I have to get these crowns to Antoine." Claude's dead, but I don't tell her. Or that I found a strange box. Paillard is missing. Aubada too. She wouldn't like to hear any of this news. She might blame herself. I was too busy baking the bread of dreams. I ran out of wood. I burnt the crowns. But that's the only reason I found the box. She might blame me. She might hate me. Really hate me.

Térèse pulls me to her. "Epi. You can't handle any of this. People. Noise."

I look around. My stomach curls against me. I am not on the bread terrace anymore. And everything has changed. I couldn't stand Térèse being upset with me. "Beauté needs water." I have to tell Térèse everything. But I am too scared.

"You're not going anywhere. Stay here. The driver will take care of Beauté."

I keep hold of her arm. "Him? No, he, he won't. You can't just leave me."

"Epi," she reaches out. "You just don't know. It's the Fool's Feast today. Do you know what that even means? No? You don't want to know. Take the cart back. The driver will take you back to Ceres. Take him back! Get back in the cart…"

"I have to find Antoine, give him these crowns." And ask him about Maman. Claude. The box.

"The Guild shop is on the other side of this square. You'll never make it." The crowd sweeps Térèse along. Her basket perches on her head. It really doesn't look like anyone could care about eating bread today.

"Take me." I poke the cart driver. "To the Guild shop."

"Girl, boy, I don't know what you are but I'll find out on the way back to Ceres." He yanks me close, rubs my chin, and frowns. Then shoves me away. He gets down off the cart. He grabs his crotch and my fleurins jingling in his pocket. He raises his nose towards the roasting chickens, and walks into the crowd, looking back and leering at me.

Beauté nods her head up and down, hoofing up the dirt where she stands. He should have taken Beauté to water. Unhitched her. I need to stay with her.

The cart driver runs after Térèse and spills her basket. Térèse pushes him away and gathers the garlic back into her basket. She squeezes through the crowd, holding her basket above her head. The driver follows her.

I should just forget Antoine and follow Térèse to Madame Bouquin's. But now the cart driver has disappeared too. What can she say to stop me? At the far end of the market square, *Place du Prieure*, the bells ring out from St. Nicholas. Vendors of olives and oils set up tables on the steps and display their wares. Scraggly wanderers push each other aside in front of the black pot of hot oil, a raging fire beneath it. They steal the fried squares of cream and almonds, then drop them, and blow on their fingers. The Guild Shop. It's not far. I can cross the square. It's not far. This is all a bad dream. A very bad dream. I should never have left.

I look at my boots. Raise one at a time. Straw and *merde* cover the bottom. Is that dried blood from Claude? Térèse turns the corner. Everything spins around me. I've got to follow her. I can't lose sight of her. The last time I was in Nerac it was this same day, my birthday. But it was not like this, this Feast of Fools. The square was quiet. Farmers baskets were heaped with pumpkins. They sold bags of sunflower seeds for the ducks. The only sound was church bells. Quiet whispering. Hugs and walks along the King's Park. The smells in Nerac are not like they were on the cart. They're worse. And there's so many people. I hate Nerac. I hate all these people.

CHAPTER ELEVEN
Bana Steals Epi's Sack

I THROW THE SACK over my shoulder and get down from the cart. My fingers run over the hitch, and the chains holding Beauté to the cart. I could ride her home. An apple hits the side of my head. I rub the thump. Another one hits. A small dog jumps on me. But his face is framed by a bonnet. I hold my head. It's not a dog but a smelly ruffian who takes my sack. I grab it back. He punches my arm and yanks my sack again. I look around for help. But no one sees, or cares, what's happening. He jumps away, like a wild hare. I fall on my knees. "Hey!" Is all I can get out. He lands on a table piled with flat baskets, full of *saucisson sec.* "Hey!" I yell. A few faces in the crowd turn and a few more slip on the dried sausages tumbling across the square, rolling under the cart and under feet and tables. Their dried and leathery skins coated with rough peppers and woodsy herbs. He runs under the arcade, past shops where hams swing, hoisted by their cloven feet, and butcher knives flash and slice at their fat thighs. The ruffian runs past the shops and then disappears into the crowd in the square.

I pull my hat down to keep the noises of all these people from filling up my ears. Behind me laughter ruffles up and down my neck. The air smells dirty. Smoked so badly I cough. Men lift frilly shirts over their head and hand them to women standing by. The ladies cackle and slip off their chemises, then fit mustaches above their lips. They tuck the frilly men's shirts into velvet breeches and sling quivers with arrows over their shoulders, and I look at each one. What if they didn't have this choice? What if their entire and every day was a Fool's Feast? Being a boy? Being a girl? I feel shaky. Why did I listen to Paillard and leave the bread terrace? Get to the Guild Shop and warn Antoine. That I'm in danger. He is too. Claude is dead. How will I tell him? And how will I explain that a small boy stole his crowns and he won't be in the Guild contest. My stomach feels so sick. I just want to go back to Beauté.

Prickles run up my spine. I squint past men puffing out their bare chests, still wearing their breeches. The ruffian plucks bright colored dresses from a pile on a table. And hands a plum lace dress to a man. When the man holds it up to his chest, the ruffian slips his hand in the man's pocket. The man slips the dress over his head, without noticing the ruffian at all, and hands his breeches to the woman. He laughs and embraces the wooden piling, his face blusters and reddens as the woman pushes her knee into his back and laces his dress tight. The sleeves fall off his hairy shoulders, and he guffaws like a mule.

"Excuse me, Monsieur, that ruffian just stole from you."

"What are you, stupid?" His gaze tells me he can't really see me, but his blindness is worse than that which affects Paillard. I point to where the ruffian turns and he sticks out his tongue. He waggles his behind and turns and runs with my sack. The ruffian dashes into a shop, the sign above, a big G with a falcon painted inside, its talons clawed around the part of the G that looks like a tree branch. I stop. I feel dizzy. This is the symbol I see every day. The falcon inside a G is just like the plaque set in the face of my oven on my bread terrace.

I hurry past a cart of glistening carp staring up at the sky, their eyes blank like Claude's at the end. I shudder. So, this is where Antoine works, how do I not know these things?

CHAPTER TWELVE
In the Guild Shop

A GENEROUS WOMAN IN a fancy dress stands in my way, peering in the door of the Guild shop. Feeling brave, I stomp my foot. She turns to me. Her face is brown as our crowns. Her nose is twisted. Her one giant eyebrow makes a shelf like at my bread oven over her eyes. I back up. She scrunches her brow and locks eyes with me. I'm immediately sorry. She makes a fist with her thick fist and punches me in the gut. I bend over, and the dark she-man wearing a dress, stomps away, scowling.

I back against the Guild door, trying to take in a breath, and it opens, the bells tinkling. I fall inside. The ruffian dances on the floor within arm's reach. He turns and sees me. He ducks away, but I grab him by the collar, his mouth full of chewing. He's eating my bread. My bread! He grins. Grins! Bits of bread fall out.

"Antoine, help! These are my crowns! He's trying to steal them!" The ruffian twists around and points at me. He shakes free and drops to his knees, before crawling behind the counter with my brother, Antoine.

I'd know him anywhere, even wearing that ridiculous Henin hat with wings and a net stretched over his face. He arches his back, and his corset pulls tight. There's a handkerchief tucked in his bosom. But even without the outfit, he's different from this distance, in this shop and not at the bread terrace or when I see him across the Gelise—he looks older than me, though he's younger. Antoine scratches his forehead, his rouged mouth set in a hardness. He looks up. Crosses his arms over his chest. A cool shiver runs down my spine. Here he is. I'm nervous. I'm not used to arguing. In fact, I hate even the feeling of discord with anyone. But this is different, I've never had to ask why someone was shot, what about this box, and oh yes, what really happened to Maman?

I turn and pull the door closed. Locks it and pulls the curtain down. "I have some questions for you."

"Open the door. This is our biggest day of the YEAR! Here, you, do something useful." Antoine shoves a mortar and pestle towards the ruffian and jar of white, green, and red peppercorns. "Pound these into a powder."

"Yes, Antoine."

"Ok. What do you want?"

"You listen. You never came back for your crowns. For the test. So, there they are." I point to the sack.

"He's lying." The ruffian says, then beckons Antoine to come closer, Antoine bends, and he whispers loudly. "I heard him with a lady on the cart, Epi's his name, everyone knows the apprentice of Ceres. But no one ever sees him."

I shouldn't like him, this ruffian, but I look at them side by side. The ruffian and Antoine are the same. Oh, one is a little taller and has more hair on his face, but that's the only difference. They both look ridiculous wearing women's clothes. Even though the boy stole from me, he's funny. He's got guts. He seems to have decided to be my enemy. But I wish he were my friend. And I don't like that feeling of someone being against me. It's something I can smell, like the driver of the cart.

Antoine is Ceres' lead apprentice and owns the rights to the crowns. The slashes are unique to our oven. I do the work. He gets the credit. So, really as far as who claims the crowns, as their entry, it's his call.

"Let the rest of the apprentices in with their crowns. They

only have till noon to enter the contest." Antoine lifts the counter and steps to the same side of the counter as me. He's not used to walking in a skirt. I would hate it too, so I can't say I blame him. He pushes the netting of his hat out of his eye. Is this why he didn't come back, he had to pick out a wimple?

"You didn't think I would recognize you in your *chemise*? Or that I could leave the bread terrace." Truthfully, I wish I hadn't left the bread terrace or recognized him. These toads jumping around in my stomach need to jump in the Baise, if there was any river for them to jump in.

"You said you would die if you left." He leans forward, the hair on his chest tufts out of his corset. "Which obviously is not true. I see the Feast of Fools agrees with you."

"That's what they always told me." My heart stirs to be next to him. I step close, reach my arm out, but he swats me away. I narrow my eyes at him. "Did you know the Guild was coming to question me?"

"This is…very strange. The crowns and ?" He opens the sack again. My sack. He closes his eyes. Juts his chin out. Closes the sack again.

"What's wrong?" I ask.

Antoine turns to the ruffian. "You know me, but what's your name, boy? You're entering these crowns to the Guild test? From what Duchy?"

"You don't know where I'm from. Far away. Down river. Upriver. Put down everywhere. I'm from there."

"I've never seen any crowns quite like these. I must know your name, boy, so I can give you the credit you deserve." Antoine asks the ruffian for his name again.

"All these *talmelier* are entering the contest?" They pound on the locked door.

"Oc, of course. They all want to be in the Guild." Antoine reaches in the sack again. "And what's this?" He points to the box. Where are my breads? Did Bana eat all the bread of dreams?

"Bana. Call me Bana. I'm named after a wheat but you won't find it here. That's mine too, the box. I made it."

"Bana, the Guild might just buy this box. Where did you find it?"

"Find? It belongs to a tree." Bana says.

Time slips away. I touch my head, pounding from being hit with the apple. I open my mouth to take in a breath but can't seem to breathe deeply. This is not how I wanted this conversation to go.

"Right," Antoine takes the box.

"Do you know this box?" I ask.

He points to the tree on the side of the box.

"Antoine, listen. What does the tree mean?"

His head swivels to me. "No, you listen. Burnt crowns and the bread of dreams and this box? Look at this. These are clearly Bana's crowns. I know they can't be mine. Burnt so badly. But this box is valuable and will get me into the Guild test. Antaia's box. Psomi's tree. But if, Epi, if they find out that you found it, you're dead, like Maman. They hated her. Do you want them to hate you too?" He holds my box that seems to have become his box, close.

I feel desperate for him to put it down. I inch closer to take it, slowly so he won't notice. "Hold on, there's a lot you don't even know. Like, if they claimed I killed her, then you have nothing to fear, right? I'm the one who will be in trouble for leaving. But, since you're my brother, they hate you, too. Antoine."

"Who hates me?" Shadows walk past the door, then cup their hands against the window to peer inside. Behind them, Beauté, the cart still attached to her, stomps across the street. Her shoulder twitches at the flies. I squint, who is in the driver's seat?

Antoine sets the box down on the counter. He leans into my face like I did with Térèse at the bread terrace. Looking in his eyes, I remember his story. Antoine's story about how the explorer from Portugal came into this shop. Pedro Cabral came to buy bread for his trip with thirteen ships down the Garonne River, shooting out into the sea, and landing in a faraway place called Brazil. Antoine's always making up stories that begin with a little kernel of wheat but then get mixed up with a lot of *merde.* Pedro probably spit outside the shop and that was all his visit, and story, amounted to.

"We're brothers. Guild brothers. Look. Ask yourself, why does the Guild want the box so badly? But we…we have it. We're not going to give it to them." I don't look at it, but my hand reaches the box, feels the grooves on the bark, and slides it over, picking up the box. It's warm, and I hold it against me. My stomach quiets. I back up. Bana is in the corner eating the bread of dreams out of the sack.

"Get out of here. I have to make money, take in the crowns. You live in a totally different world than me."

"I want you to listen. Stop." I shake the box at him. "The Guild hated her, and if anyone killed her, THEY killed her. Not me. But they blamed me."

"None of that even matters. They want me to lead them."

"That's what they're telling you? You're next in line, after Claude, I suppose. But you can't even bake bread."

"No, but you do. It's the one thing you can do. You've been living on the bread terrace."

"You don't know what you're talking about!" He backs up, holding the box. "I'm giving it to Claude."

"Claude's dead." My heart shakes, my arms, and legs. I hold the box close. "Claude's dead," I repeat. And until I told him, I didn't really feel the horror, Claude falling. His voice. Sputtery breathing. The blood pooling in the *merde* of the dovecote. His blood. Anything. He's dead. The betrayal in his eyes. I have to get the box back. The box knows all and what I need to learn. Maybe the arrow was meant for Antoine so he wouldn't take over? But that doesn't make any sense.

"Epi, stop saying that. Don't even wish that!"

"Wish? I would never wish that on anyone. yet alone your father."

Antoine shakes, clenches his fists. "The Guild needs good wheat. They're desperate. They asked me if I knew."

"Knew?"

"Knew who is making illegal bread."

"Stop yelling." I look down at the blood on my shirt. He sees it too. He quiets.

"Claude died in the dovecote."

"You're lying."

"I haven't even told you about Aubada and the woodshed. The trees are growing. Finding the box. Paillard warned me to leave. The Guild was coming. Térèse made me promise to stay. But I had to get these crowns to you. Claude said some things."

"Paillard warned you? So, you went to the dovecote? Why, you never leave the bread terrace. That's too dangerous for you."

"Dangerous for me? I didn't have much choice. But something happened. You have to know the truth."

"The truth?" Antoine grabs me by the shoulders and pushes me away. I stumble back from the shock. His jaw works back and forth. "You don't know how damn lucky you are to be alive. I don't need you, go home."

He's quiet. But I feel empty. This doesn't make sense. He looks scared. I take it in, and feel fear, a new fear. I came to Nerac to warn him, but he's warning me. "You knew? That Claude was going to be killed? Answer me."

"It's Psomi's fault, your Maman's fault. She stole the Guild's seeds, and here they are. At last, we have them back." He shakes the box. "And now, you'll stop making those stupid breads."

He means the bread of dreams. I freeze, picturing Claude in the dovecote. I cringe with sadness. Heat spreads out across my chest. I am scared for Térèse. And what about Paillard, what does he know? "The Guild threatened you, and so you gave them Claude?" A few steps away a thousand people are gathering in the square, celebrating the bread, the apprentices, the Guild. That doesn't feel safe. There's something terribly wrong here. Antoine, what are you doing? I look at the boy I love. Being protected by the Guild, meant you were safe. But being protected, did Claude feel that? I don't feel safe. I have to go home. Maybe Maman is here in the middle of all this.

"You're asking these questions in the Guild shop."

I touch his arm. "You know something. Something more." My nose burns with his aroma, like charred caraway seeds.

"Epi, you ask too much."

I step close. "Because, right now, the way I see it, we're both in trouble."

Antoine's brow knits together. The drape of fabric between the two wings of his Hennin hat makes him looks a bit like my dove, Aubada. I draw up my eyebrows. He steps closer. The peaks of his hat threaten to take down the baskets lined up on hooks over my head. He leans in and smells me like I'm a bowl of soup he's hungry for.

I duck away.

He shakes his head and looks hurt and confused. "You really don't know anything. So Térèse brought you? She can take you home. Where is she?"

"At Madame Bouquin's."

"The brothel?"

"Brothel? Noooo. Madame's is a garden shop called Le Graine." I bite my lip and swallow hard.

"You are so stupid. How are you, my brother?" he says.

The knocks get louder and the pounding on the doors, shakes the baskets on the shelves. Antoine looks at the door.

"You haven't told me anything." I say.

"I told them it was Claude. Yes. To protect you! You're stupid! Wake up! Baking the bread of dreams, right under my nose. Their nose! Get some sense! I told them it was probably Claude. Crazy old man trying to bring her back. Antaia. But I knew, I always knew you're the crazy one, and my brother, and the Guild will hunt you down, too. Get out of here."

"So, Claude was the Guild master but instead of asking him, they shot him with an arrow in the dovecote, because you told them, you blamed him for making the bread of dreams?"

"Are you listening, Epi? Bana, take Epi to Le Graine. Here." Antoine reaches into my sack and tosses him a gold *fleurin*. "Buy him a dress, to hide. People will think you're a girl dressed as a boy. And today that's not a good thing to be."

Bana's boots scuff along the floor from the back of the shop. "Try to keep up, ok?"

Antoine looks at the rattling door. "Cross the square and down to the quay. Térèse can try to take care of you. I'm done." He puts the box under the counter.

I push the door, the crowd at the front door won't budge. I push harder. Suddenly it flies open. The bell rings. The crowd steps back. I stop, looking in all the faces. Bana pushes me from behind. The crowd pushes against me, and then parts around us, rushing inside the shop.

"Back to the bridge. Under the nets. Le Graine's not far." Bana says. "I'm not wearing no dress today."

People rush around me. Maybe the cart driver is among them. Or they all smell bad. I close my eyes, seeing Claude. I didn't like him. He had gotten strange. Looking for messages. But he died for me. Because of me. He didn't know. Maybe he blamed me. I can't leave the box in the shop. It's not Antoine's. And it's clear he doesn't know anything about it. Across from us is Beauté, who Claude had sold to the Guild. I'm taking you back.

"Can you find a bucket, get Beauté some water? Bana?"

"Hey!" Bana yells at me.

I turn and go into the alley behind the Guild Shop, and snake inside. Apprentices line up and give Antoine their sacks. I watch as if in a trance. Antoine works for the Guild. He opens the sacks and takes out their crowns, examines them and reads the notes inside. So many shapes. Slashes. Raised faces. The crowns look like stones. I've never seen so many fleurins or so much food in one place. It doesn't make any sense, with all the shortages. I force myself to walk towards him. I scoop up a handful of fleurins in one hand and grab the box out from under the counter. He turns. Grabs my forearm, I drop the box. And kick it away and dive for it. He's too late. The box is mine again.

"Stop! Thief!"

I turn the corner of the alley and head back to Bana and Beauté. Above me on the Guild sign, sits Aubada. A falcon lands beside her. She hops away on her one good foot.

CHAPTER THIRTEEN

Bana Takes Epi to Madame Bouquin's

BANA AND I push our way through a crowd of Fool's. He pulls me, and I hold his hand. He stops, scanning the crowd.

"Make me taller, Epi."

I pick him up and he points. He waves us towards the next street. Ahead, Aubada lights on a roof. The falcon closes in. Bana pulls out the cheese he stole and unwraps it, he shoves it in my face, laughing. He takes a bite. And hides the piece of cheese in someone's hat as we pass. The falcon dives for the cheese, the person screeches, and the falcon flies away. Aubada escapes.

I pull Bana closer. But he struggles and I drop him. He frowns and jumps up, showing me his fist.

"I wouldn't hurt you." I pick him up again. And laugh, having survived a punch to the gut earlier. We head downhill towards the dry river. By the screeches, we're getting closer to the King's colorful and annoying birds that we heard at the bridge when we entered Nerac. They're hard to ignore, but Aubada would be safer with their noisy selves than out here with the quiet and deadly falcons.

The nets stretch over the plane trees and the walkway on both sides of the dry riverbed, enclosing the quay where the barges are docked. It's a different protected world inside. There's one Fool's Feast happening outside the nets, but another one inside, on the walkway. I see how wrong I was. The King's birds are safe, kept under the net and away from the King's falcons. I round the corner. Below us is the quay where the barges would pull in, but it's all dry and the net stretches over the trees lining the river. The King's colorful birds fly free under the net.

A flame swallower passes us. I scan the roofs above us looking for a flash of gray. Aubada perches in a mulberry tree beside a blue and green parrot, which must have escaped. We duck under the branches. Bana reaches up for Aubada, I step in the purple splats of fallen berries under the tree, but Aubada flies away. Above us a parrot screeches, how did he escape the nets? The falcon catches the bird in his talons. I cover Bana's eyes. The parrot's head lands at my feet. Bana jumps down and runs away. So, he's good at causing trouble but runs away from any that falls on him.

CHAPTER FOURTEEN

Epi Finds the Apple Tree and Meets Grigne

BANA HURRIES AHEAD, lifts the nets, and disappears inside. He leaves me with no choice and I duck under the opening to follow him.

A yellow cat with matted fur meows and scrambles in front of my walk. He hisses at me and leaps onto a barge and narrowly misses landing on a brazier smoking with fire. This drought looks bad. I don't even know the right questions to ask. It wasn't that long ago that it stopped raining. Térèse can still find water. The dust stirred up by all the carts and wagons on the road leaves a layer of dirt on everything. Fools and feasters walk in the middle of the dry Baïse. Smoke from many fires rises up through the trees and nets.

"How much farther is the seed shop?"

"Past the bridge, then three barges down. Why are you going to Le Graine? Never mind, I've heard it all."

This young boy, Bana, tips his hat and bows to the buyers lined up in front of the fromagerie stand, great pyramids of creamy, wrinkled goat cheese. He steals a log of cheese. We slip past spitted roasting birds of all sizes. Bana rips a roasted leg off a chicken turning on the spit and tosses it to me.

Sunlight slants through the houses, above us on the street in the uncovered area. We cross under the bridge. A terrible stench of urine wafts above us.

"Epi, come on, it's just the tanneries. Did you just get born?"

Four deerskins ranging from baby to old man stretch between two poles. I pinch my nose as we pass.

One barge, two barges, then three. Bana motions to me and stops at a door in the stone wall. The crowd of people behind surge and push me past Bana. I turn to my left and stop. Hoping the people will swarm around me. At a break in the crowd, I quickly step to the stone wall and follow it, my hands on the stones, hugging it back to Bana. I stop where an apple tree's branches spill over the wall, rotten apples at my feet along with bees and wasps.

Bana climbs and leaps, his legs like a frog and arms like a bird and he clings to the stone wall like a rat. He pulls on the branches that curl like old fingers around green and golden apples. Bees buzz around his head. I half expect him to snap at the bees and eat them. He lifts up, his torso over the top of the wall and his head disappears in the tree. He holds the branch with one hand and leans down, extending his other hand to help me up.

"Watch out!" I say.

Bees buzz around his head but he doesn't even flinch. "Hurry, Epi." Is it my imagination that his voice is softer since the parrot head fell at our feet? By walking to Le Graine, have we become friends? But I can't bring myself to lift either of my arms into the tree of buzzing bees.

He disappears over the wall.

"Bana? Come back!" I ignore the shivers in my shoulders and grab the nearest branch. A bee lands and crawls over the fleshy mound of my thumb and palm. I swat at it and it digs into me and stings. I drop to the ground. I'll never make it. I can't go any further. Even if Le Graine is just a few more steps on the other side of this wall.

A minute later a wooden door that is set into the wall scrapes open a little, and pushes away the apples and leaves, stirring up more bees.

Bana comes out. "Hurry up." He beckons.

My hand throbs red and starts to itch. A rowdy bunch, all wearing straw hats, stop at the wall and let down their pants and start to pee. Others notice the open door too.

I stand still. I've never been stung. Térèse gets stung all the time, and she stays calm. I'm sure she would be angry or embarrassed at my pitiful reaction. As a boy, I need to be braver. I never would have suspected that something that makes honey and is so beautiful, could hurt me so badly.

With the box under my arm, I scream and stomp on the apples and bees. They fly up. I hurry inside. I stand in the quiet courtyard, and gape at the apple tree.

Bana shouts, "Get out you idiot. No. Epi, help!"

I run over and lift the door to pull it closed, smacking the hands that snake inside. Bana picks up a rock. "You want rock fingers?" Bana acts quickly and smashes the rock against someone's fingers. He latches the lock on the inside.

It's very quiet. We are far away from the turmoil outside along the dry riverbed. I step closer, looking up into the tree, reaching out for the trunk.

"What are you doing? Lookout," Bana shoots his arm out, and smacks me in the stomach.

But I fall over backwards, my arms twirling, losing my balance. I land beside the tree trunk, and the box falls into the hole Bana warned me about. I kneel at the tree trunk. The roots wind down, like the branches wind up. They are similar, look the same, only one is above, the other below the ground. I carefully reach in, like when I found the box buried in the branches of Maman's dead apricot tree. I look down then lean my head away, to get closer, feeling around for the handle of the box. My fingers find the cool metal. I pull it out and brush off the dirt.

"Bana, what happened to this apple tree?"

"It didn't work."

"It didn't work, you mean make apples?"

"Get a clue, Epi. They tried to destroy it. Burn it down."

"They?"

"Who do you think?"

I look up at him. Then I realize the apple tree is the center of the courtyard. A path, bordered by roses, leads to a 4-story house. The branches scratch at the upper story.

"Is this *Le Graine*?" It's hidden by the apple tree, and by the wall.

"Goodbye, Epi. And uh, good luck in the brothel. Don't fall in any more holes." Bana makes a fist, as if he is going to punch me, then doubles over laughing at my face. He puts his hand on the stone wall. A shock of his yellow hair falls over his eyes, and he shakes his head to get it out of his face. He spits on his hands and rubs them together. He shakes his head, like Beauté would. But then, as if the most ordinary thing in the world, he jumps up to a branch and lifts into the apple tree. He swings over to the top of the wall. He sits on the top of the wall, turning to pull off an apple. He eats it in like four bites. Bits of it fall out of his mouth like the bread in the shop. He tosses the core over his shoulder and jumps down onto the path on the other side. I stand still, half expecting to hear his feet make a sound like hooves as he runs off.

I duck around the apple tree branches and walk up the steps. At the back door, I raise the large metal hand and knock. I hope Térèse is inside. I know she'll be pissed at me for getting stung, and for not waiting. But I'll be thankful to see her, no matter her anger. It sounds like running inside. Footsteps. I have to tell her about Claude. Paillard. I don't know how to tell her. Shutters bang open from a window upstairs. A head pokes out, then the shutters slam shut again. I press my hand against the back door, but it doesn't budge, and Bana isn't here to open it like he did at the apple tree. I lean my shoulder into the door and it flings open. I fall on the floor; the box skitters out. A woman stands over me, her hands on her hips. "*Benvenguda a Le Graine. Parlas Occitan?*"

"Madame?"

She picks up the box. "*Parlas Occitan? Connais-tu le mot de passe?*"

"That's mine. I need. Térèse?" She pulls me along, the box tucked under her arm.

CHAPTER FIFTEEN

Epi Does Not Know the Password

L*E MOT DE PASSE*? Candles flicker from the breeze. It's still night behind her. The floor is strewn with flowers, straw and heads of wheat. Footsteps echo from deep inside.

The woman who opened the door from the courtyard stares. She smells like asparagus, like peas, and a little like fish. Sunshine heated goat cheese. The perfume of spring herbs calls the hour when I would pull chives with Maman. But nowhere do I detect even the slightest aroma of roasted garlic and my sister, Térèse.

"Please. I'm looking for my sister, Térèse?"

She shakes her head no. "*Je suis Grigne*," she says and puts her hand over her heart. "Greeen-ya," she repeats as if I might be deaf. She motions to the bench in the long hallway. The front door at the other end of the hallway opens and closes. "Oc?"

"Oc?" I sit where she directs and swing my legs back and forth.

"*Cossi te dison? Me dison, Grigne.*" She offers me a glass of a frothy dirt-tinted water. She pushes the bottom of the glass up as I drink.

She takes a sip, belches, and wipes her mouth across her sleeve.

"*Moun cacalou?*" she shakes her head back and forth as if this is a joke.

I stand up. "No."

"*Arresta!*" She changes her mind.

I sit back down to wait. The box on my lap. What a strange place, with strange words. It's so dark. Why hasn't Térèse told me any of this? Maybe if I close my eyes and wish for Térèse she will appear and the rest of these people will disappear, especially Greenya. Térèse, I whisper, are you nearby? This doesn't seem like a place you would be. If I had to find my way home, I couldn't. Could I get to the river? The dry river. I wish I had never left the bread terrace. I look at the box in my lap more closely. It's very cleverly made. Without the handle I would have thought it was just another log. Could it be that there were more boxes in the woodshed? At the creaking, I turn to my right. Grigne opens the door where she disappeared. A couple of people stick their heads out and look at me. I know if one of them is Térèse she'll hurry out and yell at me. And I would be thankful. The door opens and closes several times. No Térèse.

Grigne opens the door and walks to me. A tow-headed woman who wears wool breeches, a leather sash, and black hunting cloak follows her.

"*Madame Bouquin vous parlera.*" Grigne stands between us, squints at me and frowns, introducing Madame. Grigne beckons me close, and steps back.

"*Espante.*" Madame's eyes run over me from head to toe. "*Espante.*" She grabs her own chin and holds her mouth to prevent any more exclamations.

I freeze, but Madame insists that I stand.

Grigne nods, she smiles a little now that Madame Bouquin has identified me as Espante. Whoever that is. "Grigne, meet Antaia. Antaia meet Grigne. I am, we are, so surprised to see you."

Grigne crosses her arms, back to being upset, maybe she knows I am not *Espante.* "*Mettre le ouaï!*"

"*Oc, Grigne, oc.*"

"What did she say?"

Madame shakes her head. "You really don't know? She says you're crazy to show up. Today. Carrying that box. But I, and Grigne here, are glad to see you, Antaia."

Antaia? Did they really say my mother's name? This is the best thing. And the worst. I stop like a deer spotted in the trees, hoping I can blend in to the brothel. Should I go along with them? They're glad to see her, so she wasn't in trouble, right? My hand itches from the bee sting. I scratch the bump. "I'm from, yes, I was just in Ceres. And I..thought..what about that lady..I... knew, that I know." I step closer to Madame. Her hair carries the scent of something green, a seed, maybe, like Maman's cardamom. Her cheeks are pale red apples, blotched with spidery veins. Her leafy green and yellow eyes look me over. She reaches for the box. My box. My blood rushes in my ears. What words might prove I am Antaia, hoping I remember what Grigne said to me a few minutes ago. "*Parlas Occitan?*"

She touches my hand. "Antaia, you've forgotten the password? Strange, as you gave it to me."

"I'm looking for her, for Térèse."

"Come. I can see you're in disguise. Very clever for it's the Fool's Feast. Things have changed since you were here. I don't really know if Epi survived. I've been watching. But nothing." Something flits in her eyes, anger, sadness or regret, I can't tell.

"Madame, I am Epi. I would give anything to find Antaia, my Maman. Do you know if she lives?"

Madame looks out the window to the courtyard. I can barely see the apple tree through the cobwebs. Large yellow spiders have various insects wrapped up and they are tucked away like little breads in the cobweb. Madame laughs and waves her hand at Grigne.

"Epi. You're Epi? So clever of you to ask about Antaia, since you're the one who murdered her. You're under arrest."

"Wait, wait. I would never. No, wait."

Grigne grabs my arms and twists them behind my back.

THE SECOND TALE

Taboon Breads and the Apple Tree.
Jerusalem. Madame Bouquin

*"Pain Prend La Vie Du Feu, Mais À La Fin, Pain
Donne Sa Durée De Vie Sur Le Feu, Aussi."*
Bread Takes Its Life from The Fire, But In The
End Returns Its Life To The Fire Too

CHAPTER SIXTEEN

Epi is Arrested By Madame

MADAME BOUQUIN LEADS, huffing and puffing up the winding staircase. Grigne pushes me in front of her. I stumble on the steps, this is the first staircase I've seen in years and coming up behind Madame who stops and breathes hard. Beams of light come through a window at the top of the stairs.

We enter a small room. Grigne pushes me inside. I fall on the floor. Madame whispers to Grigne, who closes the door, and turns to me. We are alone. Sweat runs down her neck and Madame brushes the blonde curls off her face with the back of her hand. Her eyes rest on me and she points, breathless, no words come out even though she opens and closes her mouth. I feel behind me and sit down on the chair. She fans herself.

"The last message we had from Antaia was, "*Calquecop Le Pa Que Be Quand Las Denses S'en Soun Anandos.*"

"What does that mean?" I don't know about Maman but I have heard Paillard say it. Has Madame forgotten she said I was arrested? I don't think I'll remind her.

"How should I know. Many things. Nothing. Oc rarely says things directly. Unlike the Guild. *Sometimes the bread arrives after the teeth are gone.* No messages have been getting through for some time. Because of the Guild. Things are terrible for the

Mistresses. You have to find her. Bring us some relief—we need her back."

They need her? Who are these people? It seems like we need her. I haven't heard her name, Antaia, said this way. I want to say, she's Maman, my mother. It feels like I am nobody to be looking for her. Yet they think I know where she is. And it makes me sad, as I am the one who needs my Maman the most. And knows the least.

I hear shuffling outside the door. Then sharp rapping.

"The Mistresses? Am I the bread? And you're the teeth?" I am so confused.

"Shh." Madame Bouquin listens, then stirs the coals in the fireplace, puts a pot of water over an iron trivet nestled in the hot coals. "Maybe. I really don't know; you could be the bread. And the teeth. But I do know the box you carry. Where did you find it?"

More knocks.

"In her woodshed…but…" Something tells me I should have kept that part quiet.

Madame lifts the box, examines the snail. "Hopefully you didn't burn the seeds. Hopefully, her tree protected them. What were you thinking? Apricot wood is very soft, don't you know anything?"

I was beginning to feel there were things neither one of us knew. "It was growing, growing in the woodshed. Her tree, the apricot."

"There. Can you see my tree? Quert. The apple tree."

She draws me to the small opening to the sky and cranks open the window. She points down to the tree in the courtyard. I barely recognized the hole, part stump and part trunk, of the tree where I almost fell. Not far away is the wall where I got stung and the door I came in with Bana.

"The Mistresses are…" She tilts her head at me as if this could help explain. "Well, here's a story. The apple tree traveled with the pear, the walnut, cherry, the fig and the plum, and they all followed the apricot tree. But then the apricot tree disappeared because it missed the chestnut tree so much."

"So, why didn't the chestnut tree come along?"

"It had been left behind to guard the horses. A lot of horses. Understand?"

I look down at her feet.

"You've heard this all before, from Antaia." She shoos me with her hand.

"I have no idea, what are you telling me? Are the Mistresses trees?" Of all the crazy things, this is the craziest. Is it just today? Maybe that's all it is. If this is what listening gets you, forget it. I have to leave. Forget having been here. Except where is Térèse?

Madame looked bright and sweaty when we first entered the room, but now her eyes were sunken in. She closed the window. "I don't have much time. Dear Epi. My Oc name is Quert, Mistress of the apple tree."

"I didn't kill her," I say.

"Child, I don't know. I have always taken in lost people, and we had the same roots, your Maman was from the mountains of Epirius. I am from Persia, I wanted to listen. I thought that was enough."

I squeeze my eyes closed. I was sitting with Maman in the branches of her apricot tree. Bees buzzed around the flowers.

"You need to find her, but the only way could be the others, they may know more. The Mistresses. When she left she might have visited them? Can you go without a map?"

"You said I was arrested?"

"I had to catch you, before he finds you."

"Who, who is he?" I run through the names of all the men I knew. Paillard. Antoine. Bana. But does he count? I'm not afraid of any of them. But then my heart skips. Except Claude. He was newly dead.

"Return in the direction she arrived."

"So, you think the message about the bread and the teeth was from her, Maman? And she is visiting these Mistresses, so that's why they know her? Why is that?" If I thought getting on a cart with strangers was hard, I doubted I would ever understand how such strange messages could help me find Maman. Or now if I have to find another Mistress to help me. Who are they? And what about the box? Is Madame trying to steal it? I can't let that happen.

"You don't need a map."

"Bana said he made the box." I was better off waiting for the Guild to question me about the bread of dreams in Ceres, right at the bread terrace. Right where roses grew and where all I had to do was disappear inside the home, they grew for me.

"My business is people. From Rome, Egypt, Mesopotamia. I go crazy, listening to them. Or maybe I listen because I am crazy. All kinds of people—speaking many tongues—pass through here on their way to Bordeaux. Or on their way to Catalonia. They stop and tell stories. They ask me about the Guild. Psomi. I tell them, the river goes both ways."

But the river is dried up and doesn't go any way at all. At least she knows she's crazy. Where are all these places? I have heard Antoine talk like this. But he's such a braggart, I don't know if any of what he says is true either. Loud footsteps stomp up the stairs. I grab the box.

"Quickly now." She pushes me toward the window. Daylight is fading.

"My sister, Térèse where is she?" I feel dizzy looking down in the courtyard, wishing for Bana to show up. I walk away from the window.

"You need to stay alive to find her! Hide now."

"Where is she, Térèse?" My stomach never felt these turns.

"Epi, the window…" Madame Bouquin pushes me frantically.

Quert, the apple tree's black spindly branches snake towards the window. The thin branches could never hold me. Madame pulls the curtain over me. I pull my leg up and hide my feet. I perch on the windowsill. The box on my lap. I turn it over and find a snail etched on it. It's so odd that the tree that was carved on it has disappeared.

A bird flies onto the top branches and pecks an apple. I ask her, where is Aubada? Pounding on the door. Silence. Then more pounding. The door bursts open. I close my eyes. Scrunch myself into a ball and steady myself in the frame.

CHAPTER SEVENTEEN

Faire Monter l'Aïoli – Stir Garlic into Everything

"HE'S GOT THE box. We have to find him," Antoine says. I part the curtain with my fingers. Antoine's with another man. He's wearing a dress too. And a beard. I've never seen anyone with skin so dark. He must spend a lot of time out in the sun.

The bird in the tree screeches and Antoine looks towards the window. He squints. I snap my head back. He scares me. I don't know what he's thinking. I let the edges of the curtain fall together and lean back against the window frame.

Grigne slides in the door too. Madame pours hot water into the cups.

"Auvillar, *bienvenue*. And Antoine, *Espante*. I'm surprised to see you. But this seems like a day for those. This drink will help you see the problem. And maybe the solution? Grigne, close the door please."

"Garlic tea? Never helps me see anything. Puts me to sleep." Antoine says.

"It doesn't work for everyone, but those who want to see, will."

I watch Grigne slurp down the drink. Is this drink making the room spin?

"Let's get on with it. I have to get back to work." Antoine sets his cup down.

I peek through the curtain again.

"Spoken like a true Guild leader. Now that Claude's out of the way. Grigne, meet Antoine. Antoine, meet Grigne." Auvillar waves his arm at Antoine and then at Grigne and encourages them to stand closer.

"What's this meeting about?" Antoine asks.

"*Empapautar.*" Grigne says to Antoine and Auvillar.

Madame translates. "Grigne says there are problems with the small mills."

Grigne speaks again.

Madame says, "*Faire monter l'aïoli, non.*"

"What did you tell Grigne?"

"Don't stir garlic into everything!"

"*Faire monter l'aïoli,*" I repeat, trying to remember these words. I want to ask Térèse. I know she grows garlic. Does she bring those seeds to the brothel? She must know this saying. I can hear her saying garlic is good for everything. Maybe I don't understand its meaning. Maybe I don't understand anything.

Behind me, there is rustling and scraping in the tree. My eyes widen. Bana climbs up the twisted trunk. He shimmies out on a limb towards an apple. He looks up and sees me. "Epi, at least I don't have to pull you out of a hole. Antoine, you in there?"

I put my fingers to my lips. "Ssshhh."

Bana frowns. "The Guild shop is overrun with nuts, and he didn't leave the key. So, I just left!"

Now Bana is here too? I steady myself. And turn back to the room. Madame continues talking. "Grigne says you have to let the dam out. The one at the conjunction of the three rivers, right? The small trickle of water isn't enough to turn those millstones."

"*Empapaouter.*" Grigne says and stares Auvillar down.

Madame shakes her head at Grigne. Grigne is very upset. Madame's words are few. Maybe she's summarizing. Maybe they talked before they saw me.

"Grigne, is it? I am so glad you came. Thank you. From what I hear you say the small mills can't keep up, and there will be an even worse glut with the bountiful harvest coming from the mountains. We all need that wheat. So, you're right, absolutely. We all need dignity. We are a brotherhood. We have to plan to improve them. Make the mills better."

"We need more millstones." Antoine scratches his head. "Don't you have one on your barge?"

"Exactly. We're sending in a team of specialists to evaluate. One of them is Antoine, here. He grew up on a mill and with Claude, one of the best millers around. God rest his soul. This new wheat needs differently dressed millstones."

I can't believe I'm hearing this. Claude was revered by the Guild. Did Antoine tell Auvillar some other story about why he died? Am I the only person who knows it's my fault that Claude died?

"*Empapautar.*" Grigne pokes Auvillar.

I don't think Grigne likes this Auvillar. And I am puzzled about Madame. How she feels. Is she keeping them all apart? Certainly, Antoine is afraid of him.

Bana scrambles closer to me, he clutches his stomach.

"What's wrong?"

"What was in your bread?" He crawls out on the spindly branch.

The door of the room bursts open for the second time.

CHAPTER EIGHTEEN
Epi is Given an Ultimatum

MY OLDEST SISTER, Margot, rushes into the tower room, pulling Térèse by her hair. "I caught her listening at the door." Térèse tumbles to the floor.

"That's some dove *merde*. Madame brought Epi in here. What have you done with him?" Térèse straightens up and puts her hands on her hips. Punches her fist in the round soft flesh at the top of Margot's arm.

Margot whimpers and pulls back her fist to punch Térèse.

"Margot, I have everything we need." Auvillar stops Margot, and pulls a linen out of his pocket and shakes it out. I put my head through the curtain. The E stitched on the sack, leaves no doubt that it's mine. Unless I can say it belongs to *Espante*.

I suck in a breath, Bana doubles over and moans. Eyes turn to the window again. I can't let Térèse think I am missing.

Bana moans. "Epi, help me" and leaps toward me. I catch him and pull him in. He's so soft. And young, and he throws up on my shirt, warm soft yellow goo on my chest. I turn and steady myself. Eyes turn to the window.

I can't hide or turn away. Where can I go? Climb out on the tree? I have to come out. Help Térèse too. I part the curtain, holding Bana like a hurt chicken. "Leave Térèse alone."

"You!" Margot comes at me, pushing Térèse out of the way. Antoine jumps at Margot. Bana slips out of my arms, pulls on and hides behind Antoine, kicking at Margot. Térèse knocks into me. Auvillar crosses his arms and stares. Grigne sits down on the chair where I sat when I first came into the room.

I scowl at Antoine.

Madame stands in front of me. "Stop. You can't just barge in here like this. Epi's not just anyone, he's, he's the...."

"Epi, see, I told you not to," says Térèse. We stare at each other—she moves towards me, but Madame steps in.

"Térèse Ssshhh." I nod to Bana, still with Antoine.

Madame Bouquin opens and breathes in the aroma of the sack. "What did we have here?"

"It's obvious," Auvillar says. "Roses. Banatka wheat from the mountains. And.."

Madame looks inside the sack. She shows me and everyone. We all look. "There's nothing."

"Psomi's bread of dreams. I stopped Claude. He was making them." Antoine says.

"Banatka wheat. Black mustard seeds. Stolen apricots. And roses?" Margot swivels and stares at me.

"Without each other, they all get sick." Térèse says.

"Don't worry, we'll put an end to this." Margot says.

Térèse's face goes white. "Claude is dead? Shouldn't we investigate?"

"We should sing the Guild song, to remember him," Antoine says.

"There were apricots, Epi?" Madame turns to me.

"I thought you said Claude did this. Antoine?"

"This is Epi's sack." Margot thrusts out her chin. "Epi did this. Not Claude."

Auvillar watches Margot. Cocks his head.

"The sack is empty." Madame turns the linen inside out. A few rose petals fall on the floor.

Bana rubs his stomach. "It's more likely that with each other, you get sick." Then he goes back to the window and throws up against the wall, the curtain covering his head. I can't help but think even though he's sick, he's smiling.

"Bana, just rest." I cringe. Feel hot. My hand itches where the bee stung me. My hands must smell like roses and black mustard seeds. Was the wheat I used Banatka wheat? I was wrong to come here and tell Antoine what's going on. Warn him? He should have warned me. I walk to Bana, crouch down, and stroke his head.

Térèse comes over to the window. "Epi, it's ok. I never wanted you to come here," she whispers. "We can just leave. Just be quiet and follow my lead."

"I can't leave Bana."

Margot pushes me. "You're making the bread of dreams? How terrible it would be if you both fell out of the window. Since he'll probably die anyway, like Maman, and you'll be found guilty and put to death this time."

I look her in the eye. Then look down. Too much is happening. What is Grigne thinking? Madame? I push Margot away, but she drags me back and tries to force me out the window. Madame kicks Margot away, but my legs won't stop shaking. Auvillar stands in front, blocking any path to leave. Antoine shakes his head no. Sit down; he motions me. I am dizzy, but I have to get out of here.

"Who are you? Your hands are full of gold rings and precious bracelets. You don't work?" I push my lips together so I won't cry.

"Without me, all of you will die. Like Claude. Or worse, starve. Be without a home." The words fall out of Auvillar's mouth and bounce on the floor as if dried millet for Aubada at the bread terrace. His words are not anger, exactly. But there is something, I feel, a power from him. "Who are you? You made these, the bread of dreams?"

Madame rolls her eyes. She scoffs. Disapproves of him. Grigne shakes her head and mutters. I don't think she can understand him, but she knows this meaning. Antoine's jaw drops. I listen. He knows this man, Auvillar. He looks as scared as when Margot comes to check on the oven, to make sure we are baking Guild crowns, or her crowns, as I am sure she thinks of them as nothing but gold *fleurins*. She doesn't eat them. She prefers honey cakes. It's funny to me that Margot thinks of herself as higher than me, but the honey cakes she has pledged her love to, are mostly made of breadcrumbs.

Antoine rises up to his full height. "Auvillar," he says, measured and quiet. "You remember, my brother, Epi?" He puts his arm around me.

"Epi, how old are you now?" Auvillar scratches his head, takes my arm, and bows.

"Epi hasn't been here for some time." Madame says. "Bana brought him."

Auvillar bows to me again. He takes the sack back from Madame. "Little Bana, what's the truth here?"

"I stole the sack and gave it to Antoine..." Bana stands up and speaks, the curtain covering him like a shroud.

"Aha, so it WAS Epi's. Admit it. Did you eat the bread of dreams?"

"What are you talking about? Can I get a drink of water?" Bana takes the cup that Antoine had and drinks down the tea.

"Stay close, Bana, or you'll end up dead, like Claude and like Maman!" Antoine says.

"I could never forget. You killed Maman." Auvillar raises his chin and looks at me.

The mouse in my stomach is furiously going around in circles. What if Bana dies? Is it too late already? I go to Bana and stand next to him. He leans his head against my hip. "I did not kill her. And if anything happens to Bana." I point my finger at Auvillar.

Madame gestures to the chair. "Epi, quiet. Auvillar, all will be revealed. Are you ready?"

"To be arrested?" I point to the box, my box, then sink into the wooden chair,

rocking back and forth on my hands. I narrow my eyes at my brother and at Auvillar. Margot leans in. Térèse stands at my back.

"Epi, quiet." Antoine leans in.

"Epi, making the bread of dreams is sedition." Auvillar holds the box.

"Epi, don't answer that." Térèse says.

By the window Auvillar has lost all the oddness he carries dressed as a woman.

His face is powdered. His beard is neatly trimmed. He motions to Madame.

"Your hands will tell us the truth." Madame Bouquin washes my hands with a warm perfumed cloth, then bids me stand.

I push out a breath. Bana sits at my feet. I look in Madame's face. I know from what she said that Grigne said, that Madame says less than what she knows.

Madame Bouquin catches my expression and laughs. "Scared?"

Her question seems the height of stupidity, but maybe it's better to say what's so obvious at my shaking legs. Grigne laughs. But from nervousness or from another side of the story, I have no idea.

"I make bread. So, you might see some flour. I had to make it. We don't have any Guild flour, you know."

Auvillar's eyebrows shoot up.

"Epi, just shut up for once." Antoine says. "Auvillar, what are you doing? I'm telling you; Epi is a guild apprentice and has nothing to do with this."

"It's not just about the breads. Epi must take the life of the fire." Madame Bouquin holds the box.

That doesn't sound like a good option to me. Auvillar steps back. Scans my face. He smiles and bunches up the sack and stuffs it in his pocket.

Madame steps close to me. "Your hands, please."

I stretch them out to her, and she takes them gently. She rubs my knuckles. Turns them over, runs her thumb over my palms and brings them close, then measures my fingers against hers. She drops both my hands abruptly, and brushes her hands together and shakes them wildly in the air, as if they were wet, or hot? She looks at me as if I have betrayed her. Wondering how to get rid of this infuriating thing that showed up today?

"Fire-handed people carry a brilliant light...they do impossible things that no one else can touch, but they leave a smoking ruin behind them." Madame says. She turns to Grigne.

Pain prend la vie du feu, mais à la fin le pain donne sa durée de vie sur le feu aussi.

Grigne nods. "Oc."

"My hands? They make *crowns* for the Guild." The sun throws scarlet and violet glints across the room. Madame offers me her arm. I reach out, but my legs mix up standing and falling.

"No." Antoine's face twists, his cheeks angry. He storms to the window and flings the curtain aside. His anger is visible, unlike Auvillar's, but I feel both inside me just the same.

"Who are you?" I ask Auvillar, though I have the uneasy feeling he was at my ceremony when I was ten.

"Madame?" Auvillar dismisses me. "Can you explain how? This? Happened?"

"I don't know you, but how did you know my mother?" My feet grab the floor as I walk, each step feels as if the floor is mud, and I might slip before I reach Auvillar.

"Call me Uncle Auvillar. I recognize her box. This tree. Inside are her seeds. Thank you, Epi, for bringing it."

Antoine struggles with Auvillar and yanks the box away. "Antaia's dead."

"So, Epi, you are her daughter, Antaia's daughter?" Auvillar doesn't yank the box away, but just looks at Antoine, and Antoine lets go.

My face heats, my shoulders, I force myself to look him in the eye. Uncle? What does that mean? I look to see if he resembles Claude in some way but can't picture Claude in any other moment except how I left him. Dead in the dovecote. So, is Auvillar Claude's brother? I just want to leave. Get away from all these people. Térèse motions me towards the door while Margot, Auvillar, and Antoine are engrossed with passing the box between them.

Térèse walks slowly. I back up.

Auvillar sits down. He rests his elbows on his knees, his hands fall in the space between his legs. "Actually, Epi. I'm not sure you can call what's in the box, seeds."

"Now that Claude failed, the box belongs to me. Finally, I am Mistress of all of Psomi." Margot grabs the box.

My stomach sickens. I watch Margot. What is this? Margot is the GUILD. I can't imagine her on the same side as Maman. As me. Madame shakes her head, "Your Oc name has been banished for centuries. You don't even exist anymore."

I stare at them both. Madame had just told me the story of the apple tree. That she is Quert, the Mistress of the apple tree. That things were terrible and I had to find the other Mistresses to help Maman. I stare at the box, this small log with a handle, which has some power I can't fathom to make Margot want to be a Psomian. But even worse, I can't imagine her ever having been one.

Do I escape or grab the box? It was only a few hours ago that I found it in the woodshed, put it next to the fire in the oven at my bread terrace. Then stuffed it in the sack with fleurins and my bread of dreams made with apricots and roses, the sack I forgot was marked with an E. Brought back to me by Paillard. Then stolen by Bana, and given to Antoine, stolen back by me to give to Madame, who only barely held it, but is now in Margot's sticky hands.

"That box was made by my father." Bana pipes up. "I lied. Before. It wasn't me. I didn't make it. Nope." He steps towards the window and holds his stomach again, but this time, I can tell he's pretending, all sheepish, he seems to have sensed I want to leave with Térèse. And I may be crazy but when I look in his eyes, I understand that he understands. He's trying to distract them so Térèse and I can escape. And then he will escape the way he came in, out the window.

"Finally, I will have the map, find Psomi and destroy it. Just how to open this damn log!?" Margot looks at the fireplace.

Grigne steps over to Margot and pushes her face close . "Fascaga."

That doesn't sound good. And I'm surprised to see that Margot does not understand Oc. She pushes Grigne down. Madame helps her up. Bana giggles as if he'd like to get in this argument too.

It's odd but I am more comforted by Margot wanting to destroy everything, than by her wanting to be on Maman's side. I don't know the Margot who wants to be Mistress.

"Where is this Psomi?" Antoine asks. The room falls silent, though there are footsteps going up and down the tower steps. Auvillar looks up.

"Margot, get a hold of yourself. Antoine, can you control your apprentice?"

Antoine looks over at me, and blows air out of his mouth, exasperated that he didn't notice and can't control what his apprentice is saying or doing. "Epiiii. No!" I push past Antoine to Margot at the fireplace. She swings the box by the handle, so I kick her hard in the shins. Margot screams. The box rolls over on the floor.

"Oh, you want to open the box?" Bana says. "That's easy. Give it to Epi."

What could possibly be in the box if it's not seeds, but could be like seeds? Why does everyone care so much, what's inside this little log with a handle?

Antoine picks it up. Fiddles with it. Turns the box over. I am not sure if Bana is lying or not.

"Ok. Epi. There, at the fireplace. Take the fireflute. Bouffe." Madame says as if it was only me and her here, and she can still tell me things I need to know. "Bouffe means breath. Maman carved it from a foot long piece of honey-colored wood as smooth as duck fat."

The stick Madame picks up is blackened with soot. Claude mentioned Bouffe this morning. How did Madame get it? And when? Claude said he knows I didn't mean it. But I don't know what he thought I didn't mean.

"Like this." Madame rubs Bouffe with a cloth till it gleams like honey in the sun. She lifts Bouffe to her mouth. The flute is carved with two forms in a strange embrace. A rush of sparks fly across my shoulders and up and down my neck. My breath stops. It's not hard to see that one of the forms is a woman. Madame's fingers cover and uncover the holes as she blows through. Bouffe breathes out notes that are wild and soft.

"You'll choose what your Bouffe is made of. It's an important choice. A tree? Or a bone?"

In the soft light of the fire, Madame looked like Maman. "Maman's Bouffe is made from the chestnut tree. Like my tree is the apple tree. Do you understand? Listen to Bouffe's words, and you'll hear the answer."

"But what is it for? This Bouffe? What are you talking about?"

Madame's knees crack as she squats near the fire. She plays a few more notes on Bouffe, high notes that sound like when the small birds twitter in the fig tree near the garden. She stops playing. Hands Bouffe to me. I see Madame as if she is Maman.

My stomach growls like a beast amidst the silent filled room, and frightens even me. Madame laughs. Like with Maman, I remembered when she wanted me to listen to the trees or the birds or something wild, I couldn't hear. I would laugh. Maman wanted me to listen for an answer to a question I didn't understand. I pick up Bouffe and blow. But this time the music becomes smoke and shapes itself into a bird and flaps out the window into the sky. A bird that lives, darkened by fire, with a soft sweetness of orange. My throat hums with the soft smoke. The smoke swirls around the box, and it slides open. I take off the lid and bend to the floor. There's a flower aroma. These bones, her bones are small and brown and sharp. My mouth opens. I smell the burning smoke from the night Maman left me.

"Boys don't cry," Auvillar says. "Even at their mother's bones."

I could never not cry. But inside the bread terrace that is different. And would it mean something different to be Maman's daughter, instead of her son? Madame seems to know I am a girl, dressed in boys' clothes as a disguise for the Fool's Feast. But she has said nothing. I hope I can trust her. I am hoping that Auvillar doesn't see me, and believes I am a boy. A longing rises in my chest to tell everyone, now, that I am Eleone, Maman's daughter. But one look at Térèse and what a shock that would be to her, and to Antoine, too, and at the same time, what would the Guild do to them to think they knew this all along. I want to, because this is the truth, but I can't, and what would happen to Epi? My heart falls to the floor.

Auvillar continues. "Maman was a special lady. Special to me as we came from Greece, both of us. But she was crazy. They're her bones, all right. We were east, almost to the Garonne, and a new shipment near the great Roman bridge in Tolosa, when…"

My mouth closes tight, and I swallow hard, trying to swallow the lump. I don't say a word. I don't tell, but something settles inside me. I remember the smoke. Her aroma. These broken bits are not her burnt bones. They're Maman's bread of dreams. Maman's story of how her wheat was born near the sea. Near orange trees. Near coriander seeds and bay leaf trees. I can't explain why—but I feel a new hope that she is alive. "Where is she?"

"You don't need them, or any map, Epi. I am sure you know, you remember, she showed you the way. Didn't she?" Auvillar says.

The fireplace burns, the logs crackle with hot flames.

"You seem to know everything." I say to Auvillar. But inside me, I question his meaning. Did he think she showed me the way when I was inside her when she traveled? I was born in Ceres. Isn't that the tale Maman told?

"But you can't be sure, can you? You very well could have been the one who killed her. But there's a chance she's alive. I see it in your face. Your shoulders. You could lead me to her. And then I don't know what's best. Yes, I could kill you in front of her. Or kill you both."

"Epi, don't listen," Térèse puts her hands on her hips and stares at Auvillar. "Scum."

"Auvillar wouldn't kill her. Or you. He couldn't. He told me." Antoine backs up, looking sheepish. "He couldn't kill anyone."

Madame's eyes hold mine, as if she doesn't know which language will best say what she needs to say. She comes close and straightens my collar. "You don't need a map," she whispers. "You know where to go."

I have no idea what she's talking about.

Auvillar says, "Of course. I see what to do. One seed nourishes the other. Margot you'll watch over him, and be sure Epi finds Antaia."

"What?" Margot says. "Forget Antaia."

Auvillar stares at Margot. "Your sister was very different. I loved her. And she taught Epi the ways of Psomi."

Antoine looks bewildered, and I feel the same. Just what does he mean, he loved Maman?

Auvillar steps forward. "Antaia was a great spirit. But she wouldn't listen. She left me one night. There was something wrong with her. With you too, Epi? You'll prove your faith to the Guild. So, find her. That's easy, if you didn't kill her. Or you'll fail. Find her by the start of Boedromion, the harvest, in the third month of the Attic calendar. That gives you two weeks. Making the bread of dreams is a crime of sedition. A great many lives depend on you finding her, including yours and your family's."

Térèse pushes her finger into Margot. And points to Madame. "I won't forget whose side you are on. The Guild allows you to live. Both of you."

Madame Bouquin hands her Bouffe to me. *Call Antaia.*

"I'll go back to Ceres." I say. "No one, especially not Margot, is taking me anywhere. Right, Antoine?" I hold Bouffe and drape my arm over his shoulder.

"Epi, I pity you. I know this river like the back of my hand. But you don't." My eyes must be burning with anger. He should be taking care of me. He can't just keep quiet and figure out what's going on. Or maybe he knows what's going on. I can't forget he gave up Claude. Is he going to do the same thing to me? He sounds just plain stupid, and I hate that I care that he's in a dangerous place.

Auvillar bends over me and studies Madame's Bouffe. So many clouds and shadows pass by in his eyes. He asks for Bouffe with his hands, and I give it to him. Then he hands Bouffe to Margot. "Keep this and I'll keep the box."

"I want the box!" Margot pushes Auvillar away.

"That's enough out of you." Auvillar says to Margot.

"Yeah. Turn around." Antoine says. "We're…."

"Taking you out of Nerac and dropping you off." Auvillar finishes.

Grigne quickly comes over and with a look of smug satisfaction helps Antoine force Margot's hands behind her back. I cringe, waiting for Margot to break free and throw a punch at all of them. I am surprised when Margot's hands get wrapped with rope and tied. By Antoine. And then blindfolded.

"Now you." He turns to me.

"Me? What? No!" Antoine ties a cloth over my eyes. I struggle against him. "Antoine, he's using you." I drop to the floor and crawl. He hauls me up by the arm. "Remember what happened to Claude."

I turn. Térèse. I feel her eyes on me. Like Madame's.

"Let me go." My hair is caught in the blindfold. And then the worst possible thing happens. I get tied to Margot. My skin crawls to feel her heavy arms, her weight.

Margot smashes my foot. "Just wait till we're alone. And no one is there to protect you," she whispers.

We start down the stairs, and I lose sense and trip, an arm raises me up. I recognize Antoine's grip.

"You can't do this." Térèse shouts. "Margot, I'll be waiting for you."

It's like another moment, with the same words and the same feeling, when I knew that the world beyond the bread terrace was a terrible and dangerous place. I don't understand why I feel it now. Hearing Grigne speak Oc is like when I pushed through the rose canes early this morning. When I stood up and saw the woodshed. Found the box. Then dropped it into the hole where the roots of the apple tree clawed the ground, digging its own grave. Was the box trying to get away or get back to something? Back to the bread terrace, with Maman playing Bouffe. And listen to Claude and Auvillar's words, when they were fighting. That's where I heard it. I remember. Maman said the same thing, *"Empapaouter"* to Auvillar. And now I picture the box, tightly held under Auvillar's arm. And Maman's bouffe in Margot's grip.

THE THIRD TALE

Chestnut Panis Focacius with Tomato and Thyme.
A Leaf From Her Tree. Trinacria. Epi.

"A cado ausèl soun nits qu'i es bèl."
Every bird thinks his own nest is the most beautiful.

CHAPTER NINETEEN
Epi Becomes Margot's Hostage

B EAUTÉ TROTS BESIDE me on the towpath, staying close. The empty panniers bounce on her back. We're both sweating from the distance we've covered since we were left on the towpath by the Baise river outside Nerac. Me, my foot throbs from Margot smashing it, and from running on it to get away from Beauté, which is not what she wants to be doing either. Is Beauté exhausted from running after me, driven by Margot? Though Margot seems to be the most annoyed out of the three of us. That part, the part of Margot being inflamed, keeps me walking, but it's made up of two parts. One part is I totally trust Beauté, but the other bigger part is I don't trust Margot at all. My skin keeps sparking like I fell asleep and woke up with a family of ants crawling all over me.

The sun is coming up over my left shoulder and I feel the heat as if I stood next to the fire at Madame's or even further back, by the wood oven at my bread terrace. We are headed south. I think. I wish Térèse were with me. She would know. How can I not know which way I am going?

It's Margot, she makes me feel like a cracked eggshell rolling down the road. Like I am not here. But about to get stepped on. So, in order to not let her forget me I keep talking in this strange way, saying stupid things that I don't feel. The things I say are not me, and not easy to think of. I don't talk to anyone but Térèse. Oh, there's a current of some kind between me and Antoine. But he's like Margot, he doesn't seem to know about this under stuff, these feelings. Even though he's not here, it feels like he is, and just keeps walking by me. Like I'm like a fish swimming in the deep water of the Baise river, while he's on the bank. I jump out of the river looking for mayflies, and he looks surprised, but he keeps on walking. So, when I talk to Margot or at Margot, it's so I can keep swimming in the cool water, and keep her walking right by me too. But Margot is more likely to aim a spear at me than talk about it.

"I'm glad, Epi. To be out here with you. You don't have time to find her, you have to keep making crowns and making me money."

"It's not much further." I have no idea how she thinks I could do that. Or how I think I know where I am but I just want her to stop talking. My gut crunches up because I can't let my guard down. She's not safe. She tries to make me feel one thing and then plunges in her knife. She's certainly not grown kindly since she pummeled my foot. And Madame set us off by the river.

"Now you know. I'm your aunt and not your sister. To think of all those years that I had to take care of you because my sister ran off with him and left you with me! And I had to pretend you were my bratty little sister."

I had to be careful. Out here alone with her. Her mouth is set in a straight line. Which way was it that she took care of me? By yelling for me on the bridge and her anger pushed me to pass by underneath. The times she came to the bread terrace. When she said, "No wonder she left you. You can't make a silk purse out of a sow's ear. You're worthless. I look at you and see her. And your father. Why were you born? Remind me, please. Remind me why I have to take care of you."

And so it began that I took care of her. To keep her away. It was easier, believe me, than even wanting her to care for me. And it can't be that she wanted to be me, be the one who got praise for baking the crowns. She was mad that I baked, mad that I was good at it. Mad when I cared for her, making the cakes she loves out of breadcrumbs that fell on the floor of the terrace. I just don't know why she hates me so much. Térèse isn't even my sister, either, not really, but she is my sister in a much better way. I don't have to say a word, and she understands. How could Margot want to get rid of her sister's child? It's not like we had any family around to belong to. Wouldn't that make us belong to each other even more? Or want to? Once you hear bad words you can't unhear them. But it's more than that too. It's like hiding, being seen and squashed. Not only in that moment but never, ever even having been born. You'd think after Maman left, that things would be good or better, that Margot might care, but it was worse.

"No wonder she left you. And I'm supposed to find her? You're worthless."

Margot blames me for Maman leaving, and yet it felt like she always wanted Maman to leave anyway. But not me, I never thought Maman would leave. Leave me. It must be my fault. So that feeling that bruise lays on top of being squished. Margot wants me to do nothing except bake crowns, but I secretly remember Maman like I want to, by baking the bread of dreams, even though it means I don't sleep much and hide in the rose canes. That's the Maman I am looking for, the soft Maman who saw me, that's who I want to find. And talk to her.

I walk ahead. Margot rides Beauté right up on me. I know Beauté won't hurt me, but I run out of the way because Margot is snatching at me, pinching my neck, shoulders. Then I walk behind her, but she turns around and comes at me. Do I have to climb a tree like Bana?

"Don't worry so, Margot, I know exactly where to look." Madame whispered something about *Condatóm*. I hope to remember once my mind clears.

"What makes you think I care at all? To go anywhere. I could care less about what they do when you don't find her. I am not helping you. Find my sister? The cause of all my problems. Besides, she's not here or anywhere near here."

Margot just talks. She doesn't have to be asking or answering anything. Her mouth moves all the time. All the time. And if that wasn't bad enough, in between when she could just let the trees sway or the birds talking fill in, she hums, an annoying habit, I've just discovered or remembered. How is she even Maman's sister? They are nothing alike! I hate her so bad! Maybe she thinks that if she rides over me, I can't hurt her. She doesn't know me or Beauté.

"Doesn't she have a decent saddle? This is intolerable."

"So, let me ride for a while." I can certainly walk further than Margot can ride. I won't lose Beauté again. Beauté trots beside me, staying close. It breaks my heart to lean away because Margot could hit me again at any moment.

CHAPTER TWENTY
Epi Ditches Margot

I WALK AHEAD TO get the lay of the land. It's pretty straight forward. Dry river. Trees. A path. But I don't know this land. Nothing here looks familiar, and of course it wouldn't. I worry that I'll see the dovecote and be right back in Ceres, having made a great big ugly circle. I glance back at Margot. I can see Beauté, but Margot looks like she's riding in the trees. I have to get rid of her. I'll punch her in the leg, which will make her climb down. I hate the thought of even touching her. I'll pretend I'm picking apples then give one to her and pull her down. Nope. That involves touching her again.

I want to go back. I can't go back to Nerac. I don't want to be found by Auvillar. But I don't know where they are, and they certainly don't know where I am. Glad to be out of that terrible room but wandering the countryside with Margot is not what I thought would happen to me. I should be feeding the fire on the bread terrace. What is ahead around the next turn of the river?

Beauté's hooves pound the dry gravel path, and Margot snorts. "We're stopping very soon. I can't go on much longer. What food did you bring?"

"Madame Bouquin said the river divides at *Condatóm*, it's just up ahead." I honestly hope so, but I don't know, since I haven't left the bread terrace for years. A hawk screeches. I cover my head.

Getting Margot off of Beauté will not be easy.

Antoine doesn't really understand that he's lived in Guild protection all his life. Like me. Except I know different. I'm a good apprentice. I'm just sick that Antoine blamed Claude for making the bread of dreams and now he's dead.

The Guild is in charge, but how far outside of Nerac? It sounds like Grigne came from far away. Where is Bana? And Térèse. I want to sit down. I look up at Beauté. How long can she keep going with Margot on her back?

"Did Madame tell you about Angeline?"

"Stop kicking Beauté."

"Wait till you meet her!" Margot keeps kicking Beauté.

"You'll see. Do what you will."

Beauté stops. Here's my chance. I shudder, little shivers run through me like a fish surfacing on the river and escape down my back. I know nothing Margot does will inspire Beauté to walk. I keep walking. Beauté whinnies. My mind spins on how to get Margot off. "Look there's a grove with apple trees."

"I hate apples. When you find a gingerbread tree let me know."

I can run and hope Beauté will run. And throw Margot off.

We round the bend of the Baise River. I bend over to catch my breath. "Get down right now. She needs water. And food."

"You think you're smart, Epi, but you don't...."

I run. Margot screams. I turn around. Beauté rears up and takes off after me.

Margot falls off of Beauté. And lays in the path. Oh god. She doesn't move. Maybe she's dead. Would I be in trouble? Now I will be wanted for killing Antaia and her sister. I could tell them so many things that Margot has done to me. But the Guild would never believe me.

We hide in the trees. I stroke Beauté's side. But I can't be like Margot, we need to go and help her, Beauté.

Margot gets up and points, and shakes her fist at us, then limps along the path.

I should have known. Margot's fine.

"Are you thirsty, Beauté?" I have no idea what's next. I couldn't stay with her but now, without Margot, what will we do? We turn off the towpath of the Baise and go deeper into the tall grasses towards the sound of rushing water. I walk ahead to get the lay of the land. This land. It's much better without Margot.

CHAPTER TWENTY-ONE

Epi on the Road with Térèse

I SIT DOWN ON the bank. A fish skeleton crushed by the rocks doesn't bode well for finding anything to eat. I look up. Birds flit through the trees, maybe they are trying to let me know that Margot is catching up. And about to find us. I walk out and slip my feet in the muddy stream. What should we do? Beauté raises her head. Someone breaks through the bushes. I drop down to hide.

Térèse bursts out of the bushes and looks behind her, as if she's being followed.

Wearing the same surprised look as she had when Margot brought her into the tower room at Madame's.

"Térèse!" I run and in the same moment that it's happening, it seems I am looking back from a distance at this as one of the best memories of Térèse, to remember how it actually was that we found each other along the thick Baise. So far from Ceres, but so close too. Maybe it's Térèse who ran to me. Or did I run to her? I have the same feeling that I had when Maman brought her home with us, long before this moment. I wrap my arms around her and lean my head on her shoulder.

"I will never lose you again."

"What's wrong with you?" She pushes me away, and bends over breathing fast. I can't hold onto her; her nature is as wild as the flowers and herbs she finds; plants that thrive in the least friendly places. But I will never lose her again.

"Espante!" I whisper, repeating Madame's Oc phrase. "I would never have known where I am. But now it doesn't matter."

She hiccups and breathes fast. "Of course, it matters. Are you ok? What did she do this time? I'm glad you got away. Aren't you tired? I'm so tired. I want to stop, but we have to keep moving. Listen, Madame said something. Oh, no, don't sit. You look completely lost. Get up. Who is this Angeline that Margot just mentioned?"

"I don't know. We're near *Condatóm*. Yes?"

"Epi, get up. What a mess we're in. Maybe we should go back. It's not far. Back to Nerac. Then Ceres."

"Go back?"

"Madame, would take us in."

"And get her in trouble too? I'm not going back. I'm surprised you think so. The only way I would do that is if we found Maman."

"What?"

"To prove I didn't kill her."

"You're not that stupid, are you? They'd kill you both."

On the towpath, Beauté pulls at the branches. Eating oak leaves. Térèse walks down a road, right next to the towpath, looking for hay nearby. The willows overhead, flutter their leaves like feathers. They brush over my hair, like Maman used to before I fell asleep. The river reflects hot tears in my eyes, that Térèse found me. I stumble ahead. Can we just stop for a minute? Can finding Maman be as easy?

Térèse guides Beauté to the haystack. We must be near the change in the river. It smells like fish. Good fish. Fish that would be even better roasted over a fire. Beauté pulls the hay stalks into her mouth. I sit down. Térèse next to me. We lean our heads together. Beauté's mouth moves, and her jaw crunches over and chews and brings the hay inside her. My eyes rest knowing she's eating. And Térèse's warmth is beside me.

The pink evening gathers, and Beauté whinnies. Crows land in, and then screech and fly out of the trees, zig-zagging across the sky. The sunflowers pick up their heads as the light descends at the edge of the field. Beauté neighs on the side of the road. We pass a sign for Moncrabeau, and beneath it says the City of Liars. "How far is it to *Condatóm?*"

We ride under the bridge at Moncrabeau. A sign for the Mill of Beauregard.

"It looks abandoned. Like ours. But this river hasn't been as dry as long as the Gelise has," Térèse points to frogs jumping.

"It doesn't make sense. Hay is growing, and not far away," I say.

"So, you never told me what happened to Claude," Térèse touches my arm.

"And you never told me how you found me and her." I don't want to think about Margot or Claude again. I was just getting used to breathing.

"Madame gave me money to find you. She said this was much more important."

"Then what?"

"Then her staying in good graces with the Guild."

"Oh?"

"Auvillar has been paying her to keep the brothel open. And keep quiet. He does his business dealings there."

"Perfect, and Margot, is she lying too?"

"C'mon does it really surprise you that they're all liars. All of them?"

I look up at the sign. I don't even know them, but what am I left to think of Antoine, my brother? There's a hot burning in me that says he isn't like this. I know what I feel. One minute he sounds like he really cares about me, but the next like he can easily discard me for the sake of the Guild. I have to show him he's wrong. And find Maman. How could one woman inspire so much love and hatred? There's so much I don't know about Maman. And I can't forget that I love Antoine. And Térèse.

"Not Grigne. She's not lying." I say. "But to make matters worse she's with Auvillar and Antoine who swear they're going to improve the problem. I don't see how they can, since they can't understand what she's saying."

"Improve the problem? What a Guild thing to say. Grigne said the problem was water." Térèse chews on some grass.

"Auvillar said the problem was the millstones." I say.

"Yeah, like that's easy."

"And Madame said something? About garlic?"

"*Faire monter l'aïoli.* Don't stir garlic into everything."

"The Guild needs a lot of garlic. And Madame said to find the next Mistress, Fabrizio. At the dovecote. Madame said it's outside *Condatóm.*" Térèse breathes and points ahead.

At the mention of dovecotes, I turn to Térèse. "Térèse I can't believe Claude died inside our dovecote. Have you seen him lately?"

"It's terrible. So sad. It's like he died years ago."

How is that possible? And what about Aubada and all the doves? Did I see them, or not? Aubada might go back to the bread terrace, looking for millet. She might get stuck inside the woodshed. No one would be there to help her. Might Paillard wander down to the bread terrace looking for me and find her body like that fish skeleton.

Around the stone wall covered with vines, Beauté leads us to a bridge over the Baïse. And there waits Bana, he's holding his arm and wincing. I run to him. He lets his arm fall to his side. He smiles.

"What happened? Are you ok?"

"I'm fine, Epi. My dad is coming soon, and you're the one who's limping."

CHAPTER TWENTY-TWO

Epi Finds Bana Outside Condatóm

BANA JUMPS UP and down. "Guess who I saw? Hobbling and swearing. She was using a branch to help her walk, but even the branch broke under her." Bana demonstrates and rolls over on the ground laughing hysterically.

"Did she see you? How did you escape?" I ask him.

"Escape? She never saw me. I was above her, going from tree to tree, my feet rarely touch the ground," Bana demonstrates by climbing a tree.

"Except when you're stealing or…throwing up," Térèse says.

"I've stolen lots of things from a tree with my father's shepherd hook."

"Right. Your dad is a shepherd. Where?" Térèse asks.

"In the mountains. Are you ok? Last I saw you; you were falling down the steps at a brothel, Epi," Bana asks. "I'll be sure to let you walk ahead, so I'll know if there's any holes!"

I'm about to answer him, when he surprises me with a hug.

"Well, just go back to the trees, Bana. We don't need you traipsing along." Térèse says.

"Hey, don't you have to get that box back from Auvillar. Your Mom's bones were in it! What part of her was it?"

"Bana, I can't believe you'd say something so cruel to Epi!" Térèse grabs his shoulder. "Get. Lost." Térèse motions her hand at Bana to climb a tree.

"Térèse wait. Bana, I didn't want Auvillar to know, so I didn't say anything at Madame's. But what was in the box wasn't her bones."

"Oh, too bad. I once saw a man's hands cut-off. And if they're real important, when they die, they put their hands or even their fingers in a box in a church. So I figured since your Mom sounded real important, and that's why they put her bones in that box."

"Hmm, could we do that to Margot?" Térèse asks, sounding excited.

"Nah, she only thinks she's important," Bana says.

"Do you mean we should put Margot's fingers in the box?" I lean towards Térèse. I know Margot thinks she's important, yet it makes me sad. I don't really know why. There's something about Margot that makes me cringe. Am I to blame for the thorn in her side?

"What was it then, in the box?" Térèse asks. "Epi? Why don't you tell me these things?"

"Maman's bread of dreams. From where she was from. And no, you can't eat them Bana," I say.

"Look for sure I can help you find the box. Or I can even make you a new box. But I can't promise I won't eat the bread of dreams."

"Remember how sick you got from eating all the breads in my sack?"

"I'm hungry enough to eat them all again, plus what's in the box. Plus the box. And the tree. And its neighbor…Where is the box?" Bana climbs overhead and stuffs some leaves in his mouth just to demonstrate how absurdly hungry he is.

I couldn't say I didn't feel the same hunger as Bana. Ahead, the path follows the Baïse on the east bank. The hamlet of *Condatóm* begins slowly, with a couple of people meandering along the river, and then around a sharp turn the lay of streets opens up before us. Beauté skirts by six carts piled high with wood. Either they're for building something or they supply the Guild ovens?

We stay to the right bank of the Baise and cross *Rue des Marroniers*, the first street.

"We're on the street of chestnuts, Epi. Pay attention. He might be here." Térèse says.

"Umm, I don't see anyone." Yesterday's crowd in Nerac was a shock. Our footsteps echo down the chestnut lined street. The wind from the river tears at the chestnut's leaves, withered and yellow. They drop at our feet, and while a few stay where they land, most swirl and brush each other's dry skins with a sh-sh-sh and flurry ahead of us, as if in a hurry to start a fire. Was there a Fool's Feast yesterday in this little village, too? Before we get too far from the bridge, three farmers sit behind tables. They look up. I look behind us, but there is no one else on the street of chestnuts, though we see people skirting by on side streets, of which there are exactly two. As far as I can tell the farmers are dressed as men and are men. On top of each table, each farmer has three short baskets spilling over with smooth-skinned brown and shiny nutmeats. Chestnuts. I can almost taste them. Though I've never had one before.

"Epi, wait." She grabs my hand, but I pull away. "Look at the trees."

"I am so hungry."

"You're hungry?" Bana says from above.

"May I?" Térèse asks and lifts the glossy brown nuts in her hands and shows them to me. They have bumps all over them.

"Where is the grove of trees, where did these nuts come from?" I ask the man behind the stand.

"Monsieur, look around you. They're dying or dead. These are the last. How many do you want?"

"They're still good, my father taught me they make great boxes," Bana claims.

"The trees, not the nuts."

"So then, don't eat them. Any of them. Please. Plant new trees, couldn't he, Térèse?" I ask. Madame Bouquin said that the apricot tree missed the chestnut tree, because it was left behind. I can't imagine walking away from these little nuts without trying to save them. Who could walk away? My stomach growls. But they must be planted, not eaten. But where and how? Térèse is shaking her head. She knows a lot more about planting them than I do.

Térèse passes them from one hand to the other, and they sound like small rocks from the Gelise.

"We will just eat them. The ground has been poisoned by the walnut trees."

"Guild trees." Térèse says.

"So, these chestnuts won't grow new trees?" I had to wonder if the Guild poisoned the ground on purpose? Or do they naturally poison everything around them?

"They would, well, maybe they would, if you take them far enough away."

"How far and how much for the chestnuts?"

"But you don't know the secret, do you? Go ahead. Plant two dozen, maybe one will make it." A man interrupts who stands next to Térèse. He's a young man, with a perfect round face of an angel, dark brooding eyes, and smallish hips. Térèse eyes him, his hands. Even I think they look soft, too soft to have cared for the doves. What had Madame said—I have fire hands. But what could his hands be? Water? There is none. Air? Leaves rustle on the chestnut trees above. Tearing them off the branches.

Térèse leans close and sniffs him. She picks a feather off his back when he leans in to examine the chestnuts. She holds it up to show me, as if this is proof of who he is, the dove-tender. She blows it away.

"Take these chestnuts for your doves," the vendor suggests offering out the basket.

"How do you know I have doves?"

"Please, I just want to…it's finished. My life as a chestnut farmer is over." The vendor looks to his right and left as if he might be being watched.

"Become a walnut farmer?" His dark brooding eyes ask the vendor. "Even if I had doves, they wouldn't eat chestnuts anyway."

I motion our new and hopeful companion, the man with soft hands and dark eyes to come closer. He stands still, a few chestnuts in his hand, and looks around him as if I am motioning to someone else. But no one else has come close to inspect the free chestnuts.

I edge closer to him. "*Faire monter l'aïoli,*" I say the Oc words. I remember these words from when Madame implored Grigne to not stir garlic into everything. I say the words confidently, as if I have known them all my life. This must be the clue he's waiting to hear. The secret. This will tell him we know he's Fabrizio. So, he will trust us.

"Oh, I couldn't." The man rubs his chin, barely glancing at us. And do I imagine he looks at my hands too? "No, thank you, but no."

The vendor stoops for something and Térèse grabs a few nuts with her rough and dirty fingers, then crosses her arms, brown from the sun, and hides them in her sleeve. She looks at me and motions me towards dark eyes. I throw down my hands and look back at Térèse. My eyes widen and say, "Didn't you see? He didn't even flinch at the Oc saying. He can't be who we are looking for, Fabrizio."

A gaggle of *talmelier,* their sacks bulging with crowns thrown over their shoulders, emerge from the same path we entered town on. They pass us and keep walking down this street. A shiver runs down my back. Where are they headed? To a Guild shop nearby? Even though the path comes from Nerac, only four hours by walking from us, the whole idea and all of yesterday seems totally out of place in the quiet and lonely village of *Condatóm.*

"Been arrested lately for stealing?" The man with a perfect round face turns abruptly and asks me.

I open my mouth to speak, but Térèse pushes me and interrupts. "So, the Guild strikes again. Once these nuts are gone, you're both out of business. But we can take them and plant them in another place, where they will grow. If you trust us?" Térèse asks the vendor and the man we still hope is Fabrizio. While we wait for their response, Térèse digs her elbow into my side.

I watch the young man's face. He refused the chestnuts for his doves. His ears fell deaf on Oc and the need to hold back on the garlic. Maybe the reason he infuriates me into seeing fire is because I saw Claude die. Or from seeing men be women and women, men. Or from learning Margot is my aunt and not my sister. From Margot not helping me find my mother. From not knowing if or where I will find her.

"Kind sir, I'm very interested in what you do to feed your doves, I'd like to hear more, maybe your doves would eat chestnuts? If you cook and mash them? Like our doves in, well, our doves eat, or I should say when they are babies, or were babies. They eat a mix of grain and sour milk called *Trakhanas*. What do you think?" I am surprised and so glad that I even remembered about *Trakhanas*, Maman's food for the doves, but mostly glad I didn't say it was for our doves in Ceres.

He looks me straight in the eye. "You, Sir, are not worth my breath."

"It's got to be him," Térèse whispers, pointing to the young man walking away. "Fabrizio. Look how he walks. I think I've seen him…no, it can't be him."

"I don't care how he walks." Beauté shifts her weight and the panniers on her back shift too, as if she is watching him move with new eyes. "He doesn't know us. Or want to. And besides. Him? A Mistress? What did Madame say again?"

"He's got doves and chestnuts. And Epi, listen. *Ecoute!* You can't let him go. How would we ever find him again?"

He might have doves, but we don't know that for sure. We do know he has no chestnuts. He's walking away. Bana stands at the corner and points where he turns. A flurry of doves flies over us and towards Bana. I haven't seen Aubada since she fought the King's birds in Nerac.

"Is that Aubada? I'm going to catch her and keep her in a cage."

"She can't find the others from a cage. And neither can you." Térèse says.

I close my eyes. I've had just about as much of this day as I can take. And it's just started. Térèse squeezes my elbow. If he isn't Fabrizio, he better damn well know where he is. I push away the urge to sleep and follow dark eyes.

CHAPTER TWENTY-THREE

Epi Meets the Mistress, Fabrizio

WE LEAVE THE one vendor market and hurry Beauté along after the flock of doves, swirling madly above us. The town of *Condatóm* disappears behind us and we enter a field of tall scratchy grass. A dozen more doves lift off from the field as we walk, they fly towards a tree. My feet push the earth behind and it flies out from my feet. I wave my hands at him. Even the cool air can't calm me down.

We head towards the fluttering. At the end of the field is a pear tree, loaded with doves. We approach quietly, but the doves lift off again. Fabrizio runs after them.

"Just a minute!" I run ahead of him.

"Don't you two have any sense? What if this was a trap? You'd be dead! This is what I have to deal with? You?"

"Don't I have any sense? You could have talked to us. Been civil. Let me tell you. I haven't eaten or slept or, and you?" I ask.

"Yes, please tell me. Like, why are you pestering me? Who are you?" Fabrizio steps closer. "Who are you?"

"My name is Epi." I had to risk it. We are here, and with a rush of cool air over my chest, I realize we could be in trouble. We're alone. Bana is above, in the tree, but would he help us? Bana *is* us now. It feels good to say my name, even if it's not the whole truth. Even so, did I just make a mistake? Not hiding who we are—what we want? And what did we want? I am so mad

I have to calm down. "Madame sent us. About the messages. This is Térèse and up there is Bana."

Bana throws a pear down on Fabrizio, that squashes on his shirt, and juices out. "That's for being mean. So be careful! I got my eye on you."

"I was expecting just two of you. But which two?" Fabrizio says.

"I don't ask permission. I just do stuff," Bana says.

"So, I see." Fabrizio says.

"Madame didn't know about Bana coming along. I don't even think—we didn't know Bana was following us. So, you knew? We were coming?" I ask.

"Doves bring messages much faster than people or even horses can." Fabrizio asks. "But since you didn't even know there were three of you, what else don't you know?"

At this question, I feel defeated. Stupid. I couldn't tell him what I didn't know. But I also feel surprised. How did he know, it did seem like there has always been three of us?

"Have you received a lot of messages? Are these your doves?" Térèse asks, not wasting a minute.

"Térèse is it? So, what kind of messages? Like, expect rain. Meet me at sundown at the top of the hill?" Fabrizio asks.

"No. Madame said there might have been a message that says where to find her, my Maman," I say. "I don't have a lot of time."

"Slow down. Who, who are you looking for?" Fabrizio asks.

"Antaia." Bana says from above. "For God sakes. Epi, just tell him."

"Look, one of you is in a hurry, the other says slow down, another, be careful. Who should I listen to?"

I look from Térèse to Bana and then hear the answer. Both. "Madame told us Antaia's last message was something about bread and teeth?" I say.

"Epi be clear, it was, "*Sometimes the bread arrives after the teeth are gone,*" Térèse adds.

"Oh, that one. *Calquecop Le Pa Que Be Quand Las Denses S'en Soun Anandos.* Sometimes the bread arrives after the teeth are gone. So?" Fabrizio asks. "The messages come in all kinds of languages. Greek. Old Roman. The Tongue of Epirius."

"So? You must know the Tongue of Oc then. And what does that even mean? How does bread arriving after teeth are missing connect the doves to finding Maman? Or growing chestnuts. What teeth?"

"I think I see what's happening. There is confusion over words. Meanings. And nuts. And no, you don't know the secret."

"So, you got this message?"

"Yes, and no. I was the one who passed it along to Madame. Since we're all learning things, I may as well tell you. The messages hold a secret. They have to. So, the Guild is never really sure what they mean. What Psomi is doing. Our big tree was the home for many doves, and now they've gone missing. Messages too. But even if the Guild takes the messages, they don't know what they mean. I was supposed to get a message from the blind man of Ceres." Fabrizio points.

"You know my Paillard? Fabrizio. I came from, we came from, Ceres. Paillard told me that the Guild was coming to question me just yesterday morning. I haven't seen him since." Térèse touches my arm, and I look at her boots, afraid to meet her eyes. I liked it better when yesterday in Nerac she was dressed as a boy too. But then I look again. Her eyes are filled with hurt that she didn't know about Paillard. And now I feel guilty that I don't know where he is. What will Térèse's face look like when she finds out I am Eleone? And Eleone is a girl like her? How can I ever explain that?

"OK, so it *was* Paillard who started the ball rolling. Then, I surmise it was Madame, the Mistress at Le Graine who sent me a message to expect the arrival of two who are organizing a Guild takeover," Fabrizio says.

I stop and look at Fabrizio. And Térèse. And Bana. "Is that what we're doing?" I get hot chills. "No. That's. Crazy. I am just out here. I must find Antaia. My Maman." I am scared that I don't understand anything.

"Woo-hoo, it's about time something happens between the Guild and Psomi," Bana swoops down from the tree, and dances.

"Easy there, Bana." Térèse rolls her eyes. "Look, Madame Bouquin of Le Graine was with Grigne. Do you know her? Grigne is a miller, and she was very upset that the waterways were too small for the harvest of wheat that's coming."

"That wasn't it at all, Térèse be clear. She said the water was being controlled," I say. "And back to these two who are throwing over the Guild, maybe it doesn't mean us. Maybe it's Margot and Antoine? I mean, maybe the message wasn't even from Madame. Is that possible?"

"Yes, you're seeing a little more now. Keep talking. So, you were making the bread of dreams? How? I mean in good blazes, how?"

"From roses, from stolen fruits, from the thatched wheat roof of the woodshed." I need to say, from things Térèse grew, stole, brought me. I look at her listening to me. I can't tell if she's sad. Or knows I am lying. Or is she happy to hear me tell her this? I need to thank her, but everything is moving so fast. And too slow at the same time. "Thank you. For…"

"No need to thank me. And this wheat that's the problem; it comes from far away?" Fabrizio says. "And what was it Paillard said?"

"From the mountains is all Grigne said, right, Térèse?" I say.

"My father lives in the mountains east of Tolosa, and he'll be so happy, man will he ever be, that we're going to take the Guild out," Bana says. "He's been waiting, like, for years for this. Years."

"The mountains? How far away are they? I never imagined even coming this far from the bread terrace. My bread terrace."

"And my garden." Térèse says.

"Once we find Maman, we'll take her back to Nerac, and then we'll go back to the bread terrace and your garden." I say to Térèse. But well, I had a sinking feeling that everything behind me, behind us, had been swallowed by the Guild. I couldn't go back. It wasn't going to happen. Maman wouldn't even know me. Last time she saw me, I was Eleone. Not this boy called Epi. "You seem to know the Guild. And what they've done."

"Epi, I listen to both sides. Read all the messages. Please don't judge me or repeat these things. Go on, what else? You have nice teeth. Your face tells more than paper," Fabrizio says.

Bana rolls his eyes. And moves his mouth, mocking Fabrizio. "More than paper? Ha!"

"I do? It does? I'm new to this message thing, so, I don't know, but does the Guild send messages too? Trying to…. confuse the Mistresses? Psomi? Maybe they have Maman, and they…" Was this what Fabrizio was telling me? Bana throws stones at the doves. I squint to see the pear tree at the other end of this field. It reminds me of Maman's apricot tree standing in the middle of our maze of trees. How we cut it down because of Guild orders and stored it in the woodshed. And that's where I found the box. I take Fabrizio's words inside me as if they are grains of rye from the field. Might they sprout in my stomach and make a new bread of dreams? Maman said the bread of dreams is best made from wild wheat and not from wheat that grows straight and obedient in rows, easy to harvest.

"How well do you know the Guild?" Fabrizio asks.

"I was raised in the Guild," I say.

"We're dealing with spies and thieves and…" Fabrizio shouts the words. I step back, but oddly, I am not scared. I should shout with him.

"You forgot murderers. They're murderers, too. And yet I was charged with murdering Antaia…" How puzzling to meet him, but maybe Mistresses are all puzzling people, the most puzzling one being Maman. What must she know, where is she?

I am more worried about her now than when I left the bread terrace yesterday.

"Aha! See! That's how they controlled you. Kept you in Ceres."

"Hmm. I never thought about that. Paillard told me to leave, that the Guild was coming, to question me about the bread of dreams. But others told me to stay."

"Yes, I did. I told you. You weren't ready. And you're still not ready for any of this." Térèse says.

"I went to the dovecote to tell Paillard that I was leaving, and I found Claude. Dead. Shot by an arrow." I say. Horrified that his death has become a topic of conversation, as if I didn't know him. Or that I even cared about him. He was Antoine's father for god's sake. He tried to be my father because, I don't know. He didn't like Paillard? But HE wasn't my father either. Sometimes it seemed like Antoine was trying to be my father. And in the mixed-up world we lived in, or that we were left in; I tried to be his father. And now the feelings that I have for Antoine, and for Térèse? She's right. I'm not ready for any of this. There is no one around to tell me. This. This is the truth. But how and why did Antoine throw Claude over for me? His own father. At least he had that much. Knew that much.

"Let me tell you something. The Guild is lies, missing messages, stupid hungry people, dying trees, and I can't even…begin to tell you everything," Fabrizio says.

"I'm stupid. And hungry," Térèse says.

It feels like all the things Fabrizio is saying are things I know but keep secret inside me. Hearing them is awful and wonderful at the same time. Like I didn't know Fabrizio until an hour ago, but now it feels like I have always known and can tell him anything. Is he my father?

"But listen, here's a strange thing too, it must have been the Guild who sent a message to cut down the huge walnut tree in the center of our square. They said it was to make troughs. But our tree is, and anyone who knows trees, can see it was a chestnut tree. The Guild just wanted to kill it. Chestnut trees grow like a dream. A dream is what they are. But one tree can't make chestnuts alone, unlike the walnut tree. Chestnuts are funny that way," Fabrizio says. "They need two trees."

"But why does the Guild like walnut trees?" I ask.

"When the Guild wants something, who am I to question it? But we all know that what the Guild wants doesn't grow on trees," Fabrizio says.

"You must mean the doves?" This didn't seem right, because maybe doves did grow on trees. Or at least, roost, in trees. And not always in dovecotes, like I thought. Nothing seems to be what I thought.

"Gold. Golden wheat. If they control that, then. " Fabrizio went on.

My stomach is either quite hungry or quite sick. I look at Bana, who had climbed the tree again after a brief stint at dancing. He was sitting on a branch, swinging his legs while eating a pear. "Fabrizio, this is all very perplexing. Where is the next dovecote? And so, do you have more messages? Can we see them?"

Fabrizio studies me. "Very well, Epi, I may as well come out and say it. The Guild not only wants walnut trees, but they are also walnut trees. Walnut trees make troughs. Bread peels. And they make fire to bake bread. Which makes the Guild a lot of money? But like your friend, Térèse here said, walnut trees poison the ground. This damn poison is Margot. Do you know her? She's always been looking for Antaia too. She was once part of Psomi, but she poisoned that as well. We have to stop her before she finds Antaia. Meet me at the dovecote, at the top of this field, at sundown."

"Margot!? Of course, I know Margot! Until yesterday I thought she was my sister, but then I found out at Madame Bouquin's that she's Maman's sister. And she's not so far away.

I was sent out from Nerac with her to find Maman." I stop and stare at Fabrizio. "She's not safe, and if we—if she—finds Maman, Here's—I mean, she lied that she even wanted to find her. So, I am sure she would kill her. Before we—got to *Condatóm*, I ditched her. She's lost in the woods. But for how long, I don't know. She could be very nearby." I feel relieved that I got away from her just in time. Térèse says it wouldn't be good for Margot to meet Fabrizio, since Fabrizio is tied to the messages. What in the world would Margot do if she found that out? She lied and made me think she didn't want to find Maman. Margot's playing a game with me. She knows things about Maman that I don't. So now what should I do? Ask Fabrizio? Could she show up here any minute? Having followed me? With a sick feeling I knew that even if she didn't find me here, I would have to meet up with Margot again. So, she was part of Psomi, as hard as it is to believe that. Would Maman be at the other end of the field, at the dovecote, to tell me the truth. The truth about why she left.

"Are you telling me that Margot isn't safe and is in danger or that you are?"

"I think you see what I'm saying. Nobody is safe around Margot." I say.

"There are a lot of sides here, so I'm glad you said it."

I move to hug Fabrizio.

"You're a very strange one, Epi." And then, he just walks away.

What else could I be? Born a girl, hiding as a boy for half my life. And now, caught in between. This is not good. I feel sick all over again. From a different kind of hunger. Before Fabrizio walked away, I was going to ask if we need to send a message that Margot is on the loose and dangerous.

CHAPTER TWENTY-FOUR
At Fabrizio's Dovecote,
Aubada Brings A Message

FABRIZIO LEAVES AND we sit beneath the pear tree and eat pear after pear. Juices and stickiness. Bees.

It's not easy to find a comfortable spot on the massive roots under the tree. Should one of us sleep while the other one watches? Finally, we decide that Térèse would sleep first while I watched. But when she woke, she pushed me awake as I was sleeping too. It's not easy for me to stay awake in the daytime, I am so used to sleeping in my nest in the rose canes when the light peers through.

We follow the field as it climbs a hill and into the setting sun. Térèse walks in one row, and I walk in the row beside her. Rows and rows of rye. Grasshoppers jump in front of us, land in my hair. Underfoot are small rocks. Then, footsteps approach and run by, brushing through the grain. Bana? I call out. I stand still, listening. There is no answer.

The field goes on and on like Ceres' North Field with the dovecote perched at the top. My stomach jumps. I don't recognize the figure. Maybe Margot is waiting for me at the dovecote? Was there even a chance that Margot had followed me? The figure climbs up into the dovecote.

"What will the messages say? We have to see them. Maybe it's Fabrizio, but maybe it isn't. Maybe it's who killed Claude." I say to Térèse.

"Epi, come on. Get whoever it is talking. What—I mean is, act like you're in charge. Not scared. Say something like where did this pear tree come from? Does he love this pear tree? Ask if this is his tree, like Madame's is the apple tree? Why is this tree, his tree? How does he know if the messages come from the Guild or from Psomi? Does he send his own messages, since he knows what they both sound like?"

"Oh, God. This is all too much. I had grasped something. Understood something. Now that disappeared. But what you just said. If it is him, does he send his own messages, how could I ask him that? He wouldn't answer." Pretend I'm not scared? I am scared.

"Epi, this is what's called talking. Sometimes people talk but don't agree."

"Then, why bother? They should just shut-up. I don't like when that happens."

"Ask him which way does he think Margot will go? When was the last time he saw Antaia? You're not very good at talking to people because, well, you haven't. Except when you talk to me. And you're not even good at that." Térèse nods over to the dovecote. "It just takes practice. And what a great day to practice and find Maman!"

"When you're so busy talking, I can't think. Bread, making bread, helps me think. Has Maman sent messages? Does she get any of these messages? What do we really know about the doves and the messages?" Not knowing who's at the dovecote ahead makes my insides cringe. This is too much. I am so tired. I want to go back to Ceres. I can't go back.

"You've got to ask whoever it is, to help find her." Terese says.

"And what happened to Paillard. We never saw him the

whole time we were in Nerac. And I've forgotten about following Aubada to find Maman. Maybe Fabrizio has seen Aubada?"

"From here it doesn't look like him, but if it's him, and if he has. We won't know til we walk further. Come on, Epi. Remember what's important here?"

"I can't remember anything. When I started out looking for Maman, it was simple. I was following Aubada, so if she's lost, I don't know how to go on."

"OK, but you know what's important. You have to find her."

I pull my hat down. "She's lost."

"Maman?"

"Yes. No, Aubada." The sun lowers itself in the sky, gently, gingerly, as if she knows this day needs an end so beautiful that it will distract me and calm me from the day of mostly unspeakable travesties; Antoine throwing Claude to the Guild to protect me, me being arrested and given an ultimatum. Somehow, I left the evil cloud of Margot behind, then Térèse found Fabrizio and even more calamities, like learning the Guild's walnut trees are poison. Poison! And then the key to getting out of this mess. Finding Aubada.

We head towards the flickering flames. A shadow stands by the dovecote at the other end of the field. We pick up pear branches and carry them as offerings to add to his fire. Bana says he has to pick just the right one. He'll catch up as he always does. Branches bend, and the wind tears leaves away, scurrying them ahead as we walk towards the fire, the dovecote, and the strangely shaped figure crawls on the ground.

We get closer. The fire crackles and sends sparks into the air. We get closer and the shadow stands and changes shape to be all of the men who have gone missing from me since I left Ceres.

Antoine, Paillard, Claude, and then Auvillar. They were all at the fire when Maman left me as Epi. Good riddance. Auvillar has gone missing. I am used to people disappearing. But what about the time I have left to find Maman. What of that? Is there another significance to these weeks, on the Attic calendar? He mentioned that there is to be harvesting then. That means there will be a lot of people on the road. Carts, baskets. Mules and donkeys. Fires. Unless there is no harvest. You can't go by people to know the answer. You have to go by the change in the air. After summer's time of growing and swelling. The slant of the sun above us says, make your best pear. Sweeten. Concentrate. I stop. We ate sweet pears, and maybe that's all the goodness we'll get today. Or all the rest of my days. Auvillar's presence closes in, in the leaves rustling, in the sun-whitened stones in the dry riverbed, and in the smoke shrouding the dark figure ahead. He leans forward. Like he's running even when standing still. Either he's carrying something on his back or he's horribly deformed. But then I remember nothing is what it has seemed since I left Ceres. What if the shadow is Maman and she's been hurt? And since Madame sent us, what of that? Didn't Térèse say that Auvillar pays her, but that Psomi's survival is more important than loyalty? Psomi's more important than me. But surely Maman is more important than Psomi since the Guild wants her so badly.

The shadow sits at the fire and feeds it, sparks fly up. It motions us to come closer. Térèse pushes me and I stumble forward. I step around the fire, smoke billows and I squeeze my eyes closed. I rub my eyes and make out his jawline and smallish frame. He's not deformed, but something is strapped to his back and covered over with a cape. I want to breathe out in relief because I recognize him. The strange figure is the same diminutive man we met at the chestnut stand. Fabrizio. But I'm disappointed too. And mad, too. Why couldn't he have been Maman.

"How is this a dovecote? Ceres dovecote is square. This one is round. But I left someone dead inside of it. Why aren't you dead? Are these the same doves, who lived there? Do you think the doves will ever return to Ceres? I've been worried about her. My dove, Aubada. I last saw her in your cage." I blurt.

Fabrizio stares up at me. "You're not making any sense. What now?"

Térèse shakes her head. "Epi doesn't know how to talk. He's a baker. Spends all his time measuring flour. Stirring the *levain*, alone. Dreaming up all sorts of things. I imagine." She points to her head and then makes a circle.

Is that how I seem? Crazy? Right now, I'm hurt, but maybe I should be proud?

Fabrizio tosses a chestnut back in the basket and puts down his small knife. He drapes a cloth over the cage. "Pigeon farms are all the rage in Rome. Outside Rome. This *columbaria* is more like the countryside, the villas. Italianate style. You'll see inside. The pigeons use ceramic pots turned on their sides for nests. But in Greece, dovecotes are called *peristeronas*. Your dove needs some rest, before she flies on. She barely escaped a falcon."

"What? Why are pigeon farms in Rome? I thought that Rome is a big city. How do you know it was a falcon? I knew something happened, didn't I, Térèse? Poor Aubada." I look in the cage as the light descends on this day. Aubada has tucked her head under her wing. Feathers are missing from her tail. I lean down and coo to her. She doesn't respond.

"Shh. You're scaring her. She'll be fine." Fabrizio picks up his knife again and slices into the chestnuts.

My heart longs to hear Aubada's quiet cooing to know she's safe. I long to see her hopping up to the woodshed roof back at the bread terrace. This dovecote won't suit her at all. It's much too crowded. My eyes take in the movements of the doves flying above us, leaving and others coming inside the dovecote. I move Aubada's cage away from the fire. Just like in Ceres, the dovecote stands alone. The fire and the fluttering calms me, and Térèse sits with her back against one of the stone columns of the dovecote. Her eyes glaze over, watching the flames. Then, they close.

"Aubada found me. But do you know how? This field is rye. Harvested in the spring. Except this year, we're waiting. Do you know why?" Fabrizio asks, he continues cutting little slits in the pile of chestnuts in his basket.

I hate to do it, but I tap her shoulder, and Térèse jumps awake. I nod at the rustling in the field. A dozen lanky men, one carries a banner with the falcon. It feels like the one who attacked Aubada. They cross the field of rye. Seeing them reminds me that the Guild is never far away. Maybe I shouldn't speak. These apprentices are the ones organizing a takeover. They threaten without saying anything. They remind me that time is passing. As if they know I have not learned enough to stop them.

"It's true. There's a lot I don't know. About Rome. Dovecotes. So please tell me. You're not harvesting because it's not yet time or what? The calendar Auvillar mentioned, is it called the Attic calendar. Is that right?" I stare at Aubada.

I don't know if I am getting closer to finding Maman, by looking for her near a rye field or if I was closer to her at the bread terrace with you fluttering in, Aubada. Where you watched me bake the bread of dreams and give them away. If I was collecting rye, and wild plants I could grind the grain and make them now, and maybe she could smell them. And find me. The aroma of the bread of dreams baking over the fire could reach her like a dove with a message. Aubada looks up as if she is listening. The setting sun spurs my whole body to stir flour, pummel herbs and knead them into the dough. Stoke this fire. Try. Keep trying. Making my bread of dreams was simple. I could do it by myself. This searching and talking, makes me need people. I don't like this method of finding her. I don't. And what if Térèse says, that when people talk, they don't always agree, happens here, with Fabrizio. Maybe Fabrizio will get angry, like Antoine does sometimes? And like Margot does, all the time. Aubada flaps her wings. Flutters around in the cage. Settles. I will always keep you safe. I can't keep you safe.

Fabrizio takes the cage and opens it. "It's ok," he coos. Auvillar is talking about *Boedromion*—in two weeks. But that's not why we're waiting to harvest the rye." Fabrizio nods towards the *talmelier.*

"It's because they're here. What's to stop the Guild from harvesting it?" I ask.

"Nothing, really, except they don't have any use for it," Fabrizio says.

Bana appears out of the shadows. A log tucked under his arm. "And you do?"

I pull him towards me. He pulls away.

"Seeds." Térèse says. "That's why, Epi. Seeds."

Aubada stretches her neck, and pecks me.

"Look! She knows you."

I reach my hand out.

"She's better now."

"No, look at her foot."

"Go on, Aubada. Join the others. Before that hawk that's been hanging around gets your other foot."

"No, no. She needs more time." I jump up, but Fabrizio opens the cage, and Aubada flies out and up to the top of the dovecote. Bana climbs after her. More doves fly in, and others fly out.

"Why did you do that?"

"She's fine, Epi. Don't worry. She needs to eat some rye."

"She likes *Trakhanas.* Look at her tail!"

"*Trakhanas?* Really? She'll come back. Trust her. Didn't you take care of her all these years?"

How could I tell him that I did, but I didn't trust her? That she was like Maman. It wasn't either one of their faults. Aubada was called by the sky. Like Maman was called by the fields. Or to return to the fire? I am not sure.

Fabrizio unstraps a pot from his pack. The vessel is black on the bottom from other fires. He scoops some water from a barrel of rainwater into the pot. And empties a basket of chestnuts into the pot. "There'll be no *Trakhanas* here. That's women's food. Baby food."

"Wait, aren't those the last chestnuts? Térèse, we need to keep some to plant!"

"Everyone knows you need the chestnuts to help cook the rye." Fabrizio stirs.

"Epi, he doesn't know shit." Bana says. "He doesn't know where that Guild is from. Look at their banners. You're all pretty much like sheep! No offense, Epi."

"What do you mean? That Guild? Are there other Guilds, besides the one in Nerac?" I ask. I couldn't understand the words on their banners, but if anyone could read my growls, my stomach had to be growling in the tongue of Oc and can now understand the pile of dove messages better. A dozen *talmelier* pound their banners into the dry ground and collect kindling. I hear crackling as they start a fire too. Is Margot with them, or maybe Auvillar or Antoine?

Térèse gets up. "I'll go see what's what."

"What? What could you possibly hope to learn? Stay here."

"You're worried about me? Look, I'll find out where they're from."

"Let her go." says Fabrizio.

Bana yells down from the dovecote. "That's very Guild of you. Send in Térèse. She's innocent, Fabrizio. You don't care about Psomi, do you?" Bana throws clods of mud at him.

Térèse walks towards the camped-out Guild members.

Fabrizio leans on me. "Who is this kid, anyway? Look, can you read?"

"He's Bana. Like Térèse, he throws garlic into everything. He took me to Madame's. Look, can you help me find Maman?" I ask. "Don't bother me with anything else. It's too much."

Fabrizio looks in my eyes. "So, you can't read. You steal chestnuts. Stink of garlic. And you're overthrowing the Guild." He laughs. "I'm kind of doubting the message that I got."

I laugh too, but it's not funny. "Hmm, do you still have the message? Look, I like being quiet, and watching, I learn more that way. But I get really lost when I talk. I know that makes me sound stupid. It doesn't make any sense."

"Yes. Yes, it does make you sound like a poor choice for this job. Keep talking. The words circle and maybe I can decipher a good path. Maybe." Fabrizio stares at the *talmelier*. "Unless they kill us all in our sleep."

"I'm not planning on sleeping. Madame was from Jerusalem and Auvillar and Maman both came from Greece."

"Auvillar is from Greece, too?" Fabrizio asks.

Footsteps approach. Then Bana's little face pokes out of the darkness, poking Fabrizio with a stick.

"I came from Rome, big deal," says Bana. "Where did you come from, Gabbie Fabbie? That's what they call you. You talk a lot but don't say anything."

Fabrizio rises up. He frowns at Bana, his hands on his smallish hips.

A fire starts in the talmelier's camp. Bana climbs the ladder on the side of the dovecote. And jumps down at Fabrizio's feet.

"I've had just about enough, you, you, *Empapautar*," Fabrizio runs at Bana.

Bana picks out a branch from the fire and swings it into Fabrizio's knees. Fabrizio falls and Bana dances around. Kicking at Fabrizio. Then he runs in circles around the dovecote.

"Bana, stop. Fabrizio?" The chestnuts float in the boiling liquid. These are the last ones. I am so hungry. And where is Térèse? She should be back by now.

"Get going. Go on." Fabrizio chases Bana.

"Get ready for the fight, Fabbie. Are you ready?" Bana runs off in the direction of the other fire. I expect to hear the *talmeliers* in the camp shouting at Bana too.

My hands tremble and my whole-body shakes. I hold my hands over the fire to warm. Something just doesn't seem right. Are Fabrizio and Bana fighting over something else I don't know about?

"I've heard worse tales from where he's from. South of Rome. And east. The mountains are full of bandits. Near another sea. And across that sea lives in Greece. The fields all began there. The dovecotes I mentioned. And this calendar of planting and harvesting. And one side who wants to harvest. Another side wants to steal it. And if they can't, then they burn it."

I shake my head. "That sounds terrible. Antaia never spoke about Greece. To tell you the truth, I can't see how either side thinks they can survive." I look at the movements at the other end of the field. My throat closes knowing that we are in danger.

Fabrizio covers my shoulders with a shawl. "Aubada knows. She's the key. You know it in your bones, too."

"What do you mean? Doves only fly home." Térèse shivers and sits next to me, wrapping us both in the shawl. "I think Bana's right."

"Térèse you're back! Bana's right about what?"

"Bana says Psomi and the Guild need to fight it out."

"It's only a dove's flight to Psomi," Fabrizio says.

"Aubada's home is Ceres. It would mean death to follow her back there." I say.

"Even though they may have been gone a long time, doves remember the landscape," Fabrizio watches doves fly in and out of the dovecote.

"The fields? But doesn't one field look like any other?" I ask.

"To us, maybe. But remember, we're walking. They're flying. It's different seeing the fields from the sky. As a dove," Fabrizio says. "Come on inside and climb to the top."

I stop rubbing my hands. Paillard said his blindness let him see the doves and follow them. I close my eyes, picturing the view from the sky; from Ceres dovecote to noisy Nerac, then down the dry river path to *Condatóm*. I picture ducking my head to go inside, climbing the ladder past the dove's nests to the very top of Fabrizio's dovecote. I haven't been brave enough to even look inside, afraid of finding Claude again. "Hmm. That sounds easier than walking."

"Over rivers!? And mountains in between," Bana rushes inside the dovecote and picks up a rake and rakes the dove *merde* into a pile. "Don't you sell this, Fabby? Dove *merde* is valuable. For making leather. For fields. For fire!" Bana jumps on the ladder. And starts up. "C'mon Epi. You got to see the field from the top."

I step inside and stop on the second ladder. The setting sun slants in a golden light when there are no doves coming or going. I reach in one of the ceramic jars and find a dove. Pull my hand out and keep going. Up. I don't worry about the *merde*. That's all down below. I reach into another jar, and find bits of rye, feathers and paper. Old messages, soiled. Madame said there was a problem. Here it is.

"So now you see. The doves bring back the messages. Lots of messages. What can I do? I don't understand them either. But this is my job. It's important to do even if I don't know why. They know why. The doves."

"But what about all these messages? Don't you want to read them?" I ask.

Fabrizio shrugs.

"I mean you asked me if I knew why you were waiting to harvest. And I learned…" I ask.

"See, he acts like he is free, But he's not." Bana says.

"I might not understand why, or agree, to wait to harvest, but here are all the messages that came before. And after. But I don't know which message came before and which came after. I can't see the whole snail," Fabrizio shares.

"Snail?" I ask.

"That's the size of his brain," Bana says.

"They say that's what the path looks like from the sky. To the doves. And isn't a snail etched on the box?" Fabrizio says, trying hard not to look at Bana.

I was so wrong. Why did I think I saw a tree on the box? Since when is a snail a tree? I should mention this, but I don't want to look stupid. More stupid.

"My new brother, Epi, doesn't have the box anymore. Auvillar took it. God, you are stupid." Bana says.

"But I still don't understand. What do the messages say?" I ask.

"Let's look. In one sense the snail sneaks up on you. I can't see the whole picture, but I have to keep communicating, even if I can't see it. I can't stop." Fabrizio stirs the pot of chestnuts and adds the rye, caraway seeds, and mustard seeds. "We'll eat in an hour."

"Snails leave a slimy path to follow. How do you even know that the messages don't all come from the Guild?"

Maman said something like that. "You think you know and see all that you need. Epi, but to understand Psomi you must listen without expecting to understand."

"Maman, said that?" Bana asks.

I get chills looking at Bana's smile in the firelight. He says Maman as if she's someone we share.

Then, Fabrizio smiles at Bana as if they've been friends all along. "Yes. What hasn't been told is kept hidden. In the spirals of the snail. In your bread of dreams. In the path of the doves flying over the rye. In the flames, you'll begin to know."

"In these flames?" The doves fly in and out of the dovecote. Could I see them the way Paillard did? I look up—I have to trust the doves. "Fabrizio, what hasn't been told?"

"Where Psomi is, what Psomi is. You don't trust me? But why should I trust you, this bratty kid, and her? Your betrothed sells garlic seeds, and wants to find tomatoes, a poisonous fruit? What did she look like?"

"Who? Maman?" I see Fabbie differently. How we are both trying to be heard and yet, to be heard, meant we had to listen too. "She had red hair. Very long, with bits of blue and gold."

"No, she was blonde."

"I grew up with her. You have to believe I know what she looks like. She isn't blonde. She's my mother. Why do you want to know now?" How long ago did I see her? This conversation feels very weird.

"He wants the Guild to win," Bana throws dove *merde* at Fabrizio, some misses and lands in the fire. Flames explode.

"No, no, I don't. Look, I'm through with you! What do I want? To make a difference, you know?" Fabrizio says.

"So that tomorrow will be different?" I ask.

"Of course. Tomorrow is where you'll find the fields and the rivers come together," Fabrizio says.

I sit down next to the burbling pot over the fire. Maman certainly is more like this field, than like a river, right? She knows planting, growing, and she would know when to harvest. It never occurred to me that when to harvest was so important. Does Grigne know this? She needs the rivers. She's a miller. She's consumed with grinding and making flour. But she needs to know this. Maman must have some idea as she traveled on the rivers too, to get to Ceres. And why did she stop in Ceres? If Psomi wants an edge on the Guild we need to harvest some grain now, to grind for flour, like Claude. But we'll save some grain to harvest later. For seeds. Goosebumps shudder over my arms, picturing where the fields and rivers come together. Of course, Grigne must be there. But also, Antoine and Auvillar. Margot? How silly of me to think any of them would care about Fabrizio and his little dovecote here. But what about all these messages? With a shudder of realization, I realize that tomorrow is where Maman Antaia is. Where Maman must be waiting. "That's where Antaia is waiting, in tomorrow. She wants to make a difference too."

"And the man. Don't forget him. It's not too far, for a dove, but for you, a long way away. Maybe. It's not up to me. Honestly, I don't think you can make it in two weeks. But it's not up to me."

"The man? What man? Auvillar?"

"Before Auvillar there was someone else."

"Do you mean Claude?" Does Fabrizio know something about his death?

"No, Claude was Antoine's father. He was way after this guy. His name sounds like the word for tree, Arb? Arber? No. Wait. Arrgghh. I hate not remembering!"

"You mean Artos." Bana says. "Fabbie, you've been out here too long."

"Who is Artos?" I ask. One of them knows the truth.

"Antaia's one true love. In Massalia," Bana says.

"Wait. How do you know that? She didn't love Auvillar?" I feel a huge wash of light over me as I ask this question.

"Artos is one of my dad's buddies. Or he was. Not sure if he's still around."

I immediately pictured Maman's bouffe, which was at Madame's. Why did Madame keep it? Was she helping Maman? It was plain she didn't like Auvillar but was somehow still doing his bidding. The strange carved embrace of the figures. Made of Maman's tree, the soft-wooded apricot. Now in Margot's hands. But why?

"So, Massalia. It's in Greece?" Térèse asks.

"No, Massalia is only a couple weeks of walking," Fabrizio says.

"Rye is no good with these caraway seeds. Why Fabbie? You ruined it." Bana pours his bowl into the fire. Smoke rises from the hot mess.

"If only we had it, Parthian duck eases the caraway, with fish sauce and ."

"Black mustard seeds?" Bana says.

"Sometimes. Ducks fly in just before the rye is harvested. Which is unfortunate. But then, that's why duck fed rye is such a specialty near Rome."

Feathers rain down. "Aubada is back. With a message!" He points his knife in the air to look.

It frightens me, that in his hunger he might mistake her for a Parthian duck and he would eat Aubada and her message in one bite.

"Oh, she did come back." I mumble, but it's just as much because I can't leave the conversation about Artos and Claude and Auvillar. I watch Fabrizio carefully, ready to jump up and save my dove. "Can I see?"

I lift her towards me. I know her still by her blue feather. She has a pouch strapped on her side. She faces away and bends her head, touching her beak to my outstretched finger. She walks out on it. She turns sideways and inches onto my other hand. Her beak tickles me as if it were a feather. I stand slowly and bring my other hand over her. Her warm body stills under my touch. My finger reaches in the small pouch strung on her side. She flies away. I sit. She comes back. I reach in the pouch again. A slip of paper unrolls. I hold it toward the light of the fire. "It's in Oc." I show it to Fabrizio.

"Take the life of the fire. *Prend la vie de feu.*" He wipes his mouth with the back of his sleeve.

"Take the life of the fire."

"Oc." He pours me a glass of wine.

"Do you think it's from Maman?" I sit on a log, watch him spoon rye into my bowl. The aroma alone is so good it could kill me. I want to eat like a crazed animal. Beauté neighs nearby. And the dog Fabrizio mentioned, barks. A shadow prances at the edge of the darkness over near the Guild fire. Panting comes across the field. Am I eating like a dove? With my mouth full of sweet chewy warmth, the grains bulge out my cheek. The chestnuts crush under my teeth. My belly rumbles at the strangeness of being filled with the rich taste of rye. I am afraid to swallow. Afraid this moment of getting a message from Maman will be gone. Did I now have the same skill as the dove, to fly over and pick the field, the one field and find my flock again? The longer I chew, the rye tastes more and more like the fire it was roasted over. Does the life of this fire now live in me? I swallow the rye. Then, I take a few swallows but spit out the wine. Phew.

"What do you think, *Oc?*"

"It's salty now," I say, pouring out my glass of wine in the fire.

"Salt? Wow! They mix salt with the grain so it can't grow." Fabrizio gestures to the east. "Where she's from, your horse. The Camargue, it's the only way to the sea."

"It's easier through the mountains, Fabbie. Then shoot down the Rhone. Less bandits."

"You might well know that better than me."

How does little Bana know this? Aubada flaps her wings. I am so happy to hear her.

Fabrizio rubs his chin. "She's ready."

"For what?"

"To show you where the message came from. Look, here." He holds up a snail shell. His finger traces the ridges. "See how the spiral winds in and out?" Fabrizio clears his throat.

"Of course, the spiral winds in and out. That goes without saying."

Fabrizio lifts Aubada. We all gather round. I hold her. Smooth her feathers. Her broken foot hangs limply. We tie the pouch on her.

"Which way will she go?"

"To Grigne. You'll follow her."

"How well do you know her, Grigne?"

"As well as anyone else. I hear she not only grinds grain, but imports long pepper, black mustard and cumin seeds and salt from the sea from far away."

"What are you trying to tell me?"

"Like the snail shell keeps going, some things have kept going that never should."

"That's a strange thing to say." Maybe he means Grigne. Maybe he means the Guild. Or me.

"You need your own. Fire flutes can be made from lots of things, not only trees. They can be made from…"

"Rye stalks, Fabbie?" I ask.

"Don't call me that. And you, you're not a little boy." He shakes his head at Bana. And turns to me. He stares a long time.

"Fabrizio. I'm 17." As if using his name along with my age, makes me right or truer, somehow. If only it were that simple. I could say, I'm not a little boy, I'm just pretending to be one so I can stay safe. And now that I left Ceres, keep everyone around me safe too. I'm old enough to be a man. Or a woman. What in the world can I say to explain? Act like nothing's wrong? Hold out till I see Maman? How can I? I have to pee! I feel like I'm in a box as well as Psomi's seeds. Or in a sack, like the bread of dreams.

"You seem younger." Fabrizio pulls the sack he carries over his shoulder to the front of his chest and unwraps a roll of strange instruments. He pulls out the smallest one. He blows through it, and it makes a high-pitched note. He hands it to me. Unlike the bones in the pouch that Auvillar claimed were Maman's bones, but were her bread of dreams, this flute looks like a bone. An actual bone. The darkness of the last night I saw Maman floods through me. Any feelings of comfort and knowing Maman is waiting ahead disappear.

"What kind of bone is this?" Tiny holes are bored into its short length.

"Parthian duck." He puts it to his mouth. And plays. My heart hurts my eyes and my throat; interconnected waterways, pathways and tears trickle down my cheeks, joining them. It's like the sound coming from me sounds far away. As if I am far away. Already at the place where Maman disappeared to, and maybe still is. What if she's not there? I wipe my eyes and nose on my sleeve.

The sound pulls Térèse out of the darkness, she comes close, sits and bows her head on my shoulder. I don't want to break the mood to ask her what she's learned.

Bana sits down beside me. He is quiet, too. The sound of the flute winds among us. Makes us sad, yet ready. For what? For more? I don't know.

"Aren't you worried that the Guild could hear it too?"

Fabrizio keeps playing. He shakes his head no. But I'm not sure if this is an answer or he just means to be quiet.

"So, Psomi is quite far? I can't let Auvillar and Antoine find Maman first."

"They'll be with Grigne?" Bana says.

"I'm sure Grigne wants to see Maman. And maybe she would lead them to Maman without knowing it. How can I get her away from them?"

"Maybe, Grigne isn't all that important." Fabrizio says. He hands me his fireflute. "*Follow the doves.* Play the flute if you get lost."

His words ring in my ears. *Follow the doves.* But how could Grigne not be important? How could that be? She traveled a long way to find Auvillar. This little bone can't compete with Madame's intricately carved fireflute. I can't imagine why I would play Fabrizio's fireflute as that would surely let the Guild know where I am. *Aubada* flies away into the night. She coos softly on top of the dovecote, matching Térèse who softly snores. Bana rolls over in the pile of hay. He burps. Beauté cocks her front hoof. And listens to the night. It's a strange feeling to be under the stars together. I've learned and spoken more than I've ever dreamed. But I still don't know where Maman is. And I'm running out of time.

THE FOURTH TALE

Chickpea Sangak with Figs, Smoked Salt,
and Garlic Yogurt. Persia. Térèse.

"Cal pos cambia un chabal bornhe per un d'abugle."
Do not swap a one-eyed horse for a blind one.

CHAPTER TWENTY-FIVE
Follow the Doves

"Térèse." I shake her shoulder. "Did you hear Fabrizio?"

"What? I need to sleep." In the dim light of the fire, Térèse pulls her blanket up. A slight rain falls.

"Wake up. Do you think Fabrizio is telling us the truth about the messages?"

Térèse whispers, "There's no us. You really are *coille*."

"Térèse!"

"Epi, you don't have it in you to see people. They're all liars."

"I'm not lying."

"Epi, something else is going on with the messages. We're headed straight into disaster. So, get some sleep while you can." Térèse lays back down.

"Bana, get up," I say. But Bana's place of straw-like a nest, is empty. I feel the hay. It's still warm.

Térèse sits up. Stretches. Beauté's reins drag on the ground.

"I wish we were with Grigne. To find where the three rivers come together."

"Actually, she said the dam sits above where they come together. All that rushing water sounds terrible."

"More terrible than Beauté coming from the Camargue, where the sea washes over the soggy land, and makes it a land of salt?"

Térèse sighs. "And where they mix salt with the grain to stop it from growing."

"Terrible too. Say, where's our third river? Bana?"

"He got up hours ago, I wouldn't let him wake you. So, he left. I'm surprised you didn't hear us. Epi, I'm not sure about him."

"About Bana, why? He's great! Says whatever he thinks." I was afraid things could never be easy with Térèse.

"He's trouble."

"But that's what you said talking was? When people don't agree?"

The feeling shifts in my heart, from despair to terrible despair.

"Help me find Bana. He's probably gone to Grigne, to get her away from Auvillar and Antoine before they suspect anything."

"Epi. More likely he's gone to Auvillar and Antoine to take them to Maman."

"That's good, though. Right? We want to find Maman! Why didn't you wake me when he left?"

"Wake you? Bana wants to win, that's all. That's all. He'd doublecross you in a minute, if it meant he could find Maman. So, it's you who better wake up!"

All I want is to feel like the sun showing its pinkness at the edge of the hill. Just when the thought of being out here looking for Maman felt real and better than all the years of not looking for her when I stayed at the bread terrace. But now, all this looking and churning of our boots in dry riverbeds had set so much dust in the air, that there was no way so many people wouldn't see our dust, and us. That's what I fear most. Being seen. Wanted for murder. Wanted for sedition. After Térèse's words, maybe Auvillar is letting me get close and then when I find Maman, he'll hunt me down with Térèse AND Maman. He still needs what she knows. But so do many others. It feels like many are on the road. Maybe like the doves. Or maybe like hawks. The doves know. And the hawks follow them. Of course, they must. They can see all of the spiral. And one thing I hadn't thought of much before. It's there when we look into each other's eyes. Maybe it is the one true thing between us; that we both were left by our mothers. But Térèse has one thing going for her that I do not. Maman chose Térèse to come back to Ceres. Why? Why else? My stomach hurts to think so, but maybe Maman was planning to get rid of me. I try to remember the day. The last day we were all together in Nerac. But all of it flies away like the dust cloud that shakes off of Beauté.

Epi Argues with Térèse About Love

TÉRÈSE AND I walk up the third hill of the morning on the narrow path called the Via Podiensis. No Fabrizio to tell us lies. And no Bana to doublecross us. A woodpecker pecks in the trees. Another swoops by as we walk along the river.

"Térèse, did you know about Artos? Did Maman just pretend to love Auvillar? Why would she do that?" It was hard to hear Fabrizio say that Maman had someone who she loved. And I had to get Térèse talking again. But I am scared to hear what Térèse might say. She thinks I should wake up. I look at her eyes, for a clue to how she feels. Was I capable of that kind of pretending or do I really love her? How can I love her or Antoine with so much unsettled inside me?

"Because love is a mess. Most of the time, I stick with caring about the garden. Love is just a made-up feeling. Men say it so they can have you. I never hear that at the brothel. And that reminds me.."

"Auvillar acts like he had Maman. Why do women say it?"

"They feel it. And to be kept safe?" Térèse says. "I have this feeling that.."

"That I am keeping you safe?" I wanted to keep her safe, but pictured her laughing.

"You're a strange man, Epi. You can't even keep yourself

safe, let alone me. I've been trying to keep you safe. But you don't listen too well." Térèse says.

How can she say I don't listen when I'm the one who doesn't talk? "Men feel it too. Or at least I do. And Maman wouldn't love someone who didn't feel it."

"What do you mean?" Térèse says.

"It seems like no one really had her. Or understood her." I certainly seemed bound for the same fate because neither Térèse or Antoine knew my feelings. How can I say more about how I feel without feeling completely stupid? I feel so confused. Frustrated. Unseen. And it all began with Maman, who I thought understood me without words, but maybe she never did and I imagined that she understood me.

"Are you wondering who bedded her? It's not the same thing as love, you know."

How would I know that? And more, how would she? Her words strike me as if they are sparks from a fire. And I know fire can destroy and burn fields, or give life, when bread comes out of it. Was the same thing true for love? And for Maman. How many men had she loved? Poor dead Claude? What was it like for Maman? Did she fall in love with Artos when she was young? And then had to leave him? Because why aren't they together? Is Artos her Antoine? I can't stop thinking about Antoine, he is not my brother, not really. He's like a fire or a sun always ahead of me, that I keep walking towards. That I have to find. I look up and feel like I can sense his heat. It's complicated. "Someone must have had her, because she had me. But then I lost her. I want things to be simple. But nothing is more complicated than saying I love you to someone."

"Epi, love has nothing to do with it."

"That can't be true. You don't..."

"I don't what, love you?" Térèse asks.

"Do you?" I'm afraid to hear what she might say. How would I know if she loves me? Just because she says so. And if I can imagine that I know enough to say I love her, does that mean she must return the same feelings? But how else could it be? The sheer magnitude of my feelings for her must be felt and known by her?

"You don't know what you're talking about. At the brothel I've seen people, love each other. Love their bodies. You'd think with the force of the love I've seen that…everything was clear. But their hearts are somewhere else. You should listen to me."

"I lost her. Is it my fault?"

"What do you mean?"

"Did I get in the way, and she went back to him. Maybe that's where she went. To Artos. Is Artos my father?"

"Oh, now, that's a good question. Your father surely isn't Auvillar, right. Yuck. I can't imagine how you could live with that. But maybe Auvillar wants you to think so? What about Claude, though?"

"That timing wouldn't have worked out. She met Claude after I was born. Oh, I don't know."

"I know you lost her. But so did I, and I also lost my own mother. But look where are they? Who knows? But us? We're out here on our own. Stick with me and you'll learn. The ways of the world are strange. Epi, love is strange. You don't need it. Shake it off."

"I still want to know what happened. Who is my father? Am I not a part of him? When Fabrizio said Maman loved Artos, it started me thinking about all of this. I've spent so much time thinking about Maman, wanting to be like her, that I never considered my father, really. Is he a sweet man? What if he's a bad man?"

"Whatever our parents do, or did, it's not our fault. If Maman left, and why she left, it's not your fault. How could it be, you hardly know how to talk or even make a decision. Of course, that's still true."

"Térèse, I promise…" I reach over and stroke her soft cheek, so different from her hands, which are rough and hard, but when they dig, they soften the earth. But her face, with the soft cheeks, hardens and tightens.

"No! Please, no promises. Each day we live to see the sun is enough." She rolls her eyes, and her face goes cold. She shakes her head and pushes me away. Stands and walks under the tree, scuffling the dirt around the roots.

"You'll always…be. Térèse. My Térèse." I run to her. Take her hand.

She shakes me off. "What does that even mean? I've heard it all before."

"Where, from who?"

"Look, whatever vision you have of me inside your little head is who I am? Where I have to stay?"

"No, of course not. You can do whatever you want. But just remember you asked me to stay. Stay in Ceres."

"Oh, I will! But it might not be what you want. And what does *my* mean then, exactly? That you own me? You can do whatever you want with me? To me?" Térèse stands, looking up.

"I just want….I don't know, you have to know, I won't leave you. I will protect you." I just want to grab her and hold her. She walks further away.

"Ha! You're just like all the rest of them! Men! What they say, what they want. It's all about them."

"Why are you twisting my words? I just want…" I am so confused. My heart beats so hard. How did what I say have the exact opposite effect I wanted to have on her? I want to let her know everything is ok. Different between us than it is for Maman and Artos. Isn't it? I just want…

"What? I just want you to know that I won't be who you want me to be. I don't care, or want your protection, because I don't need it. It…. only really helps you."

I'm just stunned to feel so far away from her when all I wanted was to feel close. Didn't she ask me *not* to leave the bread terrace, like a couple of days ago? To stay there where it was safe.

That I wasn't ready. And now we're out here. I'm scared. Térèse points at the sky. And our words drift off into the trees. I'm not ready to leave, move on.

"Look, it's *Aubada*! And she's way ahead of us. Well, aren't you going to protect me from her? What if she poops on me? Are you just going to let that happen?"

I run after Térèse. The fabric of her pants swishes together, but she's hardly going fast. But I feel so far from her. Beauté runs too. I look back at the spot where we argued hoping to see a sign from the trees to explain what happened. Branches swaying or leaves falling. But the trees fade into the distance and the grass looks brown and dried. The clouds billow and blow across the sky, leaving a bright blue expanse overhead. What happened? We move under new trees. Branches above us rustle, leaves twitch and float, then release and drift to the ground like small feathers. A hawk screeches overhead and swoops, glides and angles through the trees. My heart races. A smaller bird, maybe *Aubada*, flies out of the forest and ahead over the field.

We walk further into the morning, and further into silence. We cross *Le Garaillon*, a river that churns like all of my insides. It rushes south towards a town bigger than Nerac, called Auch and the Pyrenees mountains south even further. We meet *Le Grand Auvignon*, which isn't grand at all. It's a trickling thing. But I have lost *Aubada*, again, and with her, all the talk about my father. But I have to wonder, does Térèse already know who hers is? Or has all this talk started her wondering too?

CHAPTER TWENTY-SEVEN
The Grove of Cornelian Cherries

A SIGN POINTS TO a few stone houses at the top of the hill. Flamarens. We lean into the ground that slants up. It's so hot. And so dry that the houses look like they might crumble. I can see how the tiles of the red roofs fit together as we climb. But I worry that the tiles are too heavy for the frail houses. At the top of the hill though, the number of houses is smaller than the village name. It's as if someone in Nerac stood up and threw out a handful of stones that grew into these houses.

After the houses we trudge through a dried field and a path. We go through a grove of red fig trees. After the grove we meet an orchard of a few black cherry trees. We stop. I can't pass you, I say to the tree, as if it is a person who can talk back to me. I remember your shadows from Maman's maze of trees. And here you are, it's strange to see you growing at the edge of these fig trees, like the ones near Térèse's garden. I look around as if Maman might be near-by. This is a sure sign that Maman came this way. Your cherry branches hold long globes of dark red fruit. Why have they not been picked? Is there no one close by? The ground is too dry. Damn the Guild. The fruit should have been picked months ago, but if it had, it wouldn't be here now for us. The aroma carries a spice too, as if suddenly the bread that Maman kneaded and folded around Cornus Mas cherries and onions dried over the fire, and fried in duck fat, is here in my hand.

"Cornus mas." Térèse says. "Cornelian cherries."

"She was here and planted them. Maman." I reach up for a few fruits.

"No way. The doves planted them."

"Same thing. Right? Don't you remember the breads she made? Stuffed with cherries? Fried in duck fat? And the seeds, what were they?"

"No. These cherries taste terrible. These trees are used for spears."

"What? How do you know that?"

"Paillard told me. He was afraid of this tree, Cornus Mas. Didn't he want to? He said…"

"Paillard! Was he my father?" It seems like anyone might be.

"He was there, at your ceremony, but no, unless there's things I don't know, which isn't very likely. Besides, he's OLD. Your mom wasn't like that. Not everyone you know is a contender to be your father."

"She wasn't like what? Funny, I don't remember Paillard being there that night."

"He was with me outside. But you probably don't even remember that I was there, do you?"

"I don't remember. Antoine used the cherry tree trunk to make a handle for our bread peel."

"Ha! Bread peels! There you go. How do you know Antoine wasn't making peels and spears? Or that the peels he made aren't also spears? He's with the Guild you know. You have to listen."

"You don't say anything for hours and hours. Are you just trying to upset me?" I say.

"Epi, these things are just things I know. And that you need to know. Because you can't see anything. And you need to see everything. So, if they upset you, then, good, that's not my problem," Térèse shakes her dress and leaves fall off.

"Why don't you like Antoine? He's our brother."

"Please, Epi, I mean, first of all, you can't really believe he's our brother, OK, our Guild brother, maybe? But second of all. I see the way you look at him. I mean, I don't care, believe me, but others will. We're headed into Cathar territory. And if they think that you and he love each other?" Térèse says. "You can't not think about these things."

"Well, is that him? No! He's nowhere around, is he? So, don't worry." Térèse is what I feel about Antoine so obvious? And whatever will she think, when she finds out I'm a girl! That it's ok to love Antoine, but not her? That would be one answer. But it all scares me. I love her too. But traveling as two girls isn't safe. And wasn't Térèse the one who kissed me? More than ever, I wish I could tell her both; that I'm a girl and that I love her. But what does it matter? She's so sure of herself. I'm the stupid one. She already thinks I'm stupid. Feeling this way about her and Antoine makes me feel, I don't know, naked. Unprotected like a little fish trying to get some air. Feeling love, is that what this is? It's too risky. You know what? I actually think I hate her! I'm much smarter than she is!

I stomp away. Cornus mas's branches bend at the elbows, her fingers reaching to the sky. Her leaves loosen and float through the air. I circle the tree. The roots have smooth bark and stretch out. A cluster of new seedlings have sprouted from the roots. It reminds me of the strange roots of the apple tree at Madame's. I plop down with my back against the tree. Will your branches turn into a bird skeleton? One that I can make into a fireflute?

"Did you want me to say something?" Térèse asks.

"You? Oh no. Please. I know this tree is like the apple tree at Madame's. And the pear tree. It's just weird. And so are you."

I stand up and loop Beauté's reins in a low branch. Beauté needs hay. We all need water. I pick a few cherries. They are hard to chew. And the sour taste is so strong. I spit them out. Térèse smiles but is quiet. I hate that Térèse is right. It feels like a long time ago that we ate a bowl of rye and caraway seeds. What I wouldn't give for another bowl.

"I'm weird? How so?" Térèse asks.

"Look at this tree, or I guess you can't see it because you know it already. But to stupid little me, it feels so…quiet. Like it's thinking."

"Trees don't think, Epi."

"Something is about to happen; I know it's too much for you to believe. But we're lost."

"We're not lost. We just don't know what's going to happen next." Térèse says. "There's a difference."

"Yes, of course, Térèse. You know everything." I slide the fireflute from Fabrizio out of Beauté's pannier. I sit down and close my eyes. It's so delicate. It might break. My hands shake. I set my mouth against the tip and blow hard. Nothing.

"Not now, Epi."

"Why don't you just shut up."

The fireflute bursts out a sound, like an owl.

"See? It's a bird skeleton, too." I say.

"What's a bird skeleton?" For once Térèse looks confused, as if I might be right.

"The fireflute and this tree. Look. Those two branches are the wings, and that tall one, there is its tail. Its head is the trunk stuck in the ground. Cornus Mas. The tree of Angeline. Margot mentioned her."

"As usual you're not making any sense. At all. First of all, trees don't have heads, and even if a tree could be a bird, why would a bird put their head in the ground?" The branches above us holds cherries. Dark red, crunchy, shiny, but so very sour. Térèse looks down at me and reaches up to the branch. *Aubada* flies down to the ground, pecking at the pebbles.

CHAPTER TWENTY-EIGHT
Epi Meets Mistress Angeline

BEAUTÉ AMBLES ALONG. *Aubada* finishes pecking at the pebbles and flies ahead.

We leave the grove of Cornus Mas. *Aubada* circles and hops on the grass, then flies up again.

"Is that a mule or a donkey?" I ask.

"Male horses and female donkeys make mules." Térèse states as if she's reading a book.

"OK, but. I have never seen a white mule or donkey before."

"We could use one. Look how flat her back is. She's definitely a mule. They eat less than horses. We should trade her for Beauté."

"How do you know the mule is a her? And what, no, we're not leaving Beauté here."

"Epi? Really, you're kidding. Look again. No balls."

Smaller than Beauté, a four-legged creature with long ears hooves the field and chews at small tufts of grass.

Aubada swoops and then lands on the mule's back and pecks away. The mule arches her back, in surprise. *Aubada* flies off.

The rope around the mule's neck trails on the ground. We get closer, and closer, and the mule bellows and hoots. It sounds as if she's laughing. Beauté snorts back as if they are talking. The mule brays again and takes off. Beauté lopes behind her. Their two white rumps bound towards a long hedge of red burnished leaves. We run after the mule, Beauté, and *Aubada* circles above her. At the hedge we stop. I try to get through, but the hedge has a wall behind it. I press my ear to the stone. And hear humming.

"You first. Hurry!" Térèse laces her fingers together and motions me to step up.

"Me?" I hoist myself up, my hands touch through the vines to the warm stone. "Bees." A line of thatched skeps sits in a row on the other side, the side with a garden.

"Beans, good, I'm so hungry!"

"Not beans, bees! I see the mule."

"With Beauté? How did they get through?"

"The mule must have known there was an opening."

I lay down on the top of the wall and swing my legs over, but what can I step on? I scooch over a bit, so I won't land on the bees. With my belly on the top of the wall, I stretch my hand down to Térèse on the bee-less side. "Come on up." One bee alights on my arm. I brush it away, losing my balance. Térèse's fingers slip out of my hand.

"Epi!" Térèse says. My hands fly and grab onto the top of the wall to keep from slipping.

"*D'ont siaz?*" Someone pulls on my leg from on the other side, pulling me over the wall. I grab hold of the vines but they pull loose, my nails scratch into the stone.

"Epi?" Térèse calls.

"Térèse!" I answer.

"You better get off my land."

"I'm sorry. Who are you?" She must have seen us and waited here.

"*Me deson*, Angeline. Who are you?"

"*Espante,*" I land on the ground. Bees swarm around my head. The woman looks down at me, lifts the netting stretched over her face. Her eyes look startled, and wide, like a cat.

"*Espante?* A long time ago I built the wall because so many people passed through my land as if it was theirs. But with the wall, covered over with vines, not many climbed over. And those who do? They usually bust a leg. Or the bees get them. Or for some miserable dastardly folks, both. But do they ever thank you for helping them? Nope."

She reaches down to help me up. I don't think I should thank her or have her help me since I'm one of the ones who climbed over her wall. I am surprised and she still looks surprised too. Is she afraid of me? Because I am over the wall. What is she hiding? Or how can I get back? I hate that now I am the one again who needs help. I push my hands against the ground and stand up without taking her hand.

"Epi! Are you ok?" Térèse yells from the other side. "Oh my god, Epi? Did you break your neck? Whoever's talking, you better not hurt him!"

"Who on earth is yelling?"

"Térèse, she's my...uh, betrothed. We have to wait for her. Your mule chased our horse through the wall and that's why we're here, somehow."

"Animals are smarter than people. Look, they're together." Angeline points.

Térèse yells and grunts as she climbs over the wall. "Epi, I'm going to kill you."

Beauté and the mule walk in the field as if they know where they're going and certainly don't need us.

"Is she ok? Should we help her? Térèse, you say? I had a daughter by that name. Where are you and your Térèse from?"

"Where? Uh, Nerac is the closest town to us." How can Térèse climb over the wall without my help? Out in the field of sunflowers, the mule, Beauté and the mule walk down the middle of the field as if it's the most logical path to follow and the only path that makes sense. But they're headed to an intersection of two other paths.

"The mule thinks she's a horse."

"I doubt it. Monja doesn't care about anything but herself. From here you have a good view of three paths. Via Podiensis.

Via Tolossane, and the third way that brought nothing but soldiers, from the river." Angeline waves her hand in the air. "Come with me."

"Wait for Térèse."

"Térèse is slow." Angeline pushes a curtain of vines aside and pokes her head through. "Térèse? If you can hear us, we're over here. Oh, no! That's her? Your paramour? Your sweeting?"

I suddenly feel like Térèse shouldn't come through. Something is about to happen. But knowing Térèse she already knows what's happening. Térèse screams and lands on the ground. I rush over to her. "You could have just come through the vines! Didn't you hear us?"

"I heard you alright." Térèse whimpers.

"Is this her? Check her. Such scrawny legs." Angeline asks. She bends over, lifting Térèse's chin, then brushes the hair off her eyes. Angeline offers her arm, but Térèse pushes her hand away. Brings herself to standing, and limps.

"She's hurt. She's not very strong."

Térèse looks at Angeline for a long time. Her face reddens and she shakes her head. "Why are you here? You can start by apologizing. But, by the way, I'm just fine."

"Of course, you are. You're Térèse." Angeline says. "Lucky you, tra-la-la-ling through the countryside on your honeymoon. You have a husband to take care of you. Something I never had or wanted. But why on earth, I mean how did you find me? No one knows I'm here."

"I can't be a husband," I say.

"Why ever not?" Angeline asks.

"Well, it's obvious. We're not married. Yet." I say.

"And we're not ever getting married. Even though I've been with Epi since you left me."

"I didn't think you'd remember. You went with her. With Antaia." Angeline juts her chin out at Térèse. Whose chin will win this?

"You didn't tell me it was for the rest of my LIFE. Hah! Well, Antaia left, too. Or didn't you know that? That was ten, no, seven years ago. Seems like you both got the leaving part down."

"I didn't know that. I'm sorry." Angeline steps back.

Térèse waves her off." We don't need you. We're trying to find Antaia." Térèse sniffs. "There's lots of problems. Epi can fill you in."

"So, you two know each other?" I'm nervous to see Térèse so besieged.

"Know each other?" Angeline steps back. "I guess….but, no."

"Epi, this is my mother, a liar and what else have you done besides abandon me at the Brothel. Why are you hiding here?"

I look at both their faces, and straight limbs, bending and stomping, pounding fists, and I picture the Cornus Mas tree, and the branches becoming spears. Bees fly in all directions picking up on all their anger. I back up.

"God bless you, Epi. You found a mule of a woman to love. What you're doing takes grit. That's more than I can say for my daughter, here."

"There's really so much to tell," I say. How can things get so changed around? Térèse is the one with grit. Not me.

"Well then, we need the bees to listen too. Bees sting you where you need to heal."

And with that, bees fly in Térèse's hair and she panics. "Get them out. Mama!"

WE WALK THROUGH the field growing all kinds of grains. And down one path lined with sunflowers. We glimpse a large tree with a house held in it. My feet ache and stumble over the rocks. And stop in front of the tree.

"I've never seen a house in a tree before." I say. But why am I lying, Maman built her house in the apricot tree.

The treehouse smells like flowers, and at the top the bees circle and swarm. I don't want to be here. I am reminded of climbing into Maman's treehouse in the middle of the field, in the apricot tree.

We follow Angeline up inside the tree. In the one room, she turns and opens a window. She reaches up and pulls down a rope ladder. The bees buzz above us. Up to the top and out of the roof. A few bees light on my arm. I'm waiting for their sting.

The space and light are very much like when we were at Madame's except that here, I feel like I am trying to protect Térèse. She's not ready for this. For there's nothing she can do. She's used to raging against the earth. Tearing out plants. Climbing trees. And here, she's kind of captured. But maybe she's, ok? She doesn't like this emotional stuff. I really don't know what to do.

"Are you like a bee or like a dove?"

"What?"

"Picking up pollen along the way? Or stealing seeds? How do you digest your life? Like your food?"

"I don't, uh, I'm like a boy." I say.

Térèse smirks.

"So you're *coille*. Stupid. What you take inside needs to be broken down. Gizzards, Guts. It's a mess. What you're doing takes grit, grit to break open the seeds."

"Or you could let them grow." Térèse yells.

"Or you can die." Angeline shoots back.

"I'd rather be a tomato." Térèse says.

Angeline smirks. "Why? How will that help? We can talk all day about what we want, but you've got to work hard to be a tomato or a dove or a bee or a boy. You two are so young. And in love. And *coille*. I can see that. But if you lose someone you love, you believed and lived for—for me, it was her."

"Her?" I ask.

"Térèse. It left a big empty space in my gut, I had to fill it, then digest."

"But you—it still doesn't make any sense. You're saying you lived for me, but we both died, and THEN you left me?"

"The seeds filled the space. And then, when they grow, you heal. Or you can die. I did. And so did you. So, please. Don't listen to me."

"I'm sorry, what? Are you a ghost? How did you die?"

"The grain got a fungus, ergot. It makes you dance. But ergot only made him want it even more."

"But you said you died. Or you didn't? After you left Térèse?" I feel very sick just thinking something happened to Térèse that I didn't know but if she didn't know either, that seems worse. I wish I had never fallen over this wall.

"No, it was. Look, this isn't easy to say. It was before I gave birth. It's the Mistress way. When you are carrying someone, you didn't know about."

"What's the Mistress way?" I ask.

"If you get pregnant and don't want to be." Térèse spews.

Angeline is quiet. I look at Térèse. I'm very scared to learn something I don't want to know. But I don't even know what it could be.

"You have to understand. Or I guess you don't have to. It's a lot to take in. I wasn't planning on you. I thought it would be better if we both left this world and went to the next. So, we went to the Mistresses in the mountains, the Efta. They said they needed me and you, and they told me about ergot, what to do."

"The Efta?"

"It's Greek. It means seven."

"Seven? Seven what?"

"Seven Mistresses. Seven trees. Breads."

"But it wasn't just you. It was Térèse too." I look around at this place which is beginning to feel very small. The cherries I ate, could it have been seven of them? They are rolling around in my stomach making it sour. All this talk of death makes me want to leave. But not without Térèse. If she died here, I couldn't live with myself.

"I get it. The Mistresses have a way, they teach people how to die. But I really don't believe you." Térèse says, studying the bees.

"I don't believe you." As soon as I say it, I slap my hand over my mouth. I'd rather be on the same side as Térèse. It's probably shocking that I disagree. But she's still studying the bees as if they are the only thing that matters in this world.

"I'm not explaining this right, the Efta teach you how to die, so that you never die. I knew you wouldn't understand. After Nerac, I came here, and named the mule, Monja."

"What do you mean?" I never felt my mind working so hard to get my mouth working to ask questions. All I can think to say is *what?* It seems like there are three paths in my head as well as in the field, but something is getting crossed. Each answer or explanation Angeline gives is more confusing and heart-wrenching than the last.

Angeline sighs, "Monja means nun in Oc. The Guild visited and that was that."

"What do you mean? That was that?" I ask.

"He was young. I thought he would change. After. We spent time together. How could he leave? I thought he would change. I thought I could change him. I mean look at this place. And me, am I not beautiful?" Angleine twirls around. Her long black hair flies out in thin wisps. She and Térèse look alike and I feel like I am looking at an old Térèse and a young Angeline.

"Epi, you're so stupid." Térèse says to me. "And you're no different." Térèse looks at Angeline. "So, we should be dead, but you messed it up? Figures."

"It's not that easy. It begins with the rye seeds. Rye is an out-crosser grain and gets easily ergotized. Open flowers have more chances to cross with other plants."

"So? Stop speaking in riddles."

"Wait, you two. Back up. The Guild visited and brought rye seeds. That means everything. Right?"

"Who was it who visited from the Guild? Claude?"

"Can't you see? Must I spell it out for you? We had a seed ceremony. He's your father." Angeline sits back.

"Who's my father?" Térèse leans in.

"Auvillar."

Térèse is quiet. My head spins. Oh no! Térèse hates him. And so, apparently, does Angeline.

"We mixed other seeds; chickpeas and lentils. Sunflowers. Roses too, but they're different. All this grew with the rye, right beside the rye. I planted as many Cornus Mas trees at the other end of the field as I could. More grew because most pilgrims and wayfarers spit out the fruit—it's too sour."

"There's a seed connection between you. Térèse grew chickpeas and lentils too and brought them to me. I made the bread of dreams." I say. "Which got me in trouble." So, I'm wondering, as I look at Angeline, if she wasn't Maman's Térèse. This makes more sense somehow. Though I still don't understand about all this dying to not die.

"Let's walk in the field of rye."

We leave the house.

Before we get to the rye, we walk down rows of tall filly lentils, fat chickpeas, violet roses, and orange sunflowers. Bees circle and fly above us in a swarm. Angeline shows us sunflower stalks. And how she makes them into fire-flutes.

"Sunflowers make perfect fire flutes. Whenever I hear one, I answer. Even though no one ever answers me. I heard one just before you came. I was ready for you."

"Harrumph. You wanted it that way, besides who did you think would answer such a *coille*...thing. sound?" Térèse says. "Maybe people hear your dumb sunflowers, but they think it's a dead goose."

My heart bunches up, hearing them argue. I want to rush in, but I feel frozen. We had the sunflower field at the top of the hill over Ceres. Did Paillard know about this? Did he make flutes? Is THAT what I heard? Was he calling Madame? Fabrizio? Angeline? Why?

"No. You play them, and then throw them in the fire to burn. No one can tell. We have to stay in the open and hidden at the same time, Antaia's words." Angeline says.

"We? Great job, Mère. You wasted a lot of perfectly good sunflowers." Térèse says.

"Oh? What, daughter, what would you do with them?" Angeline asks, looking quizzical and curious and much calmer than I feel. Is this what it will feel like to find Maman? Will we talk about the apricot tree and its fruit or why she left?

"Tssk. Put them to use in the garden. Trellises for beans and squash."

"Perfect. But do you see anyone else? I can't eat that much squash."

I wish Angeline had a squash garden where I could hide. Térèse grew lots of squash. I wish they would get along. I wish we had not come here.

"Maybe people who pass by would stay if you gave them squash instead of sour cherries. You need help. And you can make bread out of beans." Térèse says.

"I don't want anyone to stay. And I don't want help." Angeline says. "Or any bread made out of beans."

"Who would want to stay here?" Térèse asks. "No one I know."

Angeline sounds a lot like Térèse. Not needing anyone. But I'm feeling—well, I don't know. Like I need them. And staying here forever, even though I feel pretty invisible as I walk along with them. So, who did I learn that from? Being invisible? I move from the middle to the outside row, closest to the edge of the field. If I close my eyes I might just keep them closed. I wish I knew how to die. If someone asked, Epi do you want to die right now, I'd say, yes please. Merci so much. I want to cry, but that will make Térèse angry. Boys don't cry she'll say. I squat, rest my head in my arms. Sadness just takes over. I can't think what to do. I pick up my head and look. Hey! Angeline and Térèse keep walking and don't notice me at all. I guess being alone when you want to be is very different than when you don't want to be.

"You're scarred. I scarred you. Look, I tried, I wanted, to help, to grow good grain, but after I came back from Nerac, I actually—see, the grain is so protected that if anyone suspects you have it, they will try to steal it, so, you begin to replace it with anything. And then the good grain becomes the bad grain, and life, it's so changed from—what you thought—what you wanted—it's not at all what it was. How it started. What you meant. What you wanted. And then—the Guild comes in and they make the good grain illegal. And they buy the ergotized grain, too, because…"

"Why on earth would they do that?" I try to follow the twists and turns in the words from Angeline about good grain gone bad. But I have a big empty space where we left off talking about dying. I watch Térèse, she shakes her head, and all the muscles in her cheeks twist into a frown. Her eyebrows rise and fall. Of course, she's angry. She looks angry. Or sad. I reach out my hand but she bats it away. And twists her head to look at me, her eyes wide and glaring. I am very confused. My stomach hurts, maybe I need to eat pebbles to try and digest all this. Though I can't imagine swallowing anything.

"Because if it's illegal, they can charge more money." Térèse works out.

"But even that is just a word, because what IS illegal? What the Guild says?" Angeline asks.

"They made it illegal so they can control it." Térèse offers.

"Oh. I guess. I see." I say. "So, why can't it just be that some people grow grain and other people cut it and others make bread?"

"But, after. They pushed the grain so far down that it died. Then, Psomi came back. And now the Mistresses. But I'm crazy, I must be, I hear other fire flutes at night. Grigne heard them too when she was here."

"I don't know how this will sound, but maybe you're still dead?" That Grigne was here seems strange.

"Are you crazy, asking that question?" Térèse says.

"It's an interesting place. Mistress Death. It's not what you think. It's more like a dream." Angeline says. "As a Cathar, it's different. You aspire to die. There's no magic. Leave this earth for the next place. But Psomi says here there's nothing to fear. After you die."

"So, should we die?" I ask. "Instead of looking for Maman?"

"As a Mistress. You must. But I didn't want that for her."

"I'm not a Mistress. Psomi is scary. *Outré.*" Térèse says. "I mean what the hell?"

"Psomi? Cathars, now, they're the strange ones." I can make Térèse so angry at Angeline, that she'll leave with me.

"And then Mistresses make breads out of these dreams. Because that's what Mistresses do. And so now, what is Psomi grain, if it's not that, a changed grain? It's not what you think. What you're looking for. Because it's changed. I've changed. What is the truth? How can we return to what we were? Or do we even want to?"

"Uh, maybe?" I say. I honestly don't know what to hope for. A rope tied to me, like on Monja, so someone can pull me out of this bewildered place. A minute ago, I wanted to stay, but now I just want to leave. It's scary talking about death with dead people.

"So, remember the doves? Most birds crack, break,—and chew their food. But not doves. They have to swallow seeds whole. A lot of seeds very quickly, and then they fly away. Because they always have to watch out for predators." Angeline says, scrunching her eyes as if she's watching out for predators, or getting tired.

"Like the Mistresses who have to watch out for the Guild?"

"Not really. These doves have a mission that's bred into their bones. The seeds, whole dry seeds, sit like rocks in their stomach. And they need rocks—grit—to digest them. The best way to find Maman is to find the Psomi fields, and to find them, we first have to look at what seeds are in the doves' stomach." Angeline yawns.

"So, how do we look in their stomachs?"

"What?" Angeline asks and stretches her arms overhead.

The doves arrive, pecking at the fat black seeds dropped on the ground in the field of sunflowers.

"Sit down." Angeline pats a spot beside her. "Look how they move. These doves ate too much. Doves love seeds. Love them. Grain. Grains are seeds. See the seeds. They gobble them up, then they get sleepy. They fly off and swallow a bunch of grit, gravel, or sand. Look for doves in the trees near the fields." Angeline yawns.

"Like your cherry trees, and Fabrizio's chestnut trees, and Madame's apple tree."

"Oh dear, it's getting late. Don't look at me. So, it wasn't my idea to plant rye with these other seeds, it was the doves. The map, the doves know it. They carry the wheat. All the wheat we need. But we're going to have to kill the doves to find it."

By the time Angeline finishes talking about the map and how the doves know more, but need to be killed for their seeds, she's slowed down. I watch the doves and wonder what else they know. Did Térèse have a sense of Angeline and the seeds when she planted them? Did Madame give them to her at the brothel and she had no idea who they were from? She's so quiet. But she's holding her hands so tightly that it feels like she's about to smash something.

Angeline's head nods, her hands folded across her chest, and falls asleep mid-sentence. Térèse moves. I sigh at all this talk being over, the sun breaks over the horizon, and a flock of dove's swoops in.

But then I scrunch up my eyes. Margot? Is it really her? I get sick to my stomach. Margot waits at the other end of the field staring back in our direction. What does she see? The tree or the house or the wall? Or are we as hidden as when we arrived and we couldn't see any of this? This whole day is so strange. "Look out there." I point. "Did you see her, Margot? We should leave before she gets here. Maybe she's after Grigne."

"Margot? You're seeing things. I don't know. I really don't." Térèse says. "Are you kidding? Angeline will never leave this place. She doesn't like horses. Especially Beauté, because she's white, like her mother, Miele, who brought my father, Auvillar." Térèse says.

"But wait, Monja is white too." Maybe Auvillar brought Monja? Oh, who cares. It feels like Térèse has changed and now she wants to leave. If the animals were all friends, and got along perfectly, surely, we could do the same. Nope.

"Maybe you're right. She'll never leave." Térèse looks at Angeline with sad eyes.

"You ready?" I ask Térèse, I am elated. Elated that Térèse is leaving with me. Maybe it's just that Angeline is sleeping, that makes Térèse content to go. Whatever the reason, who cares. I don't want Angeline to wake up. I don't mean ever. Just let her wait a couple of days after we leave is all I ask. That's not too much to expect for a dead person, is it?

"Yes. OK." Térèse says. "I suppose it's best."

"I wish you could come with us." I whisper to Angeline. "Really. But good-bye, weirdest Mistress ever." We walk away. I tip—toe. Coax, pull, and try just plain dragging Monja. Monja opens her mouth and twists her jaw, her tongue to the side. But thankfully no sounds come out of her mouth.

"No!" Térèse yells and pulls the rope from me.

"Monja will walk with Beauté." I say to Térèse.

"We can't take her mule!" Térèse snaps back, looking at Angeline.

I motion to Térèse to get on Monja. "We're going. I'll leave Angeline a note. You first. Get on, get some sleep. Don't worry. It's ok."

Térèse walks away from Monja. And kneels in front of Angeline, pushes the hair out of her sleeping face. "Do you even remember me, Maman? Why did you leave me? It's hard to ask. I'm scared, but I have to know. What happened to you?"

CHAPTER TWENTY-NINE

Epi Learns Térèse is Angeline's daughter

MY HEART PLUMMETS. I'm afraid to hear any more about how to die, so I interrupt them. "I remember the first time I saw you, Térèse. You waddled like a little duck. Took Maman's bread of dreams with the cherries and stood under the roof of the brothel, throwing pieces at the doves. You nearly knocked them out. You were so funny." I force a laugh out of my throat. I sound worse than Monja.

"I was inside at a meeting. About Margot." Angeline wakes.

I look at the far end of the field. Nothing. "What about Margot? I remember you both came over for bread. Angeline asked if we could watch you for a few minutes."

"I do remember your Maman lifting me up, Epi."

"We waited. Then we hunted for you, Angeline, in Nerac. It was dark. We left a note at Madame's where we had found you. Térèse wailed all the way to Ceres." I'm not sure if I'm telling the truth. "My shoulder was all wet from carrying you, you were heavy too, like a bag of barley."

"Maybe it was rye? Are you angry, Angeline?" Térèse asks.

"At you? No. You were mad though. And so little. And bossy."

"I had no idea you weren't my sister. Maman said you were and that was that. I just tried to not get you upset."

"Your garden was way overgrown." Térèse says.

"It was perfect. A place you could hide." I say.

"A place I could tame."

"There's something else too. I was supposed to bring him. But he ran away."

Angeline says quietly, sitting down and putting her hands on her knees.

"Auvillar?" I ask.

"Antoine." Angeline says.

"He's not really my brother." I say.

"Madame is his mother."

"No! Madame Bouquin is Antoine's mother? Does he know? Is Auvillar his father too?" Térèse pounds her fist. "I can't believe this! You should have…"

"What? Died? Before you arrived, Antoine was here. Said he'd be back." Angeline says. "He was afraid of his father. Claude."

"What? When was Antoine here? Térèse, come on, let's go." I bite my lip. So maybe it was him sneaking around and not Margot? How much more could Térèse take? I had to get her away from Angeline! Would I dare say the same things to Maman? Térèse has to leave with me. I can't let her stay. This whole situation is a mess. I just want to leave. We were so close.

"Come on," Térèse says to Angeline and ties Monja to the tree. "I'm staying with you."

What is Térèse thinking? I can't imagine why she'd want to stay with Angeline, who left her, and who died, instead of going on with me to find Maman?

CHAPTER THIRTY
Térèse Stays with Angeline, Asks Epi to Leave

I HAVE TO LEAVE with Térèse in the morning. We sleep wrapped in pine straw. The warm air cools as the evening descends. First the bugs crawl over my cheeks and then, when the sun goes down the cool air comes and blows them away.

"Haven't I been a good friend, Térèse?" She doesn't seem to remember what happened last night. The list of what we don't know is getting longer, not shorter.

"Epi, men and women can't be good friends. Angeline told me it's because of concupiscence."

"What in the world is that? Concupiscence? Is that what Angeline's dying is called?" I am afraid to learn any more. And even more afraid to hear her say it. Wait, no. I'm angry! What could I hope for? I have always felt alone, but safe. I knew Térèse wasn't far away. But now that I'm not there. And out here, I feel like, hey, I like being alone. Great. Should I thank her and Paillard? What is all this talking for then, all this talking that I don't know how to do or what to say? To help me find Maman. I may as well go back to not saying anything.

Térèse's hair swings out as she turns around. "She's a Cathar. Now she prefers death, and the company of a mule to a man. I'm kind of leaning the same way."

"Térèse, you can't leave me." I didn't know how or if this

bizarre Cathar problem of cups will help me explain more easily that I'm certainly not a mule, but a girl.

"Epi, first of all you're no man. You're a boy."

"Well, duh. And also, I'm not dead, Is that a problem for you?" I say, relieved and perplexed, I study her furrowed forehead. She swishes her hands this way and that. So much for concupity-whatever to help me explain anything.

"You don't listen! Concupiscence is like things in your food that makes you want love."

"Things in your food that make you want love. Want love? Like what food does this?"

"Like meat for one."

"Like meat? That's nonsense. Who needs or wants love? Look at all these problems. Love in your food? Sheesh. Térèse. Where's the Térèse I know? Stop being a Cathar."

"I can't stop being a Cathar, Epi. That's why I garden. Grow vegetables. Don't you know anything about me?"

Now I was really losing it. Things were spinning around. "I know you kissed me. Unless it was someone else pretending to be you because you are just pretending to be a Cathar?" I am getting confused because I am desperate to tell her, I am pretending to be a boy, but I want to kiss her too. My pretending is wearing thin outside of the bread terrace when I didn't have to see anyone. While we're on the road. We can't be two girls. And now that plan isn't working. And my "not telling her plan" isn't working either. I am so afraid. I loved Maman, and she walked away. It's not the same. I can't be alone. Not after these days. I lean over to kiss her.

She pushes me back. "Epi do you remember, you said you would always stay with me. You promised. So, are you? Are you going to forget about finding your Maman?"

"How can you ask me to do that?"

"See? You're just like all the rest of the men. Get out of here, then. I'm staying with Angeline. Go on, get out."

CHAPTER THIRTY-ONE
Epi Searches for Antoine

G ET OUT? Is that what she said? I step back as if Térèse's eyes may shoot flames at me. I want her to watch me. See how hard this is. Look at me. She watches Monja. I want her to see my face, like I wanted Maman to see me at sunset every night when I woke up to bake and she wasn't there. But Térèse doesn't look. She can't. It would be too painful for her. Or it's because she's waiting, waiting till I'm gone because she never wanted me anyway and she doesn't want to change this moment, she was just stuck with me and now, she can't wait till she is free. How can she do this?

I step back again, into the field. The cut stalks are sharp, like knives, I stumble back.

I turn to look at the path between the rows. It isn't clear. I back away, wanting the ground to absorb me. How can she do this?

"Beauté."

Beauté looks up. I call her name again. Beauté nuzzles Monja's front hooves.

"Beauté?"

Beauté—she'll be heartbroken to leave Monja.

So Térèse remembers Angeline in Nerac, but not me? How does she remember coming back to Ceres, but not how I carried her? I was still Eleone, then. I should be glad she doesn't remember me as Eleone, because remembering might put her in danger.

"Just who do you think carried you all the way from Nerac when Angeline abandoned you?"

"Oh yeah, and what prize do you want?" Térèse asks. "For doing that?"

"Freedom."

"Freedom for you? Or for me? Freedom to give up Antoine too. He's the new Guild leader. He'll be ahead—with Grigne. Face him if you can."

"No. Antoine? He's on our side." I tell Térèse.

"Our side? That's what Maman said about his father, Claude," Térèse said. "And mine, Auvillar. And who knows about yours! Is he on your side? I doubt it."

I stood. "I have given Antoine up." But to myself, I said quietly, never. Never could the boy who grew up beside me and learned the ways of Psomi be so easily satisfied by the selfish ways of the Guild. What about his promise to me so long ago? Maybe he accepted his role so he could change the Guild. Or am I the one who's blind? Maybe he's left Auvillar. When I find him, he'll tell me he needs me. He's given up the Guild.

I stomp the earth, making a new path that will be forever burned in me as well as behind me. The ceremony when I was ten is at fault for everything, where our differences began. Térèse will only accept me, as Epi. And hate me. Love, what is it? A waste of time. Térèse's right. She says I can't really possibly love her because I am leaving her. But she left me by staying. She abandoned me. I will never tell her my truth. She'll be sorry one day. I'll keep the truth of being a girl to myself. But then I stop walking. What if Térèse dies again? Oh, it's clear she never loved me at all. Ever. She wants to stay with Angeline over me. Angeline abandoned her and will probably do it again. I hope Térèse regrets her decision and wants to leave soon, and then can't find me. That will be perfect. That must be why she's staying. So, she can surprise me. But if I never see her again, I will die! That's probably what she wants. That's the reason she's doing this. She wants me dead. That's what Angeline said, that as a Mistress you have to die. Térèse doesn't deserve me. She's always been there. I stop. She's always been a part of my life. Even when she wasn't there, it felt like she was. That I was just waiting for her to show up, but then she was so damn stubborn that I had to carry her back with me. And she didn't even thank me. Maybe she wants that now. For me to carry her away. That's what men do, right? Well, no way. That's not happening. Wait. Should I? I rub my chilled arms, my hands. My legs heat and sweat. I roll up my pants. I stop again. I never considered that Maman may have died like Angeline did. What if she did? I should go back and ask. I still don't know what Angeline means by dying.

After a few minutes, I look back. Is she following me? She better not be. Hell. No way I'm going to walk with her ever again. She's sitting exactly where I left her. She's petting Monja. I think she's crying. Good. Monja brays. Beauté starts back. Beauté, come on. Forget her. And her damn mule. Monja? Ha. What a name. We don't need them. Come on!

Antoine. Like so many times at the oven, I feel his warm arm guiding me, as if he might be standing next to me. He's waiting for me up ahead at Grigne's. But we'll have to get away from Auvillar, if he's there. What a lot of news I have to tell him about Auvillar. I don't know where Grigne's is, but I'll find it. We'll find it. It must be near a river. Or a damn? But Antoine might know about Auvillar, too. Antoine will keep me from being alone. He's got to be on my side. See the problems the Guild has made. Split us all apart like some damn bread crowns. Help me. He'll build the fire. Flames crackling, just like when we were back at the bread terrace. I tingle to think I will see him. And for him to see me. Térèse thinks I can't face him. What does she know about me anyway? And he probably thinks I could not make it out here. I kick the dirt. He left me too. How could he just leave me like that? I must find him. Maybe he is trying to catch up to me. Or maybe he's ahead. I run. Stretching my arms out, like a dove. It feels good, and I fly down the hill, above me a flock of doves who swoop and dive into the field. I am grown up; I can decide what I want. And who. And that's Antoine.

CHAPTER THIRTY-TWO

Epi Follows the Doves to a Burning Field of Wheat

I'M TIRED. BEAUTÉ clops ahead and disappears over the top of the road. I climb to the top of the hill, and step into the field, and off the road. Fields cover the hill, the hills dip and rise, with more hills humped ahead. Each field winds like a snail shell. Each marked with the flag of the Guild. I remember the fields reflected in Maman's eyes on the last night I saw her at the bread terrace. But these can't be hers. There were no Guild flags in Maman's eyes, I don't know if I am going towards her or away from her. Where am I? These fields can't be her fields. I'll never find those fields, those seeds or Maman. The last thing I want to see is the Guild, or Margot behind me.

I look overhead, my hand shades my eyes. Where are the doves I was following? I stumble and slip off into a gulley. I sit down for a moment and half-wonder if I shouldn't stay here. I hear Beauté ahead. I climb up and brush straw from my arms. The grain heads bend under my hand as I walk into the field, wanting to know its secrets. I worry that this grain field knows Maman better than I do. Beauté's steps thrash to my right, and she disappears into a tall row. I could wander in here for days without ever seeing her again. I run my hands across the top of the grain. It rustles like dry leaves. Beauté keeps going. I pick a head of the grain and pull off the small kernels—squeezing some between my fingernails. The grain lets out a milky red drop, and reflects blue and green in the sunlight.

Might this grain be one of Psomi's wheats, and not rye? It makes me feel like I didn't know or can't trust what I saw when I was Eleone. We would have harvested it all by this time of year. I thought what we grew was all wheat, but I can't remember how Maman planted the field in a Térèse, or where even she got the seeds to plant the North Field? I believed it was all wheat. But I can't remember her ever telling me that. Did she tell me? It's the worst feeling in the world that I didn't hear her. I didn't pay attention. I didn't know I had to! If I had, I might know this field, what kind of wheat it is and why the Guild hasn't harvested it. I don't think it's good that they haven't, but it gives me a place to hide. But I know the Guild never does anything for no reason. What secret is the Guild keeping? Maybe this field was planted by Angeline, or by Grigne. Would they ever do that together?

The Guild might be following me. Think. Look. But I don't see anyone. And I don't have all the time in the world, I only have a week, or maybe a few days to find her. Maybe they are waiting for the full moon to harvest this field. And without the rhythm of baking Guild crowns, I can't tell time or what day it is.

How I should look, walking in the field as a boy. I kick stones along. Throw stones. Tearing at, stomping down the wheat? And now that I have left the space of Fabrizio and Angeline and Térèse, I am even more alone. And before that at Madame's. With Paillard. And Bana! With each one I leave, another part of me falls away. There won't be anything left of Epi. I wish Bana were here. Everything is worse. Much worse. I am alone again. And I miss my bread terrace. Feeding my oven. But how terrible that I miss baking crowns for the Guild. I doubt I'll even remember how to make the bread of dreams.

The flock of doves fly over me, and then I remember. I was following them. Like a cloud, they swoop over Beauté. How long since I left Fabrizio's? And Angeline? I run after them, hoping to keep up. A new field of stalks, they soften, and bend in the wind. I wonder what it would feel like to work this dough with my hands. Keep running, look for a tree where the doves have gone. The sun feels warm and familiar on my arms.

As if I am running towards the time of being a girl, back to Eleone, before Maman left. In a time when I didn't know anything. I didn't know what I would be facing. That I was someone everyone would leave. I hope at the end of the field, this field, I will find her. See her. Wisps of fog move over the field, so a river must be close by. I'm so angry that she left me alone. That Térèse left me. I'm hungry too. I wish I was a dove and could gobble up all these seeds. What happened to take Térèse from me? Why didn't she stay with me? I must be close to the time of *Boedromion* and my deadline of finding Maman. I am sorry if you thought I was going to save Psomi, or save the Guild, Maman. I haven't done either. I am just trying to find you. My heart hurts to think I let you down, I know I have. And everyone else. The wheat has done nothing wrong, only grown tall and captured the gold from the summer sky. The gold reflects another time, but if it's the time that lay ahead of me or behind me, I don't know. The field drops off to my right, and winds down like a snail shell.

I smell smoke. Or fog hovering in the trees off in the forest. A rushing sound, like stalks getting crushed, comes up behind me. I turn, and people touch torches to the field. Torches like the one Maman had the night of my ceremony. The sound of the flames crackling is like that night. Wind blows and the heat hits me like a wave, as if I had just removed the door from our wood oven. The flames behind me rush ahead, moving on my left and right. I run fast. I hope there's a river ahead. Cool water. Water that's very wet. I don't see Beauté. Maybe I should be glad. I press my tongue against my teeth and call her. Then I glimpse her, I think. I don't know. I hope that's her. That she's ahead. I have to find her. My heart stops. Remembering the fire on the night Maman left me. A flash of white, Beauté, runs to the trees ahead. I can't breathe, I cough, and trip, falling flat on my face. My knees hit all the rocks of the field. The flames get closer on both sides, I scramble up and crawl, then stand and run. Beauté rears. Her hooves silent on the ground as the flames rush over the dry field. The ground roars behind us. We run towards the trees ahead. But nets are strung between and into the trees, birds fluttering, stuck, flapping their wings, desperate to get out. I pull on the net, climbing, but it digs into my feet. Beauté's hooves get stuck. Birds cover her back as if she might save them. They fly over me and up into the net. Beauté panics, thrashing around. I grab a branch through the net. And a face appears on the other side. Bana?

"Epi? What the hell?" Antoine shouts.

"Antoine? Help me!" I let go of the branch, falling to the ground coughing. Beauté prances over me. I crawl away, trying to get under the net. I cover my head and curl into a ball.

Antoine climbs on the net, through the branches and jumps down from the tree. He grabs and cuts the net and starts to pull my arm through.

"Ouch! Forget me. Save her. Get Beauté." I pull away and shake off his hand. Beauté's hooves are tangled. He saws the knife in the net and sweat drips down into his eyes. He lifts his forearm and rubs his shirt sleeve over his face, squinting to see through the sweat. She jumps around, He thrusts the knife in the net and saws a hole. I can't watch. She falls over, the net digs into her legs. She picks her head up and turns my way. She's so big, and the hole is so small. I can't help her. I'm pressed up against the net with Beauté on the too small hole side, and Antoine on the other, free side. It just doesn't seem fair that a net, a thin net, can be the end of us.

"Hurry up!!" I panic, my throat tightening, I screech out a cry, and reach through the net grabbing his arm. He yanks away.

"Get back!"

"Into the fire?"

"Get back!"

His knife cuts the hole bigger, then slips and jabs a huge gash in my hand.

"Arrgghh!" I pull back, tuck my hand against me, and fall on my knees. The pain stabs me like a spear. Blood drips on the ground. I lay down at the bottom of the net. I close my eyes tight. Beauté makes a high-pitched scream. My back hurts. Epi don't be stupid. Beauté rears up. I don't want to get to the other side without her. I won't. I can't. The doves fly above trying to perch on branches but tumbling down into the net.

"Cut around her, Antoine, hurry! We can't let her die!" Can we drag her in the net? Can the two of us even do that? My face melts into the ground. Dirt grinds in my eyes and nose. The fire gets closer! I must be dreaming. It smells like bread in the wood oven. Fire. It's usually Antoine who makes the fire. Did he make this one? Sweat pours in my eyes too. The plan I made to drag Beauté wrapped in the net seems like a horrible idea now, when a minute ago it seemed like the only solution.

"You first. You're lucky. If she wasn't so loud, I might not have found you."

He pulls me out. I'm still wrapped in the net, doves jumping on me and flying away. "Get her." Beauté kneels on her front legs, hooves curled, head tucked down. We have to get the net off of her. Antoine grunts and works the knife back and forth, and the hole gets bigger but not big enough.

I close my eyes, and see the nets in Nerac, stretched over the dry riverbed. There were parrots. *Aubada* with her blue feather. And the King's falcons. Being hunched over like this, is, it's almost like either we are stuck in Nerac or we skipped over Nerac. Did we? Antoine keeps cutting and I think back to the Guild shop, his face when I went in and asked him to come with me. Then at Madame's. At Madame's. Térèse said he went there a lot. I can't think why he's here now. How is it that he's here now? Did he follow me? It doesn't make any sense. But maybe he wanted to find me as much as I wanted to find him.

"We didn't. I didn't." I need to tell him I haven't found Maman, that Térèse left me to stay with her mother, who is dead, and maybe Térèse too. I know those things are terrible. But they were before, before the fire, this fire. And now this terrible thing replaces the last terrible thing that happened. Who set this fire? But in my mind, I can't separate this fire from the one when we were Eleone and Antoine, before I became Epi. Then I thought becoming Epi was great. He would accept me better as his brother. I was relieved to not be a girl. But now it's different. It doesn't matter, I just want him to keep me company. I'll be anything so that happens.

"Why are you here?"

"Do you think I'm stupid? Shut up."

I cough. I'm really tired of everyone thinking I'm stupid when I'm just lost. Why are you here? I want to ask again, but no words come out. Antoine keeps cutting. Beauté rolls, neighs, rolls more, and crawls, slides pushing her back legs out, stretching the nets. They dig into her legs. "Beauté, stop. Please." I might be whispering. Antoine drags me. Suddenly I am rolling down a bank into water. Is it the Gelise? It feels so cool. I struggle up. I have to get back to her. He drags me up on the bank. Like a giant fish caught in a net. He saws with the knife, and I shrink away, I try, but can't move away from the tight net. My eyes close. He yanks and pulls and turns me. Suddenly my arms are free, the net off. He pushes me, I tumble into the water, swallowing a mouthful. Why are you here?

"Don't let her fall in the water." I walk up the bank. We have to get back to her, cut Beauté free. Suddenly she's beside me. My fingers grab the net. My hand bleeds. She sinks, and we swim with her. She's lighter in the water, and I can stand too. She thrashes around. I hold her head. The bottom drops away and my feet pump against the water. My feet touch rocks, and slip, then stand on them.

"Work your way up, cut the net off of her back. We got you, you're ok, Beauté." Her eyes are wild, rolling around. At least the bird shit is washing off. Beauté, I am sorry you are cut! She goes under the water, swims to the bank. I swim to her. Antoine swims up behind me, breathing hard. I pull the net off of her legs. She writhes in the mud. Then she scrambles up and limps away along the bank. She stands under a tree and eats some leaves. I feel my anger pressing in on me. Couldn't he have been more careful? It makes sense that I should go back to Angeline's and Térèse since she's hurt but I can't do that. I have to find Maman. Grigne. And figure out why he's here.

"You cut her! What are you even doing here?" He cut me too, but I don't say it. I hold my hand. The gash bleeds, the knife went into the flesh between my thumb and first finger.

"She's free! Finding you. Protecting my—investment. We heard Margot ditched you. So, I ditched Auvillar. And Grigne."

"You heard what? It was hardly that. Margot lies."

"Whatever. You have work to do for the Guild. You, ok?"

"OK? We narrowly missed being baked like a Guild crown. Who set that fire? I saw people with torches. Am I OK? Why are you here? Did you do this? We have to help Beauté."

He shrugs. "You weren't supposed to be in the field. You were at Angeline's. But as usual, I got you out. And Beauté, too. So just shut up."

His anger scares me. Takes me back to moments when the crowns didn't turn out quite right, and he pitched them off into the woods, so that Margot or Claude wouldn't find them and charge us, or worse. From the bread terrace I watched Beauté eating them. I half-think Térèse ate them too. How far away was Auvillar during this time? A pit of fear rises in my stomach as if all the bad crowns I ever baked for the Guild are lodged there, lumps of dough, stuck in me, turning over, but unlike seeds for the doves that can grow into more wheat, these old hard crowns must come up out of me and float to the bottom of this river like the vile mess the Guild is. My heart pounds. There is something. Maybe during those times Auvillar was closer than I thought. I bend over and retch up a bunch of green, river water.

"Why did you ditch Auvillar and Grigne? You're supposed to fix the mills." I hold my stomach. Next time I see Auvillar, will his smile remind me of Térèse, knowing he's her father? Everything reminds me of Térèse. I shudder to think I will always have this emptiness inside me because of her. But maybe Antoine can help. He won't leave me, will he? I have to be sure he doesn't. I stand up, my legs wobbly as a newborn foal. He's here and I'm here, and we're almost alone. That is a miracle. Though I hardly feel like a miracle.

He pulls me to sit down again. "Grigne?! I don't know what she's doing. Or care! Let Auvillar figure that out. So, did you come up with any new breads?"

"So, you didn't make it. You turned around. Or maybe the Guild kicked you out." What is going on here?"

"Not likely. I came to find you, protect you. Like I always have."

"From what?"

He sweeps his hand out. "From that, from fire and from Auvillar, and your task of finding Maman. You're going to fail. But I have another idea. So, hurry up. We've got to collect them. The doves—too, their seeds. Head to Tolosa."

"Wait. What's your hurry? The field still smokes. How far away can that be seen? Are you talking about the grain seeds? And is Tolosa where Auvillar is? And Grigne?"

"Duh, yes. Tolosa, forget Altivarre. And yes, the seeds of grain are in the dove's stomach, and by God, we'll have a good dinner before we head out."

All of this is too much for him too. I hold my hand over my mouth. Eat these burned doves? Angeline had said to check the doves' stomachs for the seeds to see where they had been, but she couldn't have meant this, did she?

"Oh, God. No way. Did you just see what happened? This horrible fire—the doves? I almost died. And Beauté too." I shake my head. But at the same time, I can't let him leave without me.

He brushes his hands on his pants. "Look, the doves are dead. They couldn't make it through the fire. We can't help them. But we can help ourselves. This is *Grano Arso*, scorched wheat, and I bet the Guild will pay big money for it. The Guild thinks we're burning Psomi's wheat. Psomi thinks we're burning their wheat because they don't want the Guild to get it. But guess what? There's a third side to this. You can make special bread with it. Why didn't I think of this before, I mean, Epi do you even know what we have here?"

There's a third side to this? All of a sudden, I feel like he's selling this idea to me. "Me? You want me to bake with burned wheat?" I laugh remembering that the last crowns I baked were burnt because the fire in the wood oven was made from Maman's maze of trees. "How did those burned crowns work out for the apprentice contest in Nerac? Whatever happened to that anyway?"

"The Guild was just snuffing out where the fields might be."
"And did they?"
"Sadly, no, they haven't yet found the Efta."
"The Guild will pay for burned wheat? See, they'll stop at nothing to kill things to make money. Like Claude. Someone made out from his death. I don't care. Just go. Go to Tolosa." I push him away to see if he comes closer. Help me find Maman. He thinks I've failed. I thought he believed in me. But still, he will keep me company. I sure don't want to be alone out here. Ever again. Being alone makes me feel small and reminds me of the time when Maman left. If Antoine found me, so could Margot. Margot might not have saved me. In fact, maybe Margot set this fire. I'm so tired and thirsty. Maybe if I go with him, I

can get him to change his mind. The important thing is not to let him leave. I blink and look up; he's staring at me.

"Epi, you don't care that the Guild will pay you?"

"Why do you want that? Money doesn't help you fly. I think you're confused. You want to be on my side. The Guild is only interested in you if you make money. But you care about the doves. Seeds. Growth. Come with me."

"You couldn't be more wrong. I can tell you've never heard of Grano Arso. It's new. Everyone will want it. Because of you."

"It's burned grain. How does everyone want that? You're—I think you've lost your mind. Run away with me. Help me find her, Maman. They won't like that."

"Maman? She's already dead. You can stop trying to find her. Auvillar said to forget it. I told him who you are."

"Auvillar said forget about finding Maman? Who did you tell him I am?"

"Epi. The best damn baker ever. And the Guild would be stupid to let you go."

Now why did I think he might say something like, you're my friend, or my brother or the daughter of Antaia? "Right. Auvillar who wanted Maman because she betrayed the Guild. And HE'S just going to forget about it. There's no way I trust you."

"Trust me? I'll protect you." he says. "I don't see anyone else doing that."

"Like you protected Claude?"

"That move kept you alive." He steps back, looking up and down, taking all of me in. "I kept you alive. But you're right. I gave them Claude. You owe me for that."

"So, one minute you kept me alive, and the next, I owe you? You gave them your father. How can I trust you?" I say. "Money is what's important to you. But not me?"

"You sound like everyone in Psomi. You don't know what happened, Epi, do you? I'm your friend. But you're alone. At least I found you. And saved your ass again. Hopefully before you did something really stupid." He comes closer with an angry smirk on his face.

"You're right, I am alone. Or I was alone. But now I'm with you." Who is this? I've never seen this Antoine before. "Can't we go back to the bread terrace. To the way it was?"

"Back to your little dream? You have no idea what that was like for me. I was always trying to stay away from Claude. What did you know about my life? All you had to do was stay there and bake."

I stop. It feels awful to have these words between us. Inside it feels like I want to keep running, get to the top of the hill. And leap off and yet that won't help me not be alone. "Look, I need you. To help me find Maman. And we don't have much time. Come with me." Who is this Antoine, smiling so fiercely as if he's won something? Me? Money? I owe him. He owes me! I feel very confused. And like I know nothing, again. Maybe he died. He's dead. The kind of dead that Angeline talked about.

"Forget it. Don't worry about it. You'll see everything will be fine. Let me take care of your hand, so you can bake. I can take care of you." He backs up from his anger. Gets another funny look on his face. Rubs his chin.

"No, you owe me. For all the years I baked your crowns for the Guild. You need to come with me. Run away with me." I can't bear to be alone. "I won't go back to the Guild. Or pretend to go back to the Guild. And, Auvillar never said what he would do if I found Maman. And the Mistresses told me a lot about Auvillar. Which you don't know."

"I know everything. And the Mistresses. They're just jealous. Did they help you? Aren't you the least bit afraid that they are just plain wrong? They can't. And you can't. Stop the Guild."

"You could. We could." My eyes feel like they're on fire. I reach for him. I have to make him understand. "I've been thinking for some time that we should run away."

He backs up. "Epi, we can be rich. With the Guild. You'll never have to work again."

I grab his sleeve and draw him toward me. "But in order to not work, first I have to work a lot. For the Guild? They're never satisfied. You don't believe in them. You don't care about money." His warm breath touches my cheeks. He leans in, is he softening? My eyes feel watery and sharp. My nose tingles.

"Can't you see? Listen! I can protect you from him." He storms away, then whirls around.

"Auvillar won't listen to you, he hates Maman. And sent me out here to prove I didn't kill her. But maybe he knows that's impossible because he did. Or maybe, I don't know. He just wants her to work for the Guild again. What does he want?"

"Listen, he's not that bad. I know how to control him. He and I agree about what's really important. This is stupid. And instead of dicking around out here looking for her, we need to get Grigne's crop. All the harvests. And keep our best baker, you."

"What about Grigne? What did you find out?" As long as he keeps talking. I can keep him with me.

"Let's just say I wouldn't risk my life based on any of these people, these Mistresses, backing you up. The Guild is massive, and their plan is simple."

Something about the way he says the Guild is massive that makes me shudder. Their plan is simple? Fire is simple. Deadly. But simple. Death by a flying arrow is simple. It occurs to me that Guild arrows come from trees, Psomi trees, like Angeline's tree. Feathers on the arrows from the doves. "And what do you believe? Antoine? We grew up together!" I walk away to see if he'll follow me.

He steps back. I return to the edge of the field. It still smokes. Birds fly through the knife-torn nets. He stands on the bank. Off in the distance, maybe where Angeline and Térèse are with Monja, thunder rumbles. Lightning strikes overhead. What led all of us to find each other and learn all these problems, was the search for Maman. I really hate her. First, she leaves me as Epi, and that's not bad enough. Then, there's all this mess like following pooped out seeds or charred bird guts, waterways not working, or too much water that she left behind for me to figure out. This feeling is small like smoke coming from a few sticks. Let me blow on it, to make a fire grow. Thunder gets closer. I am sad, surprised, heart-broken and disappointed at the same time. He comes up behind me. I just want to turn around and kiss him. But I wait. I want to show him how wrong he is. Show Térèse that what she says is true, and since I'm Epi and still a boy, that I can, I don't know, have sex. And with whoever I want. That all the feelings I had at the bread terrace were leading me here, to this field. Antoine is still here, and I am finally grown up enough to do something about them.

"You're not my friend. You're with the Guild." I push him away.

"I don't trust you, you're with the Psomi." He takes my arm. "So, I need to keep you close."

"How long ago it seems that we were in Nerac. At your mother's brothel." He must have had sex before. "You know she's with the Psomi too?"

"Yeah, so, what did you think? Auvillar went easy on you."

Oh my god, what does that mean? That he beat Antoine. "But not easy on you?"

He shrugs. "I know the Guild ways. They have a lot to lose here. Epi, we can come out of this ok. You and I can be ok."

What does he picture exactly? "Antoine, I know the Mistress' ways. Are they treating you badly? Is he treating you badly?" My whole body shakes.

"I can take care of him. You've been out here what, two weeks and now you know the Mistress ways?"

"Yes, like Fabrizio."

"Fabrizio is still around? Oh god. No. Not him? Did you? Did you sleep with him?"

"Did I. What?" Antoine thinks I am a boy. And I remember Térèse's warning. If anyone thinks we're together, the two of us, it could be dangerous. But this would be a terrible time to let him know I'm really Eleone. Just a minute or two more, maybe. It will be ok. He will see me as Eleone then. I won't have to say a word. He'll see. He'll be surprised. He'll be happy. He'll say he knew.

"Like I said, they'd stop at nothing to convince you. The Psomi."

"I'm, I would never, I'm Epi. But what about you? What would you do to convince me?" My fingers touch his lips, then his rough chin. I don't think he's eaten for weeks. And what is this cut on his cheek? But I stop myself from saying it. Making any of this real, because it scares me. Did Auvillar beat him? Make him come get me? If I've changed since we left Ceres, and Nerac, so must he. Margot is behind us. Is this a set-up, are we waiting for her?

"You're out of time. And where is she, your Maman? I will take care of you."

His eyes crinkle at the edges from hours in the sun. From walking? From searching?

"Come with me. I don't trust the Guild. So, why should I trust you?"

"I really don't have to say it, do I?"

Our hands lower to our sides, and I pull him to me. His palm rests on my cheek. He bends so our foreheads touch. I twist my head, our lips meet and I taste salt. There's coriander. Caraway seeds. "Ok. OK. I'll go with you." I say. But it doesn't sound like me. I've thought about touching him for so long that I fight to stand. Maybe I'm melting into him. Or dying? I can't seem to hold on to just staying in this field.

"You're scared. Of your feelings." Antoine says, taking off his shirt.

"Are, are you?" My fingers trace a long scar on his shoulder. A seam that opened him. Bits of scab flake away to pink skin.

His hand explores my face. "Your cheeks are still smooth."

My stomach jolts. He really does think I am a boy. Do I care? How could he think that? Not see me? It will be ok. I don't care. My heart beats and might explode. We lay down side by side, and I finger the leather cord knotted around his neck. The stone on the cord almost lays flat against his chest and the small hairs sprouting there. My fingers run over his shoulders, his soft earlobes.

He presses against me and throws his leg over me. His hand dips lower, and suddenly and strangely cups my breast. His eyes fly open. "Epi? What the hell?"

But it doesn't matter. Before he can push me away, I pull him to me. Somehow this doesn't feel like the freedom I thought I'd feel in choosing Antoine. All the times I thought about him, putting his hands on me. Was my thinking then, my feelings, as if I was really Epi? And now am I no longer Epi? It doesn't matter. The melting of me into him and him into me, is hard to remember. It's hard to be here. It's hard to leave and forget who we are. Who we were. Two abandoned children who found each other. Grew up to be on opposite sides. It doesn't make sense. But our anger at meeting who we are fuels all of our clothes flying off. And little bursts of fire go through me while rain pelts our skin.

THE NEXT MORNING, I wake up. I scan the trees. Did I really say it? I can't believe I told him I would stay with him. Go with him. I feel worse than before. Worse. My emptiness screams out from inside and if I could pull everything, I see into me, that would help. The trees. The next field. Beauté. It feels like someone is watching us. I look up in the trees. Waiting and cringing, but almost hoping to see Bana. Antoine still sleeps. He's got to be mad. But he never said anything. Not one word. Either time. I mean he thought I was a boy. Does he still think so? What could that be like? To not see me. Maybe he was scared. Maybe he's disappointed. Him! I'm disappointed! And so ever since I left Ceres, my life is this mind-bending void of nothing. My life is nothing. I am nothing. And here's another person who's disappointed in me. And that I gave myself to. Wanting so much. But how can I really believe that and feel it because neither Antoine nor Térèse really knows who I am! I mean, look, he's sleeping. I pull on my pants. And storm away. I think I hear him calling me. Epi. A name I will have to live with. Or maybe I'm imagining it like I imagined Maman calling me, looking for me. Only she called me Eleone. If Antoine prefers me as Epi, how can I ever return to being Eleone? I feel so stuck.

I walk across the bridge. Beauté follows me. Limping. Quietly, my footsteps set down on the next field as if the steps are already there, and I'm just finding them. Or maybe I'm dead too. Like Angeline. I could never go back to the Guild. Antoine, I feel terrible to disappoint you, but I don't want to be Epi anymore. Or rich. And so, I have nowhere to go but on. I need to find Maman and ask her the answer to all these questions. I don't know what she will say. Maybe she won't see me either. Listen, Epi. You have to find Bana. Grigne. Someone to keep from all this suffering. And fill up this emptiness inside.

CHAPTER THIRTY-THREE
Epi Leaves Antoine,
Searches for Grigne

WE PASS THE sign for Mondou. The dry riverbed sits on our left. I walk. Beauté limps. She hasn't run since the fire. It's like she's too tired—her wild eyes check every direction, and she thinks the fire is still closing in. She jumps at leaves fluttering by. She needs more water. The cut on my hand is red and puffy. We pass the sign for Altivarre. I hurry with excitement. Grigne will have the answers. But then, at the top of the hill, I stop, brushing against a stone lion jutting out from a building. Look down the street for Auvillar. Or Margot. I can't believe I'd ever be lonely enough to want to see Margot. That kind of alone makes me want to sit down, and puke. Or not move. But I can't see Antoine, I don't want to see him. Ever. Is he waking up now? I am sure he was awake when I left. And he said nothing. He hates me, I'm sure. Oh god, I feel so awful. I can never remember Antoine without adding in this new time of what we did. He didn't seem to know it was me or even care if it wasn't. Who did he think I was? Térèse?

I pull the reins and Beauté follows. Altivarre is deserted. At Nerac's Feast of Fools, there, we tripped over people. Had to push them away. Madame's shop was so full. And before that, the Guild shop throbbed with *talmelier* banging on the doors trying to give Antoine their loaves to enter the Guild contest.

I forgot about that. Isn't the Guild contest to be in Tolosa? All of them certainly need flour. The Guild certainly has plenty of help looking for wheat. The sky hovers above with clouds that threaten to drop over us like thick coats of wool. I'm certainly scared. These thoughts keep rambling around in my head like seeds, and I wish I could shake them out of my ears onto the ground so they could start growing and help me. A shiver runs up my back. We climb up the winding streets. Signs with arrows point to following the path to Compostela.

I loop Beauté to one of the posts, and run my hand over her muzzle but she steps away, a wild look in her eyes. I drop the reins and she shakes her head up and down. I go up the two steps and stand under the round tiled roof. This must be where they put up ladders and pour in the grain. The granary in Nerac looked more like a dovecote. I shudder. Might there be a body inside. I walk around the center column. There are small doors at the top around the circle. The doors slide up instead of to the side, but they are the same size as the door to our wood-fired oven. Funny that one door hides grain, and the other door hides a fire and bread crowns. They pour the grain in the top, the names carved above each door.

Orge.
Blue Emmer.
Einkorn.
Crimson Farro.
Banatka.
Richelle de Grignon.
Rouge de Bordeaux.

These grains are not Guild grains. I haven't looked in the bins yet, but when I do, will my journey be over? I breathe in and my insides rest, and maybe there's an opening of hope. So, the Guild didn't burn everything. The grain is right here. Everything is going to be good. Beauté will heal. My cut hand will heal. It's as if I've found Maman. If I could buy or steal some of these grains, we need their seeds. I could save them. Make *trakhanas*. Plant them. Do anything. Maman, you would, right? I breathe and bow my head as if I am finally somewhere. But I remember I am nowhere since I haven't found her yet.

Footsteps shuffle closer. A guard comes around the side of the granary. He jumps when he sees me. "You! Get away from there."

"What? I only want to….buy, I mean, I'm here to pick up my order." Yes, that sounds better than wanting to buy something when there might not be anything left.

"Certainly. I see. But we can't be too careful. Did your— what is your order number? Which Guild are you? Headed to the contest, eh?" His light blue eyes are the color of the sky. His thick matted blonde hair around his face argues in tufts like one of our hens, the rest of his hair twists and piles up on his head, held in place with a stick.

"The best Guild. From Nerac," I say bravely. Or foolishly.

He backs up. "You don't look like no one I ever met from a Guild. Where's your boat? Take a look—from Altivarre you can see all the way to the coast. I'm watching you. Ships are coming to pick up the grain. By rights they should be Roman galleys. Altivarre is a Roman outpost, an *Oppidum*. Look, from here you can see the whole river, everything. And stretch a little and you can see the fields where the grain came from."

"*Oc.* Yes, I see." Speaking in Oc seems like a good idea. He seems to like telling stories so I egg him on, while I keep looking around for Grigne.

"Nerac, you say? Never heard of it." He says and squints at me.

"But which fields? Guild fields? Don't you know the fields are burning? I don't have a boat. But I do have a horse. And she's the best. Because no ships can make it up this dried river. This is no Roman outpost. Sheesh. We're in Gaul."

"Have faith, young man! Altivarre is part of Rome. And this year we're rich again! Guild merchants have bought everything.

Everything that Psomi grew. Oh, I told them this would happen, if they only worked together." He skips around, his simple joy reminds me of Bana. He's dancing in front of me, but I'm sad to see him. Is Bana growing up to be like this man? His eyes are light blue and clear. He swings his head a little from side to side. On Bana this is charming, but on this old man, scary. Living in a world between the Guild and Psomi. But not seeing the dry river, the burning fields. What's really happening? He pulls me by the arm. "Look. They're coming up the river, the great Garona. See their ships? The good days are returning." His clothes are baggy. Torn. Shabby. But then I look at mine. We're dressed pretty much the same. Maybe everything is hopeless. I wish I had some food for him. And for Beauté.

"How will that help Altivarre? How can ships travel on a dry river?" I want to have faith but there is no river to speak of. I'm afraid to act like I don't notice. I'm not at all sure he's ok. The hope I felt about finding grain, and Maman, slips away. Merchants bought everything but from who? And they have no way to carry their grain. His great Garona smells like a foul river and not like my beautiful Gelise with willow trees and ducks. This Oppidum riverbed is hungry and thirsty and rolls with glass bottles, and dried-out trees that look like skeletons. What good is being a Roman outpost poised to see everything but seeing nothing. Some Oppidum.

"Your horse, she isn't going to make it. Better find a ship." He curls his hand and peers through it, scanning the river to the south. Then turns to the north and does the same. "Is that your ship?"

Beauté can't die. She swats her tail at flies. Her rump shakes too, trying to get them off. She looks out to the river. The dry river. That's scary, but it's scarier that he doesn't see it. I can't tell him. Or let him know I think he's crazy. I have to find Grigne. And Auvillar. If they're here.

"I doubt these ships are even coming. The grain is here? Let me see." I feel crazy to take this chance and be so demanding.

He shrinks back. Then shrugs and asks me to step forward. I climb the ladder to the bins. I quiver to remember climbing the ladder of the dovecote and finding Claude. Three more steps to the top. And the hinged lids to the bins.

"Pick one!"

There's so many. Seven? Ten? I stop. The bin name is *Orge*. Barley. I reach my hand in. I expected to plunge deep in the rich grains. I lean out of the way so the light can shine in. Each bin is stuffed with burned straw.

"You know so much! Let me talk to who did this. These grains are, well, they're perfect. I don't know. But it's peculiar." I search my long-ago memory back to when Maman and I stuffed the cut wheat under the woodshed roof. What happened to the *Trakhanas* that we put in Maman's box? But that doesn't make any sense. Maybe he'll tell me more. Maman, I'm sorry, I should know what these grains are, their names. I'm too *coille* to save Psomi. Find you. Anything. Solve any of this. There's so much. Too much.

"What's peculiar? The Guild has been asking for these grains for years. We finally have what they want. Blue Emmer, Einkorn, Crimson Farro, Banatka, Richelle de Grignon, Rouge de Bordeaux."

"You said we, so you're part of Psomi, too?" My plan worked. He told me which grains fill the bins of the granary. But why would Psomi burn them? To make them more valuable, and sell them or to destroy them. Did Auvillar buy them? I look over my shoulder and cringe. I put off thinking about what I can say when I see Auvillar again; his black steed's hooves clack over the cobblestones. So, these are grains growing in nearby fields. The lookout guy knows these are Psomi grains. Suddenly I become aware that even though I think he's stupid, maybe he's not at all. "My Guild, well, yes, but I can afford to buy a little to feed my family. I need a miller to grind them for me. Is there one nearby?" I need to find Grigne.

"Ha! A Miller? See, way out there? That stranded barge in the middle of the Garona? Wait right here while it makes its way to us. Ha! Oh, I figured out who you are. You're a seed saver? Come with me to the Guild leader. Antoine can help you, I'm sure. He's from Nerac too. You must know him? Come with me."

I SHAKE LOOSE FROM the old man's grip. He runs after me around the granary, but I untie Beauté and we head down the winding streets to the docks we saw from above. The docks of Altivarre stick out over the dry river, like empty rickety dovecotes. A dozen carts stand by, empty. Three men sit on the stone wall. Their faces are long and withered. They haven't moved since Beauté and I walk towards them. But now one stands up, and rushes at me.

"Millstones for sale. Cheap. That's a one-horse stone, right there. We have all the way up to five-horse and one-mule stones. Is that one stone there small enough for your horse? We can make it smaller if you like."

Beauté walks behind. I hold her rope and wave. We step over to their collection of millstones. My heart beats fast. Various designs are carved in them. Some have Térèses, like the maze of trees in our North Field. Like a snail. How strange that I lived with Claude nearby, and I never knew this. My heart lifts up again. The way the stones are carved could be a connection to Maman and the Mistresses. I run my hand over the next stone. The carved lines are like rows of beans near Angeline. Another stone has lines carved like rays of the sun. A strange calm has infected this Oppidum, this town, which makes me want to run. Clouds swirl overhead and gather in grey shrouds and mists, sending out shadows, like ghosts or spirits left and dried up in the once flowing river.

"You there, what are you doing?" A figure walks towards us from the docks, the riverbed. "Those are my millstones."

The men scatter. I recognize the voice. Her voice. It's Grigne. I hurry towards her, filled with joy. I know her. Even though I only saw her for an hour, our time together at Madame Bouquin's seems much longer. Grigne looks up. Did she just frown? I don't remember her having that much gray hair? She looks down, watching her steps, as she walks towards me on the paved stone street. She feels the same as me, glad to see me, I hope. I shade my eyes. "*Oc.* Grigne. It's so nice to see you." The bell tower chimes eleven.

"Who are you? Why are you looking for grain?"

"*Espante.* Grigne, it's me. Epi. I was at Madame's."

"Auvillar did nothing. He went off to Tolosa. If I ever see him. Or Antoine. I'll."

"No need to look for grain. The fields are all burned. But there's not much smoke here." Beauté hurriedly steps past me towards Grigne. She shakes her head, looks from side to side. Is there a well nearby? The air swims with an aroma of fish and eels, which seems impossible.

"You? You did this? Epi?" She stomps towards me. "You helped burn the fields?"

"No! I don't mean I set the fire. I, I saw it. I barely escaped, and Beauté too, look at her. Not me. *Espante.*" I back away. Who knows what Antoine or Auvillar told her in the meantime about me?

"I paid this stupid guy to guard a few bushels of grain in Altivarre so that the Guild might see and think everything is just fine. We need to keep it for seed. Or to eat? But do you know why?" Grigne grabs me by the shoulders.

Hmm, did she not hear that the grain is burned? I shake my head no, because I don't think I should tell her. "Why what?"

"The fire! I told the farmers. Revolt! Do it! Burn all the fields. Blast if we're going to get no money for our grain. We'll be the ones setting fire to it. We won't let the Guild just have it."

"Oh, but Antoine was there. So many doves got burned too." I feel really confused. Antoine was trying to save Psomi? But that's not what he said. He was burning the fields to get back at both Psomi and the Guild, he was lying to both sides. This is so strange that Psomi would burn their own fields. "And now no one has anything to eat."

"He's an *Empapautar,* like Auvillar." Grigne says.

I feel like I'm back at Madame Bouquin's. "*Oc,* Grigne. Tell me about Artos and Maman. Together, we can be stronger together." I grip her arm. I need her. As soon as I do, she pulls away. I shouldn't have touched her. It was too much. I'm always too much and not enough at the same time.

"Together? What do you know about that?"

"What?"

"I had an idea of you, but now, you—are—hmm, you're different from the you I saw at Madame's."

"Yes, my hand got cut, when I got stuck in a net. Near the fire."

"So, back up. You said Antoine set the fire?"

"Umm, he, I don't know."

"You are different. Not that you had much to lose, but it's there in your eyes. I think you lost something along the way. Aha! Your virginity. That's what you lost. Antoine ditched me and Auvillar. So, he set this fire. You weren't making that up. He was pretty upset about the fields. Now it's making sense to me."

I feel kind of sheepish. "My virginity? What about yours?"

"You can't have it."

"Why? Do you need it?" I am still not even sure what virginity is. Seems there's a lot more important things going on.

"My virginity?" Grigne laughs. "I guess not, really. It could be a bargaining chip with the Guild. Though I would rather die first. And that would upset them."

There's so much going on. I breathe. Concentrate on what I need to do. Help Grigne. Stay with her. What will help me to do that?

"What do you mean, Antoine was upset? How was he upset? He helped me. That's how I got this cut."

"Oh, I see. He helped you, by cutting you. Look, you can tell me. I saw the way you two looked at each other at Madame's. He saw a lot of men at the brothel. A lot. I have no idea what you think, but your virginity meant nothing to him. Nada. NOTHING."

We walk back to the dock where she climbed up the steps. She looks downriver and upriver.

"Good. I don't care about him." I say. Grigne's changed too. Her arms are browner than when she was at Madame's. She's harder. Which is difficult to believe and understand. Auvillar and Antoine were supposed to help her. But on the other hand, who has helped me? Everyone has abandoned me.

"Of course. Everyone says they don't care, when they really do. He's in trouble, you know. But I don't have time to spoon feed you like a baby dove and tell you what's what. I've lost everything. I need your help." The sun filters through the leaves. Her lips turn in on themselves. The corner of her mouth turns down. Is this Grigne's sad face? Am I really seeing her asking me for help?

I look at the river, and miss the gentle sound of the Gelise River near the bread terrace. The fluttering of Ausel nearby, where are you?

"They're called nestlings, baby doves." But I need to ask her. I don't want to be alone. I'm scared. Fields are burning. Térèse is gone. Where and how will I ever find Maman? "Grigne, I just, I am really scared. I really need someone. I don't want to be alone. Can I stay with you? I need you to help me find Maman." I have a sinking feeling she's not even considering it.

"Stay with me? Epi, I don't have a fancy *auberge*, or even a *Maison Closes* like Madame Bouquin. You probably can't see my falling apart barge. It's out there. In the middle of where the flood will be."

I look at Grigne's tilting barge, and it looks like Claude when he slumped over. No blood of course, but Grigne's barge has already fallen apart. "Right, so why wouldn't you move it out of the way?"

"The Guild is pretty smart; they would see that and know there's a problem. If the miller moves her barge out of harm's way."

The barge looks like it's already been harmed. And about as far away as any chance of saving these Psomi grains.

"So, whatever you're going to do. Are we going to do something in the fields?" I can't go back there.

"From what I see, how did you, how did you have the guts to even make your bread of dreams? That's what got you in trouble. When I saw you at Madame's and you were holding the box. Bana had eaten the bread and he got sick. Did he die? And where's Térèse? Is she dead too?"

"Grigne. Stop. No! Of course not. Bana is fine. Is this all that's left? I don't want to talk about Térèse."

"Oh. Good for her. She left you. You've really muffed it all up, haven't you? It's not about you. We have to keep what few seeds are left," Grigne says, walking away fast.

We walk back to the granary.

"What about the box, we'll put the seeds in Maman's box."

"The Guild took that, remember? Margot has it. Look, this is bigger than you and all your little feelings. Grow up. Psomi is starving. Farmers are dying. The only grain they get is from eating rats. And then they die from eating rats and then the rats eat them. How does that sound? I can see this is a lot for you. But you have to know. We have to talk about this. Epi, what does your name even mean? Do you even know?"

Margot doesn't have the box. Does she? I am mortified. I really do need her. I am so alone. She understands. She'll protect me. I don't understand any of this. And I don't want to talk about any of it. "I am grown up. I had sex with Antoine, isn't that grown up?"

"Oh, great. No, if you have to ask. Having sex with Antoine? Who cares? That's just plain stupid. You're being selfish. He's with the Guild. He's tricking you. To come join him. Can't you see? This happens all the time to the Mistresses. You're lucky you can't get pregnant. Epi, do you know? You're the only young Psomian in forever, or a long time anyway, who doesn't have one Guild parent. Antaia and Artos are both devoted to Psomi."

Of all the things she said, I zero in on one thing. Pregnant? I never even thought about that. But surely that's not something to worry about, is it?

CHAPTER THIRTY-FIVE

Epi Finds Grigne,
This is Bigger Than You

WE WALK BACK to the granary, and shoo the guard, the old man who's light blue eyes reminded me of Bana's. We step up on the round platform and walk around the circle of bins. Overhead is the wooden spoked roof. The bins' names.

Orge.

Blue Emmer.

Einkorn.

Crimson Farro.

Banatka.

Richelle de Grignon.

Rouge de Bordeaux.

"Can these names, is that where they came from?"

"The weather is changing and this wheat doesn't grow here. Or even close to here." Grigne says.

"How do you know?" I ask.

"Auvillar brought me some to see. Look, how small it is. The Guild wants big grains. This is a landrace wheat. Good for surviving and for small production, it takes a lot of care and people. And that's a problem for the Guild. It's inefficient."

"It makes the bread of dreams and becomes strong because it grows in isolation. Kind of like you, Grigne?"

Grigne scoffs, leans over, and pushes me. "Stop talking nonsense. This wheat grew in the Fertile Crescent. Far from here."

"We have to protect this wheat, so it isn't owned by the Guild. Where is this, Crescent?" I ask, half-joking. Epi, be more serious. And this is serious. I can't forget that all the people I love are involved in THIS. If I got here, I could get there. It doesn't matter where, or how long it takes.

"The crescent is across the sea, the Guild knows, but they can't get to it. There are reasons."

"I can imagine plenty of reasons." I have my doubts that the Guild even knows.

The Guild? We're really talking about Auvillar, and he is such a liar. I picture the sacks of flour that Antoine took to Nerac on the barges. Maybe all the wheat came from there, the Crescent. Maybe he knows. Antoine's secretly waiting to tell me.

"Auvillar worked with Psomi for a time. He seemed sincere, and we believed him. But it was only for his gain. Once he found out about your Maman's fields of Psomi across the sea, he wanted them and told the Guild and they paid big bucks. But he didn't know anything about these landrace wheats, how they grow, and how they need to be ground with a special kind of stone, and the only one I know of is on my barge."

"I doubt that he bought them from Maman." I shouldn't be shocked that this problem of ownership extends across the sea. No wonder I couldn't see anything at all from my little bread terrace, covered over with rose canes.

"Not Maman, but maybe he paid someone close to her."

"Or maybe he said he did, but he never paid anyone."

I'm feeling pretty stupid to have believed that asking why there are so many secrets about Maman could be anything but more terrible problems for all the people I love so much. And for something that they love. Bread. Its mysteries shouldn't be owned at all. I'm not sure I want to learn more. It's much easier to bake the bread of dreams, even though that is dangerous. But

I have to find Maman. And Grigne's right, this is a massive and complicated problem. I straighten up and sigh.

"So, where is the Crescent? Doesn't Psomi know? And why trust the Guild? They don't know."

"Psomi's just trying to survive. I told you, you have to go by sea. That's all I know. Maybe get to Rome. Maybe the fields are near there."

"Fields? Rome? Is that where she went, Maman? Water is the problem, and the solution to fixing this, I guess?" I lean towards her.

"Listen. It's the Crescent. The Crescent has oh, so many fields…but their faith wars prevent the Guild from going back. I don't know what Auvillar did, offended someone in the Guild? Took another wife? But there's no way to get this grain except to get to Psomi's sacred fields. That's the source. That's why he wants Antaia. Or you."

"I certainly don't know anything. I can't help him. My worry is that he was the last person to see Maman. He didn't follow her, because she eluded him, tricked him somehow. She couldn't let him find the fields. Has anyone seen her since? It's been seven years since she left. I don't want to see him ever. I just want to find her."

"He's like a crow. You'll see him again. And to find her, you have to face him, right?"

"I never want to see him."

"Maybe he actually knows where she is? Wouldn't that be something?"

"Maybe she went to the Crescent?"

"Too easy. When are you supposed to find her by?"

"This isn't easy at all. He told me I had till the end of Boedromion to find her."

"Um, the fall planting. And the ceremonies of the Efta. Depends on the moon." She looks up. holds her fingers in a triangle, and moves them over various sections of the sky. "But, aren't you lucky? That's today!"

"Today?" My heart sinks.

"I don't see Auvillar though, so you're ok."

"Maybe I could get to the Crescent from Tolosa?" This conversation is beginning to make me very mad.

"Oh, there's a bunch of rumors about finding the Crescent. Who knows which paths the Psomi invented to confuse the Guild, and which ones are worth following?"

"So, what are the rumors?" With so much confusion I have a sinking feeling I'll never ask the right questions, at the right time. To the right person. I'll have to walk out of here. My earlier optimism might come back if I had something to eat. Or if I could sleep.

"Some say it's past all the salt flats, Cap St. Marie and I don't know, you've got to get to the heel. And then, and then?" She hits her palm against her forehead. "I wish I could remember. Oh, oh, wait, on the coast is Leghorn, then Rome and then keep going south to the next sea. The sea within the sea? Or get down to the heel, then sneak out to the toe and cross over to the Crescent. So, it's one of those. Probably. Maybe." Grigne turns to me. Her dark grey eyes have bits of blue in them. Maybe from the sea within the sea in her mind.

"This is too dangerous."

"We're fools. It's true. But we've got to."

Grigne I really want to stay with you, but I don't think I can. I have to go on from here to face Auvillar. And find Maman. When I was ten, I watched Maman slip away. It was the last time I saw her. What wouldn't I give now to fear nothing and still walk after her through the smoke?

CHAPTER THIRTY-SIX

Fabrizio Brings a Message

FLAMES OF THE sun streak across the morning sky. I don't know how I can ever face Antoine again. Help Grigne? What is Antoine thinking, selling the burned wheat to the Guild. Grano Arso. I should just tell her. I should just walk on. Forget Grigne. And growing up. Forget Antoine. Her barge will never move from this death place in the dry river ever again. But I can't forget Maman, though she's probably mortified by me wherever she is. "Where are we going?"

Grigne says she'll be right back. She takes Beauté and I'm to wait in the woods. It was still early when we walked from town up to near where the three rivers come together. Keep out of sight, she says. Well, I've had years to do that, but I doubt I can remain as invisible as I once did. And there isn't anyone around to find me except those three men trying to sell me their millstones, so I feel pretty safe. I walk on. The bushes shake. Someone moans. I step back. I half expect Margot to fall out, burned to a crisp. What if it is Térèse, what will I say?

Fabrizio stumbles out onto the path. His hair askew. His pants covered with straw.

I stand still. He doesn't see me. I catch him by the arm. He jumps.

"God, why would you do something like that?"

We stand looking at each other.

So many thoughts run through my head. How did you find me? Why are you here? Did you see Antoine? Did you sleep with him too? Are you pregnant?

"You said you couldn't leave your post." Is all I can muster.

"Well, well. We all say things," Fabrizio says. "The important thing is to remain true. Keep going. But you, why are you here? Did you find Maman? Artos? Antoine?"

I squint my eyes at him at his mention of Antoine. "I'm helping Grigne, Auvillar didn't help the Psomi farmers like he said he would."

"What? Auvillar didn't help? Epi, wake up. The Psomi stole some rye and then the Guild set fire to their fields." Fabrizio says.

A shiver runs through me. I turn and see him differently. Maybe he saw me with Antoine. Antoine worried that Fabrizio had asked me to sleep with him, but maybe his concern wasn't Fabrizio being interested in me. Maybe Antoine is interested in Fabrizio.

"But why would the Guild do that? Grigne said it could be Psomi farmers, they're so fed up. But maybe it was Antoine. Or maybe she's right, the Psomi did set fire to the field, but had they harvested the wheat? The fire helps prepare the field for next season. It wasn't because they wanted to destroy the field. Or maybe other Guilds came in…" I say.

"Look, the Guild isn't giving Psomi a fair price, and they could never pay the outrageous rental sums the Guild is asking for. So, no way would they sell their precious grain to the Guild. Or…" Fabrizio takes my arm and pulls me off the path.

"The only wheat left is what the Guild stole! And it's here in Altivillarre." I say.

"But if the Psomi Farmers kept some grain before they sold it and then set fire to their own fields. They are willing to destroy Psomi to keep it from the Guild." Fabrizio adds.

"The only wheat I know of is the burned wheat, Grano Arso, that Antoine took and wants, he thinks. he's always scheming." I say.

Fabrizio watches me. "When, when did he do this?"

"The burning field that Beauté and I were caught in, who knows, maybe Psomi did it, but maybe the Guild did it?" Or there could be more to the story. Maybe the burning field is a message from Angeline? Like when I was ten and played the fireflute for the first time, and Auvillar said I started the fire. And that Maman died in the fire. And that's why I was blamed for her death. But maybe that is the same death that Angeline is talking about. The fields were burned to prepare them, not destroy them. And whether Maman died in the fire, or whether she didn't then Auvillar knows what happened. He must. Maybe Maman's death is the same death as Angeline's. And every Mistress. Did the doves…save her? The further away I get from my bread terrace, the further away I get from finding the truth and Maman.

"It's the doves. So many came back. So many died. They couldn't survive being burned. I sat and cried. She died in my lap. I knew her. Her blue feather on its wing. Epi, I am so sorry." He hands me the blue feather.

The dove with the message was my *Aubada*. Flying on, to somewhere else. And she just happened to be flying through the field and got caught like me and Beauté. Oh no, was she trying to reach me? And now my *Aubada* is gone now too. *Aubada* was called to the sky. Like Maman was called by the fields. Or to return to the fire? Why? Her death doesn't make any sense. I don't want to go on. I can't.

We sit by the river.

"How do we know if the message was from the Guild or from Psomi. I don't see how the message could get through on *Aubada* if she was burned in the field."

"It was her job to keep going. Keep carrying messages. And she did. Her message was about Bana. You see, Bana's been arrested in Tolosa. Antoine is headed there. He has to help him." Fabrizio chokes out these words.

I open my mouth. Not Bana. What happened? What in the world got him arrested, and why is he in Tolosa? Antoine is going to help him. I feel terrible. The birds rush through the branches and drown out my words. I close my eyes.

"Grigne, first I have to help Grigne. WE have to help her." I tell Fabrizio before he runs off.

Dusk settles over us, and the woods come alive. Fabrizio walks away, then comes back. He sits under the tree. An owl calls through the forest. Beauté neighs. Grigne steps out. Grigne shakes her head and her walk makes me think I didn't do a good job of staying hidden, because Fabrizio found me. But maybe that's a good thing, and she will think better of me because look, Fabrizio is here. He can help, but then, I have to keep him from getting to Antoine, who might tell him what happened between us.

CHAPTER THIRTY-SEVEN
Epi and Fabrizio Confront Grigne

"WHEN ARE WE, what are we doing? Grigne. I'm here. We're both here." I am proud that Fabrizio stayed. Not because of him, but because I brought help. But Fabrizio knows the truth. He found me. But I know he wasn't looking for me. I watch Fabrizio pacing, and remembering his words when I left the field of rye.

I can't leave. Can't stop sending the messages. It doesn't matter what they say.

So how did this message matter? This one message?

"We? Who are you?" Grigne says. "And were you followed?"

"I'm Fabrizio. Don't worry, we won't let them get away with it. But we have to leave now."

"Oh, good. Fabrizio is it? I don't need you to tell me how to get back at the Guild. Look at you two jokers. We better get going."

"Look, I haven't told you everything." Fabrizio turns to me. "Antoine. He's being tricked." Fabrizio says. "He's walking into a trap."

"Screw Antoine. He's just looking out for himself. We have to blow all three dams," Grigne says. "Look, we can try to get them to come after us. But I don't know if that will work. If not, we have to take out the guards. But there's three of us, so perfect. How is your aim? Are you good with a bow? Don't you shoot doves?" Over one shoulder she carries a basket stuffed with evenly carved sticks. And over her other shoulder are bows.

I look at one of the sticks. "These are arrows, do they come from Angeline?" I was starting to get a sense of Psomi. A different sense. "From her cherry trees?"

"Heavens no. I can't shoot a bow. You're not listening. You're going to flood the river?"

"Not one. Three! That's right. Auvillar thinks I don't know his plan. He sent Antoine to release one river in order to let the Guild ships travel. But Antoine has his own plan. Neither one is that brave. Letting out one river would be enough for the Guild to make it here and back to Tolosa. But that won't change anything. So, three. Three will flood everything. Nothing will survive. The town, the ships. The fields. Serves them right." Grigne says.

"Yeah, it will destroy the Guild but also..you would destroy your own barge? If we do that we'll be destroying Psomi too." I say.

"I told you. If I moved my barge, they'd know." Grigne says.

"Maybe they do know." All this seems kind of drastic. But necessary. Like something Grigne would do, and now for the big question. Will I help her? Can I help her? I don't think so.

"Epi this is big. Psomi's already destroyed. The farmers. They can't think, make a decision. Something has to be done. Before things get worse. We have to be prepared for their anger."

"Of course Psomi will be angry, there's no doubt." Fabrizio raises his hands to the sky. "They stand for peace. Destruction isn't their thing."

"I'm talking about the Guild's anger at destroying their ships."

"I don't fear for Psomi...or the Guild. But for all people. What's left Grigne? Even if they can't be decent. We can."

Grigne's head swivels towards him. She sits back and folds her arms across her chest. I cringe at hearing Fabrizio say he fears for all people. Grigne leans forward. She rests her elbows on her knees, her hands dangling between her knees. Grigne might just explode.

"Really? I can be decent. Fabrizio. Or I used to be. That's why. Why do things have to change."

"Please. I fear for the people we love. We have to find them, then…once Antoine and Bana are safe, then we can do whatever," Fabrizio says.

"No. No way. We've gone so far beyond thinking about any one person. Oh, maybe before they sent Epi out to look for Antaia. But now. We go along with what they want, their games. It's all games to them. You have to be prepared to kill. Or be killed. Are you ready for that, Epi? Fabrizio? Come on!" Grigne stands up. She hands a second basket stuffed with arrows to me. And one of the bows strung on her shoulder.

"You don't get it. Antoine has a plan. He has information that Auvillar doesn't. We must keep talking. It's the only answer. When we look back..we must have no regrets."

"Regrets? About what? Being dead? We have been talking. And listening. Like the Mistresses want. This world is different from the ones they saw. I'm through with waiting and hoping." Grigne says.

Fabrizio looks like a wreck. "The Psomi farmers know all is lost. Their fields burned. Their grain is about to be flooded away."

"Well, I'm not in favor of what Antoine's doing with the burned wheat." I say hoping this will matter somehow. I want to be on Grigne's side because Fabrizio can't protect me if he loves Antoine too.

"You have no idea what you're saying, Epi. The burned wheat is a plan we came up with to fool the Guild, make money for Psomi. Bana is just a boy." Fabrizio says. "He's innocent. If we stand for anything. It's people."

So Fabrizio is in on Antoine's plan. He's part of Antoine's plan. I wasn't. And my heart hurts just hearing Bana's name. I am so worried about him. Even Bana can't see that he is just a boy. He has no idea of the trouble he's in. The trouble he makes. I can't save Antoine as a boy anymore, but can I save Bana? "Psomi stands for people. People? Yes. And just so you know. Antoine and I…" If I can make Fabrizio doubt Antoine's feelings, then he might come over to my side.

"I told you, forget this stuff. We're headed to the confluence of three rivers. The Tarn, the Arratz." Grigne says.

"And the Garonne." I say.

Grigne walks ahead. "Let's go. The Guild guards all the dams. So, first shoot them, and then we can release the water. When you shoot, remember who you've lost."

"But won't we lose who we shoot? Maybe if we ask nicely, these Guild guards, they would be on Psomi's side?"

"Maybe. When they're at death's door, they might want to change, but honestly, would you believe them?" Grigne tilts her head at me. She puffs out a breath and her hair blows up off her face.

"I can't help you do this. I have to get to Tolosa." Fabrizio turns and runs.

"You'll be caught in the flood, Fabrizio," I yell.

Fabrizio keeps going.

"He's going the wrong way, the idiot." Grigne says. "We have no chance against the Guild."

Fabrizio runs off so fast, I'm not sure he hears me. In fact, I'm sure he doesn't. As he runs, his brown shirt flaps and as he disappears, like a deer, into the forest. I can't help but think of all the deer that Antoine has shot. And though he's running off to save Antoine, I'm getting ready to shoot people. And what if Fabrizio sees Antoine first? And Bana? He knows what he thinks and feels. This is the sadness of all of this. He could tell them anything. He's the one who said he has to keep sending the messages. I want to see Antoine and Bana too. And I want to tell them, what? What would I say? The Guild is wrong, and Psomi is right? I turn around.

Grigne walks in the same direction as Fabrizio, towards the dam.

"Come or don't. Either way, you'll see that death. Soon enough you'll die for Psomi, too."

CHAPTER THIRTY-EIGHT
Fabrizio Leaves Epi

WE WALK ALONG the edge of the Arratz river. Fabrizio is not happy to learn he went the wrong way. But he didn't turn around, instead he said we are the ones who are wrong. He is taking another route, making a circle towards Tolosa. It's longer, but quicker in the long run. Especially since Grigne promises that the river will be flooded and Altivarre destroyed. So I'm glad he's with us and no closer to being with Antoine. He huffs and hurries ahead of Grigne. Every once in a while Grigne runs and catches up to him, they fire words at each other, and then he hurries ahead, pulling branches as he runs. Grigne waits for me. While she watches me, I am sure she's sizing me up, and wondering if I am an equal partner to kill the Guild.

Grigne and I get to the edge of the woods, Fabrizio paces on the path along the river's edge. He throws his hands up, like he wants to jump in the water, but that would surely be death. The river speaks loudly, the water behind the dam is the answer and the destruction. How it changes when falling from the sky into the field or gently moving boats and barges along.

"Grigne, what's the plan?" I ask.

"Kill the guards and open the first dam. Then we go to the next. And then the third. Flood Altivarre. Stop the Guild ships from taking the grain they bought. Then once that area is flooded, we can close the dam on the other side and…"

"Beauté can help."

I watch Grigne talk to Fabrizio. I am overcome with feelings of possession.

Fabrizio wants to be with Antoine like I do. But we are nothing alike. Fabrizio can't possibly know him like I do. I grew up with Antoine. I practically raised Antoine. I've seen him at his worst. When he's sad. When he's so frustrated. Lonely. Fabrizio has no idea of how to make Antoine happy. Antoine needs work, and the woods to be happy. How can Fabrizio be in love with him too?

We stand over the first dam. Our faces hidden in the fog. Maman, it's you I didn't really know. I never really knew you. Never listened or heard what you said. I thought life was simple. I worry if I'm doing the right thing. I never questioned anything till we went to Nerac's market the day I turned ten. You went into Madame's. I don't know if you made me heir to Psomi to protect me, keep me safe. Or if you knew then that you were leaving me, and you had to use me to leave and keep yourself safe. I can't imagine standing in front of Maman and asking this question. I don't know if you ever wondered if you were doing the right thing.

"It's time." Grigne says.

"Wait. Stop. We can't do this. We'll just go north, away from Tolosa, gathering wild grain. We'll look there for Maman and more Psomi fields. Has anyone even tried that?" I say.

"We can't," Grigne says. "Let's go."

"It's a trap. We'll be killed for sure," Fabrizio says.

"Probably. Many Psomi farmers died."

"We have to go to Tolosa. How could you live with yourself for not saving Bana and Antoine?" Fabrizio says.

"We'll stay put. Keep out of sight. Let what happens, we don't need to do anything," I say.

"I can't just sit here." Grigne pulls an arrow out of her quiver. She lowers her bow, and places the arrow, then raises the bow, her left arm stretched straight. She widens her stance, and aims for one of the guards. She lets the bow string go, the arrow whizzes and disappears. It bounces off the dam. The guards look around and point at us. They run around and gather their own bows and arrows.

"Get up." Grigne shouts.

I pull at Fabrizio's arm to stand. I hand him a bow from Grigne. I don't want to be shot like a dove. "Grigne's right. I don't like it either. But we have to do this." I do not know what else Maman did for Psomi, even while she was pregnant with me, but I can do this. Because Grigne needs me. Psomi needs me. And Maman must need me too.

CHAPTER THIRTY-NINE

Epi and Grigne Attack the Guild, Beauté and Grigne Fall in the Water

A FEW ARROWS WHIZ past us, but the guards won't leave their post. We crest the dry path, and there on the other side we see the Arratz River. The Tarn, and the Garonne. They boil and crush against the dam.

"Grigne, this will flood Altivarre, and the granary. And south, how will we get to Tolosa?"

"We? You'll have to figure that out."

I let Beauté go. She bends to get a drink from the cool water churning on the one side of the dam. Grigne climbs on her before she's finished.

"No, Grigne! What are you doing? Get off of Beauté. Let me help!"

Grigne ignores me. She rides Beauté farther out along the top of the dam. Farther. On one side the water churns. On the other, the dry river bed. Grigne rides Beauté towards the guards. She waves her fire torch. They wave theirs back. Maybe they can't see her. Maybe they think Grigne is their relief. They walk closer to her. Maybe they know nothing about Psomi. But a white horse in the Guild must seem unusual. Maybe to them this is just another Tuesday.

Grigne shouts and curses. She waves the fire torch in front of her, then heaves it, yelling Psomi. She throws it out and the guards watch it fall like a shooting star, as it thuds into the empty river bed. They laugh. She draws her arrows. Shouts. The bridge makes five humps across to the east bank. The dry branches in the river bed catch fire from the torch.

I can't imagine what Grigne will do. What the churn of the water will do. I step away, then run onto the stone wall of the top of the dam. I stop. Scared to look at the water. In the deep empty bed below, where a small fire burns. The Guild guards point at me, then toss their flamed torches in the river bed. Grigne kicks her heels into Beauté's side, and she bolts ahead across the top of the dam. Grigne draws her arrows and shoots one of the guards. He falls in the dry river bed, missing the fire, but screaming from breaking his leg. A second guard shoots an arrow into Grigne's leg, but she keeps going as if an arrow sticking out of her isn't a problem. I walk further out on the dam.

Grigne gallops on Beauté, clinging to her side. Grigne and Beauté ride closer to the last guard. Grigne draws an arrow on him. He gets down on his knees. But her arrow pierces in his arm, and he jumps in the water. A new guardsman comes from the other side of the dam, and shoots an arrow, hitting Beauté in the chest. Grigne quickly goes to the wheel of the dam and turns it, but nothing happens. She pounds on it, and kicks it, till it turns, opening the large metal door. It slides open and the water trickles, then rushes out from the Tarn and the Arratz. Beauté and Grigne plummet into the churning water. My feet disappear as the water rises, I sip off, the water from one side joins the other, and I sputter and cough and swim as hard as I can.

CHAPTER FORTY

Epi Almost Drowns

I'M SWIMMING AND floating and dodging doors, some float, some rush by. I feel more like a tree than like a fish. I don't belong here. It's sunset. I'm not sure if the mauve-lighted glow comes from the sky or from my headache. The tile roofs swirl up a hill. I reach my fingers out to catch the dock, but it comes loose, and I swim under it, to let it go.

"Come on, boy. You look awful." The man lowers his hand to me. But the river has other ideas, and pulls me on. His fingers harden and stretch, then he let's go. Trees sway along the quays. The Garonne River is full of all the things I saw scratching the throat of Nerac. I expect to get smashed between the overturned boats. And that will be that. I dive down and find more boats pushing up, and trees. No, I didn't find her, Auvillar. I come up to the surface but maybe I should look below for Grigne and Beauté. I get a grip and climb up on a boat. And fall on my belly. Shivering. Cold. The boat drifts towards a brick walkway. It hits and I roll off onto the warm bricks. Gashed in a hundred places by branches. I've never been so thankful for the sun. Or hungry. I close my eyes. The Guild couldn't survive Grigne's flood. How can a flood cause all those fires? My eye travels to the first street across the bridge. Smoke lifts from a blackened hamlet. Not a fragrant wood fire for bread, but burning furniture, straw roofs, dung, and stables. A man throws a broken chair on the fire, and flames shoot up.

"They say it was the burning fields that caused the flood."

"What a foul stench."

The Guild had to know Psomi would come. And now Psomi will be the ones being shot at. Above me, the bells toll. Men dressed in brown burlap, like flour bags, march toward the boat. Ropes tied around their middles. They hold baskets of burgundy and gold chrysanthemums, and throw them in the water. I scoop some up from the water. Beauté, where are you?

I get out of the water and approach the man with a sign. Wood for sale. I have to find Bana. Fabrizio and Antoine. My chest hurts. My shoulder bleeds from a gash. From what I ran into, but I don't know what that was.

"Where are they taking prisoners?" I ask.

"Are they dead like you, or alive?"

Three-storied, half-timbered dwellings crowd along the river, and a pebbled incline winds up the street to the blackened houses. A man shakes a paper while perched at his open window. "I don't want her to get anything," he says to a man below.

In the oldest part of Tolosa, I stamp my feet, the cold air sloshes away. The scent of burning wheat hangs in the air. Is it from the roofs? The sign on the building announces, "Cathars" with a big red x over the word. Across the street, on another building, there's another sign. "St. Sernin."

I wipe my eyes with a discarded burlap rag. My mouth drops at the flux of so many people, their complexions as rouge as their cloaks. I cross the one bridge, push through people in ragged tunics. The Garonne River swirls below, as wide as the sea where the path ends. I want to sit in the sun. I lean against the warm stone building.

My heart jumps. I see Fabrizio. Auvillar leads, Antoine follows. I feel sick. Oh so sick. Antoine stops, his back to us. He waits. People pass him. Antoine slowly turns. His face holds anger, regret, sadness, and then goes blank. My mouth opens to shout. But I don't know what to say. Stop thief. Betrayer. Guilder. Brother. He drops my gaze and leaps up the steps of St. Sernin. I don't think he even recognizes me. Antoine steps up as if in charge. Antoine beckons everyone up the stairs and opens the door.

CHAPTER FORTY-ONE

Epi Arrives in Tolosa

Tʜᴇʀᴇ's ᴀ ᴅᴏɢ on the step leading up to the church. I look more closely. It's cold and still. I go inside the church and duck under the scallop shell carved into the stone above the doors. Just inside, two men guard the next set of doors.

"Aren't you the lucky one?" one says. "You're just in time."

I step in. The rose-colored sky streaked with yellow and apricot warmth disappears as the door closes behind me. The room of the church is cold, cold as stone. In time for what?

"You're entering the Prison of the Guild, in Tolosa, and we need a few more prisoners."

"You don't want me," I say.

"Aren't you the lively one? Of course we do. What's your name?"

"I'm not who you want."

"We especially want you."

"You can keep shouting but it doesn't matter."

They grab me. I push them away.

"You won't escape this time. You're under arrest for treason."

His voice is quiet, but I'd know him anywhere. I turn around. Antoine.

"Treason? You said I could save the Guild."

"By causing the flood?"

I want to say no it wasn't me. I want to say how could you. I want to say didn't I love you enough? But then, I stand up. Hearing about Fabrizio and his undying love. "Yes. Too bad Grigne didn't shoot you. Then maybe the Guild would be saved."

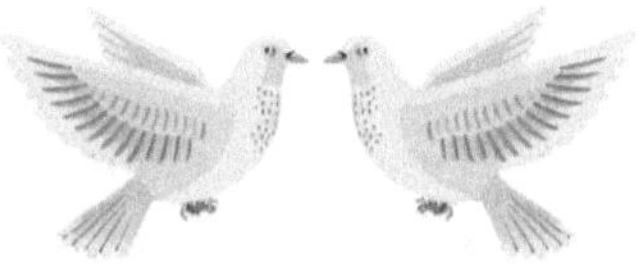

CHAPTER FORTY-TWO
Epi Thrown in Tolosa's Prison

BRIGHT GREEN, RED, and blue diamonds lay out on the floor beyond the scallop doors. I'm nervous about where we're going, because the Guild, hasn't it been destroyed? My heart races. "Look, the Guild. They're just people, just like Psomi. Right? Aren't we all people?"

"Be seen and yet unseen? Like Maman told us." Antoine says in a sarcastic voice. He pushes me.

We go down the steps, billowing with a putrid stench. I want to fix this time. I want to smell wild and sacred seeds and grains being ground between stones. Their scents fill the air. My thoughts lean away, my hand smooths along the stone wall and it becomes the stone of the wood oven on my bread terrace, a fire burning inside. I want to return to where we once lived and everything was ok. Or I believed it was. On the morning of my birthday I finished crowns of bread for Antoine to enter the contest. And filled a sack with the bread of dreams wrapped around apple and caraway seeds. With cumin and wild onion. I'm handing the sack to Térèse just before dawn. She smiles, actually smiles. I touch the stone wall again, going down more steps. Térèse walks to the bridge with the bag of my bread of dreams. I look up and there's a guard. The bridge leading from Ceres, our lives then, and what I believed, disappears.

I am shoved against the entry door, divided in four leather sections and embossed with the snail. The guard pushes my shoulders and the door opens. Silence, and the strong scent of rot leads the way. Antoine and I grew up, pretending to be in the Guild. Now I know, he wasn't pretending. Only I was. I feel stupid to have believed in him for so long.

A row of cells. Someone whistles.

"Bana, is it you?" I stretch out my hand, and reach his face. "You're alive. Even Grigne will be glad. Well, she would be.."

The guard shoves me inside the cell next to Bana. Slams the door shut and turns the big iron key in the lock. Antoine turns and walks away.

"Grigne, pah, she doesn't know everything. Psomi could grow all it wants. No one's stopping them. So they have to get a permit, apply, then pay the tax. The Guild could protect them." Bana says.

"Protect them, from who?" I ask.

"Epi, really? With all this money at stake, you don't think there's just two sides, Psomi and the Guild?"

I had never thought there was a third side to this. "So, who else does Psomi needs protection from? You're leading bandits to go between the Guild and Psomi?"

"Me? The Guild can't see anything, unless it's their way. And Psomi can't see anything either. They're stuck in the old ways of the Efta. What good are they? They hide up in the mountains. Everyone went there. I would check there for your Mom. She's got to be with them. Hiding. She was one of them. But there is someone else who knows both sides' secrets. That's who you have to worry about. Take back what's yours, Epi. They stole it from you. I know the way. My Dad is coming. He'll get us out of here…"

He's got more to say. I think for a minute. "What was stolen from me? The box?"

Bana sighs. "Auvillar took it back. Or he thinks he did."

"What do you mean?"

"My dad can tell you when he gets here. But then, why wait? Let me tell you. He made the old box. Gave it to your Maman at the meeting. That's what he told me. He helped them, the Efta, but then, he's old like them."

Bana digs in his cell and swears. He digs more and unearths something, he pulls it out, rubs off the dirt. I used this chisel and the hatchet to make another box from a fallen chestnut log I found in Fabrizio's Forest. My dad taught me how. And I buried the new box in dirt so it would look the same. That new box is what that idiot, Auvillar, has now. Except that his box has the snail on it and not the tree. The one with the carved tree, that's the real box."

I vaguely remember there was a snail on the box at Madame's. And the carved tree on the box Maman and I filled with Trakhanas. I never questioned it. I wished for any and every possible turn of events, so I won't have to see Auvillar. But now with the news of more boxes, I picture Auvilar's darkness at my ceremony when I was ten years old. The same Auvillar who is Térèse's dad, ignored her crying outside the bread terrace. Margot, did she know? How can I see Auvillar now and not see Térèse? Hating him, and loving her. I don't want to see Térèse in him. I just won't look at him. Is that footsteps? I look over to see Bana scraping dirt with the chisel. I'm relieved.

"I'm telling you. If Psomi doesn't get off their ass, I'm not going to stress over it, I'll make a deal with Margot for this box. I'm not stupid."

"It's Margot." I say, and my gut feels the truth. Margot is the third side.

"This is a war. I want to be on the winning side. So right now, who that is, who knows. This will show them. I'm tired of everyone sitting around talking, talking, talking, arrgghh, it's dead already! Do something."

"Margot? She's the other side. What do YOU want? Grigne certainly did something."

"Yeah, thanks Grigne. Old girl. She certainly caused a lot of problems. Not bad for a start. Or for an end since she's dead now. You were there? What happened? Tell me everything."

"Bana, what? It was horrible. Beauté was lost. And Grigne too. They died. DIED. You see these bruises on my arms? I barely swam away. But what about Margot?" It's not like Bana to lead the conversation away from something.

"You think it's easy for the Guild? They just want to feed people. Make money. Why is that bad?" He picks up the hatchet.

"Bana, it's kind of bad if the Guild kills the people they say they want to feed. And besides. They arrested you. How did that happen?" My intuition tells me that since he has no loyalty, maybe Bana is being paid by the Guild to find the Efta. And maybe in Nerac, the whole scene between Bana and Auvillar was just an act. But if I still want to find Maman, and even knowing that Bana might be trying to trick me too, I still want to keep him safe. Not sure why. Does he remind me of Antoine when I first found him at Madame's. Maybe. Or maybe it's because he's so smart and clever and doesn't care what anyone thinks. I keep telling myself I have to know him and see him for who he is. Because I have been wrong about everyone.

Bana cocks his head, "Don't worry, my dad is coming. He'll get us out of here."

Suddenly the door opens, and Antoine enters with another shadow. Auvillar steps into the light. "Antoine what do you say? Am I an idiot like Bana thinks?"

"Epi, he's why I am here." Bana shouts and points.

"Yes, he's an idiot." I say.

"No, not Auvillar. Antoine's the one who arrested me."

CHAPTER FORTY-THREE

Auvillar Threatens Eleone

A FAT IVORY CANDLE flickers shadows on the wall. Wax runs down the iron pillar, hardens in the cool air and hangs like an icicle.

"And you, what do you say?" Auvillar steps to my cell, reaches through and cups my chin, and forces my face towards the light.

I pull away from Auvillar and look at Antoine's face. "Antoine, you did what? Bana's just a little boy. How could you arrest him? And not tell me?" As soon as I say it, I realize I said too much. It's so much more than Antoine not telling me about Bana. As if that wasn't enough to make me want to kill him. I'm not used to speaking out. The room sounds funny. Looks funny. As does everyone's face as they think, who was that speaking? Antoine had the power to protect me or not. He arrested me too. He knows I am a girl. But everyone else here thinks that I am Epi, and a boy. If I reveal I am a girl could I protect him from getting in trouble about being with Fabrizio because surely that's not what Antoine wants. I know deep down he wants to be with me.

Antoine stares at me. His eyes wide open, as if I'm crazy. "Bana is where he belongs. And so are you. Auvillar, you missed the proceedings. Epi is in the Guild now." Antoine says. "It doesn't matter about finding Antaia."

It doesn't matter? Everything is moving way too fast. So, Antoine is protecting me. Wait, is that even true? How can that be true? It hits me that he's not doing it to help me. He's doing it so I can still be in the Guild and make him money. But maybe that's just his cover. Maybe he's doing it because he can't say his feelings. And keeping me in the Guild is the only way he can stay close to me. That must be it. Antoine actually looks scared. Of me finding out his true feelings? He would be too vulnerable if he told me he loved me. It's ok, Antoine, I understand. But then I shake my head. No, he doesn't care about me, because he betrayed me. He can't have arrested Bana and keep that a secret without knowing how much I care about Bana. Bana is not innocent of being mischievous, but for god's sake, he doesn't deserve this, not this. This likely means execution. And what did Antoine think would happen when I found out that he arrested Bana before we slept together? I wonder if he thought sleeping with me would make arresting Bana ok?

"Since when does it not matter about finding Antaia, finding her means finding the fields? What world are you living in?" Auvillar scowls at Antoine.

"Bana's where he belongs? In Prison?" But now I feel sick watching Antoine turn and face Auvillar's anger. And get shut down. But how did he expect this not to all come out? Maybe he believed Auvillar. Maybe he never said anything to him at all. Another betrayal! Bana bends his head and laughs. He seems to be enjoying this whole thing. Something from our past comes back. The questions I have about who is protecting who. It began on the night I turned ten and Maman walked into the fire; when I was left with the feeling of even though I watched something happening, I still didn't believe it. And watching this all unfold is like being back at Madame Bouquin's.

Antoine calmly says to Auvillar. "You're being stupid about this. You've gotten old. It doesn't make any sense to give up our best baker to find someone who's dead. Probably dead. With Epi we can recoup our losses."

Auvillar turns to me. "Antoine has forgotten something. I know your truth. I see you."

A strange heat runs through me. I feel sick. And frozen to reply. It's not about me at all. It's about power here. I try to locate the conversation I had with Antoine the night we slept together but it was all a blur of burned feathers and his sweat and my arms that didn't want to let him go.

"Antoine said that it didn't matter and that I didn't have to find her. That I was the Guild's best baker." I might just throw up, from feeling too much. Like when I first went to Nerac and couldn't fathom all the people. I will just stick with being the Guild's baker. All of these betrayal's are confusing. But no, I can't just go along. Faced with his anger, I want to agree, and escape, say anything just to get out of trouble. I want to be like Bana, and not care. I look at Bana, he smiles. Then Auvillar smiles at me. Looking at Bana included him in our argument, or agreement, our horrible problem. And I realize I just let Auvillar know how I feel about Bana. I close my eyes and cringe. Bana giggles. Giggles. I can't believe he would do something so foolish. Something happens inside me. A spark, a turning, "I see you too, Auvillar. You don't care about anyone, least of all my mother!"

Margot comes down the stairs. "Ah, Epi. We're here. Together at last. There are so many reasons to be thankful."

With Margot's arrival, Bana stands.

"Antoine's right. You have made many beautiful crowns for the Guild. Do they sometimes join together in the oven? Like we're all gathered here? Look around. Bana, Antoine, you."

"No. Never." I won't admit to any wrongdoing. He's trying to put the blame on me instead.

"Epi? Tell me the truth now. You know your name means ears. So listen carefully to my question," Auvillar says. "Do the crowns sometimes join together in the oven?"

Margot smirks. Bana leans his face against the bars, his eyes following the conversation.

"Why is that important? Sometimes they do. Sometimes we have to split them apart, but it's not because Antoine's done anything wrong. It's not his fault. I'm the spare Guild apprentice. Talmeleier."

"Yes, yes. Split apart, you each carry the *baisure,* the scar. Under the same sky, the wheat joins you and tears you apart." Auvillar says.

Hmm, yes, the sky. The scar. If I hadn't looked at Bana, maybe Auvillar would have forgotten him. And forgotten how angry he was with Bana. With Antoine. With anyone in his way. Everyone. I am not sure if he's saying the wheat is me and Maman. Or me and Antoine. Or Angeline. Or Térèse, his daughter. He has a lot to gain by splitting us apart. But he must be so sad inside. I look at his face. The deep lines and sun-weathered skin. I step close to the bars. Auvillar stares. He scares me, but it doesn't make sense that he would hurt me. He needs me. I know he does. Now that he's lost everything. He steps away.

Margot stares at me. I have no idea if it's to kill me or save me for her purposes. Whichever would bring her the most money.

"The Guild knows you burned the fields near Altivillare. And you were supposed to keep Grigne from doing anything stupid. But you failed that too." Auvillar turns to Antoine.

"HE burned the fields. But he arrested ME." Bana shouts.

"Antoine again, for god's sake, why?" I say. "Blaming a little boy for this?"

"I like you, but, Epi…" Bana says. "Epi..sit down."

"You're so stupid, Epi. It was before you and he were together that night. I couldn't believe what I saw." Margot says.

"He?" Auvillar asks.

So Margot WAS watching us. But I don't trust her not to play some kind of trick. Whatever would help Margot.

"Yes, him." Margot points. But not to me. To a man waiting in the candlelight. Fabrizio.

Auvillar steps back. Shakes his head. "Antoine, at one time you were like a son to me, and I had such hopes. But now, I see. I am so disgusted and disappointed. The Guild doesn't tolerate such liaisons. But you'll be the perfect sacrifice. Just like Claude was for you," Auvillar says.

"What?" Antoine turns. "Oh, no, that's not happening after all I did for you!"

"I am truly sorry. I had hoped for more too. But I have no choice…after you double crossed me. And now with this little dalliance, with Fabrizio. You will be…."

"You can't be serious. We had a deal!"

"Executed. My true son is Epi." Auvillar says.

The guard opens the cell next to me, and pushes Antoine inside.

CHAPTER FORTY-FOUR

Epi Confronts Antoine about Fabrizio

A GREAT RUSH OF confusion passes through me. The candlelight flickers over Antoine's face and he looks like when he was a little boy, like Bana, in Nerac and at another fire, our first fire, when I first met him in the market square and we tended the fire that Maman left me to feed.

Young Antoine poked me. "Is this your first fire?"

"My first fire? What?" I slanted my eyes at Antoine. Little thief and trouble-maker. But then he looked up at me again. There was something in his green eyes. I knew. He was hungry. Probably in his belly. But mostly in his heart.

"When it slows down you have to feed it small wood, not throw on a big log, like that, and crush it."

"If you're so smart, can you read the fire, Antoine?"

"*Oc.*" He used Maman's word. "*Le feu.* So nice to meet you. I'll feed you, much better than him."

"Him?" I asked.

Many people scurried past us, up the steps and into the shop where Maman had gone. When Antoine's eyes met mine, I understood. The *him* he meant was me. I had a second to decide. How did he not know I was a girl? How did he mistake me for being a boy like him? It's strange to remember this and realize that he always saw me as a boy. And from that moment on, in our likeness but extreme difference, even before I became Epi,

I wanted to be like him, please him, protect him and save him, like a brother. My brother in the Guild. I didn't know any of that then. But then who I was when I met him disappeared, and had to stay a secret. I didn't know how long I would have to bear it. Be Epi. I was so sure Maman would come back for me. For all three of us. And now I see Antoine had a secret too. The fire, the job of feeding it, is what drew us together, held us together and now burned us apart at the same time. We are like two crowns that joined together, their skins touching in the hot oven, only to be pulled apart and left with the *baisure*. The scar.

On that day in Nerac when we first met, Antoine and I fed the fire and waited for Antaia. But we ran out of wood. "You have to go in there to find her. I'm not." Antoine said. And pointed at the smoke coming out of the chimney of Madame Bouquin's. Why did I have to do this? My stomach felt sick. Paillard was packing up his plants and seeds at his stand across from us. More people were headed inside, where Maman had gone with Auvillar. I had never seen a man with skin the color of tree bark.

But the Antoine in the cell next to me has grown circles under his eyes, as dark as Auvillar's skin.

"It's the same problem as the day we met, you still have to go in and find her," Antoine says. "Antaia."

"So, Antoine. You and Fabrizio? You were with him before you held me close all night? Or maybe Margot is lying because she needs me to get her into the same Psomi fields that Auvillar wants. Neither one of you cares about Maman, you just need her to help you make money. But I'm not who you think I am."

In the light of the torches, Margot's face blusters. She blows out a huge breath.

"Epi, I always thought you were a boy. I only saw what I wanted. And I wanted to make Fabrizio jealous."

But why would Antoine exchange his freedom for the Guild. There's no way I can get him out of here, too. Not for me, but for him. I guess I do know why he wanted to be in the Guild.

Antoine didn't like being left. Being lost. He wanted to belong. Even belong to something as bad as the Guild. To be wanted. Fabrizio's face falls but he reaches out his hand. Antoine takes it. Tears stream down my face to watch Antoine look at Fabrizio, wishing he would look at me like that. Wishing I was that person and that he could see me without my secret. And that he would want me, like he wants Fabrizio. But he wouldn't want who I am without my secret, Eleone.

"I could never be your son. I have always been, and will always be, Antaia's daughter." I say to Auvillar.

CHAPTER FORTY-FIVE

Epi Reveals Her Identity

AUVILLAR TURNS TO Margot. "This is your fault. When you lost Epi, that's when he got out of hand."

Margot stands staring at Auvillar. I get a strange feeling. I remember him sending her with me along the Baise from Madame's. But I can't think of anything better than both of them getting imprisoned along with Antoine.

I say. "Is that what she told you? I ditched her outside of Nerac. She's not safe to be around. None of you are. I can't imagine what you did to Antaia to make her leave. My mother is the only one who ever protected me."

"Your mother protected you?" Margot opens her mouth, rests her hand on her hip, shakes her head, mumbles something. I cringe at what she might say. After an awkward minute she says "You're Epi, what do you know? You lived inside a rose cane for seven years. And became the Guild's best baker. So know your place. Epi just works and doesn't talk."

"But I'm not Epi. I'm Eleone."

"Listen, Epi, this tidbit won't change anything. Did you think being a girl could save Antoine? The truth is that by telling us that you're Eleone, you not only didn't save Antoine, but now you condemned Bana, too. Because he worked with a girl baker and didn't tell anyone, Bana's just as guilty. He's got to hang too. And once they're both gone. No one will ever know poor Eleone. And you'll always be Epi, working for the Guild."

"You just want to kill anyone who stands in your way. I'm sure you had something to do with me being charged with Antaia's leaving and her death. Can you imagine what that did to me? It made me want to hide and keep baking bread for the Guild." I was born a girl for a reason. I spent years with Antaia for a reason. So you both kept me prisoner in the Guild.

"Actually it wasn't me who turned you into a boy, but I can say that was brilliant thinking on the part of my sister."

"Your sister is nothing like you."

"Here's another shitty truth you don't know. You're MY daughter."

"You? You're my mother?! My mother?" How can that be? I must not be hearing this correctly. I look at her. My legs tremble like a little mouse that's been found eating grain. But then I feel myself slipping through the door like the water in the dam at Grigne's. Margot turns the wheel to open it wider, until I flow through. Antoine chose Fabrizio. Térèse left me, and I am stuck with the worst of them all. Margot! And the only other woman I believed in wasn't mine at all. Never was. I sit down. Térèse chose to stay with her mom. I look over at Antoine in his cell, he's staring straight ahead. Did he know? What would his mother, Madame Bouquin, say about this? *Espante!* Who cares, I mean Antoine gave up his own father for the sake of the Guild. He's mired in his own *merde*.

"I never planned to tell you. But then—."

"So did you give me to Maman? Or did Maman take me away from you." The question spurted out of me, before I considered if I really wanted to know.

"I gladly gave you up. But now you're useful."

"So it was you. You had everything to do with Maman's death, and with blaming me." I can't believe this. It hits me. I can't even say Maman. She is Antaia. She was not my mother. And neither is Margot. I had no mother.

"Claude was easy to buy."

Antoine frowns. I wondered how he feels about Claude now.

"You wanted to get rid of Antaia," I say.

"I had to."

"She, she was everything to me." I say.

"Antaia was teaching you about Psomi. Wasn't she? How much do you know?"

"That's why Antaia had to be so quiet. You were with the Guild. I wondered why she was, why she never spoke to you." I had two mothers close to me, but it's like I didn't have even one. I sit down and stare at Antoine. He looks at the floor.

My ears would close down when Margot yelled at me. Especially when she beat me if I didn't bake enough crowns. Eleone listened to Maman, I mean to Antaia. But it was a kind of listening that let all she said flow into me. I was safe with her. I thought I would always be able to ask her. To tell the stories again. And listen. I tried to save Antoine by telling everyone who I am, as if by becoming Eleone again I could change everything. But here's Margot trying to take that away from me. Even saying I am Eleone can't change anything. And why would I want to return to being Eleone, since that's who I was when both my mother's left me.

"Did you ever meet Angeline? And apparently you know Fabrizio."

"Both of them are such putan's. Basing their lives on Psomi nonsense." Margot crosses her arms. "You have a lot to make up for, daughter." Then, Margot watches as shadows go by my window. "But don't worry, I won't leave you behind like she did."

CHAPTER FORTY-SIX

Antoine to Be Executed, Auvillar is Arrested

"*C*ADUN BIRO L'AIGO DEBÈS SOUN MOULI. Everyone diverts water to their own mill, that's what I think. Psst. Bana, I'm sorry I got you in this mess." Antoine watches Margot go up the stairs, and says. "With the Guild. I was trying to get you out of the way. But did you? You know? Save them? The seeds?"

"Yeah, I did. Who knew Grigne would really flood that town. And this one, too. Good thing I was arrested by then, and had already buried the box in my cell. Don't worry, my dad is coming. His sheep hooves will get us out of here," Bana says.

"Bana, who will send the messages now that Fabrizio is here?"

"Ha. Who knows? Margot, will she?"

Antoine shakes his head. "She's worse than Auvillar."

"Where did she go?"

"Who knows. She ran out of here like a dove about to be shot." Bana says and pats the box.

The door opens at the top of the stairs. We all turn to the footsteps coming down. Maybe Margot is going to throw Fabrizio in the cell next to Antoine. Since it's really all his fault.

But it's Auvillar and he is alone except for the big iron key he's jingling. He stops in front of Bana. "Keep talking. You'll be next."

He passes Antoine's cell and stands in front of me. "By the time I come back, you'll wish you were the first one to be executed." Auvillar fiddles with the keys, trying to find the right one.

He moves to Antoine's cell. "I have nothing to say to you. Let's get this over with." Auvillar unlocks Antoine's cell.

Antoine looks over to me. I look over at him. At this moment I see all of who we've been to each other. How far away and how close today is to the day we met outside Madame Bouquin's. Everything crashes together. Auvillar was there that day too. He said I was his true son. But the man is so confused. Antoine was his Epi. I didn't know we were both training for today. Auvillar opens the cell and Antoine walks out and stands in front of me. He seems frozen, and in his eyes. Gone. Why doesn't he try to get out of it? Make a deal with Auvillar. Or break down. Or fight? Auvillar puts the chains on his wrists. I hate him for what he's done, but I love him for who he is.

"Wait." I shout. "Antoine, say something. This isn't the time to go mute."

"Auvillar, you made promises to me. This won't solve anything." Antoine shakes. "I can make it right with the big guys."

Again, the door opens and closes at the top of the steps. Loud voices argue.

"I'm telling you he's here." Margot shouts. "Down there."

"You have him? I don't believe it." Big voices boom down the steps.

I shrink. Surely, I am the him they are coming for.

Margot tromps down the steps with three well-dressed merchants behind her. Fabrizio follows them. I turn my back. I don't want to see any of them.

"So now you see, here he is." Margot huffs.

I can't believe she would really give up her own daughter. And now I have been given up by two mothers. Great. Grigne promised this is bigger than me. Everything is bigger than me.

"Not him, HIM, you idiot."

I turn around and watch Margot snag Auvillar. Auvillar quickly slips out of her grip, and runs into the first man, his sleeves puffed out, who wears velvet breeches. Auvillar tramples him and pushes Antoine out of the way, but Antoine pushes Auvillar into what was his jail cell. Antoine closes the door, trapping Auvillar.

Margot smiles at Antoine. "It looks like we're just in time, gentlemen. He's just where we want him. And he's all yours."

I can't believe Margot would do this to Antoine. But I should believe it. Why isn't Fabrizio doing anything? He must be in danger too. I never thought I could hate Margot more, but I do. My own mother.

Margot gestures to Auvillar. I step back in my cell watching Auvillar cower. But then Margot unlocks my door. I back up. So she is turning me in, too, as Epi? She can't be. But that must be it. My own mother!

But the two men stop in front of what was Antoine's cell, and fight with Auvillar to open the door. After much swinging back and forth, the iron door opens and they pull Auvillar out of the cell, pushing him between them, and poking him.

The merchant who was trampled a minute ago pushes Auvillar. "What do you think you're doing? Executing the Guild's best workers? Then you plan to run out on us after losing everything and screwing everything up for years? You've tried to trick us I don't know how many times. This is it for you."

"You don't understand. She's who you want. Antaia's daughter." Auvillar points at me.

"More lies, Auvillar? You told us they both died years ago."

"I was wrong. They tricked me." Auvillar looks panic-stricken.

"Take a good look at this loser. He's responsible for the Guild going down. And she's going to save it." And with that, the well-dressed merchants take their well-dressed merchant, Auvillar, away.

The door closes at the top of the stairway. The silence is deep.

"What are they talking about, who's going to save the Guild?"

"Actually, I'm the only one with an answer for Antoine, Fabrizio, and everyone here," says Margot.

"This I gotta see." Fabrizio says.

"You will," Margot says to Antoine and Fabrizio. "Come back to Nerac and *Condatóm* and head up the new Guild. I don't care that you're together. You both wear pants anyway, so who cares. Just make money. But if you're caught, I won't save your ass."

"Hey I'm glad, but don't even ask me. I ain't selling out." Bana sticks his tongue out at Margot.

Antoine turns. He reaches out to Bana. They shake hands through the bars. Then he stands with Fabrizio.

I listen. I can't tell if it's the wind. A bunch of doves lift past the window. I watch them fly away. So that's it? I followed the doves and this is where I am? Fabrizio and Antoine were bought out by the Guild because they want to be together. And now I'm alone.

"I'm coming back for you. We have our differences, but you are our best baker. And I am your mother. And listen, you're going to obey me, for once." Margot says.

"There's no way. I'm never listening to you." I say.

"Whatever, you don't have any choices." Margot leaves.

CHAPTER FORTY-SEVEN

Epi Says Good-Bye to Fabrizio

"EPI, YOU CAN come too. You must be hungry, like Antoine. You grew up together. And you both had a secret." Fabrizio says.

It's not fear, but acceptance, something I didn't expect to see in Fabrizio's eyes. It should feel good that they're both saved, for now, and going with Margot. But hopelessness sweeps out over me. So many things just don't add up.

"If you believe the promises Margot makes, then you are doomed, too." I say.

"What if the Guild and Psomi could work together? If we could, Epi. Could we? What would it be like? Antoine believes that. And his plan, it can work, he just needs, we need more money. And Margot—we can control her."

I swallow hard. "Who are you? You told me you have to keep sending the messages. Psomi Isn't about money."

"Who are you now?" Fabrizio asks.

I sit down. Look at Bana. He shrugs. He can't tell me. No one can. I don't want to be Epi in the Guild, and I don't know if my connection to Psomi or to Antaia is still alive.

"The Guild will never change. They want to own everyone. Maybe like Antoine thought he owned you? Or you, did you think you owned him? Look, I don't care. Just go."

"Get to the port of Massalia. The ship Auvillar was going to take, it can take you." He squeezes my hand, then takes his hand from my grasp.

"Take me where?"

Tears run down his face. "Be careful. Margot knows."

"Just go." With my eyes closed, my breath slows; keeping my fire going inside. The fire that I fed with Antoine outside Madame's when we were ten. Margot? This is just perfect.

"I'll stop Margot from following you." Fabrizio says. "I… and one more thing."

"Fabrizio, I'm so angry. You disappoint me." I have to give it up. Give up thinking it could still be different with Antoine. I'm so angry. Give up thinking that I could find Maman.

"He forgives you. He wants you to know." Fabrizio reaches through the bars and touches my hand. I pull away. If I forgive him now wouldn't that mean that everything I ever felt for him was a lie?

Outside my cell the first big flakes fall. How quickly it covers the grass and the branches. The air grows still. Birds fly to the pine branches. Their feathers ruffle out. They bury their beaks in their wings. My hands are cold and I rub them together wishing to make a fire. Being this cold reminds me of Ceres, and the only home I know. I laugh. But I feel crazy. I don't know which I would choose. To stay inside these bars with no snow falling on my head or be outside of these bars with the birds so I can be with them and freeze. The sum of the bread terrace was so little. The iron trellis. A white rose that grew as my fear grew, big enough to hide me. And there I lived inside my cage with visits from *Aubada*, Térèse, Antoine, and Paillard. But they all left. They're gone. I feel ashamed that secretly I was always glad when they left. I don't feel glad now. I feel anything but glad. What I wouldn't give for any of them to visit me now. Except maybe for Margot. Margot, my mother.

Fabrizio stands. How quiet he is. Not at all like Antoine.

I can't give up searching for, and finding Antaia. Because she's the reason we stayed and the reason we left. The reason I stayed. And I left. She is everything to me.

"Maybe one day you can forgive him. I'll watch out for you. You're family."

"Never." I say, but then I hear myself and can't believe how cruel I sound. "Fabrizio, we're nothing like family. At all," though this is what I want most. I don't understand why I can't say ok, let him win. Maybe he needs family too. He's been alone like me. With Antoine coming to visit him. If I could remember when Antoine stopped coming to the bread terrace. And visiting me. I hate that he chose Fabrizio over me.

Fabrizio stands and leaves. But two shadows climb up the steps.

"So, what's going to happen to me here? Bana, to us?" I think back to the conversation between Antoine and Bana. It makes no sense to me. I don't know what to think about Antoine.

"You took them, didn't you? Who did you give the seeds to? Auvillar? Margot?" I ask Bana.

"Took what?" Bana shrugs.

"Zeiai, Olyra, Einkorn, and Emmer. The seeds that were in the doves that you stole. And you and Antoine had made a plan. It wasn't the fire that was the problem. It was that the fire covered what you were doing. What were you doing, Bana?"

"I like you, but Epi, you're crazy!" Bana jumps down from swinging on the ceiling bars.

Footsteps approach. "Margot, I told you I'm not going." I say and turn away.

Bana jumps up. "Abrasar? Is it really you?"

"Tsst! You don't even remember my name." The man shakes his head. "What on earth? You haven't changed. Thank God.

What did you do this time? I've looked everywhere but here. Here?! Bana! Come here."

"Oh, right. Pàisser? This is Epi." Bana gestures to me, and walks to the bars and shoves his fist through. The man bumps it gently with his.

He hands me a nut.

"What's this?"

"That's a chestnut from your tree. From Antaia, if you ever made it this far. I'm Ispanek. Not Abraser or Paisser. Bana's father. I hope he hasn't been any trouble."

The sun sends curls against the sky in colors of ripe plums, apricots, cherries, pears and apples. The sky lifts like a bird high over Maman's maze of trees. Ispanek turns the key on Bana's cell and mine next. Bana comes in, dancing a jig, but I pick him up and he struggles, but then he leans into me. His bony arms wrap my shoulder. We shake together for a long time. I forget how to breathe. But it's too much for him, I know he doesn't like this side of me. I can never let him down. What can I tell him to make him understand all these sides. My sides. His sides. Nothing. Nothing at all.

He wipes his eyes and looks away. The box tucked under his arm. I still haven't seen if it has a snail or a tree on it. We hurry through the garden of the church, where the leeks lift themselves and the pumpkins nestle down in their furrows.

BEFORE WE GET in the cart, Bana hands the box to Ispanek. We push to leave Tolosa behind, but it pulls us back. I swallow my tears, reminded of the day Térèse and I left Ceres on a cart. Then, left Nerac. Left *Condatóm*. Left so many places. So many people. And leaving myself to return to Eleone. I listen to the wind. Hoping I can hear Eleone returning like Maman told me I would.

"Shhh. In seven years you will hear Eleone returning. Your tree, the chestnut is…the center of the spiral. It's on the box. It will help you find the fields, the Mistresses." Maman picked up her Bouffe. She brushed it off. She played and the music curled around me as if it was a snail shell, taking me home. Or keeping me home. The melody took me to the maze of trees where we would dance. And while playing, her eyes left again. What place was she staring off to? The place where I could hear Eleone returning?

"But Maman, is the snail or the tree the place where Eleone will return?"

"It's not a place out there.."

"I don't understand any of this."

"Once the trees of the maze came down, everything changed quickly, and why the doves are unsettled, they are getting ready."

"For what?"

Maman sighed. "To take the seeds to the Mistresses. I'm keeping our box empty. But if it gets opened you must act surprised."

"I don't understand. Stop telling me things. I don't under-stand. And don't want to understand"

"Listen without fighting the words. Understanding will come. Bread_takes its life from the fire, but in the end returns its life to the fire too. So you too are like a bread of dreams, and when you walk through the fire, you will take your new life from the fire."

"New life? I don't want a new life."

"You are two people, Mistress of Psomi."

"I won't!"

"You'll die and be reborn in the fire. You'll understand me in 7 years."

It's ONE THING I forgot. Antaia telling me I will die.

In the back of the cart, we bounce down a street. Loud voices lift up and bruise the sky purple. The sky may not be the best place to look for the answer. Bana stretches out, looking up too. The trees swirl in a circle, and we go back towards the church. I look up to the sky. We leave to the east, the sky smokes with clouds that pass over the moon. Where will we be when the sun rises? If it rises. A horse nickers beside us, pulling their cart ahead. People lean out of windows above the street, pointing at us. We pass a fire, and the scent of meat roasting rouses me.

"Where are we, can you tell?"

"Crossing the big river."

"Oh no. The Garonne." The Garonne is the river I fell into and crawled out of to go to prison. Behind us, smoke hovers over Tolosa.

WE CROSS THE Garonne safely. After we get to the other side, we hurry along the towpath. The bridge sits behind us. Feathers float above us, as if from the dovecote, and when Claude died. Soft and white, they float above us. Soon, I realize it's snow, not feathers. The flakes lift off from the big clouds overhead. How can I forget Antoine? And Margot. Nothing is what it seemed to me when I was ten. Or yesterday.

"Epi, I'm scared."

Bana, scared? "I'm here, Bana. I see you."

Ispanek thrashes the mule and we rush, slowly, along. The trees shiver with their bare branches. Another cart passes by, and I nod, pull Bana to me, tuck him in my coat. How can I go on knowing Antoine will never be a part of me? Or Térèse.

The flat lands hug the chilled air down from the mountains and it rushes over us quickly, greets us and knows us better than we know ourselves.

The mules' hooves pound the road and heats our steps, and I shiver a little from her warmth. We pass a green sign for Salvetat-Lauregais. A wide bridge carries more carriages and carts, with a small footbridge beside it and the rushing Vendenille River below. We feel far from Tolosa, but at the same time, not far enough.

There's no room in the sky for the sun. The sky is a never-ending blanket of clouds, grey upon grey, sinking down and filling the land and its furrows with a hard cold hand that breaks the ground. Psomi wheat could never grow here.

More carts and more boxes. Will they ever end? So many people have died because of the flood. The Guild's fault and Psomi too. And before that, Antaia. Angeline. Madame. Paillard, too. Claude. There are so many whose names I don't know. The Efta?

"Where are we going?"

"Where you need to go. To the Efta. Or you can come with us to Greece. Or you can decide to come later"

With Bana tucked and snoozing in my coat, we move as one. Our mule's breath billows out, her back moist with sweat. Another cart passes. How will I find Antaia? When I lost her, I gave up Eleone. To find her I gave up being Epi. Who exactly does that leave me to be?

Bana and Ispanek Take Epi to the Efta

DAWN SLIDES OVER the hill like last night's red blazing sunset over pink Tolosa. But the bridges over the Garonne have gone up in flames, and so the way to find them, and Antaia, is gone.

The path spills us down, and with no other choice, we descend. We walk beside terraced vineyards. In the distance we see fields. With their task complete, their grapes harvested, the leaves rejoice with flames as red as a fire in the wood oven. Fabrizio spoke of them in *Condatóm*. The thick black vines against a purple sky. Relieved of hanging from trees, Bana sleeps in my coat. The wheat fields are slow to arrive. But not so our hope for food. That stays with us always. I look for the chestnut groves that Fabrizio spoke of but see only grapevines.

At a gate, our breath pulses out in a fog. We pass under the arch. The mules' hooves clack on the stone. The sounds carry up the street.

Castres' doors are lined in bronze and inlaid with gold. But they stay strong and silent, letting no snow slip inside when we knock. Signs hang on iron rods and creak in the wind. The mules' back sweats despite the chill.

In the fading afternoon light, we pass houses marked with the signs of tanners, weavers, and dyers. People rush along the banks of the Agout River. Hurrying men wear bright wool hats—curly haired ones like the coats of the sheep. We follow them both to the square, a giant marketplace.

In the center of the square, a fire smokes with thick sticks and dry manure, blocks of straw. A grey cat bounds over to us, He's very skinny with an odd growth in his ear like a cepe, a forest mushroom. He pushes his head against my palm.

I stroke him, pick him up, but he claws and fights. He jumps away. He prefers to rub against the mule's legs and hooves. A large man turns a long spit over a great fire. He lurches a grin at us. The sign strung around his neck proclaims: *Volailles de Montespieu*. He smiles a big smile and offers Bana a spitted bird. I'm shocked when Bana says nothing and takes it.

"They grow fat on grain." The man offers. And as if to prove his point he turns the spit again. The birds' little heads, eyes blackened and dripping juices, flop on the thinnest of necks. He turns the handle and the flames lick at the fat birds and reminds me of running in the field with Beauté', the fire behind us. How Antoine cut me free from the net. A sob bursts out of me.

"Look what you've done now. No kidding. These came through Tolosa," Bana says. As he opens the bird, and the belly is full of steaming grain and pebbles.

Nearby, a wooden board holds brown bread. Above them, a sign reads *la Reine des Châtaigne*. Queen of Chestnut.

"This bread, is it made of chestnuts? And where does it come from?" I ask. Wiping my cheeks and blowing my nose. I can't help but think of Angeline. Térèse. Fabrizio and Antoine.

The man points ahead. "It's not for me to say."

"Then Fabrizio was right."

ISPANEK WEARS STILTS and makes footprints—marking a path up the hill. The stilts have sheep hooves fastened on them.

"Of course. I am doing this to hide the field. Keep it secret from the Guild. There is a whole system. The doves are hateful birds, destroying and eating everything. But they bring the seeds. Not in their bellies. That's stupid."

Bana jumps up. "No, Papa. It's true."

Ispanek kneels down. "Son, stick with the old ways. Let the trees do it. Nets in the trees catch the doves. Then, read and burn the messages. Write new ones. I always say, if you don't like the message. Change it."

Bana stands by me, looking up. "See, Epi, I told you! Take back what's yours."

"You did everything right. Just next time don't get caught," Ispanek says softly.

"But that was the plan. Antoine's plan." Bana says.

"Next time you make your own plan." Ispanek says.

"How did you know where to find Bana?" I ask.

Bana, "He followed the doves, it's what he taught me."

"So you change the messages, Ispanek. Does Fabrizio know that?"

Ispanek says, "Don't let anyone define you. And you know, I'm not always sure what language will work. I search for words. Oc words. Words of Gaul. Guild words. They're all flowing in me. Like the sea far away. I'm a regular poet. You did everything right. But next time? Don't get caught."

After meeting Madame, Fabrizio, Angeline, and Grigne, and Bana, it's clear. "I see now. You're a Mistress too. Like Fabrizio. But wait. Did you die? Like Angeline?"

"I am NOT, definitely NOT now like Fabrizio or NOT ever will I be a Mistress."

"Maybe not you. But your son, Bana, is."

"What? Epi, you're crazy, why are you telling my dad that I'm a Mistress?"

"But, Ispanek, you were at the meeting, right. The one at Madame's, where Margot was put out. Is that when you last saw Maman? With the Efta? I need to find her."

"The meeting, that was the first and last time I saw her, Epi."

In the hills above Castres, we meet a man. He holds a scythe like a shepherd's staff.

"Are there chestnut trees ahead?" I ask.

"*Calquecop le pa que be quand las denses s'en soun anandos,*" he says and smiles a toothless grin.

"Sometimes the bread arrives after the teeth are gone." The man motions ahead. It's hard to tell if he's come from Castres or headed there himself.

At one time the saying sounded strange, but now it's comforting. "Paillard said this all the time. It's an old Oc saying," I tell Bana.

"What does that mean?"

"Are the Efta near the chestnut groves? Over these hills?" My head feels hotter than ever.

"*Cal pos cambia un chabal bornhe per un d'abugle.*"

"He only knows riddles. Listen, he's crazy, "Don't catch fish when you don't have worms?"

"Maybe he's from the Efta. He says "Don't swap a one-eyed horse for a blind one."

The man picks up his scythe. "This land lay between you. Don't ever depart. Each other." He grips his scythe and swings it around our legs as if we might be grain.

I raise my hand, and listen. He backs away. Which is strange since he has the scythe. I lower my arms and ponder what he might mean. Or even if I should care. I do care that this land surely lay between me and Antaia. But really it does lay between me and the Efta. The Guild too. Of that, I care. Maybe he means that Ispanek and Bana and I should never depart each other. Or that the bread and the teeth should stick together.

Then he walks down the hill path, into the sun. As the sun sets, he stops at the gate of Castres, stands, and waves his scythe at us for a long time. Maybe his hope is that this will surely make his meaning clear. I wish it did.

WE TURN FROM the sun and follow the path up the hill. The Agout River still pushes us, and we chase the silver thread from Castres. Tall cedars flank the path. We need to find the chestnut groves, where he last saw the Efta.

The path along the field bears to the right. The wind rushes past. The field is full of harvesters, chopping the frost-nipped shafts. I wrap Ispanek's coat closer and get down off of the mule.

"These are the fields Grigne talked about. The seed that grows near the chestnut trees?"

"We're getting close. Too close. We have to stop here. But you keep going."

"You want me to go alone?" I point to the vast mountain. "To where?"

"To night, to the snow. To the Efta."

"No, wait. I can't."

"You have to." The wind picks up, and echoes the scythed man's words. *Do not swap a one-eyed horse for a blind one.* But I don't have either.

Ispanek swears. "*Le vent Tramontane!* Cursed wind! You're never satisfied, are you?" He raises his fists. "Ha! Tell her, le Cers, old man!"

Maybe I am an old man now. It doesn't sound strange. I move with the stiffness of Paillard. And after they leave, I will sit down and die right here in this cold. Little snowflakes fall from the sky onto my eyelashes.

I close my eyes. Ispanek bends and shouts in my ear. "It's *le vent Sirocco*, little sheep. Sirocco, try a little harder, climb harder up the face of this mountain, just try to keep us from coming down or her from going up, you coward!" he yells.

I am not sure if he means the wind is the coward—I surely know I am. I would do anything to make them stay. But then I remember how many times that didn't work. How many times and how hard I tried to not be alone. How heartbroken I was to find Claude dead. To walk away from Térèse. Watch Grigne fall with Beauté' in the water. Watch Antoine walk away.

I grab Bana to steady myself. He hands me a pair of sheep hoof stilts. "Epi, we'll go up to that ridge with you. Walk like this."

I slip on the ice.

"*Autan*," Ispanek implores the air. "Hurry before *Noir* rises up over that ridge," he booms, then jumps up in his stilts. If I wasn't so sad, I'd die from laughing. This is Psomi's trick to keep the Guild from finding the fields? If I had worn sheep stilts when I left Ceres, my tracks would have been hidden and just maybe I would have found Antaia by now.

"Go on," he says to me. "Hurry."

"I need my horse."

"Speak up." He snaps.

Snow swirls around. A horse comes down the trail. The mist covers her. I hear her hooves, slipping on the rocks. She runs right past me. I slip and tumble to the edge of the path.

Bana leans over. Reaches out his hand. "Take back what's yours, Epi."

Through the white cloud of flakes the horse turns around. The horse runs close to me, and I scream. She disappears into the falling snow. Wait. I hear her hooves again, she's coming back. She stops in front of me. Breathing heavily. Is it really you, Beauté'? You didn't die. I really don't want to go on, because if I go further, maybe I'll die. Maybe I did die. I can't see what's ahead. Maybe Grigne. Maybe Térèse. I get up. I have so much to ask her. Tears run down my cheeks and freeze.

Ispanek's hand fights to keep his hat against his brow. He holds the side of the mountain and digs his stilts into the snow covered muddy path. Beauté follows, trotting. He shrugs, ditches his stilts and climbs up on her. And turns back around. "Do you hear that?"

The wind howls.

"*Le Vent Marin*—you witch, you haven't been heard from for ten years. It was you who cursed me, brought me here from the Mediterranean. But help guide this little ewe out to the path."

He snaps her reins. Beauté wears a frayed rug across her back and steps ahead. The mule slips on the rocky path. Ispanek lights a stick, and it smokes, filling the air around us. He stands with me, and we look out over the valley below. Early yellow light creeps across the snow.

What river is that? The force of the River Jaur passes through, cuts the mountains, and circles a small village, he says. An odd bridge burns with torches. It humps over the river like the wide wings of an owl.

A green signpost says Olargue. An arrow points down toward the humped bridge. Such certainty should give me comfort.

He nods. "Afterwards you take her back home, to the sea." He holds up his hand, missing a finger, and slaps Beauté as she runs by. "Four days from here."

"Beauté came from the sea?"

He takes a draw from his pipe. "She did. You can't remember. We came together ten years ago now."

As if questioning what he means, the wind howls in the distance, baffled at his persistence.

He stubs out his smoke. "Walk down to the bridge. But listen, no matter what you hear, only cross it in the light of day."

"You said we came from the sea? I don't remember any of that. But perhaps Antaia does. Maman."

"Little sheep, I followed the wind around Trinacria, a three-sided island shaped like an eye. It's there that these cursed airs begin. The wind tries to cool the great fire on the island."

I grab his arm. "Don't leave me!"

His eyes darken. "I'm sorry. You belong here."

I could only hear Antoine's words when we were in Tolosa's prison.

Bana belongs here.

"Bana! Don't go. You're leaving me alone. I'll die. I know it."

"Little sheep, listen. Don't let anyone tell you shit." Bana reaches up and touches my face.

The wind howls and screeches. How did I not notice Ispanek's left ear is pierced with a fishhook?

I step away and squint into the snow for the place where the path winds down.

He grabs my coat. "Not so fast. Only in daylight." His eyes twitch nervously.

I sweep my hand toward the bridge. He's Ispanek, prone to telling stories. He's Bana, prone to mischief. Who wouldn't be, to pass the time in these mountains?

"Remember, pass only by day," he grins, his teeth gleaming.

"Bana, you've got to. Find Térèse." The wind swirls our words, every uttering, rushes them over the peaks into the vast sky. "Will you? Send a dove to tell me."

"To which dovecote? It's impossible."

"Fabrizio could do it." My sheep stilts land at my feet. I turn and run after them. But already they are gone.

THE FIFTH TALE

Kesra Matlouh, Snails from the Date
Tree, in Morocco. Paillard.

"A Cado Ausèl Sou Nis Qu'i Es Bèl"
Every Bird Thinks His Own Nest is the Most Beautiful

CHAPTER FORTY-NINE
Epi Walks Alone

A NARROW PASSAGE RUNS between two stonewalls toward the river Jaur. Thick snow shakes off the branches of acacia at the entrance, tangling Beauté's mane. She steps away. I struggle with the branches stuck in her mane. She panics. I break the branches so she can be free. We angle down sideways. A few steps more send me slipping, slanting down. My hands slide along the cold walls. I crawl on the cold ice, unable to stand up, reaching out for Beauté and a strange darkness and lightness of snow falling. Down, still down, like the Allées in Nerac before getting to Madame's. How I wish I was still there. What I would ask Grigne. Antoine.

Beauté clears the passage, and light streams in, and I tumble out and land at the foot of a pine tree, boughs tipped with clusters of cones above my head. The wind shouts and slaps. I pull Ispanek's coat closed. The midday sun tires in the sky and reaches through the snow and looks like a candle coming from some far-off home. There isn't much time left to worry about being warm.

By late afternoon, we come out of the pass through the mountains. I wish for the stilts as we climb up, Beauté ahead, she gallops after the cloud of grey sheep that wear bells and disappear into a hillside forest blanketed in snow. The only sound is of the snow falling. We come out of the forest on the other side. Only to find a new mountain ahead. Snow blows in my face. Beauté?

I find her above a stream that rushes across big stones, and we climb the next mountainside together, huddling close. I forage for cress and onions beneath the snow. Then we catch up with them. The cloud of thick-fleeced straw-flecked sheep. As if nothing dangerous has ever approached them, and they expected us, only one dirty sheep slips behind and coughs out a raspy bleat. Beauté and I slip into their midst, their cream-and-straw-colored rumps, black muzzles, soft and chilled floppy ears. I rub my fingers through their wet wool.

At nightfall, the bridge Ispanek warned me about sits below, we climb and come upon an abandoned sheepfold hidden in the side of the mountain. The cave is ripe with straw and sheep dung, circled with stone and moss. The sheep duck their head and crawl inside on their knees. Beauté follows. And I wonder if she is reminded at all of the fire in the field, and crawling towards the nets. Once inside the fold, the sheep heap upon each other like a litter of fat kittens. The massive ram, his golden horns curled like great snail shells around his ears, sleeps in the gateway of the fold, snoring and protecting the ewes. Stray bits and pieces of something Paillard told me one winter flood back to me.

"The spiral lives everywhere. Doves eat the snails to help them see, the spiral keeps going." And then Paillard handed me a snail bread, wrapped around a handful of chopped dates and spices that he claimed had come from Morocco.

"Why Morocco?" I asked.

"I stayed one winter when the doves flew south. It was where I lost, we lost, Ausel."

I didn't know he had tried to follow Maman by following her dove, Ausel. What of Maman's imperative? *Listen. Follow the doves.*

I followed *Aubada. And* she died to bring the message about Bana having been arrested. I take off my boots. And peel back the blue fabric from my feet, but it clings. I pull harder. Underneath, the hills of my feet are nothing but blisters and raw valleys. Tears wet my cheeks. There is no one. No friend. No food. I hear her call, the owl. She sits in the tree outside the cave. The bird turns her head. Her two wide eyes search us, wondering why we're disturbing her hunt. She spreads her wings and flies off, going further up into the mountain.

I crawl to the front of the cave. Footsteps and voices pass below us on the bridge. Ispanek was wrong about crossing the bridge. Maybe he was wrong about the Efta. Maybe I got it wrong. Maman always said to listen, but it's not easy to do, when there's already so many thoughts crowding your brain, and your only hope, and you only want to not be alone, and to get warm in the light of a fire.

A frozen fog blankets the river. The torches on the bridge below burn their halos well into the night. My eyes close, and breathe with the sheep. But the bright light keeps me from sleeping. But maybe not sleeping is all that's keeping me alive.

In the morning, the light flattens, razed to a thinness like the delicate white flesh of a pig. The wool hat covers me, scratches my ears, as I climb down to the bank, Beauté ahead. At the foot of the bridge, I stop to question the tired-looking man begging. He bangs a silver cup against the bridge.

"Good morning, monsieur. Of course, you are troubled."

"What?"

"The look on your face says it all. With so many people parading up and down the bridge every night..who could sleep?"

"Are you crazy? No one crossed this bridge. I was here all night. Alone."

Leaving his bald head open to the cold must have taken away his knowing. I climb up on Beauté.

"Get down. Let your horse cross first. Watch what happens to her," the man yells.

Flurries of snow circle and I get down from her back. The wind gusts me up against her as I walk past her front legs. I fight to keep my hat, but it blows away and dances up before it plummets into darkness. I stand in front and take her reins, handing them loosely in my hand.

We walk out. Thirty-eight, thirty-nine. Beauté blinks against the wind. I pull, but she won't budge. I drop the reins and rub her soft nose. "We're going to…be.."

My words sweep off into the mountains and fall into the gorge.

"One step more ." I walk backward. We share our breath. Warm like smoke.

"Look only in my eyes," I tell her.

Her eyes flame with saffron and flecks of crimson fires, as if lit from a burning apricot tree. Clumps of snow fall from the bridge to the river. Her front hooves slide out on the ice. Beauté, no! Don't give up. I know you need food. How will I help her stand? I am afraid.

Behind Beauté, our steps fill in quickly with snow. The man from where I came, waves his silver cup and disappears in the storm. Maybe he was never really here.

I can't see either side of the bridge—where we're headed or where we left.

Beauté's ears flick off the snow, listening hard. But not to me. I kneel and put my forehead against hers. Her muzzle is frosty. Beauté's eyes reflect the sky.

On the afternoon before I became Epi, I remember Maman. "Where did Beauté come from?" I asked her as we took the sawed logs from the maze of trees off of Beauté"s back and stacked them inside the woodshed.

"A long walk from here."

"What part of Psomi is she?"

"What a good question. The horses from the sea are one of the three Térèses."

Maman pushed her hair, with bits of straw caught in it, behind her ear. Leaves crunched under Beauté's hooves, as she skipped towards me. She was young and trusting. She learned how it felt to be roped to the millstone and walk in circles all day for the Guild, for Claude. Young Beauté scraped the ground and leaned down, getting on her knees, then fell, surprising herself and me and Maman as she rolled around against the flat earth. Maman's knees cracked as she squatted and stroked the forelock off of Beauté's eyes. *She's looking for her home, the sea. Look only in my eyes, and you will find it.* And then Beauté and Maman stood up together.

Beauté's ears pick up and slant forward. The sticks still stuck in her mane make her look like Maman on that long ago day. She gets up.

Whistling comes down the bridge. A figure appears at the other end of the bridge, snow swirling around her as she walks toward us. Her face—she's short. No, tall. Wide, no, slim. The snow melts on my cheeks. I hope for Térèse. I hope for Maman.

CHAPTER FIFTY

Epi Meets the Efta

ON THE OTHER side of the bridge, the ladies sit on the snow-covered rocks. I count six, no eight. But then again, and see seven. Each lady holds the reins of a horse; some mostly black and some off-white, and some with pearly gray muzzles.

Grigne is one of them and breaks the ice in the troughs. Strong warm arms grip me. Waves and waves of grey hair. Beauté steps in and drinks. "I know you. My brother, Epi." she says.

"Grigne, how is it that you're here?" I am not sure why she is calling me her brother. She doesn't remember telling me I had lost my virginity. She doesn't know I am Margot's daughter. But I want to ask her if she walked here or came directly from falling in the flooded river. Or simply, is she dead? Did she die and end up here, and me, am I dead, too? I must be since she told me I would meet death soon enough.

Grigne shrugs. "*Oc.* I did nothing wrong. But you, I am not surprised that you're here, Epi."

Another lady stands nearby, her long arms cross her chest. She raises her equine nose high.

The dark one smiles. A tiny, tiny waist. Blue-black velvet hair covers her beautiful eyes, her round cheeks, her shoulders.

Up ahead on the path, slightly behind the ash tree, stand two more, arm in arm. Twins. The same face, but one is old and crinkle-boned. In her arms, she holds her likeness, a babe. I step closer, and they circle me, drawing me to the center. The old lady twin sets her squirming baby down. Her apricot mouth opens in innocent laughter, and she crawls, then totters to her feet, and runs to me. I clasp her hands, and they are warm as hay and soft. She drops mine and runs away. "Too cold," she laughs.

The morning sky is dark blue. No sun. We walk far away from the bridge.

They touch my face. My hands. Maybe I fell off the bridge and death is where I have landed. I am dead. I must be.

"Come and sit." Grigne's long grey hair has a golden cast.

Beauté steps back. Her ears flick. I hope she's not remembering dying with Grigne.

"How did you get here?" I ask.

"I came from the north." Grigne twists her hair and piles it on her head. It stays up, in a complicated system of coils.

"And I came from the east." The horse lady shakes her head up and down, mirroring Beauté. Her bangs fall in her eyes, she moves them with her long-boned hands.

"How did you find us?" Their hands feed the sticks into the flames. Eyes flutter and blink and their mouths whisper. Their elbows nudge.

My hands stretch over the fire, but I doubt they will ever warm again. "I came from home, the small bread terrace, I thought that was home. But wherever *she* is, that is home." I say.

Shorter than me, she pushes forward, moving around the circle. Her blue-black hair flashes in the firelight with a scent of crushed black pepper and nutmeg. "From all directions, home is found in our bread of dreams. But there is more to tell."

"Yes, I want to tell you everything. But where to begin?" The bread of dreams is easy to make, but to touch the emptiness I keep hidden inside me is much harder. Does it even make sense that making the bread filled in the holes that bread made in me. Who I left. And who left me. I am too tired and cold and hungry to think.

"Of course. The *she* you mention as home, is she Antaia? Térèse?"

"Térèse stayed with her mother, Angeline. Térèse is my home. I lost Antaia in the fire I made." My cold fingers stretch out to warm in the fire. I sit in my hunger and the tears flow out of me. Without Térèse to tell all this too, it doesn't matter. I don't need my stomach at all.

"Epi, our home is here, and yours too. The lands of Psomi. My first land is Persia, Jerusalem, then Greece." Her skin takes on burnished light, like leaves of the chestnut leaves near Fabrizio's.

"Tunisia. Istanbul," whispers Grigne.

"Cimeria," says the old twin. Her eyes command a mix of greens, like the curly lettuce in Térèse's garden.

"Thessaly, then Thrace." The horse lady turns, her equine nose points in the direction of her home.

"She had a lot to do." The dark-haired beauty speaks, necklaces of silver jangle when she pokes the fire.

"HE has to keep moving." The old twin says, her breath takes on pink tones in the firelight.

"Mine." The young twin with curly, red hair, like Antaia, ruffles my hair.

"Look. Her coat of sheep can't hide who she is." Grigne crosses her arms.

"She has to stop. She's seen death." The old twin says.

I laugh. "You're the only one who said I was a he a minute ago, and now you call me, she. Talk to me. I'm here." Is my confusion so obvious? It must be.

"I had the same problem. I had to hide. And eventually I didn't know what I wanted to be. Until I came here." The old twin admits.

This changes the air around us, and the snowstorm clears away. They blink. They come close, hug me. And I soften into their folds, their soft, clean scents like new milk and hay.

"Your hair, umm, smells like toasted coriander."

"Oh, you are Antaia's daughter. There is no doubt. Is she with you?" the horse woman asks.

"Is she supposed to be?" I ask.

"What have you done with her? I told you! Antaia never made it to my home, Rome." The old lady twin sits down hard on a rock.

I slump down to this, and everything collapses again. One minute passed. But here is the question I set out with. Did I kill her? I still don't know.

Her red hair floats out, furious, around her shoulders. "What about her sister?

"Have you met her yet?"

"Margot? They forced me to walk with her. She's mean. I lived with her. And.."

"Margot never came here. But you did." Grigne totters closer. She hovers, it seems, like a bird, and sways. She touches my hands, opens them and rubs circles with her knuckles on my palms. She leans close.

"When I last saw Antaia, at the meeting at Madame's," Grigne says. "She was happy. And when you came in, I thought you were her."

"Was she? Happy?" I had not felt the weight and loss of Antaia until I spoke of her, but in the time between me looking for her, and wondering if I had killed her, I had one vision in mind. I knew I didn't. I couldn't. How she was when I was ten years old. How she was for me. To me. But now *that* Antaia and *that* time were gone.

"That Antaia you're thinking about? She is dead."

They are right. But I hope not because I killed her. Here, with the Efta and in the mountains, she lives. Maybe she came here to die, unlike Grigne who died and then came here. I am safe. Am I safe? Margot is surely looking for me. I look up and they are all standing by, their eyes turned on me waiting for me to say something. As if I am the keeper of Antaia, my Maman, instead of Maman keeping me.

The grey, black and white horses, the mares of the ladies, nicker in the stand of trees nearby. Snow falls off the branches onto their hooves. Beauté moves closer and talks with them.

We huddle close. The ladies build a fire from trees, like Maman did from the maze of trees in the North Field.

Plum. Fig. Apple. And Walnut. Then we gather and sit at the foot of the flames. We poke and stir sleep from the ashes with smooth tipped branches, and throw more wood on the fire as easily as if their trees were as light as sheaved wheat.

They hand me a branch of the apricot tree, and I toss it in the fire.

"What I think," the small one with blue-black hair begins, "Is that Antaia wanted your father, Artos, to journey with her to Ceres, and that he loved her. But she understood he couldn't leave. She loved him anyway. It's too bad how Margot got involved."

Oh my god, my father, Artos. And Margot. I am shocked. Artos was who Antaia loved. Maybe. I think of how I argued with Antoine. And how I feel about Fabrizio. Was this the same? Maman let him go, but she took his child he had with Margot. Me. So, that might have been hard for her in so many ways. Except, no, Antoine didn't love me. Did Artos love Maman? My hands look old in the firelight. Beauté rests, her one hoof cocked against the ground. She seems gone from this world.

"Maman trusted everyone. Too many," I say.

The old twin makes a harrumph in her throat. "Too many!"

The flames curl around the apricot log I had thrown on the fire. Was Maman trapped in her tree? "Where is she?" I ask.

The small twin sits across the circle, rests her face in her hands. "*Prend la vie de feu.* Look for her in the fire."

"Is she alive?" I ask.

"You tell us. Try to see her," says the lady from Persia, her burnished skin reflects the fire.

"Both are there. Safely held inside. *Mar i Cel.*"

They fall quiet, all of them nodding. *Mar i Cel.* The sea and the sky. Such an old tale.

"There's a tale?" I whisper and the ladies repeat. Chanting. Then the tears come.

"Each of us keeps a sea and sky inside."

"It sounds like something Antaia said. But I can't remember."

"Does it now?"

Sheep wearing bells pass by. Ispanek's sheep? Or maybe it's the wind tearing my thoughts away, and rebuilding them in the deep dark. Maybe this is the place I heard, so many nights when I leaned out of the bread terrace. It can't be. There's no music. No feasts. But I am so hungry. The old one snores, and the young twin pushes her over on her side. She hands me a paper wrapped piece of cheese. I nibble at it like a mouse. It's hard. And crumbly. It's not cheese, but it is sour, with many seeds. Then it hits me. It's *Trakhanas*, like the seedcakes I made with Antaia. Like the ones that disappeared from the box during my ceremony. The voices and footsteps cross the bridge, the *pont du diable*, in the distance, long into the dark. Finally, I sleep.

IN THE MORNING, the air is cool. I love sleeping outside with only the sky over my head. I sit up. Rest my arms on my knees. The six ladies' rouse from their straw piles and scoot close to the fire, surrounding me, and holding their hands close to warm them. It's nice but scary too. What do they want? I smile but I wish I could just hide under the straw again. Before I got here, I was alone for a long time. Then on the way here, I didn't want to be alone. But now that I am here, I'd still like to be alone. Maybe I can trust them. I need them. I do. I hate that. I don't know how to not be Epi. The boy who brought me here. All this way. What do the ladies want to teach me? Or, I swallow hard. Or maybe I am supposed to teach them something. Ispanek said I need to be here. I am glad to be here. I don't want to need to be here. I don't want to think about anything they have to tell me.

One lady shows me her work as she pushes a thick needle in and out of rust-colored leather in palm shapes. It feels as natural as can be to work outside under the sky. Like it did with Maman.

"Help us make more gloves so we can pick chestnuts. The trees live on the other side of the forest."

Our tight circle joins hands. On this side of the *pont du diable*, the air warms from the fire. Flakes of snow swirl in the sky above the trees. The wind takes the snow back across the bridge. The fire crackles with trimmings of apple, cherry, fig, walnut, plum, and pear. The fire consumes them, and new trees will grow from their ashes.

"I did what you said. I tried to see her in the fire." I hand them more wood. They put a pot on the fire and pour in a bottle of wine. It hisses and they all stand around and breathe it in. Grigne throws in whole garlic cloves. Uses a giant wooden spoon to stir it around, some splashes out of the fire. Grigne still stirs garlic into everything.

"Add the rosemary."

"Or maybe this isn't the right fire. Is Antaia on an island called Trinacria?" I remember what Ispanek said.

"That's possible," Grigne says. She furrows her brow at me. I don't know if she's trying to be helpful or if she's lying. Maybe since she's dead, she doesn't care.

One stands, hooks a basket over her arm, and goes to the bushes that line the path that winds up into the mountain. She plucks something from the bushes and drops them in the basket.

She walks back and shows them to me. Little snails from the spiky bushes in the early morning light. Wild thyme, mint and rosemary branches in the basket too. She turns them, and when her finger touches their wet moist flesh, they retreat.

She plops the snails in her boiling garlic broth, floating with dried fennel seeds and shoots of wild onion. I remember what Paillard said. Doves eat snails to see further.

"Antaia's wisdom has grown in you, but it is not yet over."

"You liked it well enough the other night. You're making it too hot. Move it off the fire. Stir *Trakhanas* until it's thick. It will thicken your child."

"My child?" I didn't think I could keep being Epi and pregnant at the same time. But then if they think I'm pregnant they might already know I'm not a boy.

"Eat more. It's happened to all of us."

I don't know which part they mean happened to all of us. Being a boy and becoming a girl or being pregnant. I stir the sour milk with onions, and thyme, black cumin, a little coriander. How different this feast tastes, than when I was ten and with Antaia in Ceres. We made this the night of my ceremony when I became Epi. I look over and imagine Antaia sitting cross-legged next to me, our knees touching. I open my palm, and their fingers prance over the lines. "Eat. There is still much water between you and her," they hand me a bowl heaped with *Trakhanas*.

"This needs more broth. So, she's across the sea?"

"All the Mistresses make *Trakhanas* differently. It's possible that's where she is. But you should stay. Antaia could still come back. We love being with you. Besides, you need rest, and to wait for your baby to be born. Antaia would say the same thing."

Grigne pounds raw garlic, and her gray hair flies forward with the effort. She rubs threads of saffron between her palms over my bowl. "Do you know how we get it? Where it comes from?"

"I don't have any idea. But one thing I do know." I point to the mortar and pestle where she's pounding garlic. "*Faire monter l'aïoli.*"

"The saffron is pulled from their safe world. Their world inside the crocus, their brittle beings are both sharp, fragile and sweet." Grigne says.

I feel both shocked and amazed that saffron can be so small and be so many things. And looking at the threads makes me feel just as small and as fragile as when I was pulled from my little world, too, the bread terrace. Looking at them, I forgot their question about Maman. This world is safe and though it's in the mountains, from here I can see a larger world. The world with the ladies is small and safe, delicate with perfumes, sacred with understanding, too. I know this is the feast I smelled and have been headed towards for a long time. With the Efta I would always, and could always be fragile, sharp and yet sweet. Everything I need is here. But I forgot their question.

"Yes, but don't forget, *Prend la vie de Feu*," she mutters.

"Of course. *Prend la vie de Feu?*" I laugh. And repeat it to myself. It gives me chills. *Prend la vie de Feu.* I remember this. I know this. But it feels like it's been so long since I heard it that it feels as if the words have changed, as much as I have.

"*Oc, Prend.*" she insists. "Take the life of the fire. This wind makes it possible to take the life of the fire on the island…

"Follow the path to the grove of chestnut trees."

"It's not a grove. It's one tree big enough to protect a hundred of our horses." The ladies look up. Their hands cover their mouths.

"Take the life of the fire, say it together." We stand and dance.

"Take the life of the fire."

"What does it mean?"

"Burn the earth. Return to Spring. Fire can destroy. Or grow new things."

Around the fire, they blow through flutes carved from trees, sunflowers, and bones, the flames go crazy. The music hits me in the small place where I find Eleone. It's a dangerous place to feel like Eleone, a girl, and now a woman. It's also dangerous to stay Epi. I wonder about Madame Bouquin. She knew Grigne, Antoine, Fabrizio, Auvillar. Angeline? Madame kept the strange fireflute of the man and the woman. Maybe it was more than just a fireflute. Maybe she needed to keep the fire flute close because she kept the secrets of so many men and women in Nerac, and of all the Mistresses. I shake my head and return to listening. If I can listen openly to the Efta maybe I can hear more of what Maman told me when I was little Eleone.

"Epi means ears. You have to listen. Follow the doves."

"The sky can send gentle wind to feed a fire. But the sky can also send fierce winds and kill the fire."

Feed a fire, or destroy the fire. The line between the two is very close. The fire in the field the night Maman left came from the fire we had made the bread of dreams over, earlier. That fire helped Maman get away. Maybe the Mistresses all blew on that fire, that helped her get away. It was the bread of dreams that helped her leave. The fire in the field the night with Antoine, helped me find Eleone. And the next minute the great winds in the mountains rush down. I try to hold my hair down, but they grab me, and we hold each other, falling over, our coats closed and we laugh, holding each other and smashing out sparks in our hair, when the wind blows the flames of the fire high into the sky. Then just as quickly, the wind blows the fire out. In that moment I feel as strong as the sky. I feel as if I can be the sky, and send a big wind to spread the fire, or a small breeze to feed the fire; take the life of the fire. Whatever is needed most. I am filled with the same feeling as the night before Maman left, how wonderful the fire is, the closeness and understanding, being seen by the Efta. And just like Maman leaving, the knowledge that it can quickly change.

"So, wait. Did Antaia take the fire to the island of Trinacria? Is that what you're saying?" I could stay with them. I wouldn't have to be alone. I wouldn't have to be a boy here. I look down at my pants. My shirt. How long has it been since I bathed in the river without being afraid? Never. I could dress as I wanted in ever expanding colorful wraps of cloth like the Mistresses. I could be Eleone. I could be finished with my journey. But I look up at them. Kind faces. Stern smiles that soften. It's kind of like being where I was at the bread terrace. I'm getting one life, but not what I set out to find. This life would be an easy life. Companionship. Peace. No conflict. Except with Grigne who is angry with me. I know she is. Here I would be cared for. And I could learn to care for them. Trust them. I could stop driving to keep going. I could stop. I would have a place. It wouldn't be my place though. It would be turning my back on what I thought I wanted to return to. That was their question. It was Angeline's question too? I need to return to me. If I stay, I'll be content, I will have to be. I would give up being lost. That would be nice. Give up feeling lost without Antaia. I've been lost for so long. But then I realize it's not the same. I want to give up being lost. But I still need to learn the answers. Because without the answers, I won't be found. And neither will Antaia. The name makes my heart feel soft. I don't know why she decided to be my mom. I just want to hear her story. To listen. I don't think I am but if I am pregnant, that's easy. I have to go. Because I have questions for Antaia. I can't keep to the mold of the Efta and stay. I want to make a commitment to my child. And if I am pregnant, I see another side of how complicated it must have been for Antaia to take me and Térèse. And for Angeline. I have come too far to stop. I can't not keep going like a dove. See the spiral. Follow it. I have to know if Antaia's still alive.

I feel sad too, as one of the women wraps a round of cheese in hay, then in linen, and warms it in the coals. It catches fire, but she pats out the flames and gives it to me. "Ewe's milk is good for vision."

"Thank you. Is it good for listening?" I share the roasted hay with Beauté and taste the rich flavors of the cheese. In the fire the faces of the sheep from the mountains appear, their eyes full of deep trust.

"Why did Maman start her journey?" I say, wiping my mouth.

"Because of the seeds. She left them for you. In the thatched roof. In the doves. Was there a box?"

"Both boxes are gone, too." Quiet, I stare at each. My eyes fall on the young twin. "Antaia's leaving and losing the box, both of them, was—it's all my fault."

"Not at all. If it's meant for you, it will return." The young twin speaks.

"We follow the Orb River, to where the chestnut trees grow along the wind-dried path to the sea. The trees came from your tree. Antaia planted them to guide you."

THE ORB RIVER flows like a silver thread and winds and meets the River Jaur. The Jaur flows into the Orb. We walk sometimes and ride sometimes, the horses keep along the rocky path of the Orb, stones fall and meet the path below us as we wind down out of the mountains. I might forget everything about the River Jaur. Except it is still with me, as it was the river Beauté and I crossed to meet the Efta, and so it is still part of the Orb. How does a river decide when to disappear? We walk through the towns of Vieussan and Roquebrun.

"This day, today, proves that we can move ahead, even without Antaia."

For them to mention this, seems telling. I know how they feel. Then, the wind bites back, and it is a cold wind that reddens their cheeks. When the wind bites hard, I feel the hollow places, the lost moments, even more. Move ahead without Antaia. I wish Térèse was here to talk to. To listen to. I wish I knew that Ispanek and Bana aren't lost. To know what they know. Or maybe just different things.

"Epi, I hope you're proud." Grigne says. "I know I am less angry with you, brother."

"Don't call me your brother. You hope I'm proud, and you are less angry with me?" I almost fall into her; I am so tired that I can't stop walking. I nod, out of habit to agree and not cause problems. But then I shake my head, no. I can't go along and not say anything. "Why should I be proud? And why are you angry with me? I haven't done anything. In fact, I did what you said."

Grigne's face brightens and falls. "So, it's your fault. I died. I'm here. And you are too."

"No, I came here. I looked. It's different. But you're angry. Because what you did caused so much death."

"So what, that is true for what Antoine did and how Claude died."

I listen. I hear her. I don't want to argue with her. Maybe the best I can do is tell her my truth. "Look, I don't like it. This is bigger than you. Than both of us. You told me that once."

"I don't like it either. Can you forgive me?"

"And how about what happened to Beauté because of your action?"

Grigne says "She's fine. Everything we do impacts someone else. So what? I made a choice and I'm ok with that. Because, do you know why? If I had made the choice to not blow the dam, then, well, who knows what might have happened? You have to decide and then move on down the road. Accept that."

"Or move on up the road to the Efta. Here. How many times have you been here?" At that moment I didn't think I had changed at all. The Efta could see inside me and see the change about to happen, like when one day of sun can change a plum flower into a red plum, juicy and ripe with purple softness.

"We're stopping." All the ladies sit. "The seed ceremony, let it begin tonight."

"Thank you." I sigh and feel relief. But one look at Grigne and I knew it wasn't over between us.

"The ceremony, it's for you. You must stay. Your eyes, look ahead. But you have no need to leave."

I am tired. But more and more I feel sad, because I can choose, stay or leave, and that makes me think I must. But I don't want to be running on, just running away from Grigne, or for the sake of running to the next mountain. Or the next field. The next tree. Or Mistress. But I have to tell them I'm leaving. I'll tell them tonight.

For one whole day, we walk and search for the grove of chestnut trees. Their nuts. For wild onions. I think of what to say to them tonight, while we bend and pick wild plants to grind. We hold hands on the steep trail down. For me there's never been a more perfect moment. The sun falls over the late afternoon. They sing. The scent of rosemary drifts from our hands to our hair. They are good. They are.

Then, the old lady twin with copper hair and skin falls. We wait, pick her up and check her legs. She limps and we put her on Beauté's back. The horses go slowly. We pass a large rock outcrop, and we hug close to its cheeks and go down the neck, the southern slope, as the sun glows behind the clouds. The smallest, the apricot child, holds my hand, tightens her fingers through mine. Her eyes are luminous pale blue, like the sheep's. Her red curls bounce along her cheeks, plump with a hint of red sun like the fruit in Maman's fragrant apricot tree.

We find the grove of chestnuts. And it's wide and expansive. The trunks of the trees wind with the roots. The branches like arms wrapping us. The forest, ancient. Listening.

As I build the fire that evening, the young twin drags a log toward the flames, and I lift the other end with her, and together we drop it on the burning twigs. It crushes them, and sparks shoot into the evening. She might be a Mistress about to be set free. Or one starting over. Maybe she doesn't know. Tonight, it's not even important.

They pierce bitter oranges and squeeze the halves, the juices run over the roasting *lapin*. Their rich skins form a crust, crackly sweet and salty, and at the last minute we all crush the long peppercorns on the wood with our stones and dust the roasting meat.

"In the fire, we find Psomi," the lady from Jerusalem, Persia, and Greece says. "And you will, too."

"You can choose, to stay Epi or become Eleone. Mistresses come here to have babies. Angeline had Térèse here. And Antaia left with Angeline, you and Térèse."

"Was Margot here too?"

"No, when Antaia was here with you, you were 3 or 4 years old? I forget."

"Look, I see no signs that I am pregnant. I ..only ..once."

"We do not say in this moment or that moment that there is right or wrong. No right and no wrong. It is just a moment. And there will be another one. Yes, just now. See? Another moment."

"It's your choice."

"And we will be here, if you come back. Like Grigne does. We see her all the time."

"But Antaia never did. Never came back?"

"You're right. Never."

"There is a vision of us outside of here. We can't fix anything. Solve anything. You can stay here. Make fires. Make a bread of dreams every day. Pick onions. Grow trees. Make honey. The hand things connect the spirit things."

"What's the deal with the fire," I ask."

"What do you think?"

"I don't know. Fire is like a moment."

"Like people."

"People can't be controlled. Sometimes people destroy, like fire."

"Sometimes people change, like fire transforms. Changes," I say.

"Instead of trying to reclaim old things, make something new. Let go. Who you were, let him go. Return to the fire."

"I have to keep going. Finish my journey. But I can't just leave Epi, Either. He got me here."

"Epi will teach you how to remember Eleone. Or how to be Epi and Eleone. And for Eleone, how to bring Epi along."

The wind picks up and makes the flames of the fire stronger. There's a space in me that says maybe. Maybe I am stronger than when I left the bread terrace. No one can decide but me, who I am, or need to be. Epi or Eleone?

The trees sway overhead, and out of the corner of my eye, the trees all turn to being Mistresses. Each lady brings out a bread of dreams.

One crust is pressed with purple rosemary, borage and yellow flowers of tarragon. One bread holds the delicate scent of saffron with wheat berries.

Grigne steps forward with a gorgeous flat bread.

"You trust me, don't you?"

She cracks off a piece. Inside sleep soft garlic cloves.

"Faire monter l'aïoli."

The old twin moves to me, and I take up her bread drizzled with green oil, salt and honey.

"Burn the earth and return to Spring."

They stand around me in a circle. Each places a new bread in my hands and I break it apart and pass it along. I chew each taste, rich with sweet spices and fire, the bitterness of walnuts. The roots are earthy with dirt, fruits are tender like they are from the trees in Antaia's maze, our maze. The trees that we cut down together and stored in the woodshed. Building the woodshed. All those moments of the field. The fire. The wood-shed. The ceremony that went wrong. But all these paths led me to the Efta, to my family. And suddenly, I realize Antaia is my mother. Her care of me, choosing me. Eleone. Choosing me. The ladies sit next to me, in this circle. It's not that I think Antaia was heartbroken to leave. She didn't belong in Ceres. Once she stepped away from me, she could protect Psomi. But by leaving me as Epi, she protected Eleone. And planted the seeds to listen, to return to the Efta, and return to the place

where she is my mother, one day, and even, maybe, to find her.
I can call the Mistress, Antaia, my Maman again. And I long
to tell her. I am listening. I hear you.

They give me a linen wrap for the fougasse, lined with lacy
green leaves.

"Seaweed from the Camargue."

Beauté excitedly sniffs.

"And what have you brought?" asks the lady with burnished
skin from Persia, she reminds me more and more of Madame
Bouquin.

"My bread of dreams with apricots and roses." I say. "Is your
name Quert?"

"I have many names."

It doesn't matter, her name. "I brought trouble. No one likes
to answer these questions."

"No one can. So, stay. There is no reason to leave."

I think of Antaia's box, which was empty at my 10 year old
ceremony into Psomi, that I found in the woodshed so long ago.
And Bana's box that he made. If I had that, I could answer these
questions. Feel like I have done good. Something right. Tears roll
down my face. "Who am I to be here? I lost them, the seeds."

"What we lose we must set free."

"I lost the seeds, and me too. I was lost, and yet, and maybe
until I find her, I will always be lost."

"Let me assure you. Antaia is smart. There wouldn't have
been just one box."

I stop at hearing them say this too. Bana, he might still
have the box.

"And you are not lost, not at all. For here you are. You found
us. You lost her, and so you must set her free."

Could I do that? Not look for her. I must look for her, ask
her, and then, I don't know, is my task to set her free, as she did
me. I don't know. But something new bothers me, what if she
didn't set me free either?

"What if she wonders where I am?" My stomach settles when I ask that. I just don't think she knows, and maybe she wonders too. And I don't think she died either.

"You must stay. You have no need to leave."

I bend my head and think about this journey. Making my bread of dreams. But after so long of waiting, missing my time at the dough trough, grinding the seeds and the plants, chopping herbs, folding and pressing the apricots inside and lighting the fire; will my hands remember this work? But I know in my heart. I want to wait to make the bread of dreams. Wait until I find Antaia. My fingers itch to pull the reins back on Beauté', her warmth between my legs. The land unfolding before us. I long to do what I must, head down the mountain and out to the sea. These Mistresses have been so generous. Taken me in. Even though Maman isn't here, and they haven't seen her, I don't think she's lost. They helped me find something I didn't have before. Or someone. Eleone. How to do this? How can I leave Epi, who's brought me this far? Being Eleone means not being afraid to leave them, like Maman left me. Or maybe it's the difference in seeing and listening to the world, like I did when I was with Maman. Like when Epi was with Margot and had to shut out her cutting words. Maybe Eleone tells Margot to keep her words. And maybe Eleone has been with me, and longs to ask Maman to share her tales, again, the ones I heard but didn't keep, and live in her world. Like the sea and the sky.

In the morning, I will, Eleone will, tell them I'm leaving.

We pass a young apricot tree pushing out from a crack on the mountainside.

"What do you need to make your bread of dreams?"

"It's not what, it's who."

"Find your way to the great chestnut tree. The fields live beyond that."

"The tree lives as a grove near olive and blood oranges, across the sea. This old tree gives still and remains for another thousand years. In spring, her trunk splits with four, and then five, slender green trunks."

Doves roll in the red dirt; it dusts their feathers like flour. *Prend la vie de feu.*

"Close your eyes and walk. From these mountains take the winding path, look and see easily. Like a dove."

"But how does no one know this chestnut tree? How will I know where to find her?"

"Her tale says the tree lives on a hill."

"That's not true, the tale lives at the end of the field where our wheat grows tall."

"Pah, it's in the middle of an open meadow filled with wild garlic."

"That lives on the way to Mt. Etna."

"A meadow can live on a mountain?"

"No, it's in a field surrounded by the sea."

"What I knew when I started, is very different from what I know now."

"You've been searching for her fields, her wheat."

"Many Mistresses, long ago, stayed in that place, and lived. Where they are now, I don't know."

While we prepare and pack to leave for Roquebrun, I uncover my feelings about Antoine. Who was he when I left Ceres? I am sad that he isn't with me, but he has the chance to find himself. But then again, who am I to say if he has or if he hasn't?

I take the new *fougasse* from Grigne and wrap the bread, shaped like a leaf, with the seaweed linen. The openings in the bread mark the path. Or maybe the openings are the water, and the bread forms the path. There's something about it, this bread, which makes me feel it is both. That I am both.

We finish the last pair and pack the hand-stitched gloves for picking chestnuts in Beauté's pannier. We all gather branches and twigs from fallen trees and carry them. I kick the dirt over the smoldering coals with the horse woman. Inside my boots, my feet are cold. The horse woman takes off her boots, and I push mine off too. We walk over the ground with our bare feet, the earth is cool, but if I stand still I can feel the heat beneath. One minute more and my feet will burn. We step out on the path, our boots over our shoulders.

Eleone couldn't say anything. That she was leaving. That she was happy. I slip my boots back on and with Beauté, we lead the Efta. The herd plays and nicks at Beauté's heels, and we gallop ahead on the path, the shade of trees to the north and the sun to the south. Maybe then.

"It will take five days for all of us to cross the mountains. Five days to reach the village of Roquebrun and the chestnut trees along the Orb River that leads to the sea."

I could go more quickly alone, but I'm listening. My ears are the spirals, the maps. I think of other questions to ask about Antaia in this time. But the wind tears them away. Once we're in Roquebrun, I will say goodbye.

"It's going to rain, you know. And I should not be walking at all." The old twin with coppery hair says the next morning. She wrings her hands, twisting them together. The others walk ahead and disappear. But I slow and walk with her.

"Oh? We can stop."

"No, just pass me if you wish." The old twin walks each step as though it were her last, but her eyes glow like the polished wood of Madame's bouffe, fireflute. Her skin gleams, rubbed with almond oil. "I will walk last, behind you, and protect you from your past."

I walk a few paces slightly ahead, but then slow to her rhythm, stepping beside her and leaning close. Of all the people I have met on this journey, they all have a past that they need protection from. Except maybe Bana. He would stomp the ground and chase it away. As we speak, I take glances behind us. There is only one set of footprints.

On the path ahead, the fallen leaves curl up, their edges tipped in frost; they lay against each other for warmth. Grigne appears in the distance, stopping at the hawthorn tree. She shouts and stoops to the ground. Her long fingers caress the roots, her nose piqued over the fallen branches. She calls out again and points to a hoard of tiny flies, then uncovers a forest of mushrooms.

These mushrooms have a lot to say, she informs us all. A kiss of pepper and, if some is left in the goat skin, an aged wine in the pot.

I smell them greedily, these roots of trees, for their perfume hints on things buried and gorgeous and deeply haunting; the wild boar that plows up the woods is in search of them and will not stop. I sit up and see the sun setting and know that all the beauty I have seen and felt in visiting the Efta is like the tender and soft garlic cloves—once fire-y and tipped with green, but then softened in the fire. All the Mistresses have been hurt in fighting the Guild. Once I was Epi, but now as Eleone, the measure of who I am has changed inside, too. And outside of me, the hard things like the wild boars with tusks, and the sharpness of the Guild, is never thwarted from taking the mushrooms that grow next to the tree roots, and so too that means that Margot must not be far behind. When I see her, if I do, I will know by how I feel if I am Eleone. But then I shake my head, no, I am Eleone with or without seeing Margot. I don't need to see Margot or Maman to know I have returned to being Eleone.

Love, they say. Love, always. Never be afraid to set it loose, for it to come back.

CHAPTER FIFTY-ONE
Epi Arrives in Massalia

Navettes Of Marseilles—Anise Seeds
and The Apricot Tree. Maman.

"Better a wren in the pan than a goose in the sky." *Ibal mès un repetit à la padeno qu'uno auco que bolo à la sereno.*
The next morning, I walk around the circle they make. We are leaving, I love you, and I will set all of them loose.

I don't know if Mistresses tell each other these things. But I will. How much I will miss them. But I don't have to ask how much they will miss me too. They link their arms with mine.

Maybe it isn't even possible to measure all the love, all the ways that Maman felt. Antoine. Térèse.

After I tell them, I lift up on Beauté's back, she stands taller, her back is straighter. We crossed a bridge to meet the Efta's world a lifetime ago. Rocks tumble down, as we walk into the forests puffing smoke along the mountain path. Forest villages sit on the foothills, and a light dusting of snow falls over their few houses and trees. We pass through their stone gates, and out again, always moving to the south.

The sea comes closer, its briny sting sets in my nose. The air slows Beauté's hooves. Shades of the fire and sunflowers in the sky.

Another river, the Rhone. How much water yet lay between us, Maman? Ispanek said that he followed the wind around the three-sided island of Trinacria, the wind that tried to cool the big fire. What about Antaia's saying, "Take the life of the fire." Is this the fire she meant for me to return to? I have never been to this fire. I have been so focused on what I need that I never even considered whether Antaia needs me, and not the other way around. Grigne taught me it's bigger than me. And it is. Who knows how Antaia is and what she needs? On my last morning on the bread terrace Paillard came to warn me about the Guild. Paillard said, "It keeps going. The shell, the snail feeds the doves. I am blind, but I see everything. Close your eyes. Find the doves. Follow their path to the fields. There in your mind's eye."

Paillard is a Mistress too. I lived with him nearby for so many years but never saw him. Never saw his truth. Blood rushes through me, I am so foolish! It's even more important to find Antaia, and see her. See who she is. Before it's too late.

I have followed her path in reverse. How many of Psomi's grains were planted in the North Field? Maman would not foolishly plant all of Psomi's seeds in one field. There were fields near *Condatóm* with Fabrizio, then more fields near Angeline & Grigne. How many fields is that? The fields leading to the Efta. Antaia kept the seeds in the box, but which box? If they are safe, they can still grow. *Follow the doves* to Antaia.

Flies buzz and dogs' bark. I rest my hand on Beauté's rump. If I let go, I'm afraid I'll collapse. I stand tall and walk straight. I fight what she is feeling. How did she get better from our time in the mountains when I feel so tired? Beauté, let the sun warm us, this age of sun beating down along the shore, la Gacholle. The russet red flesh of the salicorn grasses crunch underfoot, as if we were crunching coals left from the fire with the Efta. I walk with her along the Camargue. The land moves by us, slowly, like a dream. The mounds of white that were snow near Olargue now sift through my fingers as if my new flour. These hills look pink.

"Beauté, go." I can't hold on to her if she truly needs to go. Herds of white horses follow the black bulls across the sand flats. Beauté gallops ahead with the white horses. The bulls stay at arm's length. Slowly, I follow. Carefully. Beauté's nostrils flare, steam escapes. I follow her, walking beside strong haunches and hooves through the salt marshes. Every mouth feeds on the grasses, showing Beauté what to do. The clouds mingle with blue sky, each rolling over each other, hurried by the salt and the wind. Beauté eats the fleshy grass. Her white legs swim in the sea. The saltwater washes my feet.

In the evening light, I sit on a small hill above the beach under the pines. Birds glide toward the orange sun, their wings spread wide. I sit a long time. Night begins. And the stars come out. Térèse what did she say, to always guide us? The Milky Way? I sleep next to Beauté where the bulls melt into the sky and the dark sea.

WE CROSS THE Grand Rhone delta, and salt fills our breath. My thoughts move east toward Massalia. We cross the Golfe de Fos. I scramble on a boat, then a cog full of horses and goats. We get dumped in the port of Lavera. Beauté and I escape being sold to another ship, and bend around a curve of land, Cap Couronne. As large as Tolosa, the city ascends up into the hills. The sunlight falls over it.

At Niolan, another boat guides us between the great rocks. I know it's crazy to trust him just because he looks like Paillard. But when he takes Beauté on board and not in the barge transport for other horses, I know it's ok.

"Steady in the middle, don't hold the sides. She needs to suck in her breath through the Calanques," the seafarer says.

"Is this Trinacria?"

He shakes his head. "You might as well ask for Greece, my home. Trinacria is nowhere near here."

The seafarer turns back to steering, his boat, armed with nets and hooks gets caught on an island of rocks. Their will to hold us is as strong as ours to get away. The waves splash up, and the salt makes my eyes shriek with blindness. Like Paillard. I try to see in my mind's eye what might be next and how to get to Maman.

The tip of our boat wedges into the rocks. The boatman scoops the nets up and dives in the water. He brings fish aboard, and an eight-armed creature he calls *polpi*. White squawking birds perch and smash the curled shells, like snails, in their beaks on the rocks. My feet and Beauté's hooves rest. The sky swirls with calling birds pushing our boat, and quiet waves steer us into the horseshoe-shaped port.

THE BOATMAN SQUEEZES our boat next to others, bobbing and swirling. We plonk down the boards and stumble onto the land. Massalia settles over us like a veil of hot breath. Creatures, snails of the sea, fall from the baskets of fishermen and crawl a path back to the Mediterranean. Houses rim the port. Grand ships with Greek names sprawled across their belly, rock in the water.

Beauté and I carry the *polpi* and we reach Place de Lenche. Huge, flat black pans steam with rice, oil, lemon and garlic.

"It's the style of Phocaea. My people from Delphi founded Massalia long ago, and this is their way." I didn't ask, but the woman behind the brazier offers up her story. I can't help but wonder if she knows the Efta. "Where can I find a ship to Trinacria?"

Birds caw above us. Our fisherman's *polpi*, from the rocky Calanques, splays out on a metal grid held above a fire. Men mend nets, tend shops of lanterns, and stir boiling pots of snails in their seaweed-covered shells. Beauté drinks heavily from a barrel of fresh water.

In front of me, clerics herd lines of men bound together in chains toward the docks and board the ships. Windmills circulate air over *Cimitiere le Py*.

Outside the empty granary, hard-looking men shout. "Where are the grain ships? We were promised!"

I walk away quickly with Beauté. But then I come back. "The Guild ships were destroyed by the Psomi."

The men remind me of Ispanek. They raise their hands and shout. They hug each other. Once I might have felt unsafe around them, but now I see them as family. I'd rather walk with men or women who wear tattered clothes. Their faces sunburned. Their hands are rough with work.

SUNRISE OPENS OVER the port of Massalia. Not dark and burning like Tolosa, the pink and ochre houses absorb the golden sunlight, and radiate it back to Beauté.

Words that Paillard spoke, and that the Efta said stay with me as I reach the end of the path.

"Think like a dove, big. It keeps going, the spiral. One dove can't fly forever. But many can fly over big expanses. They guide ships, too. The captain sends one on and then another to follow."

I did follow *Aubada* from Ceres to Nerac, and then into *Condatóm*, but she died. A horrible death. It seems unlikely that a Captain on a ship could follow a dove across the wide sea to Morocco. But maybe a ship could follow a flurry of doves.

On Rue Gambetta, I close my eyes. The scent of bay leaves and orange and a wood fire calls me. I turn back. I look up and feel the heat of each person passing by. Like at Madame Bouquin's when Auvillar tried to convince me that Antaia's bread of dreams was her bones. I raise the metal knocker shaped like a fist and knock it against the heavy blue door. A net bulging with oranges hangs from a bay leaf tree. How can I find the right ship? Boxes of breads are stacked against the wall. Filled with Maman's bread of dreams. I close my eyes tight. Maybe I am imagining this. I lean against the door, listening to steps approaching. I step back.

A small man sizes me up and knocks on the blue door. "I am ready." he squeaks. The baker hands him boxes full of the breads.

I look at the small man. "I am looking for a ship that…"

His face crackles and laughs. "You are in the right place! When the moon leaves, and the wind dies, ships will take to the sea again. Follow me."

A black and white cat slinks against my legs. She meows. The baker pours milk in a bowl. The cat laps up all the milk, her tongue flicking drops on the wooden box. I stoop to pet her head; she jumps up on the box. The sky grows grey and violet with a light at the edge of the horizon. I bow my head. Then stand and follow the man with the box of breads ripe with the perfume of orange, herbal scented bay leaves, and coriander. Words from the Efta come back in the wind. "Whatever you leave empty, the sea will fill."

I WALK ON the dock, wind circling. So many currents rush through my body. Inside my pants my legs turn to fire, wanting to run.

Is it really, might it be her, my Térèse? She gets up and walks slowly away. Last time I saw her, she was pretty angry. I half-expected, hoped to see her, but now I search for what to say. My mind fills with fires and trees and fougasse. I unbuckle the straps of the pannier on Beauté's back and lift out Grigne's bread. My heart pounds. The part of me that was Epi and argued with her wants to run before she sees me. She doesn't look angry, but she might be. It's not possible she's looking for me. I'm still wearing Epi's clothes, but feel Eleone growing in me, and I plant my heels firmly in the wooden dock and keep walking. Térèse disappears again.

I only survived Antaia's leaving by working for the Guild, baking crowns. But with the Efta I got something back. Not Maman, but me, Eleone. Even though I still don't know where Trinacria is. I know where I am.

Along the port, open fires are tended. My legs have a mind of their own and won't rest. I hold her lead close. Beauté walks on my left. I look behind. I lean closer to Beauté. Beauté stops. She's under a fig tree. It is Térèse. I am sure now, she looks in our direction. She finishes talking to someone who's wheeling burlap sacks away. I want to run over to her. Térèse! Térèse. I slow down. I can't go slow enough or fast enough. I might yet remember the way she looked, her face, on the day she kissed me on the bread terrace. I have come so far and so has she. Térèse.

Beauté whinnies and raises her head up and down, and she hurries over.

As soon as Beauté sees Térèse, Térèse sees Beauté, and I know she sees me.

"Stop crying. Wait, who are you? Epi's sister?" She frowns and then smiles.

"Térèse!? What? How can you make a joke now?"

We grab each other and hug for a long time. The bag slung over her shoulder slides off. Beauté stomps next to us.

"I ran into Fabrizio and Antoine. They told me you would be here. Epi. Are you well? Walk with me a little."

It's like I am seeing her for the first time. Térèse is Auvillar's daughter. His daughter. How different can family be? She's not the Térèse I knew. How could she be? I am not who I was. I have never prayed for anything so hard. But all I can do is listen. See her.

Small boats arrive and unload. A cart goes by filled with fish.

Her cheeks flush red, sunburned. Dark circles under her eyes. "Please know. I was angry. I never told you." She says.

"You're alive, Térèse. Get on Beauté."

"Am I? Luckily, Angeline—that is what I call her. She helped me." She reaches out to touch my hair. But then pulls her hand back. Climbs up on Beauté. The bag slung over her shoulder is stuffed with twigs.

"I never thought I would see you again."

We go up a steep embankment of rocks to the crest, walking above. The sea, the port, below. The wide path winds down. I want to tell her about Antoine. And how it is that I am carrying his child. What we said about love. We argued that love held you in a place where you couldn't change. Beauté struggles. Térèse gets down. She has changed. Have I changed as much to her?

A seabird cries above, flying and perching from boat to boat. But none of these boats look ready to sail.

"Are you still angry with me?" I ask.

We sit under the fig tree.

"I told Angeline you walked thirty kilometers a day, but who knew in what direction? A little bit east, a little south, then west, and north. You made a Térèse, just like a snail in my garden."

"Or like a dove. You didn't answer me."

"It's not possible, I could never be mad at you."

"I, oh, somehow I don't believe that. I have to tell you everything."

"I said a prayer for you and Antoine. Wait, oh god, does he know?"

"He knew I turned down Margot's offer to join the new Guild. And that I was going on."

"Epi, I mean does he know you're not a boy?"

"Now. But not until after…" Was I still Epi? I had to answer this for no one but me.

"The Guild has hired all kinds of people to find her. Look at these ships. Never say it, never mention Trinacria."

"Too late. Should we go on together? Or go our separate ways?"

"How important is it for you to find Antaia?"

"I can't believe you'd ask me that. What did you learn from Angeline?"

"Where Antaia is."

"The three-sided island. Trinacria."

"How can we get there?"

"Together. It's an island, Epi. So.." She gestures out to the port. One rowboat bobs in the water.

"You don't have to get on a ship to find the place where Antaia is your mother."

"She's not my mother."

"I was not sure how to tell you, especially since we haven't seen each other for a while. I didn't know if you knew."

"I want to hear her story. See her face. Will I know her? I must see if she's ok."

"You're Eleone. She'll know you."

"It's been too long."

"Angeline knew me."

"You should stay here because you're safe and not ready to leave." I say, wanting to brush the hair off her face.

"Like when I told you, that last day we were on your bread terrace in Ceres, right?"

"I didn't listen then, and you won't listen now."

"I can't. There's so much to catch up on. So, where is Antoine?"

We walk around the port. The moon fades in the sky. "Antoine is…with the Guild." I have to tell her. And I can't tell her. I'm pregnant. I say it to myself to see how it sounds.

"You have to say it. He's dead, isn't he?"

"No, that's not it. Térèse, I am just like all the rest of the Mistresses, as it turns out." I feel so very tired. And holding on to all that the Efta taught me. Fishermen lift their nets and dump hundreds of shiny little fish, they spill all over the dock. I hold my hand to my mouth.

"Like them? No. No, you're not. There's nothing wrong with them. But you are like you. It is not at all the same. This battle has been going on for a long time, Epi."

"My stomach feels like the ocean is lapping up my throat."

"What?"

"Can we move, that smell…" I bend over and throw up in my mouth.

"Epi, oh no! Come on, sit down. You need something to eat."

"I'm pregnant. Just water." Beauté follows us. We sit on a box of salt cod. Their stiff bodies look bleached by the sun and stick out of the slats, poking our legs.

"When's the last time you slept?"

"Sleep? That's all I want to do. Didn't you hear me? I'm pregnant. But it's not what you think."

"I heard you. What do I think? I will kill him myself."

"He thought I was Epi."

"Auvillar, that swine! He's my father! How could he? Of course, you weren't Epi."

"Oh no, it wasn't Auvillar." Now I'm really sick, though how close was I to this happening? If Margot hadn't arrested him, is it possible that Auvillar would have taken me? "No, it was Antoine. He thought I was Epi. Believed I was. And I loved him as Epi."

"Hmm. Really? This is a lot to digest. Of course, you were Epi." She swings the bag off her shoulder.

"A minute ago, you said I wasn't Epi."

"If you're going to go by what everyone says, you'll never know what to believe."

"Not everyone, but you, what you think is important. To me."

"And so, what do you think? Why must you stop being Epi?"

It was a good question, and it made me sad. Her eyes explored mine, but it was more than the way they blinked and comforted and smiled and accepted at the same time.

A small boat comes in and docks. The fisherman jumps ashore. He unloads a net and tips it into a wooden barrel. Fish jump and roll away, and some flip back into the sea.

I reach for her hand. She lets me hold it. It's still rough and weathered, calluses on her palm from digging into the earth. I know Térèse really sees me. The moments of living as Epi were my best moments, because—who knows what is ahead? And if I forget Epi, in my hurry to return to Eleone, didn't allow myself to feel all his fears and joys, be him, then I would lose Térèse, too, and the Epi that I was with her. My best moments with her. She knew me then, and now. Would she love me as Eleone? I didn't know what lay ahead for either one of us. What did any of it mean? I hadn't stopped being Epi. I had a great deal to thank Térèse for. And to thank Epi for, too.

"Epi will always be here."

"I think we are a lot like those fish. We got away."

"You knew all along I was Eleone, though, didn't you?"

"No. No, I didn't. But I love whoever you are."

My eyes widen at her. "So, did you want to kiss Epi or Eleone?"

"It didn't matter to me. You, you're both." She leans in and kisses my cheek. She places the bag that was slung over her shoulder, on her lap.

"I'm sorry I keep asking you questions. I can listen. Please, go on, tell me?"

"That sounds like a question."

Térèse twists her fingers at her mouth, then pulls her closed hand away and blows in it to release whatever words she was going to say. The motion reminds me of Fabrizio or Paillard releasing the doves into the air. Sending them on with a message. Or back to Morocco. Or Maman when she was silent and wanted me to listen.

"What if I still haven't seen everything, understood everything. Why can't I get answers? And what if this is my last chance, and I still don't find her."

"Maybe she isn't in any place out here, but she's here." She holds out her hands.

I take them.

"You have everything you need. Do you know why?"

"Because I have you?"

"No, you can never have me, or anyone."

"What, why would you say that after all this?"

"Because you already have everything you need." Térèse says. "You."

"Seems like I'm always too much, or never enough. I must know why she left. You're right, I can't ever have anyone. But I see who you are. You see everything. You survived everything. Like Beauté. And even though you didn't go to the Efta's, you're a Mistress too. You're my first Mistress and last. And that's part of why I must find Maman. She knew we would need each other."

"Like Antaia and Angeline needed each other too."

When Térèse says that they needed each other I feel a twinge of needing to know why they each left, so I don't leave. Do the same thing.

"They're for sure just like the sour cornelian cherry and the sweet apricot tree. But, I never did understand the damn trees. I mean what's that about? Why those trees? A Mistress for each tree. Protecting each tree. Each tree in Maman's maze. A tree for the doves. And their messages."

"I don't know. Can we talk more about it? On the way to the place we can't name."

A cart of fish goes by. I hold my hand to my mouth, twist it and throw away the feeling that something more is unfinished. I trust that I have time to talk to her.

"*Oc*, and so forget that I was the Mistress of the fig tree. I'm the new Mistress of tomatoes. And a bag of pepper. I brought ..pepper." Térèse walks to a stand piled high with red fruits, tomatoes with hints of purple and green. Térèse picks out two and weighs them in her hand. She lets Beauté sniff. She puts those back in the pile and picks two others. Beauté favors one, Térèse puts the other one back and finally settles on another with bits of yellow. We step back from the merchant.

We walk to another merchant with a table-full of colorful cloths. The piles have a slight dusting of salt from the sea-breezes. We each pick one. Mine is the color of pomegranate and Térèse's cloth is a deep bronze woven with bits of purple thread. Then Térèse picks out a small beige linen sack. She opens the bag she's been carrying and takes out a knife, cuts the tomato in half, and squeezes the seeds into the small beige sack.

"And to think I was hungry. Is the tomato bad?"

"This is for our new garden, Epi." She opens the bag and pulls out a huge fireflute. Or maybe it's a fig tree she's going to plant. It could be any of the trees from the Mistresses. She just stands there with it. She holds it out to me.

My hands shake as I take it by the handle. I turn it over and look at her. I don't believe it. It's not a log. It's the box. The box I found in the woodshed, which started it all. It's polished smooth. It looks different. Clean. If anything, the tree carved on its bottom has grown.

"How, how did you get it? Ispanek?"

"Fabrizio, when I saw him with Antoine. Bana had both in the prison."

I laugh and my stomach settles. The sky over us is still cloudy but a few rays of sun burst through and land on a distant spot of water out of the harbor, out on the open sea. Like when I was looking for the Efta, and the sun shone through the snow, like a candle lighting the way.

Térèse folds up the linen bag of tomato seeds. "Bana's not bad for a little Mistress, huh?"

I tie the pomegranate cloth around her hips. "I'm ready, I want to listen to Eleone."

Térèse takes a bite out of the second tomato as if it was an apple. She laughs, and hugs me, wiping her chin, and feeds me the heavy yellow and orange fruit.

"To all the new breads of dreams you'll make," She ties the beige and purple threaded cloth around my waist.

I have not had this taste before. It's a little sweet and juicy, salty too. I close the box and hesitate. I should give it back to Térèse. But then, I drop it in the burlap bag and toss it over my shoulder.

CHAPTER FIFTY-TWO

Epi and Térèse Search For Passage to Trinacria

CHARRA MEDFOUNA—DOVE STUFFED AND BURIED
IN VERMICELLI AND THE WALNUT TREE. BANA.

"WHO DRINKS BITTER cannot spit sweet."
Qui beu amarguent pot pos escupi dous.
We walk around the port of Massalia again.
It's horseshoe shaped. Dozens of ships are docked for the winter.

"We are in need of a ship, a vessel of magnificence," Térèse says.

"This is a ship of such sort." A burly curly rough man insists.

"A ship of such sort is not what we need." Térèse turns away.

"Before you, a great ship. I chose most of the trees myself." The man twists his long beard.

"He lies. I did!" Another man, tall like Madame's apple tree, insists.

"Logs cut straight from the chin of the Carnic Alps and the arms of Rhaetian slopes north of Venice." The curly man rubs his arms and the sound is like leaves rustling.

"Hmm, of what manner is the keel?" Térèse bends to look.

"The shipwright was like a magician to be sure." The man waves his arms. On his arm is a tattoo of a tree.

I shake my head. "Is this ship, a grain ship?"

"How did you know? Her ribs are made of chestnut wood."

"I don't know. It is just not quite right for us." I pull Térèse away.

"Wait," the bearded man implores. "Do you bear the mark?" He pulls us back and rubs his chin.

"The mark?" I ask. "What mark?" Does he see the *baisure*, the scar on my hand from Antoine's slashing the net, and freeing me?

"Your hunger, I see it. You want *lonzu, ficatellu*, or *brocciu sec*?"

"The air of Algiers smells clean. Sweet as spring," the burly man promises. "On the voyage there you can fold a heavy *sanbusak* around some spicy roasted lamb." He kisses the tips of his fingers.

My mouth waters,

"Brother, look. They would appreciate Constantinople more." The bearded one lifts the scallop shell around my neck. "Or Jerusalem."

"Phew on Constantine. Byzantium is nicer this time of year."

"We need to go to Trinacria," I blurt suddenly.

"Never! You don't want to go there."

"Why not?"

"Pirates, thieves and ruffians—live there."

"Sounds pretty much the same as here."

"And everywhere."

"The island is unreachable."

"And soon you can just walk there. They're building a bridge of boats and barrels."

I am not surprised. I am so close to finding Maman. The ships strain to get out to sea. "Why didn't you say so, that's what our specialty is. Building bridges." It wasn't entirely untrue.

"Do you have room for pepper?" Térèse asks.

"Pepper?"

"Surely such a ship has room for one or two quintales. We have to get to Rome. But you didn't hear that from me."

"Certainly."

"And our horse, Beauté?"

"Is she a working horse or a pleasure horse?" The tall man says, vying for the title of the worst ruffian in Massalia.

"What do you mean? She needs to rest." I say.

Térèse elbows me. "Beauté's crossed lots of bridges."

"Fine, then you can sleep in a berth. Bring the hay for your horse."

The ropes strain against the heavy ship, anxious for the sea.

The burly man says, "I don't think she'll make it to…where we're headed."

I step back with Térèse. It feels like when we met Fabrizio but didn't know who he was. "She's working?"

"Horses need work. Just because you love her doesn't mean she's like you." Térèse says.

"Quarrels, oafs, and blasphemes are forbidden on this ship. But we will supply you with bows, arrows, and lances."

"If my horse works then I am a paid passenger. I won't fight."

"What about her? Or is this your husband?"

"You'll not sell me at an Arab port?" I demand.

"No. Only Greek."

"Agreed."

"Wait. Maybe we should take two different ships?" I ask Térèse.

"After all this time? Are you crazy? No." Térèse answers.

"Sign here."

"How far south will you go?" Térèse pushes the black hat back on her forehead, rosemary branches tucked in the brim.

"South? We never know till we're out on the sea, then we look at our orders. "Where the sea meets the sky. At the turn of spring!"

"That's far too long." Térèse looks at my belly.

"The further south we go the closer spring gets. It's only a few weeks."

"We need time to gather a few supplies."

"We leave tonight. Feel that warm breeze? Spring is approaching."

"Help me." A man brings another cart, heavy with our promised bows, arrows, and lances. He gestures to Beauté. I want to say no, she's not made for this work, but what part of this journey was she made for? Carrying Margot? Going over the dam with Grigne? Saving us in Tolosa? Walking to the Efta?

"Hurry." I say to Térèse.

Beauté pulls the cart up the ramp while I hold the rope. One hand covers my eyes, the sun blinding. The air whitens, damp with salt and the beings of the sea.

On deck, the ship feels as wide as the port that holds it. Several dozen men mill about beneath the sails. Three masts spring from the deck. A great flag waves at the bow of the ship. It unfurls.

I turn to Térèse. "We got on the wrong ship. I know we did."

"Hmm, I don't think so. Besides, which ship is the right ship? They're headed out of Massalia. Or maybe they'll turn right around. No one on the ship knows where the ship is supposed to go until they are out on the sea and read their orders."

"Your berth…is down there." A bent man with sun-frizzled gray hair points to a door and stairs that lead to the ship's belly.

"We paid for two."

"I know! Thank you! You can share!"

I lead Beauté down the ramp next to the stairs. Down in the belly, the cavity sweats as much as the men above deck. Someone breathes heavily. I stand still. Chickens with feathered hats scream, their clawed feet scratch my arms. Sailors squeeze past me with sacks slung over their shoulders. One of them is our pepper—and they stack them on pallets below deck.

THE SIXTH TALE

Manaqish Bil-Kishik. Fertile Crescent. The Efta.

"Fai un pan con tantos buratos, podemos estar xuntos, no centro."
Make a bread with so many holes that we
can stand together in the center.

CHAPTER FIFTY-THREE
Térèse and Epi Board the Phantome in Massalia

TÉRÈSE HURRIES BEHIND me. We inspect our berth. The musty smell makes it seem more like a nest for a dove. One of us fits. We decide to take turns sleeping. If I can even sleep.

We climb up and stand on deck. We breathe the salty air.

We're foolish to have boarded a Guild ship.

After all this time, what if I am the one bringing the Guild to Maman. When Auvillar was arrested, they said she was dead. I keep telling myself, they don't know it's possible. That Antaia and the fields still exist.

"Maybe Maman was just an idea I had when I was ten. My stomach turns over. I am so scared to face her. If we get there. I have no idea who Maman is."

"Eleone, come on." You wouldn't make something up like your mother."

"I don't know, there are so many moments and lies, that that's entirely possible."

"You're scared. But, you're right. You should be prepared."

"For what? Not finding her?"

"Shhh. Of course, that, but maybe worse."

"What could be worse?"

"Maman has given up and has turned to the Guild?"

"That's why everyone has lied to me. They never wanted me to find that out. And they never thought I'd get on a ship to go find her for myself."

"We don't know where this ship is going. Isn't that exciting! And you're far from being alone anymore, but don't go thanking me just yet."

"Great."

We push out of Massalia's harbor. So many ropes to pull and untie. Sails flutter and billow. The men on board belch and fart. And most are stone cold drunk.

We slip around *les Iles d'Hyeres* and cross the path of water into the Ligurian Sea.

Beauté looks up. The moon slips behind some clouds, it's so tired.

I retreat too. Our berth is near a small porthole below deck, and sweat soaks my cocoon of purple silk. I dream of Margot. She might be on board. Unable to rest, my legs swing over the side, but the deck swims under my feet. I lay back down in my cocoon. My lips taste like the salt flats of the Camargue. From my berth, I long for the moon, and the cold wind to return, a reason to turn around.

Such blue in the winter sky. Faces drift over me in the strange light.

Antoine.

Fabrizio.

Bana.

Ispanek.

Maman.

Bana.

Madame.

Claude.

Auvillar and Margot.

Bana.

Angeline.

Térèse.

And then I remember. Térèse. She's on board. I leave the hold and push up the stairs. On deck, I stare out over the horizon. But still the sea wretches green. The winds drop into breezes, as we smooth along the coast. In that time of rolling waves, fish swim along our sides. The waves spray as we leap along.

"So many days you've been asleep. It feels like we're still leaving. An island. More coast. Then..."

"What have they said? And where are we headed?"

"They run from ships. They spread out maps. The men say Tunis. Cagliari." Térèse whispers, and frowns.

"But that's not where we want to go."

"Do you feel ok enough to eat?"

I hold out my hand and take the black cake from her.

"It's lupini beans."

They're dry and tasteless. It seems at odds with all the spices we are carrying in the hold. The sun beats down on our heads. I lick my fingers, and when the breeze lifts my hat away I shiver to remember Antoine, and wonder what he would say or do if he knew I was carrying our baby. The wind cools. How does time pass so slowly at times and so quickly when you need more of it? A few stars come out.

"Look, it's Casseopeia, " I point up. "This is how you said we'd arrive to her."

"A three-sided island takes time to find." Terese leans against me.

"Especially if you can't say that's where you're going."

"And if you're carrying someone else, too. especially then."

"Just mentioning that makes my stomach sick."

"I'm not a sea-faring man, but the stars don't seem to say we're near Tunis. She won't leave the land without a fight."

I wondered if the she Terese was talking about was the ship or my baby, and the time of leaving was when my baby would be born. Térèse goes below deck to rest.

We squeeze around an island then careen, fighting the sea to leave it behind. I sleep on the hard deck, a bag of pepper for my head. The next morning a large city hovers on the horizon. Rome? Or did the sea pull us back to Massalia?

"Little sheep," I remember Ispanek saying. "When *le vent marin* pushes the sea from the sky. Watch for the spiral of water. You have to get past that to find her."

A BOLT OF lightning cracks through the clouds. A storm overhead swirls the ocean. It is hard to tell if the sky threatens the waves, or if the waves have so infuriated the clouds. How many other Guild ships have tried to reach the place we can't name?

"Everyone hurry," the burly man slaps me on the back.

My heart races, it's so busy on deck that I miss the steps down into the hold. Térèse comes up from below and rolls a barrel of oranges and lifts them over the side. Chickens escape the hold and squawk past me. If they fly up, the ship will lighten enough to get away. They lift off and fly into the mast, then flutter down into the waves. Their feathers matted and wet. They bob up, riding the white crests of foam then disappear into the angry green sea.

Beauté's hooves clop by, bags with spices tied on her back. Térèse's bag slips off, lands at my feet. The strings loosened. I pick it up and push the box back inside, but it's as if the box knows it was made by Bana, and tries its best to sneak away.

I run after Beaute, grabbing at the ropes to release the sacks from her. A crate of apples tilts, and slides to the edge of the deck. the red fruit bobs into the sea. Clouds and more clouds drift overhead. The sea rises and rolls waves against the ship, lapping at us. Beauté leaps overboard, toward the jagged rocks. The sea is foam. And churning bodies and barrels of malmsey wine. Chickens. Pigs. Cooking Pots. Crates of Castilian Wool. And fish fly out of the sea into the sky.

I come up for air and keep pushing away from the ship. Boxes spin out in the waves, like chickens and bob in the sea. The sea washes the burlap sacks; pepper and red spices. I close my eyes, rub away the seaweed. When I open them, I squint from the salt in my eyes that makes it hard to see. The waves are so strong they might have pushed me back to begin the journey again. I thrash to stay afloat. Will I wash up at the millhouse in Ceres, never having begun? Or when I fell in the great Garonna when Grigne flooded the dam. Or worse than possibly drowning, willI I wake to find myself as Epi walking beside Beaute with Margot beating me with a stick to keep walking. Is that Térèse?

Across the waves, a head breaks through. The sea sprays from Beauté's nostrils. Beauté swims toward shore, but then she splashes into the spiral of water.

CHAPTER FIFTY-FOUR

Eleone Lands on Trinacria

THE BOOTS THAT walked with the ladies over a bed of hot dirt are ruined, and I take them off. I don't know where we are. Maybe this is the island we saw approaching. Or maybe the sea has returned us to Massalia and the Guild that we escaped from.

The hot sand rubs my feet and removes the skin hardened from walking in these boots. The sea lurches out of me onto the sand. The waves wash away my retching and then try to pull me back, back to the water as though I have gotten away too easily, and the sea has reconsidered if I deserve this last chance to find Maman.

My side aches to breathe in and out. I stand but fall backward as the waves crash into jagged rocks. I remember falling into the water with Térèse and Beauté. I did not lose you. I can't have come all this way only for that to happen. Beauté, you must have swum ahead. The sea spouted from her wide nostrils. Térèse and I strained toward shore. But where are they both? The cook's words haunt me, *the sea keeps what is too frail for the land.*

A wave rushes up and knocks me down. My knees carve little gullies in the wet sand, the waves lapping behind me. If I stretch I can reach the dry sand. It will feel warm, like sleep. And how I long for deep rest. On my back, the sea seems so wide and far away. My stomach heaves up salt water. The sky, full of storms.

"Térèse! Térèse?" I don't see her.

My hands flatten out beside me, the golden sand is warm. But further down the jagged rocks meet the crashing waves. The sea swims with wooden boxes, some as big as the coffins we saw when we left Tolosa. Some as small as the seedbox. Pieces of wood. Branches. A log bobs by. And then another. I reach into the churning foam, but it slips by. It could have been Bana's box that Térèse carried a long way to give to me.

I hold my belly. My head really hurts. I comb my hair with my fingers, stiff with seaweed. I pull a clump of green from my hair, and my hand smears with blood. A gash on my forehead.

The sun glares off the water, days gone and days yet to come. The waves break, smashing against the rocks a few strokes into the sea. Against Térèse if she's still out there. She's usually ahead of me. I grab my boots and turn toward the land. But even with my hand sheltering my eyes, the sun is so bright. The hills rise up again, and I have to wonder if this is the last climb on the last mountain, where I will find Maman.

My knees press the warm dry sand. I step slowly, the sand is so warm it reminds me of the hot earth I walked over with the ladies. Burn the earth. Return to spring. My foot perches on a smooth round rock. Up the hill, rocks cover the landscape like a stack of a hundred more crowns of bread.

I walk to Beauté. My hand rests on her white rump. I circle her. She turns her head and her wide eyes peer out from her blonde mane, stringy and matted with seaweed, too. A stalk of wild fennel juts from her muzzle. The roots hang down at her hooves, the yellow flowers in her mouth. She crunches, her jaw working from side to side.

I rub her back and rest against her belly, but with her wounds, it's too much. I walk beside her. Her hooves crunch ahead of me against the pebbles under the almond trees.

"Beauté, you are the horse that cannot die. I want to look in your eyes. And Térèse's eyes. And follow the dove's path, like Paillard."

Morning threads a light along the shore. We cross through vineyards, sloping down roads lined with pomegranate trees. In the distance, a path opens toward a white-capped, smoke-circled mountain. My mouth longs for the cheese in rich green oil that I ate on the ship. My feet feel a little better now.

Around the bend sits an apricot tree, her slender branches filled with pale blooms and, cracked by lightning, she lies across the road. Beauté steps back and raises each leg. She shakes her head up and down. She steps over the branches and the pink blooms scatter on the road.

We stand under a tree with branches that tuft up like a hat of chicken feathers into the air. A sticky brown fruit with wrinkles hangs in clusters from the golden tree. It is hard to chew, but sweet with crunchy seeds inside. I remember this taste, and her tree outside her garden in Ceres. Figs. Térèse has to be near.

"Excuse me, where is the hundred horse tree?"

"How about a twenty-horse tree. There." He points up to the mountain side. A large grove of trees begins at the base and circles to the top of the mountain.

"There's a town and then a forest. Or, I can't remember, maybe it's the vineyard, then the town, or a grove of fig trees." He sighs and scratches his head. "Then the other fields, and then the tree."

"Is the forest actually a tree? A tree they say is large enough to protect a hundred horses? And how far is it?"

"Not much further. It's from here to here," he squints and his fingers measure from the sea in the distance to the sky. The sun comes out and a beam of light through the clouds guides us through a door beyond the wall. It reminds me of the wall surrounding Madame Bouquin's. The new sun edges into the puddles. I hold my back, arch and stretch. The last half-mile disappears under my feet. I breathe the sweet orange air. If I don't see anyone else, did no one else from the ship make it? A white cloud swells, as if it's stuck on the mountain above.

We walk and the sun lowers in the sky. I sit and throw my legs over a wall that circles a grove of pomegranate and olive trees. The round red fruit feels heavy in my hand. Térèse will like this one. It doesn't seem right that I haven't found her. The red fruit tears open easily to reveal pockets of seeds and red juice. A bird in the tree tilts its head at me. I leave the opened fruit on the wall, and it flies down to eat. On the other side of the wall, the street bursts with people scurrying by. I pick three more and store the pomegranates in Beauté's pannier.

"Hello, hello." I wave to a man with three camels.

He stops rubbing the camel's legs, the oil fragrant with almond, laying his palm on his heart, and bows slightly. "Me?"

"Yes, you. Can you tell me, please, where is the large chestnut forest?"

"Follow the path up to the great fire. Etna."

I head up the hill and twist an orange from a tree. Beauté leads me up a cobbled street. A sign at the end says it's the *Corso Umberto*. The last stretch of street disappears into a dirt path up the mountain. At the top the path curves and opens up into a field. I walk down a row of farro with Beauté's reins wrapped in my hand. We walk out of the wheat and wind through an olive grove, and then another grove. Dried cherries litter the ground. Pink flowers and hand-shaped leaves burst out of fig branches. Beauté eats hay from a wrought iron feeder. Hay, it must mean that more wheat fields are ahead. Auvillar wanted them so badly. Spring wheat, Banatka wheat would have been planted in this field about the time that I left Ceres. Maman has been pulling me closer in this way, the whole length of my journey. Or the wheat could be the *farro grande* or camel's tooth wheat. We climb through a terraced vineyard. I chew on a few dried grapes, sweet and chewy, hidden deep inside the vines, missed during fall harvest.

This path up the mountain winds and at the top, and my feet keep up with the switching, zig-zagging, jagged turns, as if the path can't stop till we go over the steep rocks. At the top fields open up below. We wind down the hill quickly, running to meet the rose bushes growing, marking the end of each row of wheat. Green rose canes stretch up the iron trellises, like the one arching over the bread terrace in Ceres. Bright red and green shiny leaves burst out of the canes. Beauté and I keep going.

THE SEVENTH TALE

Ferro Di Cavallo, The Horseshoe of
Sekhnet. Freekeh. Psomi. Perpetua.

"Dabant la mort èle foc nou i a cap de benjenço."
Against death and fire there is no revenge.

CHAPTER FIFTY-FIVE

Eleone Finds a Bread Terrace
in the Hundred Horse Tree

THE LARGE CHESTNUT tree we've been walking towards after we passed the fields is not one, but many trees. Near the top of the tree, I move the chestnut branches, yellow flowers drop at my feet. I reach for the iron handle of a door but pull back. Beauté neighs below. The handle is cool, where the handle on the door of our wood-fired oven on the bread terrace in Ceres was always too hot to touch with just my fingers. I pull open the door and have to put my foot on the tree to open it. It's swollen shut, but it opens, and I step inside. My eyes squint at so much light coming in through the window.

An oven sits in the corner of the room. In the space below, instead of wood there sits a basket filled with crescent-shaped weaves of olive branches. I laugh. My first impulse is to take it to Beauté, who would wear it as a crown, or shake it off into the fire. Like with the Efta. The crowns could each be a thought or a wish like when we were with the Efta. A wish for winter to burn away. I take them and hold them. I look in the oven, it looks like it hasn't been used in a long time, and a spider scurries away.

I hold my hands close, as if I could get a sense of who lives here, if Maman lives here or another Mistress has stepped in. The stone feels warm, and my stomach growls, I am so hungry. But that doesn't stop the tears. Have I walked far enough to find her, far enough to believe in Maman? The fire is where it all began. And what she told me to do. How to return to myself. Take the life of the fire. Suddenly I pull my hands back. What if fire's not good for my baby? I step back. It wasn't good for me. Was it? To take the life of the fire. I would never let fire hurt my baby. Antoine's child. But Mistresses, please. I stand up and lean out the window. How true is it that my child, our child, is here because of fire? I run my hands over my belly. The ripples across my stomach make me smile. You are here because of fire. Because of the fire, Antoine and I were together. He saved me, and I thought I had returned to the fire and that made me into Eleone that night. Tears slip down my cheek. I was more scared to walk away, and not let him know. To not touch him. What truth would that have been? For all those years of loving him to not tell him? But what wrestling truth am I now? The truth is fire kept me alive all those years, while Maman was gone. Fire gave me back my life. Feeding the fire gave me life. And now fire has given me another life. I feel crazy to be this close to finding Maman. Maybe she is climbing through the vineyard towards me. Maybe she already sees my footsteps. I stop and lean out the window. Moving the vines aside. The vineyard is empty.

What did it feel like to Maman to disappear into the fire? It's very hard to give up the idea—the feeling—some belief that as my baby lives inside me, that I lived inside Maman. But instead of that the truth is, I lived and grew inside Margot. I know this, I have known this for a while, but having enough time to rest, to digest it, as Angeline would tell me. My baby moves and sends waves across my belly. Is he or she beginning to wonder, to look up and out?

I sit on the bed by the window. Smooth my hand over the rough blanket. I still can't believe my mother is Margot. To say that feels like the worst possible part of me, but that I am here because of her and Maman, maybe—I don't know. I can't think about this too much anymore. I'm here. I'm here. Maybe the best possible moments of my life are before me. I lie down on the straw bed. Close my eyes. A bee buzzes outside the window and flies in and then out, and in again, around the yellow flowers of the tree branch stuck in a vase. I lay back down, turn on my side and look out the window.

A LITTLE WHILE later I struggle to open my eyes. I push a hand away, and squint to see. Térèse? No. She looks like Maman. She keeps her hand on my shoulder then runs her hand through my short hair. "Chestnut flowers, like the dried ones on the shelf of the oven, sit in your hair. But you're not little anymore."

I fall back to sleep, a breeze flutters across my cheek. Before my journey I was so used to falling asleep and dreaming about her. Why she left. And even worse, why she didn't return. Maybe her being here is a dream I'm still having. My dream. Maman died. Doesn't exist. But this dream, this dream is one that I've had for so long. That I would find her. This is what I left for. Left my little bread terrace for. The further I got, the more complicated the story. Why did so many lie to me? If I don't find her this trip won't have been in vain. To leave and search means I took the chance to find her. Or not. Someone touches my hair. But now I don't know which is better. To find her and ask her. Or not find her and never know the answer to why, and what happened to her. And why I was alone. But then, one thing, one thought opens my eyes. I am not Epi; I am not the little boy/girl she left. And she was alone too. And my heart grieves that I was not there. Or here. That I was so afraid that I did not hurry after her. I sink down in the blanket. I smell smoke. Hear crackling. The last night I saw her, I know I turned around to go back to the bread terrace. Surely she wouldn't leave me. I remember. I felt alone even though Térèse and Antoine were there. It slowly comes to me to open my eyes.

The light warms my face. Makes it hard to see. With so much light it's so hard to believe how long I stayed at the bread terrace. In such darkness. The strong light of Trinacria hurts. But maybe like the vines, it's helping my baby to grow. I close my eyes again. I am so tired. My arm falls off the bed. But the breeze is sweet and floats around my head like a bee. Someone rubs and pats my hand. And I go back to my ceremony and the last time I saw her, and when she took my hand and squeezed my fingers.

"*Prend la vie de feu.* It's the first time a mother and daughter will be inducted at the same time. You think you know and see all that you need. Epi, but to understand, you must listen without expecting to understand. What hasn't been told is kept hidden. Listen. Listen with your spirals. Your ears. In your bread of dreams. In the path of the wheat growing around our trees. In the snail shell. In the finger-size scrolls of the doves. And when your hands shape your bread of dreams, you'll begin."

"When will I find you?"

"Epi, is it really you? How is it that you're here?"

I open my eyes again. Antaia. Does she have the right to call me Epi, even though she was the one who cast me as a boy, named me, to keep me safe or keep me away from her? My Maman from Ceres. Her hair is wild and long-curly and grey. I feel small again. What can fill up this space? Who can say? Ten years ago, I wanted to walk with you, but you left. But meeting you again is part of this world. I try to hold on to what it feels like, what this is. I feel sick. So sick and let it go.

"Why did you let go of my hand?"

"Epi. Things. There are many things you don't know."

I want to remember how I made it here. Slow down each step. But not enough to go backwards. "I had chestnut flowers in my hair when I was little?" If I knew I was headed towards her—did she feel somehow the same thing, that I was getting closer? As she told me to listen that my name meant ears, what is her skill?

It must mean that she wanted me to listen to her calling me. But she never said that. What does Antaia mean? How did she look for me? Did she have some blind hope that I would hear her?

"It was not my job to call you. What if I called you and they followed you? The Guild. To the wrong place? As a mother, I wanted the best for you. To hear everyone, all the Mistresses, and for you to decide. What good is it for me to tell you what to do?" Antaia says.

"But you aren't my mother."

"I asked to be your mother. It wasn't an accident. When we came through groves of chestnut trees in the mountains in Langue d'Oc, we were with the .."

"Efta. I was still Eleone then, before you made me Epi."

She smiles. "The Efta showed us, me, a world, a big world. I did not understand what it meant. I would never put you through that."

"But Antaia. You did. Leaving Ceres was the hardest thing in my life, harder than leaving the Efta, months ago, alone."

She uses a wooden bowl and scoops flour into the bread trough. It looks smokey dark with hints of gold.

"Grano Arso? So, he learned that from you?"

"Who?"

"Antoine."

"Oh, Antoine. Was he that boy from Madame's? Your brother in the Guild." Maman says.

"No. He was never just that boy. Antoine is many things. Many things."

What I didn't say was that he was the father of my child. Couldn't she see that I am pregnant?

"Was? Is he dead? Oh, Epi."

"No, I mean, he isn't. He went against the Guild and that didn't go well for him, at first. He was supposed to be executed because he loves a man, but he and Fabrizio are making a new life."

"A new life. He loved you, I see. Love though, all love is good. I left, for love too, to draw the Guild away from you."

I must tell her that my mother, Margot, saved him. It feels like Maman is making excuses about why I was left in the Guild. I bend my head. Like my heart is radiating out light, because I found her, but it's breaking me apart too. Hard to know where to begin, but I must.

"You changed my name to Epi, so I would be a boy in the Guild, so how did that draw the Guild away from me?" Trying to understand that she didn't know or remember Antoine, how is that even possible, or right?

"By the Guild, you really mean Auvillar. Did he follow you?"

"The Guild took him away."

"Epi, sit down. Tell me you found the seedbox, you must have."

Asking me to sit down, that's nice. I want it to be enough. I feel like I was so wrong. What do I want if I find her? What do I expect? To go back to the way it was, so I could be a child again. I don't want that anymore. I don't need that anymore.

"Maman, I found your box, your seedbox, in the woodshed. It was the box that made me decide to leave. The box seemed to tell me that you were still alive. It seems like it's taken years to find you, since I left on the day of my 17th birthday." I don't know which time passed more slowly. The years at the bread terrace since she left or this moment when I am waiting for her answer.

"Epi, look at you. You're how old? In the woodshed? I buried it. In the field, near the dovecote."

"How is that possible? I feel terrible and ungrateful to say this, but it doesn't matter. I didn't come all this way to talk about the seedbox. The important thing is when I found it, it started me looking for you. I tried to remember what happened. I didn't think I could find you. Or that you even wanted me to. There are a lot of people looking for you."

"So you know then, you understand, you're…"

"Some, yes, but no. I mean here you are. I need to look at

your face for a thousand years before I can understand. Why did you come here? Why did you leave?" I didn't ask why she left me.

"I can't be that person that left. Look, I'm sorry. I don't remember."

What did Maman look like before? I can't see her, but I see pain on her face now. What is her story? So many of the Mistresses have a story that goes far back. Maybe she felt the same when she left home as a girl too.

"That person? I don't need you now. Not to take care of me. My sister was more of a mother to me." The words were out before I could stop them. How long had I wanted to know where she went, what happened? I look away. This wasn't coming out how I wanted it to, all soft and flowery and wanting to know that she needed me.

Her face falls. "Epi, stop."

My heart falls. If there is anything I want more than being seen by Maman, I don't know what it could be. Her voice calls me Epi, and puts so much distance between us again. We were so close just before she named me, Epi. But now I am invisible to her. Again. To call me Epi, when I am not him. Why would she be calling me that? I worked so hard to please her, to be Epi, when she wasn't there. And I worked so hard to not be Epi anymore, but when I hear her call me that name I go back to the beginning of when I became Epi. The beginning of all my doubts. Who I was. It was the last thing she called me that night.

"No, I won't stop. I'm not ten anymore. You named me Epi. But I am not him, can't you see that? Epi. Did you think that I would forget? I've been Epi till a month ago. People said you were dead, Maman. That I killed you." No one was more surprised than me to hear my words spilling out on her bread terrace, so far from my bread terrace. The one she built. So many fields between us. Her face is old, but the way the light hits her cheeks, she is still beautiful. I can't decide from her face, from how she looks, or what she's feeling. Is she ok?

"You didn't believe them. Those people."

When I only had myself, I was empty, like her box was empty of seeds. but I am not empty, now. All the things I thought on my way here. Why she left? Maybe she was hurt. Did I even exist to her? Has she taken other daughters since, too? Did I just happen to be her sister's daughter?

"People?"

"Claude."

"He loved us both. I hoped he wouldn't turn on you."

"You mean get bought out by the Guild. But you left me anyway. He was one of the only people left there in Ceres. You were my dream, my mission for so long. To find you and ask why. Why so many lies?"

"Epi, you knew you were coming, but I'm not prepared for this day. I was getting ready for you, but I didn't know if you'd come."

"Neither am I. There were no signs that said this is the way here. Here is your mother. But on the way to her, you'll find out that she's not your mother." Why couldn't I speak clearly to her? I didn't know who she was anymore. I only knew who I was, or I thought I did before this moment, before seeing her.

"How I mourned never seeing you."

"You mourned me? You didn't love me. You couldn't. I wasn't even yours."

She looks at me. "You were never anyone else's."

"By anyone, you mean Margot."

"Margot is not as nice as Térèse, but then I didn't choose Margot to be my sister. Angeline was so much more like a sister. I had to help her, so I took Térèse. I hoped you'd have each other. But don't you see? If you hadn't wanted to get as far away from Margot as possible, you might not have come this far. You might not have had this journey if it hadn't been for her."

"Or you." I say.

"He told me you were dead."

"He told me I killed you!"

"Sweet Claude, he told you that?"

Sweet Claude? Chills go through me, I look up at Maman. "What are you saying?"

"Auvillar, he looked, he told me you were gone. He didn't leave me for a long time. He helped me accept that you were dead."

"Maman, what are you saying?"

"He told me you died in the fire. I wanted to go back. But he convinced me to keep going to the fields and save the seeds. And that would be a way, the best way, to save you. But he promised he only wanted the seeds, to save them, not to grow them. Did he ever come back to Ceres?"

Come back? Her question reminds me of what the Efta said. Never be afraid to set love loose so it can come back. But I don't think that's what Auvillar was, love. Maybe he did come back to Ceres. I mean he must have. Was it love that brought the box to the woodshed? Or did it get there the night she named me, Epi, the night she left? Bees fly in and out of their skep. The dove on the branch hops along. Maman holds out her hand, and the dove hops on her outstretched finger. Something strung on her side.

"I prayed you'd never meet him."

"Praying didn't work. There are many things you don't know." I say.

"What matters most is that you, you're here." Maman looks up at me. Then she opens the pouch on the dove. Petting the dove, cooing to her.

"That matters a lot, but there's a lot more that matters too." I say, moving close. I knew a part of me would never be satisfied with her answers. Unless I could go back to that night. And see her again as she was. She's not the same Maman, and neither am I. How could I expect her to be the same or remember, when I couldn't either. I didn't want to go back to that night. To being Epi. I sit down beside Maman.

She turns the pouch upside down. A cake of *Trakhanas* falls out into her palm. She hands it to me. All pebbly and coarse with seeds and grains.

"The Efta gave it to me to eat. To thicken my child."

"Antoine's baby?"

"This is how you sent the seeds. How you saved them."

"From the seven fields of Psomi. Have you figured it out?"

"The sacred fields. I'm guessing you're a dove."

THE EIGHTH TALE

Touarits (Semolina Breads with Chakchouka)
and the Cherry Tree. Tunisia.
Grigne & Angeline.

"Cadun biro l'aigo debès soun mouli."
Everyone diverts the water to his own mill.

CHAPTER FIFTY-SIX
Epi Finds Antaia

IT WASN'T TRUE that Antaia was a dove.

For several minutes I walk around the edge of the field, nervous about what might happen. I remember finding seven fields of Psomi. The North Field. Fabrizio's field. Angeline's field of beans. The fields near Grigne. More sacred fields on the way to the Efta. The fields I walked over wearing sheep stilts.

But in this field, the green tall stalks of wheat sway and thrash against me, leaving my arms and legs damp. I take the sickle from Térèse and cut, and then throw them on the fire with her. Térèse. Steam turns to smoke, and pours out of the pile. The scent is more like spinach cooking rather than like bread baking. The spring rains brought us so much grain that we are making bags and bags of freekeh, scorched green wheat.

As the smoke billows, I squat next to the fire and remember two other nights in my life when I was in one of the sacred fields and my life changed. When a different burning aroma surrounded me.

The night I turned ten, and I lost Maman in the fire in the North field.

And the night, three years ago when I ran with Beauté from the fire in the field near Angeline's, when I found Antoine, and my daughter, Perpetua, was planted in me.

With Beauté, I ran in the field towards the nets. I was Epi, and Antoine saved me. I was angry and wanted the fire to change me. I didn't know I wasn't ready to find Eleone, and return to her. Antoine saw Epi, and the smoke helped hide Eleone. Epi was who he wanted to see. But when I looked at Antoine, I saw who I wanted to see, too. I could blame the smoke, but that's not fair to him. A complicated fire still grows inside me, from both those nights of fire and loss, and how those nights changed both of us.

I walked into the first field the night Maman left, as Eleone, but left as Epi, and walked into the second field as Epi, but left as Eleone; carrying a child, our child. That never would have happened if Antoine saw me as Eleone. Now that I am far away from him and that night and on Trinacria, and found myself, I can admit that he didn't want me. The me I so desperately wanted to return to.

But what of Epi, who begged him close. Epi made it possible for us to meet in that field. In the field we were both brothers in the Guild, but only I got pregnant. We both hated it, both alone, both overloaded with impossible choices. We needed and understood each other as young children do who have been left. I had no need to be Epi or Eleone. I was both.

In this field with Térèse, there's nothing to forgive. Except maybe, myself. I haven't thought about who Antoine was when he entered the field and who he left as. Antoine walked away to return to Fabrizio. He escaped Auvillar and death, and the Guild. Much more than just escaping a prison cell in Tolosa. I am glad he isn't running away, or dead. I am thankful that he is Perpetua's father. That will be her name if our baby is a girl.

Antoine, maybe if you had been the Antoine I wanted, I would have stopped there. I would not have continued on. I wouldn't have journeyed to the Efta, or to Trinacria. Or found Maman. I would not be here. I have to thank Epi for that. You said you remembered burning the North Field with Maman;

and when the seed heads were dry enough, we ground them into flour. That's what we are doing again, and it feels right, as though you and Fabrizio are here with us as we continue the work of Psomi.

Térèse, my heart aches for the times in Ceres when you were so near and yet so far from me. And for Antoine who was so close but who I knew nothing about. We each lived alone, in our lands, day and night, and we loved them so well. On this walk to Antaia, we've been brave. And afraid. Ready to die. Maybe we did die. We found deep paths that crossed our hearts and our hands and joined them together. It took a lot of seeing like the doves to understand each other's fields, our lands. My bread terrace. Térèse's garden. Antoine's trees. We all lost what we had when we left Ceres behind, as if we returned to the fire too. Who we were. But when we returned to the fire, we found who we are. We can see each other, and say yes, I see you, I see who you are. And Epi, where would I be without you? Or without Térèse, and those two little girls who needed each other so much, believed in and made the *Trakhanas*, and planted them in the box.

And when Maman planted the box of *Trakhanas*, it grew into Psomi.

June 1, 1566–Psomi, Sicilia

THE *LEVAIN* IS a little thick. I ladle in some water and the *levain* swims between my fingers. I keep turning and squeezing till it feels like mud. I scoop from a bag of rich flour, smoky from the chestnuts from my tree. The peaks sift and meld into a new bread of dreams. My eyes make out the blade Maman kept in the crack of the table. I take it out, the handle carved of bone, and slash the openings in the fougasse. We lay the map of bread in the ashes. Not too far from, but not too close to the fire.

In the middle of June, day pushes night away. Fields of emmer and einkorn linger in the color of ginger. They grew from the *trakhanas* cakes, the last that Maman did was plant them before my daughter was born, when the chestnut tree bloomed with yellow flowers.

Outside the *caseale*, the house, the garden sends shoots of wild green onions. I rake the earth with Térèse. Who is just as fierce as the sun and even though she's still a Cathar, she's moved to believe that love is possible.

"Don't step on the onions! They made it here from Angeline's."

I step back, stumbling on rocks.

"Not there either, that's her spinach, lettuce, and peas."

I walk a few steps back, squinting at Térèse.

"Epi, move! You're crushing the little tomato plants. And

courgette. And red orach and black radishes. They have to last for when you leave me and the full, hot sun is my fair and only companion."

"She's ready," I tell Térèse, but she knows I am not leaving, just as she knows I would never leave my daughter.

"Is she?" Térèse crosses her arms. "And you? Are you? This must be so hard."

"Of course, if only Maman was here. How do I explain to my daughter that when she was born, Maman left? I am sad they never met. But I want Perpetua to feel safe and loved. She won't ever have to pretend to be someone she's not." I don't know why my mind didn't rest on this before, but has Antaia gone to the Efta at last?

"Feed the fire slowly." I nod.

We carry the branches of apple to the small smoking fire. Her branches tangle and twist, refusing to come. They look light, like skeletons, bird skeletons, dry and withered. They curve and claw the ground, as if making furrows for seeds.

In a few weeks, the seeds will burst and stretch their green shoots to the sun.

A sliver of moon hangs over us. Beauté's little horse, Neptune, was born three days after my daughter, Perpetua. He pulls our little cart. It bumps down the hill toward the canopy of the chestnut tree.

The *ferro di cavallo*, the horseshoe shaped bread of dreams, was baked in the ash of the fire and speaks of Sekhmet, a surge of Mistress energy to push winter away, and draw up the green shoots.

Last night, it was the first time on her own. My little Perpetua pulled the rested dough out of the trough. Her hands tumbled it against the table, full of air, alive. It gave me goosebumps. We kneaded and shaped the little birds. The dough released a fragrance of Antoine's caraway seeds. Then later, under the night sky, we smelled Angeline's cornelian cherries and even Margot's walnuts drifted through the smoke of the logs in the oven.

"Slow down, so you can really taste the dream. Bread of dreams made over the fire fill your hungry places." Margot's shadow lurked but disappeared in the smoke.

This morning, we step out into the garden and wind our way to the center of the maze of trees. Perpetua runs ahead, and we hear the voices of the ladies before we arrive.

Vines with pink blooms climb the stone walls. Walls protect the garden from the fields in case a fire escapes. Or from tomatoes that want to be free. Laughter spills over as we build the fire that will make Grano Arso, burned and smoky wheat for Perpetua's bread of dreams. This celebration is not a ceremony. No name changes. Perpetua won't ever have to hide who she is. Her bread of dreams says everything; tells her tale, where she came from.

We are staying.

My eyes dart to the small log on the shelf, the green leaves sprouting. Our new box.

Three shells perched on top hide the handle.

She grins and pushes back her sleeves, picks a few dried fig sticks, and tosses them on the crackling fire. Salty breezes drift up from the sea and stir the fire.

The next morning inside the *caseale*, the tree-house, Perpetua's eyes half open on our straw bed. I fold back the new woven linens and she jumps up, laughing.

"I forget, how old are you now?"

She scrunches her brow at me. "Listen, Maman." She holds up her fingers.

I touch each one. "One. Two...."

"Free," she shouts.

I hold out the back of my hand, and she raises her hand and turns it to do the same. She touches mine, all serious. Then, I worry that my joy will scare her away, just like I didn't understand Maman at all. But I must risk being who I am. Loving her too much. I walked too far to not risk this small thing. This morning the sun filters through the trees and shows the fields running up the hill, and beyond the sky opens up to the sea. I must share my joy, to be with her. It's ok if she feels too much. Is too much. I take her hand. Open it and trace the lines of her palm.

"You have many paths ahead of you."

"Stop, Maman. No tickles."

I fold her hand closed, gently and squeeze it. She squeezes back. I bend down, cup her hands in mine, and kiss her little fists.

"Maman?"

"Listen, little bird. *Follow the doves*."

Outside our caseale, the sky bands with the hot yolk of morning. A searing pink sky circles Mt. Etna. The fire we have taken and the fire we have returned to.

Perpetua's eyes sparkle with gold flecks mixed in a deep sea, and her long bone fingers.

"Is there one for me?" Térèse blows Perpetua's fire hair off her face.

"*Follow the doves!*" Perpetua stands on her tip-toes and shouts these words that carved my journey back to Maman, but also back to me, to Eleone, and now a Maman myself. She gazes at the canopy of the tree. Birds fly overhead and further up the slope to Etna. I grab her hand.

"Wait." How could I implore her to do something that caused me so much pain, to find Maman? Maybe following the doves isn't the right thing for Perpetua. I scoop and lift her to me. My chin rests on her head. Her warm body is a comfort, her weight is welcome in my arms. Her fingers and palms are long with water, not wood or fire. Only in time would she know what was right for her.

"Surely it won't take a whole day to get to the beach." Térèse leans into her. "Even as slow as your Maman is."

I swat Térèse.

"And because it's your birthday we're…"

"Going swimming?"

"In the sea."

In the green of Perpetua's eyes, I see Antoine, her father. And I am reminded to forget the past and remember it at the same time. To learn how to keep her close and to know her at the same time. I tuck her bread of dreams, the dove, in her hand. We hurry toward the tree, before the light arrives, and stand at the edge looking down. The hundred horse tree canopy below.

"*Oc.*" To the mountain of fire. I hold my daughter on my hip.

"Like this, Maman?"

"Remember, throw the dove far enough into the sky for your message to go on."

My stomach lurches as her bird falls away from the flock flying over the tree. Her bird skips twice and thuds on the rocks, falling into the sea. She looks down, searching the water. Then up at me. We turn away, walking further along the rocks.

I tell her, "Prend la vie de feu."

"What?"

I kneel down. "Even when it looks like it isn't working, keep going." The look in her eyes brings back how I felt when Antaia told me to *Take the Life of the Fire* at my ceremony. Confused. Disappointed. And then my Maman was gone, and I was alone.

"*You must listen. Always.*"

"Look, Maman!" A dove shoots out of the waves and flies west toward the sunset, where the fire began.

And then she smiles.

THE END

Glossary

Dear Readers,

The language, besides English, used frequently in the novel is Languedoc, which has roots in, but is not spelled exactly like, or pronounced the same as, modern French. If you find words or phrases you'd like to see added to the glossary, let me know, and I'll add them to my website.

Four banal. French Communal Oven

Auberge. Inn

Maison Closes. Brothel.

Psomi. Direct translation from Greek is bread. In the novel it refers to an agrarian cult similar to the ones founded in ancient Elysium.

Oc. Yes.

Oppidum. Roman outpost, usually on a hill.

Espante. What a surprise.

Mettre le ouaï! Make trouble.

Talmelier. Bread apprentice.

Calquecop Le Pa Que Be Quand Las Denses S'en Soun Anandos. Sometimes the bread arrives after the teeth are gone.

Faire monter l'aïoli. Don't stir garlic into everything.

Touti li persouna naisson liéuri e egali en dignità e en drech. Soun doutadi de rasoun e de counsciència e li cau agì entre eli em' un esperit de frairessa." All human beings are born free and equal in dignity and rights. They are endowed with reason and conscience and should act towards each other in a spirit of brotherhood.

Mot de passe. Password.

Le Baisure. The scar.

Empapaoutar. Swindler. Imposter. Fraud. More blatantly; a fucker.

Grano Arso. Scorched Wheat.

Lonzu. A smoked pork delicacy from Corsica. It is customary and necessary to eat *lonzu* in the spring as an appetizer like prisuttu (Corsican raw ham) and is served in thin slices. Some accompany it with goat's milk tome , cut it into shavings in an omelette, in a pasta dish, in a stuffing.

Ficatellu. The pig's liver finely chopped is salted and peppered, then one incorporates some crushed cloves in it. One sprinkles then the preparation of wine red or rosy (slightly scented garlic) and one threads it in fine bowels of pig before smoking *ficatellu* during a few days. One can eat it fried in a frying pan, but one traditionally tastes it roasted slowly on ember, and served on a mound of polenta made from chestnut flour. The sweet-salty-po-lenta called *ficatellu* is rarely found.

Brocciu Sec–According to Corsican legend, there was once an ogre, the "Orcu", who lived in the mountains and terrorized villagers. One day, a young shepherd fashioned a trap—a giant leather boot filled with a sticky substance—which he left outside the Orcu's cave. Sure enough, the ogre got stuck in the boot, and in his struggle to escape, toppled over. As the shepherds rushed at him to attack, he offered them a secret in exchange for his life: a recipe for a cheese he invented, which he called Brocciu.

Le vent Tramontane. The wind, Tramontane.

Efta. Greek word for seven. In the novel it refers to the gathering place, home, collective, community, foundation, or body of Mistresses in the mountains of Languedoc.

Poulailler. Chicken coop.

Ecurie. Stable.

Abri de jardin. Garden shed.

Merde. Shit.

Pain prend la vie du feu, mais à la fin pain donne sa durée de vie sur le feu aussi. Bread takes its life from the fire, but in the end gives its life to the fire too.

Columbaria. Roman dovecote.

Peristeronas. Greek dovecote.

Mar I cel. The sea and the sky.

Lapin. Rabbit.

About the Author

WITHOUT A SHADOW of a doubt, a hurricane that swept through my family's life years ago downed so many trees, exposed their muddy red clay roots, left twisted branches, broken twigs, and stubborn stumps that kept me building three, then four and then five fires and kept them burning for weeks just to keep up with clearing them away; but it was the force of wind and destruction and ultimately regeneration that mimicked my own life, but I didn't know that, then. I wanted to understand and express the extent of my confusion about roots, fires, demise, loss, and ...of what, exactly?

Ok, great. But not great. Why this story?

In history, Ceres is the ancient Greek Goddess who presides over grains. Her daughter Persephone is trapped in Hades for half the year. Mother and daughter are reunited in the spring and summer.

This mythological tale has always entranced me. And ever since I was a little girl, I've felt like something of a gypsy. I had the pleasure and the peril to have four mothers, and so legends about, and the search for mothers ignited my imagination and sent me wandering off into the deepest forests.

After the hurricane I dreamt of a forest, and a mysterious village. I searched and found Gascony. And a beautiful 14th century millhouse, La Belle Gasconne, in Poudenas, France.

The pond was like a mirror. I looked at my reflection as I stood on the ancient stone bridge. The Gelise River poured through the auberge and ground wheat into flour, before winding on to join other rivers as they made their way to the Mediterranean.

Smoke twirled from the wood-fired oven and touched everything with a delicious heat. The path of wheat and different breads spoke to me. Not baguettes, though, of course, baguettes were everywhere. This was ancient. About unheard women. Surviving. Searching. Preserving. Secrets. Southwest France was at the crossroads of many paths. I only had to open the door and step out, to follow the winding path that began a few feet from the millhouse.

After that visit I sat down to write my way home.

DORETTE E SNOVER

DORETTESNOVER.COM
INSTAGRAM: @DORETTESNOVER